D. W. BRADBRIDGE

The Winter Siege

www.dwbradbridge.com

First edition

Published by Valebridge Publications Ltd,
PO Box 320, Crewe, Cheshire CW2 6WY

Cover design by Electric Reads. Cover images courtesy of Cliff Astles, and Flickr users, ingermaaike2, Naval History & Heritage Command, kladcat, Radarsmum67

Typeset for print by Electric Reads
www.electricreads.com

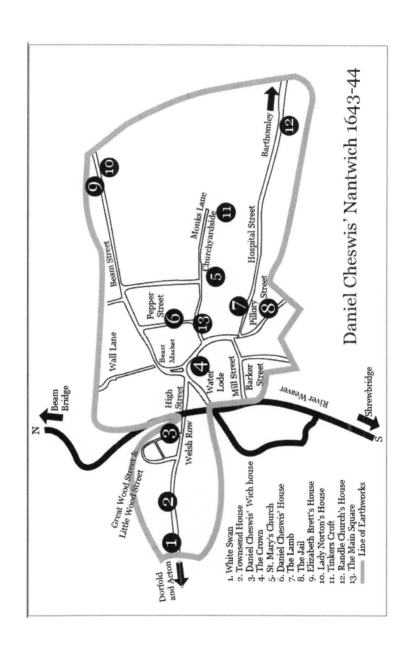

Daniel Cheswis' Nantwich 1643-44

1. White Swan
2. Townsend House
3. Daniel Cheswis' Wich house
4. The Crown
5. St. Mary's Church
6. Daniel Cheswis' House
7. The Lamb
8. The Jail
9. Elizabeth Brett's House
10. Lady Norton's House
11. Tinkers Croft
12. Randle Church's House
13. The Main Square
— Line of Earthworks

Prologue

In 1643 England was in the bloody grip of civil war, parliamentarians against royalists. During the early part of the year, the King had made progress, both in the South-West and in Yorkshire. However, by the autumn, the impetus had ceased, and it had become clear that the royalists' opportunity to capture London would be missed for a second year in succession. In September, the conflict entered a critical phase, with both sides looking further afield for reinforcements in an attempt to gain an advantage.

In Scotland, the King's Commissioner, the Duke of Hamilton, was forced to watch helplessly as the Marquis of Argyll signed the Solemn League and Covenant, by which the Scottish Covenanters agreed to provide military aid to Parliament in exchange for money and an undertaking that Presbyterianism would be enforced in England. Hamilton, whose role it was to prevent such a treaty, realised he would be forced to flee his homeland and contemplated with trepidation the reception he would receive when he arrived at the King's court in Oxford.

Meanwhile, the Duke of Ormond, the senior general of the royalist army in Ireland, had negotiated a cessation of arms with the Irish Catholic Confederation, allowing him to repatriate the King's Irish Army. As autumn turned to bitter winter, four thousand of Ormond's infantrymen landed on the Flintshire shore, and, after a brief sojourn in the royalist stronghold of Chester, where they joined forces with a thousand cavalry from Oxford under the leadership of Lord John Byron, they began to march on Nantwich, the only remaining parliamentary garrison in Cheshire.

1

Kinneil House, Bo'ness, Scotland
– October 1643

*T*he small group of horsemen pulled up in front of
the imposing sandstone towers of Kinneil House,
allowing the riders to survey the scene in front of them.
The gateway shimmered in the haze of the unseasonably
warm October day. It was a true Saint Martin's summer,
and the horses sweated uncomfortably with the exertion
of the long ride.

"So, we have arrived," said the lead rider. In his late
thirties and clean-shaven, though showing several days
of stubble, he bore the upright demeanour of a seasoned
veteran. His once-handsome face, now craggy and lined,
betrayed his years in the field, but his blond curls fell
over his shoulders like those of a younger man. Wearing
the ubiquitous buff coat over his shirt and breeches,
as well as bucket-top boots, he looked every inch the
royalist cavalryman, though, as it happens, he was not.

His five young colleagues were of considerably
more humble appearance. Clad largely in the clothes
they enlisted in, they gave off an unassuming air; and

intentionally so, for their aim was to remain inconspicuous in what was, for them, unknown territory. They were, in fact, not cavalrymen but dragoons, mounted infantry seconded from the Duke of Newcastle's forces to guard and guide the older man to his destination.

One of them put his hand to his forehead to shield his eyes from the sun. "It seems we are expected, sir," he said. It was true. Behind the gateway, men rushed to and fro in frantic activity. Heads and muskets started to appear at the top of the fortified tower house. The lead rider nodded sagely.

"Then let us sample some Scottish hospitality," he said, spurring his horse forwards.

The gateway was unguarded, but as they trotted down the wide avenue leading to the house, a servant appeared from the three-storied wing to the right of the main tower and waited for the soldiers just within the building's musket range.

"State your business, gentlemen," he called, in a lowland Scots accent, as they came within earshot.

"My name is Ralph Brett," replied the cavalryman. "I would speak with the Duke of Hamilton. I come at his lordship's request. My colleagues have accompanied me from York. They are the Duke of Newcastle's men."

"Wait here," said the servant, curtly, disappearing from whence he came. Two minutes later, he reappeared from the doorway and strode over to Brett's horse.

"Welcome to Kinneil, Colonel," he said, holding the

horse's bridle to allow him to dismount. "Your colleagues may rest and recuperate in the main building. An ostler will take care of your horses. If you would care to follow me into the palace block, the Duke will see you now."

Brett was led into the east wing of the building and upstairs to the first floor.

"My name is Mackie," said the servant. "If you need anything, I am at your service. The Duke is awaiting you in the Arbour Room." Mackie opened a door at the end of a corridor, and Brett stepped into a spacious room, overlooking the gardens and main gateway to the east of the house. The room was opulently furnished, but the first things that caught Brett's eye were the walls, which were covered in exquisite murals depicting biblical scenes. Brett recognised some of them – Samson and Delilah, David and Bathsheba, Abraham and Isaac. They were all clearly by the same artist, and Brett wondered who it was.

"Valentine Jenkins," announced a voice to his right, anticipating his thoughts. "One of your countrymen, I believe."

Brett turned around to see the familiar face of the Duke of Hamilton.

"He painted the Chapel Royal at Stirling, so I'm told. My mother commissioned him to redecorate this room about twenty years ago. Wonderful, don't you think?"

"Indeed," said Brett, taking the hand offered to him.

"It's good to see you again, Colonel Brett," said the

Duke, clapping him on the shoulder. "How long is it? Ten years?"

"Eleven, I believe, my Lord," replied Brett. Despite this, the Duke did not seem to have aged much since the last time Brett saw him. His shoulder-length brown hair had, perhaps, lightened with age, but behind the neat, pointed beard were the same amiable features he remembered. Today, the Duke was resplendent in a slashed red and gold doublet, breeches, and tall boots.

"Eleven? By Jesu, indeed it is. Those are times that will live long in the memory."

Brett nodded. In truth, the Duke's campaign to the Oder and Magdeburg to support King Gustavus Adolphus of Sweden had been a disaster. Hamilton's army of 6,000 Scots and Englishmen had been decimated by disease and starvation. Brett had fought bravely as a colonel under the Duke's command, and, after Hamilton's return to Britain in 1632, he had experienced five more years of bloody conflict before returning to Nantwich in 1637. He had left many a friend behind in Germany, and he still baulked at the memory.

Hamilton noticed Brett's discomfort and changed the subject.

"I trust your journey went without incident?" he enquired, eventually.

"The ride from Nantwich to York was not the most enjoyable I have undertaken," admitted Brett. "Avoiding patrols was not always easy, but since York, it has *been much more straightforward, thanks to my Lord Newcastle's help."*

"That is good to hear. Now, I expect you're wondering why I have summoned you here."

"I must admit, I have been intrigued by the nature of your request."

"Then I will enlighten you. But first, make yourself comfortable."

Brett was led to an oak table and two armchairs situated by the window, and Mackie arrived with two glasses of wine. Outside, the afternoon was still bright. In the middle distance, Brett could see the small but bustling port of Bo'ness and, behind it, the waters of the Firth of Forth, glinting in the sunlight.

"It's a fine view, is it not?" said Hamilton, his hand stroking his forehead. "It's a sight very dear to my heart, but I'm afraid it's a sight I may not be able to enjoy for too much longer."

"How so, sir?"

Hamilton turned round to face his guest. "I am afraid," he said, "that events in Edinburgh have overtaken me. Last month, the Marquis of Argyll signed an agreement to support Parliament in the war in England. The Solemn League and Covenant agrees that the Covenanters will provide Parliament with an army of eighteen thousand foot and three thousand horse and artillery, in exchange for thirty thousand pounds a month and an undertaking that the King will work with the Kirk to uphold the true faith and to rid the land of popery. Although the Covenant does not actually say as much, the inference is that presbyterianism will be enforced across England, Wales, and Ireland. As the King's Commissioner for Scotland, this is something that my brother, the Earl of Lanark, and I would have been expected to prevent."

"Then why didn't you?"

"The truth is that ever since the Antrim Plot two years ago, it has been impossible to influence events. The King made a serious error of judgement when he wrote to Ormond in Dublin, asking him to make a truce with the Confederation and to raise an Irish army for use in Scotland. Argyll is no fool. He is a Campbell, and once he saw that the King was not only plotting to flood Scotland with papists, but with a force led by a cousin of the MacDonalds, which would be likely to attack Campbell lands in the west, events were beyond my control. It's no surprise that the Scottish Council was furious, dominated as it is by Covenanters. The die had already been cast. The problem is that both my brother and myself will be expected to sign the Covenant."

"Which of course, you can't do."

"Precisely. We will be forced to leave Scotland and go cap in hand to Oxford, where our reception is not likely to be one of conquering heroes."

The problem facing the Count had become clear to Brett. "You are likely to be accused of treason, I think," he said.

"Quite possibly. Not that I am unused to this accusation, of course. If the King dies with no surviving children, then I will be next in line to the Scottish throne, so I am used to people thinking the worst of me. You will recall this was also an accusation levelled at me in sixteen-thirty, when I was raising Scottish forces for the King of Sweden."

Brett did indeed remember, clearly. Hamilton was almost extended family to the King, which was probably why he had retained his trust for so long. However, the signing of the Solemn League and Covenant would be a disaster for him and a political opportunity for his enemies. Men like the canny Argyll and the Earl of Montrose would be quick to capitalise on his misfortune. Brett took a swig of his wine and looked up at the Duke, who was still standing by the window.

"Where do I come into this, my Lord?" he asked.

"I will tell you," said Hamilton, "but first, I must ask you a question. You are an experienced soldier and yet you have not taken a command. Why is this so?"

"When I returned to Nantwich in sixteen-thirty-seven, I'd had my bellyful of blood and gore. I got married and promised my wife that I would lead a normal life and devote it to her and our son. I took over my father's mercers business when he died a few years ago. Nowadays, I spend my time thinking about fabrics, not warcraft."

"That I understand," acknowledged the Duke, "but

pray tell me, are you for the King or for Parliament?"

Brett inclined his head and looked Hamilton in the eye. "I do not admit a loyalty for either side, if the truth be told," he said. "My loyalty is to you and to my wife and family."

Hamilton smiled inscrutably. "Then I believe you are well-suited to the task I have in mind for you," he said. As he spoke, Brett became aware of a presence behind him, and he turned to find that Mackie had slid, unnoticed, into the room. He was carrying a leather satchel bearing the Duke's coat of arms, which he laid on the table. Brett glanced at the satchel and raised his eyebrows.

"This," said the Duke, "is my safeguard. You will find that the pouch holds a number of personal letters written by the King to me, in which he expounds his views on many things, but more particularly, on his desire to raise an army in Ireland to support his campaign in England. The appearance of letters such as these, exposing his Majesty's duplicitous nature, will not be good for his standing in England."

"But this is treason," breathed Brett. "Why would you want the existence of such correspondence to become common knowledge?"

"Because these letters will consolidate the Covenanters' position with Parliament and, if I am imprisoned, a swift win for Parliament might just be enough to get me freed, as would evidence of my support for the Covenant."

"Your aim is now to support the Covenanters against

the King?" asked Brett, amazed.

"No-one is more loyal to the King than I, but I must protect myself and my family. I may need the support of the Covenanters should the King lose the war."

Brett slowly began to understand, and a grim smile broke out on his face. "And my role in this?"

"All I ask is that you take this satchel back to Nantwich and keep it in a safe place. Do nothing unless you hear word from me, at which point you may release the letters into parliamentary hands. Will you do this for me, Colonel?"

Brett grasped the satchel and looked inside. He took out the letters one by one, looked at them briefly, and then replaced them carefully. "There's one thing I don't understand, my Lord," he said, eventually. "Why me... and why Nantwich?"

"There are not many men I can trust," replied the Duke, "but you are certainly one of them. As for Nantwich, it is a parliamentary stronghold. It is under the control of Sir William Brereton, a man of radical beliefs, who is no friend of the Covenant. But there is a young colonel under his command, George Booth, a moderate and a good presbyterian, whose grandfather, Baronet Delamere, is well known to me. Colonel Booth, I understand, has been entrusted with command of the garrison, while Brereton is absent in North Wales. It is to him that the papers should be given, should it prove necessary."

Brett seemed satisfied. "Then I will do it, my Lord. Is there anything else I should know?"

"For the sake of security, be certain that you secrete these documents in a safe place and make sure you gather a small team of trusted people around you, in case some misfortune should befall you. I presume there is no shortage of trustworthy people in Nantwich committed to the parliamentary cause?"

"I can think of one or two people," confirmed Brett.

"Good," said the Duke. "I am in your debt. There is one more thing, though. Do not reveal the fact that you have the letters to Colonel Booth unless you feel you are in danger. In this case, you may tell him that you have important papers, but not the precise nature of them. For this purpose, I have written a personal letter to him carrying my seal, which you may give to him, should the need arise."

Mackie stepped forward with a bound letter, which Brett accepted and put inside the satchel with the rest of the correspondence.

"If Booth is informed," warned Hamilton, "I suggest you are particularly diligent as to where you hide the letters, just in case he decides to take them anyway."

Brett nodded. "I will protect them with my life, my Lord."

"That is good," said Hamilton, turning to look out of the window. "The afternoon is already passing us by. You are welcome to avail yourself of my hospitality

tonight. I suggest you take some time to relax and enjoy the gardens here. I look forward to your company this evening, and tomorrow you can start your journey afresh. Mackie will show you to your chamber."

Brett was more than happy to rest up in Kinneil overnight. A good meal and an evening in the company of the Duke offered welcome respite after several days in the saddle. However, when Brett returned to his bedchamber that evening, he did not notice that the leather satchel was in a slightly different position to where it had been before dinner, and the next morning, when they set off on the long ride homewards, neither he nor the band of dragoons were aware of the lone figure on horseback who was tracking them at a discreet distance.

2

Nantwich – Saturday December 9, 1643

I was at home in my cottage in Pepper Street when the first body was found. I often mused that, had I been on duty that Saturday morning, instead of the town's other constable, Arthur Sawyer, things might have turned out differently – and not necessarily for the better. But perhaps fate had ordained it so.

It was market day in Nantwich, and I had risen early to set up my stall. The cheese and butter that I had collected from local farmers during the course of the week lay on two small tables in the hall, waiting for me to summon up the enthusiasm to move everything to my designated area in front of the house, ready for the first customers. Outside, fresh snow had fallen, and, although the streets in the centre of town were beginning to come alive, the bitterly cold weather that had plagued us for the past two weeks deterred me from venturing outside until absolutely necessary.

Mrs Padgett, my housekeeper, had prepared a simple breakfast of porridge, bread, butter, and ale, and I was just sitting down to eat when I noticed soldiers on the street outside the window.

"It seems as though you are in demand," said Mrs Padgett, as she poured me a mug of ale. She gestured with her jug towards two musketeers, who were outside my house, standing their weapons against the wall, before preparing to knock on the door. I groaned inwardly at the prospect of my office imposing further on my time. It was now a year and seven weeks since the Michaelmas Court Leet of 1642, where Sawyer and I had been appointed as Nantwich's two town constables for, supposedly, the following twelve months. At the time, I was happy to take on the role, knowing that, as a local tradesman of growing, albeit still modest, stature, I would be expected to fulfil the task at some point over the course of the next few years. My thinking had been that, at a time when business was likely to be curtailed by the war that was about to take place on our doorstep, now was as good a time as any to get this particular responsibility out of the way.

I had, however, misjudged the situation. Within months of my appointment, local government, as we knew it, had collapsed. Quarter sessions had ceased in January, and Cheshire had fallen under the control of the 'County Committee', a wartime administration managed by Sir William Brereton, head of the parliamentary forces in Cheshire, to whose officials, the Deputy Lieutenants, I now reported. The Committee's interests, it seemed to me, were focused on raising men and money for the war and not on the day-to-day concerns of a petty constable. What was more, it was made clear to Sawyer and I that elections to find our replacements after our year in office were to be delayed until the political situation had stabilised.

This may not have been such a disaster, were it not for the fact that the establishment of Nantwich as a parliamentary garrison town earlier in the year had actually resulted in increased custom for my business. In addition to the population being boosted by around a thousand foot soldiers and cavalrymen, the extra security offered by the garrison had started to attract all manner of puritan and parliamentary sympathisers, largely from Chester, which was now firmly in the hands of the King. The arrival of four thousand seasoned troops from Ireland, to support the King's cause, had not helped either. Stories of the atrocities committed by the papist hordes had been rife, forcing even more terrified folk to seek safety within our walls. With a rapidly increasing number of mouths to be fed, business had been good. As such, on market day, I needed to be working and avoid the burden of onerous civil duties.

Indeed, my responsibilities went far beyond law enforcement. My many tasks, shared with Sawyer, included such varied roles as maintaining the pillory, stocks, and cuckstool, overseeing the practices of innkeepers, the apprehension of vagrants, restricting unlawful games on Sunday, tax collecting, and drawing up muster rolls – in other words, plenty of opportunity to make myself unpopular with the local population. I could, of course, call on the help of friends and other townsfolk, who responded with varying degrees of willingness. Nevertheless, I had been counting the days to when some other unfortunate would have to take over from me. Now, I was uncertain whether that day would ever come.

I motioned for Mrs Padgett to open the door, and was greeted by a blast of icy air and a flurry of snow. The two men framed in the doorway, one in his late thirties, the other younger, perhaps mid-twenties, introduced themselves as Carter and Hughes.

"We have been sent by Major Lothian," announced Carter, the older man, rubbing his hands against the cold. "It is Master Daniel Cheswis that we seek."

"Would you disturb a man at his breakfast table?" scolded Mrs Padgett. "You would do best to come back later."

Unsure of themselves, the two men hovered on the threshold, but I waved over to my housekeeper. "Let the men in, for goodness sake," I said. "They will freeze to death".

Grumbling somewhat, Mrs Padgett stepped aside and allowed the men to remove their hats and take a seat by the hearth. They were grateful for the opportunity to warm themselves by the fire.

"You must take no notice of Mrs Padgett," I said, as

she disappeared into the kitchen to fetch some ale. "She means well, but I'm afraid she could sometimes be mistaken for my mother."

It was true. My relationship with my housekeeper was certainly somewhat unorthodox. Many would have said that the owner of a single wich house and a fledgling cheese business was living beyond his means having a housekeeper, but at the age of thirty-three I was still unmarried, and Mrs Padgett, a slightly plump but energetic widow of forty-eight, had, together with her nine-year-old grand-daughter, Amy, shared my house for the past eight years.

Mrs Padgett was a cousin of Edward Swindells, the childless previous owner of the wich house I had acquired, whose apprentice I had once been. Indeed, on the culmination of my training in the salt trade, it was made clear to me that one of the conditions for the eventual acquisition of Swindells' business was that I provide Mrs Padgett with a home.

Not that I minded. Mrs Padgett – Cecilia was her given name, although she had always been Mrs Padgett to me – was a kindly and organised woman, who had suffered the misfortune of losing both her husband and her only daughter within the space of a month, both in tragic circumstances. The husband had died in a freak farming accident, bleeding to death after cutting himself with a scythe, whilst the daughter had succumbed to the rigours of childbirth. Mrs Padgett had the mildly irritating habit of mothering me, sometimes taking liberties when she shouldn't, but I tolerated this, accepting that her positive characteristics far outweighed the negatives. Her cooking, for example, was extraordinary. Her veal and ham pie, to which I was particularly partial, was one of Nantwich's best kept secrets. If one thing could be said about Cecilia Padgett with absolute certainty, it was that she kept a good table.

Her granddaughter, Amy, was a quiet child, who kept herself to herself much of the time. However, I had always been good with children, and over time she had begun to accept my role in her life. It was inevitable, I suppose, that these circumstances would result in us practically living together as a family. It was an arrangement which was perfectly understood by our closest friends and relations, but one which was often misunderstood by outsiders and sometimes needed clarification.

The two musketeers glanced at each other, somewhat embarrassed, but said nothing. I cut myself a slice of bread and spread it liberally with butter.

"So, how can I be of service to Major Lothian?" I asked, taking the initiative.

"A body has been found near the sconce at Welsh Row End," replied Carter. "We don't know who it is yet, but it would appear to be a townsman. Major Lothian says it is a civil matter, and so he has requested the presence of a constable without delay."

I looked at Carter with interest, making a mental

calculation as I did so. Welsh Row was on the other side of the River Weaver from where I lived, and the sconce, the earthen fortification constructed at the end of the street, would take fifteen minutes to reach at least, especially with a fresh fall of snow to negotiate. I still had my market stall to set up, and my apprentice, James Skinner, was already late. I was going to be pushed for time.

"You have tried Arthur Sawyer, I presume. He is supposed to be on duty this morning."

"Yes, sir," responded Carter, "but he is not at home. His wife told me I had missed him by no more than five minutes."

I sighed. "Very well then, tell me more. Where exactly was this body found?"

"In a ditch by the earthworks," interjected Hughes, the younger man. "I was nearby when the body was found, sir. He was half-covered in snow. Some bastard had smashed the poor fellow's head in."

"And nobody saw this happen? Ever since the Irish army landed, the town has been teeming with soldiers."

"No sir, it was snowing a blizzard last night and we couldn't see five feet in front of our faces. The body also looks to have been dragged into the ditch. It looks like he was killed somewhere else."

"I see. And you say Sawyer is nowhere to be found?"

"No, sir, and Major Lothian wants the body moved as soon as possible."

"I'm sure he does."

Major James Lothian was not a man given to inefficiencies of any sort, and it was no surprise to hear of the urgency he had placed on the removal of the body. Lothian was Sir William Brereton's second-in-command and one of his most trusted advisors. As well as being responsible for training new recruits in Shropshire and Cheshire, he had been instrumental in the skirmish the previous January, whereby Sir William had taken control of Nantwich. A Scotsman by birth, Lothian was considered to be a ruthlessly efficient officer and, with Sir William absent in North Wales, he was now a vital advisor on military matters to Colonel George Booth, who had been placed in charge of the Nantwich garrison. I took a mouthful of ale and turned to face Carter.

"I need to set up my market stall and await the arrival of my apprentice," I said. "Please tell the Major not to move the body. I will be with him in an hour or so."

3

Nantwich – Saturday December 9, 1643

Although my activities in the cheese business were not my main source of income, it was no accident that I became involved in that particular trade. I grew up in Barthomley, a small village six miles to the east of Nantwich, where my parents leased twenty 'Cheshire acres' of land from Lord Crewe. We grew wheat, oats, and turnips and produced meat, cheese, and butter, a standard mixture of produce, in those days, for farms of our size.

I was the second of three sons, and, by the time I reached my late teens, it had become clear that my elder brother, George, was going to inherit the farm. So my father, who for some reason thought that the future lay in Nantwich's status as a salt-producing town, bought an apprenticeship for me at Edward Swindells' wich house. To be fair, my father made a shrewd move, for Swindells was an ageing widower with no children, whose main motivation was to make sure he was taken care of in his old age. When I finished my apprenticeship, my father lent me the money to make an unusual arrangement with

Swindells. I would continue to operate the wich house and make sure Swindells did not starve in his dotage, in return for which, I would inherit his business on his death. As it happened, one Sunday in 1637, Swindells dropped dead as he walked to church, and at the age of twenty-seven I became the owner of a single wich house with six leads, with the responsibility for Swindells' cousin and her grand-daughter.

The life of a brine worker never really appealed to me, though. The salt trade in Nantwich operated like a co-operative and offered little chance for development. There were too many restrictions, especially for a bachelor like myself, so I started looking for ideas for an alternative method of employment.

My inspiration to become a cheese merchant came from a chance meeting with my father's landlord, Sir Ranulphe Crewe, who had bought one of my father's finest Cheshire cheeses and taken it to London, where it had been received with considerable enthusiasm. Sir Ranulphe, now in his eighties, was a self-made man, the son of a Nantwich tanner, who had risen to become both Attorney-General and Lord Chief Justice of the Court of the King's Bench. Nowadays, he spent most of his time in comfortable retirement in Westminster, but was still occasionally to be seen riding his piebald gelding through the Cheshire countryside with his sons, Sir Clippesby and Sir John. Sir Ranulphe was held in great regard in Nantwich, and it was an honour to have him as a patron and advisor.

Sir Ranulphe had explained to me that the old full milk cheese that he had taken was considered far superior to the Suffolk cheese that most of London ate. Suffolk cheese had originally also been full milk cheese, but as demand for butter had increased, local farmers had started to skim off some of the cream, with the result that the quality of Suffolk cheese had deteriorated over time. Sir Ranulphe said he believed discerning gentlemen in London would be prepared to pay up to a penny a pound more for our Cheshire cheese.

I saw the market and made my plans. Shipping the cheese by land would have cost between £5 and £10 a ton, which would have made it unprofitable, as the value of cheese itself was only around £20 a ton. I therefore planned to transport whole cheeses by ship from Chester or Liverpool, the cost of which would have only been £1 a ton. In the meantime, I developed my business locally. I offered to sell my brother George's surplus cheese, allowing him to buy extra cows as he saw my business increase. I then started approaching other farmers in the area and started buying up their surplus too. I sold cheese from my stall on market day and build up a local clientele amongst inns and the larger houses, who tended to buy from me when they ran short of the cheese their own livestock had produced.

Unfortunately, the onset of war in 1642 changed everything. The growth of my business beyond the boundaries of Nantwich was stymied, and I was forced to bide my time. Chester was in royalist hands and I would have to wait until more stable times before I could realise my ambition. Fulfilling my debt to the town by taking on the role of constable had seemed a logical step at the time. On days like this, though, I had seriously begun to doubt my sanity.

Once the soldiers had left me in peace, I put on my overcoat, gloves, and hat and ventured outside to set up my stall. My house was located in a strategic position on a slight bend, halfway up Pepper Street, meaning I could see both ends of the street from my front door. To the right, less than a hundred yards away, was Beam Street and the Beast Market, and to the left the square and St Mary's Church.

About three inches of fresh snow had fallen overnight, but this was already being disturbed as local farmers and traders began to enter the town to set up stalls. Soon, the town would be teeming with all kinds of people trying to sell goods. A pale sun shone above the thatched roofs of the houses. Steam rose from the thatch, and smoke billowed from the chimneys. It was bitterly cold, and my breath froze instantly on the light breeze that blew right to left down the street.

Although the centre of Nantwich was relatively new, having been rebuilt in 1583 after a devastating fire, which destroyed almost all of the town on the east side of the river, the closely crowded buildings still gave off an aura of fragility. I mused on the fact that all that was required was a stray spark and a strong wind, and lives could be destroyed again in an instant. It was a reminder that life was constantly on the edge, even more so now that Nantwich was one of the few remaining parliamentary strongholds in Cheshire.

Market day in Nantwich was a well-organised affair, and traders were located together according to what they were selling. Stalls ran all the way through the town from one end to the other. Livestock, as one would expect, was largely sold in the Swine Market and the Beast Market, but the butchers were located at the end of Pepper Street by the square, the offal being transported down Castle Street to be dumped in the river. Fish was also sold on boards around the square, whilst the drapers were all located in the Booth Hall nearby. Pillory Street was mostly full of tanners, shoemakers, and potters, but the far end of the street, next to the Beete Bridge, was reserved for vegetable farmers. My own street was largely inhabited by milk maids and farmers selling eggs and other dairy produce. Various other traders, such as quacks, booksellers, spice merchants, and the like, fought for space where they could.

I was fortunate in that I had been able to persuade the town officers to give me a position right in front of my own house, making it easier to transport my wares into position. I would store my cheeses in a cool place in the rear of the house until Saturday morning, when I would simply transfer them onto tables by my front door.

I dragged the two tables out of the hall and started to load them with the eight cheeses I had to sell. On the left-hand table, I placed a single 10lb cream cheese and two new milk cheeses of the same size. The cream cheese, which I sold at 4d per pound, was the most expensive cheese and was usually only eaten by the more affluent townsfolk. New milk cheese, made of full, unskimmed milk, was 3d per pound. On the other table I placed two flett cheeses and a large tub of butter. The flett cheeses, slightly smaller at 8lb each, were made of skimmed milk and tended to be eaten by servants and the poor. Flett cheese sold at 1 ½d per pound. The remaining three cheeses, one new milk cheese and two flett cheeses, were placed in the parlour to be brought out later if required. I calculated that, if I managed to sell all my stock, I stood to make about 5 shillings profit, more than acceptable for a morning's work.

I took great pride in the layout of my stall. Each full cheese was positioned exactly four inches from the front of the table, and each cheese was placed three inches apart. The neatness and perfect symmetry of the stall pleased me, although Mrs Padgett thought me too fastidious in my approach. My obsessiveness was the work of the Devil, she said.

"But how can order be the work of the Devil?" I would respond. "Surely the Devil rules over chaos, not order?"

Once the cheeses were in place, I fetched my scales, some knives, and some plates, and started to cut the cheeses up into 1lb blocks. This was a task I usually entrusted to my apprentice, James Skinner, but the boy had still not turned up. I cast my eye anxiously down the street, but there was no sign of him. If he didn't arrive soon, I would have to ask Mrs Padgett to look after the stall, whilst I dealt with Major Lothian.

Skinner, a thin, gangly youth of fifteen with a pale complexion, had been working for me for nearly three months now. He came from a large family of brine workers and was recommended to me by one of the walling overseers in charge of the brine-making process in my own wich house. I was already regretting the decision to take him on. Often disinterested, he bore a constant hangdog demeanour and needed more supervision than he should have done. He was certainly not suitable as a future partner, and I had left the walling overseer in no doubt as to my opinions of his recommendation. Today would be the first time that I would have to leave Skinner on his own, a thought which filled me with trepidation.

Presently, he ambled round the corner of Beam Street and made his way slowly up the street. He was exchanging a degree of banter with two milkmaids, who swished their pails as they walked. By the sound of the cackling being emitted by the girls, it was the kind of crude, inappropriate conversation of which I disapproved. After a few seconds, he caught my eye and, no doubt chastened by the glare I gave him, abruptly ceased his conversation and quickened his pace.

"You're late," I growled, as he made his way behind the tables. "I've had to set up everything by myself."

Skinner apologised begrudgingly. "I'm sorry, Master Cheswis," he said. "My father is not well and I've had to help my mother with some of her tasks."

I had no time to lecture Skinner on the importance of punctuality, so I let it go and focused instead on making sure he understood exactly what was expected of him whilst I was away.

"You know the prices," I said. "Do not, under any circumstances, leave the stall unattended. If you really need help, call Mrs Padgett."

At that moment, my housekeeper poked her head around the door to check how I was getting on. I pulled her to one side.

"Keep an eye on him," I whispered. "We have a lot of cheese to sell and we can't afford any disasters. I'll be back as soon as I can."

"Can you not leave a man to care for his *own* business every now and again?" scolded Margery Clowes. It was meant half in jest, but she had a right to complain. I had been taking up much of my best friend Alexander's time of late, and his wife was starting to become irked at my constant requests for his services as an assistant, to help with my constabulary duties. Today she stood with her arms folded, barring entry to her hall. Three doors away, Skinner looked up from the table piled high with cheese and smirked, quickly averting his gaze when his smile was met with a glare from my direction.

I peered behind Margery into the semi-darkness of her hallway and was rewarded with a view of the grinning face of Alexander Clowes, who was drawing his finger across his throat in mocking glee at my discomfort.

"I'm sorry for the inconvenience, Margery," I said, truthfully, "but today I have a good excuse. A body has been found by the sconce at Welsh Row End. I need someone to help me investigate."

Margery rolled her eyes and was about to say something, but my friend's not-inconsiderable frame had already appeared out of the gloom and he was looking at me with interest. "A body, you say?" he interjected. "Does that mean we have a murder to investigate? Who?"

"I'm not sure yet," I replied. "One of the townsfolk, as yet unidentified. He was hit over the head. Seems he took a proper basting."

Alexander emitted a low whistle and ruffled his shock of sandy hair. Margery, giving up in exasperation, had already turned back into the house.

Alexander Clowes had been my best friend ever since I moved to Nantwich. He was the same age as me, but, unlike myself, was blessed with both height and bulk, very useful attributes in a constable's assistant. Despite his size, though, Alexander was of a genial disposition, a gentle giant in every sense of the phrase, and I enjoyed his company. He ran a chandler's shop, but also held the position of the town's bellman, a role his father had held before him and which had often prompted him to jest that he was the town's primary supplier of both sound and light.

Alexander had been happily married to Margery for four years and had two young sons, Nicholas and William, who, as a godparent, I treasured dearly. Alexander rarely wasted an opportunity to recommend marriage to me, but it was his shoulder that I had cried on when I lost Alice ten years previously. He understood why I had remained a bachelor, but it didn't stop him trying to persuade me to find someone else.

"Cecilia Padgett has her good points as a housemate, but a full belly isn't everything," he would often say, as I smiled indulgently. He was right, of course.

Alexander grabbed his cloak, and we walked down Pepper Street, through the snow and into the Beast Market, which was already teeming with farmers and their livestock. Talking to one of the farmers was a short, stocky man with a neatly trimmed beard, who I recognised as Will Butters, head servant at Townsend House, one of the town's larger private residences. Butters was one of my regular cheese customers, and I hailed him as we approached.

"Good morrow, Will," I called. "What's new today?"

"There's some kind of bother up at the sconce,

constable," he said, acknowledging my greeting. "Some poor bastard found dead in the snow, so I hear. I'd get up there quickly if I were you. I'm told Major Lothian is demanding the presence of a constable."

I nodded my thanks and headed off through the throng of market-goers, taking care to avoid the carts trundling round the corner from the direction of Town Bridge; the wooden structure which spanned the River Weaver. The majority were bringing goods into town for the market, although one or two jaggers' carts, laden with coal for the wich houses on the other side of the river, were fighting against the tide and heading into Welsh Row. The ground was frozen solid, which was good for the carts, but experience told me the road would become a morass once the snow thawed.

We crossed the bridge and passed the salt-making area on the west bank of the river, heading out of the town centre. After passing a row of workshops, alehouses, and modest tenements, inhabited largely by brine workers, we approached a number of more elegant residences. On the right was Townsend House, a substantial brick property with bay windows and a walled garden, the walls ornamented with armorial bearings and figures. Townsend House had been the home of Thomas Wilbraham, one of the town's most prominent gentlemen and a respected supporter of the crown. Nantwich people still talked about the visit of King James to Nantwich in 1617, when Wilbraham had played host to his Majesty.

But times had changed. Thomas Wilbraham had died in October, and the estate had been left in the hands of his sons. Young Roger Wilbraham was stood by the gate as we walked by, and I bid him good day as we passed. From Townsend House it was not far to the earthworks, beyond which lay Dorfold House, the home of another branch of the Wilbraham family, the village of Acton, and the main road to Wales. Not that I could see far into the countryside, of course, because the imposing earthen walls at the edge of the town were four yards high, three yards thick, and had been built to withstand the heaviest cannonballs. Atop the earthworks which encircled the entire town was a wooden wall and walkway, accessed by wooden ladders. On the other side of the wall was a ditch. At the end of each street, sconces had been built, star-shaped fortifications designed to enable soldiers within the walls to fire at attackers from behind.

As we approached, I noticed Major Lothian waiting impatiently by the sconce with several other men, who were stamping their feet and blowing on their hands. He broke off his conversation and turned to me.

"What sort of timekeeping is this?" he barked, in his thick Scots accent.

"I came as quickly as I could," I replied, unperturbed. "There are only two constables in Nantwich, and I have a living to make. At least your men managed to locate me. I understand Sawyer was nowhere to be found."

Lothian grunted. The sharp-eyed Scotsman was a short

man with angular features and slightly greying hair. He had a reputation for being dour, but he was undeniably an excellent soldier. Efficient and highly regarded, he bore the unmistakeable demeanour of a professional. He was most definitely not a man to be crossed.

"Follow me," he said, motioning towards a group of people huddled together fifty yards or so to the right of the road. "I have some work for you – and for you too, master bell ringer," he added, turning to Alexander. My friend acknowledged the comment. As the town's bellman, he would be responsible for the process of lating on the morning of the burial of the poor soul lying by the roadside, ringing his bell to invite mourners to the funeral.

Lothian led us to a ditch behind a barn, twenty yards or so from the earthworks. I took a quick look around me and made a mental note that, despite the ditch's proximity to the fortifications, the body was actually out of sight of anybody patrolling the walkway.

I took a look into the ditch and grimaced. The dead body had been a tall, thin man in his early thirties. I didn't recognise him, but that was not necessarily surprising, as the left side of his head had been staved in, perhaps with a rock or some other heavy object. The body was in a grotesque position, arms splayed and half-covered in snow. Tied tightly round his neck was a large, crimson silk scarf. I took a closer look at the ugly wound on the side of the man's head. There were some bloodstains in the snow, but nowhere near enough for the catastrophic injuries that had been inflicted on the victim.

"Who found the body?" I asked, eventually. Robert Hollis raised his hand. He was the barn owner, a balding, middle-aged man, a local farmer who I had known for some time.

"Tell me what you saw, Robert," I said.

"I saw nothing," said the farmer, with a shrug. "I came by the barn at around six this morning to feed the cattle and found him lying here. He was stone dead."

I nodded and turned to the group of soldiers who had been stood there when I arrived.

"Did *anybody* see or hear what happened?" I asked. The soldiers looked at each other but said nothing. Eventually, a stocky musketeer with red hair stepped forward and spoke.

"It was dark and there was no noise from this direction," he ventured. "We can't see behind the barn from here, and we were keeping watch for people outside the town, not for those within it."

I looked at the dead man again.

"This body's been moved," I said. "There's not enough blood for him to have been killed here, but I can't see the drag marks in the earth because of the snow. Does anybody have a spade?"

Hollis nodded, and a couple of minutes later he emerged from his barn with a suitable implement. Two soldiers, meanwhile, returned to the sconce and found two more spades. Standing on the edge of the ditch furthest away from the earthworks, I slowly began to scrape away snow from the edge of the pit. As I did so, I noticed boot-marks on the edge of the pit and lines in the earth, leading away at an angle towards a wall to the rear of a tavern about fifty yards away. The lines were indistinct, for the ground had been close to freezing the night before and was now rock hard. Nevertheless, they were distinct enough.

"Here. Clear a line in the direction of that wall," I shouted to the two soldiers with spades. As they did so, I saw that the drag marks extended for quite a distance.

"Looks like he's been dragged from the tavern," said Alexander, striding off in the direction of the wall, leaving myself and Lothian in his wake. We soon found what we were looking for. A perfunctory glance at the top of the wall revealed numerous blood stains, whilst the snow on the other side was stained a curious shade of pink. Ten yards away, a stone about a foot square lay crimson and bloody, having been ditched in the snow.

"Does anyone know who the victim is?" I enquired, on returning to the ditch. The soldiers looked blank, but Hollis spoke up.

"I think you'll find it's William Tench. He's a tanner from up Hospital Street, I think."

"Do you know him, then?" I asked.

"Not well, only by sight, but he was in The White Swan last night, drunk. If I were you, I'd have a word with the innkeeper."

"That I shall," I said. "Does he have any family?"

"He has a wife. She's a maid in Randle Church's house. They live in one of Mr Church's cottages nearby."

I considered what Hollis had said, but, at that moment, my thought process was broken by a commotion coming from the direction of the sconce. Presently, a soldier came running in the direction of Major Lothian, and six bedraggled-looking men were manhandled into the open, where Lothian could see them.

"What do we have here?" scowled the Scotsman, looking at the newcomers with evident distaste.

"They claim to be deserters from the Irish army, sir," said the soldier. "They say they've marched from Chester and want to change sides."

Lothian glanced at the sorry-looking group of men, who were shivering miserably. Ambling over to them, he addressed their apparent leader, a broad-shouldered man in his late twenties.

"What say you to this?"

"He s-speaks the truth, sir," stammered the man, in a local accent. Several of the onlookers eyed the man with surprise when they heard his voice, but Lothian showed no reaction other than to look the man up and down.

"At least you are not an Irishman," he said, eventually.

"No, sir. My n-name is Samuel Pratchett. I am from Warrington. All my f-friends here are from Cheshire or Shropshire, as are most of the men I have served with.

There have been only a few Irishmen amongst our number."

"I see. And why have you deserted, may I ask?"

"It is one thing to fight for the King against the papists, sir. Quite another to fight against your own people."

Lothian smiled almost imperceptibly.

"So it is, Mr Pratchett," he said. "You and your men are welcome in Nantwich."

The six deserters breathed an audible sigh of relief, but one of them approached Pratchett and whispered something in his ear. Pratchett listened carefully and nodded to his colleague.

"Is there something the matter?" asked Lothian.

"N-no, sir. We thank you for your hospitality. It's just that Will Sparrowe here was concerned that this m-might be how you treat recruits from the King's army." Pratchett gestured towards the figure of Tench lying in the ditch. Lothian's brow clouded for a moment, but I understood Pratchett's meaning and stepped in.

"I think our friend may be referring to the scarf around Tench's neck," I explained. "Is that not so, Mr Pratchett?"

"Yes, sir," the man replied.

I had been so preoccupied with working out how Tench had ended up in the ditch that I had failed to pay any great attention to the eight-foot-long crimson sash that had been tied in a tight knot around the dead man's neck. Made of silk twill and with embroidered gold fringing, it was clearly a particularly ornate example of the kind of scarf used by officers to denote their allegiance. I tried to loosen the knot around Tench's throat and realised that, had the rock that had been embedded in Tench's skull failed to do its job, the scarf would have surely succeeded. As I finally loosened the knot, I saw a bright red mark stretching all the way from the back of Tench's neck to his Adam's apple.

"A red scarf," exclaimed Lothian, who had clearly also not recognised the sash for what it was. "A sign of one of the King's men."

"Indeed," I concurred, "but this is no ordinary scarf. Look at the fine finishing on it. If this was used for military purposes, it belonged to someone of high rank. Why on Earth would a humble tanner be found strangled with such a thing?"

The Scotsman shook his head ruefully but didn't answer.

"Perhaps the answer to that question lies in The White Swan tavern," suggested Alexander.

"You're right," I said. "Perhaps it's time to pay the landlord a visit."

4

Nantwich – Saturday, December 9, 1643

After asking Lothian to summon the coroner, I left him to his job of debriefing the group of deserters, who were already being marched up Welsh Row in the direction of the town centre. Food and warmth, no doubt, awaited them in The Lamb, the inn at the top end of Hospital Street that served as the garrison's headquarters. I permitted Alexander to return home, but asked him to check on my cheese stall on the way back. Once satisfied, I made my way to the front of The White Swan and headed for the door, which, I noticed, had been left wide open, presumably to let the stale smells of the previous night escape into the winter air.

The White Swan had always struck me as a curious place. Situated on the edge of Nantwich, it mainly attracted brine workers or local farmers on their way into or out of town. Although there were sufficient bedchambers and adequate stabling to meet the needs of paying travellers, most of the space had been occupied by lower-ranking officers from the garrison. I stepped inside and caught a strong waft of sweat, beer, and stale tobacco. I found the innkeeper, a short, squat man by the name of Edmund Parker, by the bar, sweeping the floor. He glanced up and registered my presence, but said nothing.

I had come to know Edmund Parker only since I had become a constable, and I was not particularly impressed. In my office, I had become responsible for a number of tasks relating to alehouses, not least for maintaining order, but also for their relicensing. I had split this task with Arthur Sawyer, taking responsibility for all alehouses and taverns east of the river, in addition to those on Beam Street, Swine Market, Pepper Street, Churchyardside, Monks Lane, and the High Street as far as the Square. Everything else was Sawyer's domain.

I had found Parker to be less than helpful when it came to maintaining law and order in his premises. Although he could not be accused of being openly hostile to me, he made it clear that my presence was welcome only when absolutely necessary. This approach was no doubt due to an incident which occurred during my first week as a constable, when Alexander and I were called to attend to a disturbance between an off-duty soldier and one of Parker's regulars, a farm-hand called Briggs. Alexander, who was not a man to be messed with, had ejected both men single-handedly, banging Briggs' head on the door on the way out. Despite the fact that Briggs had been much the worse for drink and had clearly been the main aggressor, Parker had not welcomed the intervention, pointing out that he could handle any disturbances in his tavern by himself and did not appreciate his regular customers being set upon by the town constable and his lackeys. For my part, I had responded that I was unlikely to allow his license to be renewed if he did not co-operate with me while I was doing my duty.

Our relationship was, at best, strained, and therefore it was no surprise to find Parker ignoring me.

"A moment of your time, please, Mr Parker," I ventured, attempting to break the ice.

"Just so long as that loutish chandler is not with you, constable," came the reply. "What do you want with me? You should know by now that I keep an orderly house here."

"Not last night, it appears," I replied. "One of your customers was bludgeoned to death in your back yard, and his body has just been found behind Hollis's barn near the earthworks."

Parker stopped his sweeping and looked at me evenly, leaning on his brush. "What happens outside these four walls is none of my business," he said. "Who was the unfortunate fellow?"

"A man called William Tench, a tanner from Hospital Street. Do you know him?"

Parker shrugged. "What makes you think he was here?"

"If you'd care to examine the bloodstains on the wall at the back of your yard, I think you will find that it is easy enough to prove his presence on your land," I said, irritably. "It's been said he was drinking here last night. I wanted to know whether you noticed anything unusual."

"The alehouse was full last night. I can't be expected to keep an eye on everyone."

I took a deep breath. "Look, Mr Parker," I said. "I don't particularly want to cause you any trouble, but I do require your co-operation. If you prefer, I can always close your tavern until the matter is clarified. What is it to be?"

Parker gave me a sullen look. "What do you want to know about Tench?" he asked.

"So he *was* here?" I said.

"Yes. He comes in here every now and again."

"Why would a man from the other side of town come to The White Swan, instead of going somewhere closer?"

"I can't tell you that. But he did have the habit of talking to the soldiers. They were a bit wary of him. He would ask them questions about their soldiering – you know, a bit more than would come up in normal conversation. It seems he would do this in other alehouses too. Folks had begun to wonder whether he was a royalist scout or something."

"Really?" I said, amazed. "Why on earth has this never been reported?"

Parker shrugged. "Nobody could ever prove anything, and he never hung around long enough to make himself a proper pest. In any case, the people he spoke to were generally too drunk to care. I didn't want any trouble, so if he started to bother the customers, I generally told him to move on, and I wouldn't see him for a few weeks. In any case, he was usually careful not to antagonise anyone."

"And do you remember him from last night?"

"Alright. If you insist, yes I did. He stood out because this time he was in a blazing argument with John Davenport."

I stared at Parker with surprise. "You mean John Davenport, the brine worker from Great Wood Street?"

"How many other John Davenports do you know?" came the caustic response. I pulled aside a chair at one of the tables and sat down for a moment. If this were true, then I was no judge of character. John Davenport was well known to me. He was the owner of the wich house next to mine, and I counted him and his wife amongst my friends.

Parker looked at me with an amused expression. "A friend of yours, is he?" he asked.

"By the look on your face, I suspect you know that already," I said. "What were they arguing about?"

"I don't know," replied Parker. "The tavern was noisy, but Davenport was as white as a sheet. He was deadly angry. I could have sworn he was going to hit Tench."

"But he didn't?"

"No. They talked for a while, and then Davenport got up and stormed out. Tench finished his drink and left about ten minutes later."

I considered the situation. I had done plenty of contract work with John Davenport over the years, and I thought I knew him well enough to think that he could not possibly be responsible for the violence inflicted on Tench. Nevertheless, I realised that I would have to interview him. I got to my feet, thanked Parker for the information, and headed for the door.

With the market now in full swing and the need to locate Arthur Sawyer ever more pressing, I decided it would be prudent to return to town via an alternative route. So, once across the bridge, I skirted to my right down the Water Lode, the narrow lane that led to the fordable part of the River Weaver. In order to avoid the crowds, I followed the line of the earthworks past the bottom of Castle Street, where butchers' lads were busy climbing the walls to deposit meat scraps into the river. From there, I passed the end of Barker Street and eventually arrived at the bottom of Pillory Street, where the onion sellers and other vegetable farmers had set up their stalls.

The town on market day was always a seething mass of humanity, and not knowing the whereabouts of my colleague, I realised I would have my work cut out for me if I were to make it back to my stall in time to relieve Skinner.

My first task was to deal with two vagrants who had been caught begging from the townsfolk as they shopped.

With the help of a couple of grateful stallholders, they were quickly ushered into the town jail, located halfway along Pillory Street, to wait until such time as I could deliver them into the next parish. The next problem was a dispute over weights and measures between a customer and an onion seller, who had come into town from one of the nearby villages. The two adversaries had almost come to blows when I arrived on the scene, and neither was in the mood to be calmed down. Far from being pacified by my attempts at mediation and my suggestion that the issue should be settled by the town's leave-lookers, the stallholder carried on in a shameful manner for fully five minutes, before deciding to take a swing at me. He too had to be bundled, cursing loudly, into a cell alongside the vagrants, whilst the market inspectors did their work. I could see it was going to be a long day.

As I battled with the ill-tempered market trader, my eyes fell on the unmistakeable pock-marked face and bulbous nose of the man I was seeking. Arthur Sawyer, a short, wiry man, was stood with an amused look on his face by one of the cell doors. Towering over him at his side stood the town bailiff, Andrew Hopwood, who nodded a curt greeting. Unsmiling and taciturn in nature, the tall official cut a gaunt figure, dressed, as he was, soberly, in the Dutch style.

"Good morning, Cheswis," chuckled Sawyer. "You seem on rare form today. Two wastrels and a well-cankered farmer – and all within ten minutes. The jail will be fit to burst if you carry on at this rate."

"It is not the vagrants that bother me," I replied. "As a bangbeggar I am now well-practiced, but I'd be pleased to avoid having to put up with being assaulted by swindling stallholders and angry market-goers quite so often."

"Well said, my friend, but it seems you are only too keen to place yourself at the mercy of angry tradesmen. It is not even your turn to be on duty. Why are you not at your cheese stall?"

I thought it somewhat rich to be spoken to in this manner by a runagate like Sawyer, who seemed to prefer gossiping with the bailiff to keeping order within the town, so I let my feelings be known. "You're nought to brag on," I said. "The only reason I'm here now is because you were nowhere to be found this morning. A man has been murdered near Welsh Row sconce and Major Lothian required someone to attend. I was hauled from my breakfast because you did not leave word as to your whereabouts."

Sawyer looked at me evenly and snorted. "I was doing my rounds, as we both do," he said. "I heard something had happened on Welsh Row. What's the news?"

"The victim is a man called William Tench," I explained. "He was a tanner from up Hospital Street. Seems he had a reputation for frequenting a number of different taverns and asking awkward questions. Do you know of him?"

Sawyer's eyes had widened in surprise. "Tench? Yes.

I've spoken to him once or twice. He's one of those people who tries to befriend everyone but really is liked by no-one. He knows where to draw the line, though. If he upsets someone, you won't see him for days."

I nodded. "On this occasion, it seems he upset someone rather more than he bargained for," I said, drily. "Do you know where he worked? Did he have his own workshop?"

"He used to, I think, but he ran into money troubles and had to close down. Had no head for business, I'm told. You might want to talk to the Comberbachs. I think he has been employed by them for the last year or so."

I thanked Sawyer and, after making sure the irate onion seller was safely locked away, made my way back into the crowds. The Comberbach family ran the town's leading tannery business, and I would pay them a visit in due course. For now, though, I had a cheese stall to take care of.

The bells of St Mary's church chimed one o'clock as I weaved my way through the crowds in the square and back down Pepper Street towards my house. When I arrived, I was surprised to find Alexander stood there, serving cheese. Skinner was nowhere to be seen.

"He's buggered off home," grumbled my friend, by way of explanation. "Some excuse about his father being taken ill, or so I hear."

"You mean you haven't seen him?" I asked, angrily.

"Apparently, he disappeared with one of his brothers not long after you left. Left poor old Mrs Padgett to hold the fort, which meant she was unable to do her own shopping. She left five minutes ago to see if the stall holders have got anything left. Simon has turned up, though. He's inside, getting more cheese."

At that moment, my front door burst open, and the familiar figure of my younger brother appeared, brandishing the last of the new milk cheeses.

Simon was fully ten years younger than me – my baby brother, but in almost every aspect he was my direct opposite. Whereas I was dark-haired and often described as being of studious and reserved character, Simon was outgoing, humorous, and sported a long mane of straight, blond hair, which fell loosely over his shoulders. Women tended to find him attractive, and he had turned many a young girl's eye in Nantwich, but he had recently become betrothed to a young seamstress called Rose Bailey, who lived with her parents towards the end of Beam Street. Simon had always been a spontaneous young man, a trait which had a knack of getting him into trouble from time to time. However, I was pleased to see that there were now signs that he was beginning to settle down.

Simon, like myself, had been apprenticed to a local tradesman; in his case, to a shoemaker called Simkins. Like me, he was not particularly enamoured with his lot. It was a hard life. He was usually away from home between Thursday and Saturday at the market in Manchester, so I was surprised to see him on my doorstep.

"Your produce has sold well," he said, laying the cheese on the table. "There are only a couple of pieces of cream cheese left, and the flett cheese ran out over an hour ago. Once this is sold, you'll be fair cleaned out."

"It's good to see you, brother," I said, clapping him on the shoulder, "and thank you for the help. But why are you not on your travels today?"

Simon shrugged. "Simkins decided not to go to market this week because of the weather, and, with news of the Irish landing in Wales to support the King, he was concerned we might not get back safely."

"But Manchester remains strong for Parliament and the King's army is still in Chester," I said. "The road should be clear enough."

"I know. But Simkins is a cautious fellow and he is afraid of the papist hordes. He has heard all manner of stories of their barbarity. He believes it will be safer to trust in the protection of Colonel George Booth."

"Let us hope that that is so," I said.

I talked in this manner with Simon for the next half an hour whilst we sold the remainder of the cheese. Despite our age difference, Simon and I had always been close, and it was good to have the opportunity to converse with him. It seemed as though we never had much time for such things these days. Before the last portions of cheese were sold, I wrapped up three pieces, one each for Alexander and Simon, and one for Rose Bailey's parents. Alexander muttered his thanks, but his mind was elsewhere.

"You know, Daniel, these takings don't quite add up," he said. "You should have more money than this."

"What do you mean?" I asked, sweeping the crumbs from the table and gathering together my scales.

"Well, allowing for waste and the pieces you have just given us and assuming you made a couple of shillings for the butter, you should have about sixteen or seventeen shillings in total. You only have fourteen shillings and sixpence here. It looks like about five or six pounds of cheese have gone missing."

I cursed. This was not the first time that stock had gone missing on market day. It was usually only a couple of pounds at a time, but there was always something. I had begun to suspect that James Skinner was secreting some away each week, but I hadn't been able to prove anything. Surely it was no coincidence that the first time I had needed to be absent from the stall, a larger amount had disappeared.

"It's that good-for-nothing apprentice of yours, I'll wager," said Simon. "If I were you, I'd let him feel the weight of your boot on his arse on Monday."

"What's your view, Alexander?" I asked, seeking a second opinion.

Alexander sucked his teeth and looked up. "I don't have the best impression of him," he admitted, "but don't go jumping to conclusions. He's nothing more than a young lad and, according to Mrs Padgett, the stall was unattended for a couple of minutes before she was able to come out to help. The town was busy too. Anyone could have stolen a couple of pieces."

I exhaled deeply, unconvinced. "You're too kind to him," I said.

"Perhaps," conceded my friend. "If it helps, I'll make a few enquiries. Skinner lives up in Snow Hill, so I'll ask a few questions in the taverns thereabouts. You never know. I don't hold out much hope, though. It is only a few pieces of cheese, after all."

On any normal Saturday, my work for the day would have been finished once the market had closed and my stall had been cleared away. However, I had rapidly become accustomed to the fact that the work of a constable is never done. After thanking Alexander and Simon once more for their help, I returned to the jail to seek out Sawyer, in order to attend to the matter of what to do with the two vagrants and the market trader who had assaulted me.

I had already decided that the latter would rot in jail until he could be brought before a judge. The vagrants, however, could not wait. In principle, our duty was to whip all tramps and beggars before transferring them into the safekeeping of the constable in the next parish, with a pass to return them to whence they came. This was one of the duties I disliked the most. I had always possessed a keen abhorrence of corporal punishment, and so I usually left this task to Sawyer, who seemed to have developed something of a taste for it. Today, however, I managed to persuade him that the most efficient course of action would be to get both of them out of town as quickly as possible.

This was my responsibility, as Sawyer had agreed to be on duty in the evening to deal with any trouble that might occur in the taverns. Fortunately, both vagrants had arrived in town from the same direction, so I only needed to take them as far as Acton. Nevertheless, it was fast approaching six in the evening by the time I had fulfilled all my duties and was on my way home.

It was a clear, crisp evening when I arrived back in Pepper Street. Orion was prominent in the winter sky and an invisible blanket of icy air had settled over the town, biting at my exposed cheeks as I made my way through the snow. The effect would have been invigorating, were it not for the fact that I was utterly exhausted.

The house smelled of cooking as I entered, a mixture of roasting meat and baking, and I thanked God for Mrs Padgett. I threw my hat down on my chair next to the hearth and ventured into the kitchen. Amy stood by the table, engrossed in rolling out pastry for her grandmother. Mrs Padgett herself was preparing vegetables, and she turned to face me, wiping her hands on her apron as she did so.

"You are a sight for sore eyes, Mrs Padgett," I said. "That smell is a welcome worthy of a king. You are indeed a wonder."

"That may be so," came the answer, "but let us hope we don't have to welcome this particular king to our parts any time soon."

I acknowledged the riposte with a wry smile.

"And as for you, Master Cheswis," she continued, "you look fit to collapse. Mark my words. You'll be dead before you're forty, if you carry on in this manner."

I considered this. There was certainly a modicum of truth in what my housekeeper had to say. A year as a constable is enough public duty for any man, and the rigours of civic responsibility had begun to take their toll on me. However, Mrs Padgett was not taking into account the restorative properties of her cooking. After sampling her roast capon, root vegetables, and apple cake, I felt much more inclined to face the argument which I knew was coming next.

"What you need, Daniel Cheswis, is a wife," she said, filling my wooden tankard with a serving of small beer. "Now it may be none of my business, and I may be doing myself out of a job and a home, but you would do well to find yourself a good woman. There is more to life than ambition."

"You are right and you are wrong," I replied, with a little more force than was warranted, for my housekeeper meant well. "My marital status is certainly none of your business, but as far as your position in this household is concerned, you need have no cause for worry. I would not see you and Amy destitute under any circumstance. You must know this."

Mrs Padgett pursed her lips in annoyance, as she was wont to do on occasions when her mothering ways failed to achieve their intended aim. She said nothing, but I could see she was struggling to hold her counsel, so I relented.

"The fact is, I cannot see where a wife will come from," I said. "I simply have not found the right person."

This was, at least, the truth, but it was meat and drink to Mrs Padgett, who jumped on my lame response like a hungry dog on a bone. "Those are the words of a man whose head is full of bees," she exclaimed, with a vehemence that caught me off guard, adding "if I may be so bold," as an afterthought.

"And how do you come to that conclusion, pray?"

Mrs Padgett's cheeks reddened as she warmed to her task. "You need to free yourself from the past. It is ten years since you saw Alice Bickerton. She is long since married and settled in Shrewsbury with a family of her own. You must forget her before your obsession with her ruins your life."

It's funny how women often have the knack of getting right to the nub of the problem. Mrs Padgett spoke the truth, although I was loath to admit it. Alice Bickerton had been the love of my life and the fact that I had lost her still rankled, even though it was nearly a decade ago. I knew that I would have to pull myself together if I were to avoid becoming a middle-aged bachelor, but it was not easy. I could not rid myself of the hope, deep within me, that Alice would one day come back, and things would be as they once were.

I had known Alice Bickerton since I was a small child. Our respective fathers, both being farmers, were neighbours and friends. We occupied Greenbank Farm, which lay in the centre of Barthomley, next to St Bertoline's church and opposite the village's only inn, The White Lion. John Bickerton's farm, Stony Cross, was half a mile up the hill on Audley Road. As youngsters, Alice and I had been schooled together by the village rector, Reverend Fowler, and in our spare time, being the same age, we had played in the fields together too. Even as we grew older and developed groups of friends of our own genders, we saw each other regularly.

Neither of us could remember exactly when it was, but sometime during that difficult year of 1631, when the country was beset with harvest failures, I noticed something different about Alice. Perhaps it was something in the way her blonde ringlets fell across her face, or the way she smiled, revealing her slightly crooked front teeth. It could even have been something to do with the way she said my name – as a small child she had been unable to pronounce my name properly and had called me 'Danull', a form of address she had kept ever since. Whatever it was, one day during that summer, everything changed and Alice was no longer just a friend.

The feeling, it turned out, was mutual, and we would have married if we had been allowed, but John Bickerton told me to sort out my apprenticeship first and to come back when I was in a position to support his daughter. And so I was packed off to Nantwich to work in Edward Swindell's wich house.

Alice said she would wait, and every other weekend for three years I would return home to Barthomley where we would make plans for when we would eventually be united. But then, one day in August 1634, I returned home and Alice wasn't there. At first, people would not say what had happened, but I knew something was wrong, and eventually it was the Reverend Fowler who told me. Alice had fallen in love and eloped with the owner of a printer's workshop called Hugh Furnival. I was devastated. How could it be that we were as good as betrothed one moment and separated the next? I struggled to comprehend what there was about this man that had brought Alice to betray me in this manner.

There *had* been a letter, but I could only bring myself to read the first few lines. I tore it up and threw it down the well.

Furnival was also from Barthomley, but he was seven years older than me. Being so many years his junior, my dealings with him were scant, but I recalled him as a thin, weasely man with a prominent forehead and straight hair as black as coal, which hung strangely forward over his cheekbones. My brother George, who had been a burly youth, remembered him better, having beaten him up in an argument over a spinning top, despite being four years younger.

Hugh had left Barthomley when I was still small and had gone to London to take up his apprenticeship. There he had learned his trade and become active in the production of newsletters and pamphlets, largely espousing arguments of a puritan persuasion. He had made something of a name for himself, and perhaps it was that and the lure of the capital which drew Alice to him. I did not expect to find out, though, for since the letter, I had never seen Alice again.

I eventually learned, through my parents' friendship with the Bickertons, that Hugh and Alice had married and now had three children. Furnival himself had continued to be successful as a printer and had eventually moved to Shrewsbury, where he had established a printing press, the only one in that part of England. Occasionally, I caught sight of his pro-parliamentary pamphlets in the taverns, but I did not trouble myself to read them in detail, not wishing to be reminded of what I had lost.

As for other women, there had been one or two liaisons but nothing serious. Those relationships I did have broke down when I realised that the kind of feeling I had for Alice was absent. This, however, was not a subject Mrs Padgett needed to concern herself with. She was, after all, a servant in my household and she occasionally needed to be reminded of this. Placing my tankard on the table, I drew myself up to my full height and looked my housekeeper squarely in the eye.

"Mrs Padgett. You always have my best interests at heart, and I thank you for that. But I am a grown man and I do not need advice on whom or when I should marry," I said. "And as for Mrs Furnival," I continued, deliberately using Alice's married name, "she is, as you say, out of my life and, as I see no reason for her to make an appearance in Nantwich, I fully expect her to be perpetually out of my mind."

Satisfied that I had stated my point and reasserted my authority in my own household, I took a mouthful of beer and let it swill around in my mouth before swallowing. Mrs Padgett said nothing, but as I looked up from my beer, I saw that she was smiling.

5

Nantwich – Sunday, December 10, 1643

Sunday morning dawned bright and fresh, although the air was still freezing cold and the snow on the paths had turned to ice. Thanks, in no small part, to my exertions the previous day, I had slept well, and so it was with renewed vigour that I made my way through the square, my boots crunching on the frozen cobbles.

Having made little progress the previous day, I had decided it was time that I spoke to William Tench's widow. I was loath to disturb her on the Lord's Day, but I felt the need to get what I anticipated would be one of the more unpleasant parts of my investigation over with the utmost expediency. With that in mind, I stuffed the crimson scarf found on Tench's body inside my cloak and set off to find her immediately after breakfast, hoping to do so before the first churchgoers started to descend on St Mary's for the morning service.

I headed off down Hospital Street, the main thoroughfare, which led more or less due east out of Nantwich. Mrs Tench, whose first name, I had learned, was Marion, lived at the far end of the street in a small cottage that she and her husband had rented from her employer, Randle Church, whose own magnificent half-timbered mansion lay only a few yards away.

A knock on the door of the cottage resulted in the appearance of an ageing couple dressed in workers' clothing, who I took to be the parents of either Tench or his widow. Behind them, I caught the sight of Tench's body, laid out in the front room, ready for burial. The father, a balding man with an unkempt beard, appeared to recognise me.

"We've been expecting you Master Cheswis," he said. "You'll be after Marion, I imagine? You'll find her over at the house with Mr Randle."

I nodded my thanks and, not wishing to impose on their grief, walked the few extra yards to the end of the street.

Church's Mansion was a fine, moated residence, located on the right-hand side of Hospital Street, just before the earthworks, which ran in a broad curve round the back of the house and its ample gardens. The building's striking black and white gables faced the street and seemed even more imposing due to the overhanging first floor, which seemed to reach over and engulf anyone who approached the front door.

The mansion, among the grandest of the houses belonging to Nantwich's merchant families, had been built in 1577 by Randle Church's parents, Richard and Margery, and it was their faces, engraved either side of the oaken front door, which greeted me as I entered the porch and rang the bell.

At first there was no response, but eventually I heard the sound of shuffling feet, and the door was opened by an ancient servant, who eyed me suspiciously.

"My name is Constable Cheswis. I would speak with Mistress Tench," I said. "I understand she is here with Mr Church."

"You'd better wait in the hallway a moment," came the gruff response. I stepped inside the oak-panelled vestibule and watched as the servant shuffled off towards what I assumed must be the drawing-room. My attention was drawn by the sound of raised voices, which seemed to be emanating from behind the door and which ceased as soon as the servant opened it. After a couple of minutes, the servant reappeared and I was ushered in.

The room's main feature was a large brick fireplace, surrounded by intricately carved oak panelling. A log fire glowed in the hearth. Facing it were two oak armchairs next to a low table. It took me a second or two to accustom myself to the light, but once I did so, I noticed a slim, dark-haired woman wearing a red and black jacket standing next to the window to the right of the fireplace. She looked up at me, and I saw that her face was streaked with tears. I was about to address her when I heard a voice emanate from behind one of the armchairs.

"So, Mr Cheswis. You would disturb a poor widow

the day after her husband's demise?" Randle Church was now in his eighties, an old man with wispy grey hair. He may have been infirm, but his face showed an alertness that belied his age as he swung his chair around to face me. I stepped forward to help him, but he waved me away with a brush of his hand.

"I'm sorry for the disturbance, sir," I said, "but you know it is my duty as a constable to seek out the perpetrator of this crime. I understand the sensitivity, and I will take care not to impose on either your or Mrs Tench's time more than is necessary."

Church grunted in reluctant acquiescence and motioned for me to continue. I turned to Mrs Tench, who cast a sullen glance in Church's direction.

"I am very sorry about the loss of your husband," I began, noting with interest the strained atmosphere in the room.

The poor widow dabbed her eyes with her kerchief and made to sit down in the other armchair. "I thank you for your sympathy and concern, constable," she replied. "Life will be difficult without my husband, especially with a young family to take care of. However, I am grateful to Mr Church. I have my job and the cottage. Mr Church has assured me that the roof over my head is safe."

I ventured a glance over towards where Church was sat, but he showed no reaction.

"I have to ask you a few questions," I continued, "but

I will try and keep it brief. Were you aware of your husband's whereabouts on Friday evening?"

The widow shook her head. "I don't ask. I've learned not to. He is out most nights."

"I know he was in The White Swan Tavern on Welsh Row at some time during the evening. Is there any reason why he would be over in that part of town?"

"I have no idea, constable."

"He was observed arguing with the brine worker, John Davenport. Is there any reason you know of why this would be so?" At this question, I noticed a slight tightening of Mrs Tench's lips. She then uttered what I thought was a rather strange response.

"I know of no such thing," she said, "but you can be sure that if William had business with Davenport, my family will take care of it."

I must admit to being slightly taken aback, for I didn't know what to make of Mrs Tench's words, but I continued with my line of questioning nevertheless.

"Did your husband, to your knowledge, have any enemies who might have wished him harm?" I asked.

"He spends most evenings in the tavern," came the reply. "I dare say he may have got into arguments from time to time, but I am not aware of any specific grievance held against him."

"He appears to have had a reputation for visiting different taverns and asking awkward questions. What were his politics, would you say?" At this point, Randle

Church made to intervene, but Mrs Tench was too quick for him and answered anyway.

"I know nothing about that," she said. "I keep well away from his private business."

I was not convinced that Mrs Tench was being entirely truthful with me, but I could see that pursuing this line of enquiry any further was unlikely to be successful.

"Then I will leave you in peace," I said. "Please let me know if you think of anything which might be relevant." For the first time since I had entered the room, Marion Tench smiled.

"I certainly shall," she said, hesitating a moment before adding, "William was a good man, Master Cheswis, a good husband. He did what he thought was right."

I nodded and was about to take my leave, when a final thought struck me. I put my hand inside my cloak and pulled out the crimson scarf.

"Do either of you recognise this?" I asked, taking care to watch both Church and Mrs Tench attentively. For a brief moment, I thought I saw a flash of recognition in Randle Church's eyes, which flicked almost imperceptibly to Mrs Tench, but it was only for a second, and he quickly recovered his composure. I turned to Mrs Tench, who was unmoved.

"Where did you get that from?" asked Church, evenly.

"Do you recognise it?" I responded, answering a question with a question.

"No, I was just curious."

"It was found around the neck of William Tench," I said, fingering the scarf's gold-embroidered border. "The point is, it's rather ornate, is it not? Not just a run-of-the-mill scarf that any royalist officer would wear."

"It is indeed," said Church, "but I'm afraid I can't help you identify to whom it belongs."

"No, sir," I said, "but please be sure to let me know if anything comes up." And with that, I made a tactical retreat and left Church and Mrs Tench to finish their argument.

I must admit to having been somewhat discomfited by my audience with Randle Church, which had raised more questions than it had solved. What had Church and Marion Tench been arguing about before I entered the room, and why was Church so protective of his servant? More importantly, what was the connection between Church and the crimson scarf? I was so lost in thought, as I strolled back into town behind the first of the churchgoers, that I failed to notice the two figures stood by the entrance to The Lamb as I arrived at the top end of Hospital Street.

"Master Cheswis, a word with you, if I may."

I shook myself free of my thoughts and realised I was in the presence of Colonel George Booth, the garrison commander. With him, and displaying his customary impenetrable countenance, was Major Lothian. Both men were dressed for church and had positioned themselves by the earthen walls that had been raised to protect Nantwich's second-largest coaching house from royalist artillery. In that position, they were able to greet anyone approaching the square from Hospital Street or Pillory Street.

Colonel Booth was a young man, barely twenty-one years of age, but as the grandson of Sir George Booth, Baronet Delamere of Dunham Massey, he had risen quickly to his position of authority. Clean-shaven, save for a small moustache which caressed his upper lip, he was of athletic build and possessed a long mane of light brown curls, which fell over his shoulders. Those who had an interest in such matters said that he had spent the years before the outbreak of war in France after quarrelling with his grandfather over his marriage to the daughter of the Earl of Lincoln. However, on the outbreak of war, he had returned to England and fought under Sir William Brereton during his advance into North Wales. Now, with Sir William again on the march, he had been placed in charge of the garrison in Nantwich. He was the very epitome of the young, ambitious officer, but he lacked one thing – experience – and this was provided by the battle-hardened scot who stood by his side.

"Good morning, Colonel," I said, acknowledging Booth's greeting. "How can I be of service?"

"Major Lothian has advised me of the details of yesterday's unfortunate incident at Welsh Row End..."

"You mean the murder of the tanner, William Tench?"

"Indeed. It is not my wont to meddle in civilian matters, but I am given to understand that there are some circumstances surrounding the man's death that may be of relevance to the military."

"I'm not sure, sir," I replied. "I think, at this stage, any assumption would be merely a matter of speculation. I take it you are referring to the scarf that was recovered from Mr Tench's body?"

"I am indeed," affirmed Booth. "You have no doubt heard the same rumours as me about Mr Tench's activities. I would like to discuss your findings with you."

"Well, I think that's a little premature, sir. I've barely begun my investigation."

"I realise that," answered the Colonel, with a smile, "and today is not the day for it. Tomorrow afternoon will do fine. I will await you in my office in The Lamb at two p.m." And with that, Colonel Booth turned abruptly on his heels and headed off in the direction of the church, leaving me standing, open-mouthed, in astonishment.

"Aye, and try not to be late, laddie," added the Major, before marching off in the Colonel's wake.

I must admit I was more than a little irked by the arrogance of the Colonel in presuming to meddle in a non-military matter, for until a firm link could be established between Tench, the scarf, and the King's forces, that was precisely what it was. Nonetheless, I was curious as to Booth's interest in the matter. Pulling my cloak around my neck, I resolved to ask the Colonel a few pertinent questions the following day and headed off in the direction of the church, weaving my way through the crowds that had begun to assemble outside.

The octagonal, red sandstone tower of St Mary's made an impressive sight in the winter sun. Set against the backdrop of the snow-covered trees, which lined the edge of the churchyard, the splendour of such a fine church in a town as small as Nantwich never ceased to amaze me.

Entering by the main door, I sat down at a pew at the rear of the nave and surveyed the scene. The great and the good of Nantwich were already in their places in reserved pews – Thomas Maisterson and his wife near the cross aisle by the pulpit, young Roger Wilbraham next to Maisterson, occupying his elder brother Thomas's pew, representatives of the other leading families in the town – the Church's, the Mainwarings and the Wicksteads to name but a few. I noticed the three Comberbach brothers enter and take their seats in the middle range of the North aisle of the Church and made a mental note to call on them the following morning. Colonel Booth, Major Lothian, and a number of other officers were also in the congregation.

Presently, the minister appeared and made his way to the three-deck pulpit attached to one of the pillars in the nave. The low murmur of the congregation died down in anticipation. The matter of Sunday worship in Nantwich had become a much more serious business of late. Since the establishment of the garrison, the town had become a magnet for the ostentatiously pious, attracting such people from all over Cheshire. It was no longer unusual to see a whole family marching down the street singing psalms on their way to church. The servants of the more affluent families found themselves expected to take part in twice or thrice-daily family prayers and had grown accustomed to having to tolerate instruction from their masters on how they should live their lives, in order to best serve the Christian faith.

The influx of the godly into the town had also resulted in more travelling preachers and an increase in public meetings on theological matters for those who wished to further expound God's word. Sunday services had become more lengthy affairs too, especially since our minister, the respected and well-loved John Saring, who had served our parish for ten years, had been prevented from carrying out his work. Saring had been a popular figure, whose one weakness had been to be a royalist. He now languished in jail in Stockport, having been convicted in April of colluding with others to betray plans for an attack by the garrison on nearby Cholmondeley Hall, which was held by the King. His unelected replacement, a man called Welch, was much more in line with the expectations of the local puritan laity.

Today's sermon, unsurprisingly, consisted largely of a justification of the parliamentary cause as a religious struggle and was aimed as much at the soldiers of the garrison and at strengthening the moral fortitude of the average townsperson as at the godly elite.

"Is it not a sin for a king to enforce his subjects to worship false idols?" he preached. "Is it not a sin for him to show contempt for his most faithful servants, those ministers who would follow the true faith? If this is true, is it not divine providence that has brought the misery of this war down upon the King's head? If this is true, is it not right and just that the forces of good should raise arms against a king? Brethren, I urge you to resist idolatry, do not profane the Sabbath, and unite under the banner of Jesus, and good will triumph over those who would mislead our monarch."

Once the sermon was over, the majority of the congregation proceeded immediately to act contrary to the words of the minister by profaning the Sabbath and heading straight for the nearest tavern. For my part, I lingered outside the church and watched as the crowd gradually dispersed. Alexander and his family nodded to me as they ambled back across the square in the direction of Pepper Street. My brother, Simon, was also there, the very image of sobriety as he attended Rose Bailey and her parents. This, I suspected, was not a state he would be in for long, and I fully expected him to be found in one of the alehouses on Beam Street just as soon as he had finished paying his respects to his future in-laws.

I was just about to head for home myself, when my attention was caught by two women and a man, who were stood in conversation by the church wall. I don't know what it was that made me look in that direction, but as I did so, my heart lurched. Even though she was turned away, facing the wall, there was no mistaking the blond ringlets of the woman dressed in green on the right.

Alice Furnival must have realised somehow that she was being watched, for, after a few seconds, she looked over her shoulder and caught my eye. She said nothing to me, but turned and spoke to her companions, who both glanced nervously in my direction. Alice then touched her female companion gently on the arm and walked slowly over to where I was standing. As she approached, I noticed she looked a little older. There were a few lines around her eyes and mouth that had not been there when I had seen her last, but she was still beautiful. She also appeared to be reasonably well-to-do, her dress being clearly of the best quality. I felt a mix of emotions upon seeing her again; happiness for being able to see her face once more, but also anger for what she had done to me and, above all, frustration, for I knew I would not be able to say to her what I really wanted to say.

"Hello, Daniel," she said, taking care to use my real name, rather than the pet name I had become accustomed to hearing.

"Mistress Furnival," I said, returning the greeting with the formality I felt the occasion required. "I did not expect to see you again."

"Nor I you," she replied. "Time has passed us by. It

must be ten years."

"It will be ten years next August. That much is etched in my memory."

I thought I saw Alice purse her lips slightly at my response, but I could not be sure.

"That is certainly a long time, Daniel," she said, "but there is no need to address me as a stranger. You can still call me Alice."

I nodded in acknowledgement.

"Please accept my apologies, but please also understand that this is difficult for me. The last time we spoke, circumstances between us were rather different."

Alice lowered her eyes in a manner which one might have taken for contrition, but which I was in no mood to accept as such.

"I promise you I will explain everything someday," she said, "but today is not the time. I understand you have done well for yourself."

"I have my own wich house and a cheese business, and, as you can see, I am now fulfilling my duty as a constable. Life is treating me tolerably well. Tell me, what brings you here, Alice?"

"My father is my main concern. He has become ill of late and I wanted to be nearby, not least because it appears that the area around these parts will soon be a target for the King's army. It is this development which also draws my husband to Nantwich. The demands of his newssheet means that he is required to be close to where there is some military activity to report. Wars provide much work for publishers and printers."

"I am sorry to hear about your father," I replied. "I shall endeavour to pay my respects to him the next time I am in Barthomley. But what of your husband?" I asked. "He is not here?"

"Hugh has some business to attend to in Shrewsbury, but he will be here in a few days. In the meantime, I will be lodging with my sister and brother-in-law." Alice gestured to her two companions, who had not taken their eyes off us since the beginning of the conversation.

"And your children? You have not brought them with you?"

"Hugh, Edward, and Alice are eight, six, and four. They are growing up quickly, but we did not wish to uproot them and considered it safer to leave them in Shrewsbury. It is quieter there since the King left. They are in the safekeeping of our housekeeper, who we know we can trust. We plan to return as soon as we can."

After wishing Alice and her husband a safe and productive stay in Nantwich, I walked back home in a black mood. The return of Alice into my life was not something I was prepared for, nor was it welcome. The knowledge that she would be living in Nantwich, both married and unobtainable, was almost too much to bear. But it wasn't just that. I could not help thinking that her return was somehow unnatural, that she was not meant to play any future part in my life. I could not quite put my finger on it, but I was plagued by a nagging feeling that this was a bad omen – the start of something of which no good could possibly come.

6

The next day, I awoke to be greeted by a dawn so grey and misty that I could have sworn God had chosen to tease me by reflecting my mood in the cold dreariness of my surroundings. Frost hung heavily in the air and livestock huddled closely in their sheds to escape the icy bitterness of the winter's morning.

I had slept fitfully, tossing and turning, my mind plagued with alternating images of Alice standing in her green dress by the wall of St Mary's Church and the unsettling vision of the crimson scarf wrapped tightly around William Tench's neck.

"God's teeth, Daniel. You look like the very image of hell," said Alexander, as I opened the door to him. "Did you sleep last night?"

"Barely," I admitted, stepping past him into the street. "I had things on my mind. I didn't eat much yesterday either. Mrs Padgett thinks I'm sickening for something."

"Worrying about how to track down William Tench's murderer?"

"Yes, but not just that. Alice Bickerton is back in town.

84

I saw her outside the church yesterday."

Alexander shot me a sideways glance. As my best friend, he not only made it his business to look after my welfare, but was fully-apprised of my previous relationship with Alice. "That is not good news," he said, struggling to keep up with me as I marched off in the direction of the square. "Why is she here?"

"To be closer to her father, who is ill, or so she says, and so her husband can report for his Shrewsbury newssheet on what happens when Lord Byron shows up here."

"Then I advise you to give her a wide berth. That woman is not good for your health, I'll swear it. Look at the state of you already." Alexander was right, of course. I did not require my friend to tell me that attempting to renew any sort of romantic relationship with Alice was absolutely out of the question. Despite that, I had a hunch that staying out of her way might not be quite as easy as I would have liked.

The ever-indulgent Alexander had joined me that morning because my prime objective was to interview John Davenport and I needed both a witness and, potentially, some muscle, should an arrest be necessary. However, our first visit was to William Tench's employers, the Comberbach family, whose thriving tannery business was located on Barker Street, which ran almost parallel to Pillory Street, but a little closer to the river. The family's workshop was run by three brothers, Thomas, Roger, and John, and it was the second of these,

Roger, a fit, wiry man in his early forties, who greeted us at the entrance to his yard.

"You are here, I take it, to make enquiries about William Tench," he said, coming straight to the point.

"Indeed I am," I confirmed. "Had he been in your employ for long?"

"Not long. A year or so, perhaps. But he was a good worker who knew his trade. The Tench family have long been active in this business."

"I'm aware of that. So you have no grounds for complaint with him?"

Comberbach shrugged. "Complaint? Not at all. Why should I? He was occasionally the worse for wear for drink, I admit, but, as long as his work was not affected, I turned a blind eye to it."

I nodded and fastened gratefully onto the information volunteered about Tench's drinking habits. "His partiality to a tankard of ale is well known," I agreed, "but it is also said that he had a habit of poking his nose into the affairs of others, particularly those of the soldiers of this garrison. Do you know anything about that?"

Comberbach gave me a sharp look. "I don't know what you mean," he said.

"Let me put it this way. Did he ever express support for the King's cause in this conflict which plagues us at the moment?"

Comberbach opened his mouth as realisation dawned as to the direction my questions were taking. "So you suspect him of spying for the royalists?" he exclaimed, a grin spreading slowly across his face. "I don't know about that, but he was always very complimentary about the King. His wife works for Randle Church, and everyone who is associated with the Church family supports the King in some measure. Mr Randle's son was Sergeant-at-Arms to the King, you know."

"Really?" I said, interested.

"Yes, but that doesn't mean a thing on its own. Half of the gentry around here are royalists. They just have to keep it quiet at times like this."

I nodded. "Did Tench have any enemies that you are aware of?" I asked, more in hope than in expectation.

"Not to my knowledge. There is one thing you might wish to be aware of, though. John Davenport came around here early on Saturday morning asking for William Tench. When I explained he was not here, he left a leather pouch for him."

My eyes widened. This new revelation was something I had not expected. "At what time would that have been?" I asked.

"About eight o'clock."

"And do you still have the pouch?"

"Yes. I'll fetch it for you." At that, Comberbach turned on his heels and disappeared inside his workshop, returning a few moments later with a small leather purse, which he laid in my hands. I looked inside and was surprised to find coins amounting to about two pounds in value and a small piece of paper folded twice. I carefully took out the paper and unfolded it. I gasped as I read the note written on the inside.

"This is the last time."

I looked at Roger Comberbach in puzzlement. "Have you any idea what this note alludes to?" I asked. "A payment for work done on behalf of your business, perhaps?"

"No. It can't be that. Tench knew that all payments needed to be handed over to me personally."

"I see. In that case, Master Comberbach, I fear it is time to pay John Davenport a visit," I said. "It is fortunate that he was to be our next port of call anyway. Good day to you."

With that, I pocketed the note and turned on my heels, leaving poor Alexander to return the pouch and to apologise for the abruptness of my departure.

"This is a strange turn of events," I said to Alexander, as we turned into Mill Street on the way to Davenport's wich house. "Tench was already dead on Saturday morning. If Davenport is guilty of his murder, why would he drop a pouch of money off for him afterwards?"

"Perhaps it's a bluff," suggested Alexander, "a ruse in order to appear innocent."

I stopped and looked down the River Weaver towards the bridge as I considered my friend's words. "It would be a strange ruse indeed," I mused. "Handing over money in this way does not diminish suspicion. It merely increases it."

A freezing mist had descended over the river like a shroud, bleak and forbidding, as Alexander and I approached Town Bridge to cross into Welsh Row. Icicles hung like daggers from the rooftops of the houses lining the Water Lode, threatening anyone who dared walk beneath them. It was still early, but the streets were oddly quiet save for a lone dog searching for food, sniffing down by the river bank at the last of the butchers' scraps from Saturday's market. Sensing our approach, it slunk noiselessly between two of the houses, a piece of semi-frozen offal clamped between its jaws.

Crossing the bridge, I noticed that 'Old Biot', the brine pit responsible for the historical prosperity of Nantwich, lay deserted, the gnawing cold having discouraged all but the hardiest souls from venturing far from the warmth of their firesides. Despite the weather, I might have expected to find a few brine workers huddled around the edge of the pit, but today, the only evidence that anyone had been there at all were a number of footprints in the snow around the rim.

Located a few yards north of the bridge and no more than fifteen feet from the river bank, the brine pit was a twenty-foot-deep scar in the earth from where the brine would be lifted in buckets or transported in wooden pipes called theets into the wich houses, which lined the edge of the river in Snow Hill and along the Water Lode. On the opposite side of the river, in Great Wood Street and Little Wood Street, more wich houses were located. However, only one theet crossed the river, this running through a gap between two buildings into a gigantic common cistern, which ran in between the two streets for their whole length, storing brine for over fifty wich houses. From here, myriad theets rose like giant spiders' legs, leading into the individual buildings.

I glanced across the river and saw that just one of the wich houses in Great Wood Street was emitting smoke from its chimneys, indicating that it was the only one with a kindling on that day. This was the wich house of John Davenport, which stood next door to my own. The other buildings in Great Wood Street were all quiet, little more than salt warehouses.

"It grieves me to see so many wich houses standing idle," I lamented, as we made our way into Welsh Row. "Salt made our town rich, but walling is no longer a trade for young people."

"I fear that is so," agreed Alexander. "It is a sign of the times. Nantwich salt is no longer in demand as it once was." My friend was right. Advances in salt-making techniques had meant that the evaporated salt produced in Nantwich was considered inferior to that manufactured in other salt-works, which had begun to use a Dutch process called '*making salt upon salt*,' involving the purification of the salt by blending it with high quality salts from France or Spain. Even before we had had such competition to deal with, the pans Nantwich used to produce salt from 'Old Biot's' brine tended to emit a malodorous stench of sulphur, causing many to consider the end product barely fit for human consumption. It was also frowned upon by physicians, who held poor quality salt at least partially responsible for pulmonary ailments. As a result, salt from the Cheshire wich towns attracted lower prices than other salts and was used mainly by the poor.

This was, however, not the main cause of my disillusionment with the salt trade, which lay more in the antiquated and regulated manner in which the industry was organised. Salt manufacture in Nantwich was organised according to the so-called '*Customs of Walling*'; ancient salt laws which went back as far as anyone could remember and ensured that 'Old Biot' remained a public resource to be managed for the benefit of the whole community.

The laws specified the exact number of wich houses allowed in the town – two hundred and sixteen, all of which had to contain the same number of leads, the large kettles used to boil the brine. With each of these two hundred and sixteen wich houses came a right for twelve days walling per year, each walling consisting of twenty-four hours plus a two hour allowance for cleaning.

Because wich houses came with walling rights, over

time the rights were sold, with the result that a wich house was not necessarily a physical entity. Some wich house owners had bought rights from others and could therefore produce more salt in their own buildings. Others had closed their wich houses completely, but still held walling rights and sub-contracted these rights to other wich houses.

This might have been acceptable to me, had it only been the amount of salt produced per wich house that was limited. However, the ownership of walling rights was also rationed. Married men were allowed thirty-six leads, the equivalent of six wich houses, whilst single men and widows were limited to half that amount, another reason, according to Mrs Padgett, why I should hurry up and find myself a wife.

I fully understood that the customs of walling existed in order to maintain the use of the brine pit for the common good of the people of Nantwich, but it stopped people like me from developing and expanding their businesses. The result was that wich houses stayed idle for much of the year and the only way to make money was to contract walling work for those who had walling rights but no wich house. Salt-making was truly a business for men with no ambition.

Anyone trying to beat the system by dishonest means was taking a great risk, for walling was heavily policed by four Rulers of Walling elected from those who had walling rights. Like my own position as constable, the rulers were elected at the Michaelmas Court Leet and served for a year. John Davenport himself had previously held one of these positions and it was a role I knew I would be expected to carry out myself sooner or later. The role of the Rulers of Walling was to estimate the price of salt and to allot the time of each person's walling in order to make sure that no wich house was disadvantaged. This was carried out during a process known as '*making meet*'. The Rulers also had to be present at the start and the end of each kindling to make sure the rules were adhered to. Anyone not complying with them ran the risk of being ostracised by the community and having his wich house pulled down.

All these factors had combined to bring me to the realisation that the life of a brine worker was not for me. My ambition was to develop my cheese business to the point where it could support me on its own, and then to sell the walling rights and wich house to somebody else. In the meantime, though, until that dream could be realised, I would need to continue to work my allocated walling and make as much as I could from what was essentially a stagnating business.

That being the case, my first task before calling on Davenport was to visit my own wich house. So, having turned right into Great Wood Street, Alexander and I stopped short of the building with the smoking chimneys and entered the one next to it.

My wich house was laid out exactly the same as all

the other wich houses in the town. Down one side of the building stood the ship – the huge wooden trough used to hold the brine, enough for four days walling or one kindling. In front of this stood six hearths, each with a large iron pan about a yard square. Behind the hearths were a series of stone pipes, through which heat was funnelled to an adjacent storeroom where the wet salt was stored and dried in barrows, huge egg-shaped barrels made of wicker, which allowed the leach brine to drain out.

It was here that I located James Skinner, who was busy stoking the fires, in order to make sure that the storeroom was warm enough to dry out the salt produced during my last kindling, which had been completed a few days earlier.

"Good morning, Master Cheswis," he said, as Alexander and I entered the room.

"Good morning, James," I replied. "You are on your own here?"

"Yes, sir. Mr Robinson is next door with Mr Davenport. He left me to stoke the fires and ready some salt for shipment. I am to report to him as soon as I've finished."

Gilbert Robinson was my head waller, responsible for all production within the wich house. Like many such people, he was contracted to several wich house owners, one of whom was John Davenport. I had no problem with Skinner being used to help Davenport during his kindling, as the favour would no doubt be returned the next time I had a kindling of my own. What I did have a problem with, though, was Skinner disappearing whenever he felt like it, so I made sure I took advantage of the opportunity to quiz him about his whereabouts on Saturday morning. Skinner, for his part, had clearly expected to be chided for his absence and was ready with his excuse.

"It was my father," he said. "He was taken ill. He suffers from the falling sickness, and on Saturday morning he was taken with a seizure and fell into the fireplace. If my brothers hadn't been there, he'd have been badly burned. I was sent for to help tend him." Skinner's excuse was no doubt a good one, but I was not feeling particularly charitable that morning.

"That's all very well," I countered, "but you can't just abandon your work at a moment's notice. You inconvenienced Mrs Padgett, who could not do *her* work, you inconvenienced Alexander and my brother because they had to take over the stall. What's more, a number of pieces of cheese were missing. I can't afford to lose half my profits to thieves."

Skinner gave me a sullen glance and, avoiding looking me directly in the eye, mumbled a further apology. I sighed in frustration as Alexander looked on.

"I have to be honest with you, James. You are no use to me as an apprentice if you cannot be relied upon. You need to think carefully about where your best interests lie."

"Yes, sir."

"Then be sure to finish off your work here and hasten over to Mr Robinson. I have a feeling the Davenports will need every spare hand they can muster this morning."

Skinner poked at the fire once more, and shrugged.

"The work here is more or less finished, Master Cheswis."

"In that case, you can make your way over there now. I'll finish tidying up." Skinner laid down the shovel he was using to put coal into the furnaces and scuttled out of the room.

Alexander looked at me with raised eyebrows. "I think you were a little hard on Skinner, there," he ventured. "His father was genuinely ill, so I hear, and, after all, he's just a lad. If you want to nurture an apprentice who will eventually buy this business from you, treating him like that will get you nowhere."

In contrast to my own deserted building, John Davenport's wich house was a hive of activity. With four days walling work to be completed, brine workers from across the town had descended upon Davenport's premises like bees to a honey pot, and they were now busy carrying out the various stages of the kindling, with the five-hour boiling process at each of the six leads having been staggered to ensure maximum efficiency.

At the nearest hearth to the entrance, workers were filling one of the large iron pans with brine and surrounding it with clay and bricks, ready to begin boiling the brine. At the adjacent lead, I noticed the short, square-jawed figure of Gilbert Robinson adding a mixture of brine and cow's blood to a full pan of boiling brine. Once he had finished doing this, he moved onto a third lead, in which the brine had already half-evaporated. Into this he added a mixture of brine and egg-white. Then he approached the fourth lead and poured a small beaker of ale into it. Whilst this was happening, I noticed that James Skinner was stood beside Robinson with a large scoop in his hand and realised that my apprentice had been entrusted with the job of cleaning the scum out of the second and third leads as the brine gradually evaporated.

As soon as Robinson moved away, Skinner began frantically scooping out the scum from the pans and transferring it into a trough already half full of scrapings. This would eventually be sold by the cartload as manure.

Robinson now moved onto the fifth lead and instructed brine workers to reduce the fire so that they could ladle in the leach brine. This process was already well underway at the sixth and final lead, where a number of female briners were busy with their loots, the special wooden rakes used to scoop out the salt that had gathered in the corners of the pans and deposit it in the wicker barrows waiting nearby.

Once he had finished, Robinson caught my eye and waved me over, simultaneously wiping the sweat from his brow with his other arm.

"Warm work, Gilbert?" I said.

"Yes, Master Cheswis, but better than being outside on a day like today."

"That it is," I concurred. "I see you left Skinner to the job of stoking the fires."

"Yes. I'm mortal sorry I had to leave him, but I needed to be here to supervise Mr Davenport's walling and to be present when the Rulers arrived to watch over the start of the kindling. I thought a little responsibility would do him good."

"Well, you've certainly rewarded him with the best job in the house now," I said, as I observed the youth sullenly depositing the detritus from the kindling into the trough behind him. At that moment, a thought struck me. "You said the Rulers have already been. You mean there was more than one of them?"

"That's right," replied Robinson. "I thought it odd too. Normally there's only one of them, but today both Mr Wickstead and Mr Kinshaw turned up. They said something about the need to keep a closer eye on walling activities to prevent fraud, with the market being so low and all." Robinson was right that this was rather irregular. There had been, I remembered, only one Ruler present at my own kindling no more than a few days previously. Still, I mused, Wickstead and Kinshaw must have had a good reason for tightening up their monitoring activities. I returned to the matter in hand and asked where I could find Davenport. Robinson motioned over towards the storeroom.

I was not looking forward to interviewing John Davenport, for I had known him ever since I had begun my apprenticeship. Although he was ten years older than me, he had helped me considerably with my business over the years and I considered him to be a friend. I had shared a table with him, his wife, and his four daughters and felt uncomfortable about having to question him, in the knowledge that he might be guilty of murder.

I found him stripped to the waist, manoeuvring the remaining barrows from his last kindling to one side, in order to make way for the new ones that would be produced over the next four days. It was even warmer in the storeroom, and Davenport's shoulder-length brown hair was tinged with sweat as he manhandled the heavy containers of salt across the room. He nodded in recognition as Alexander and I walked through the door, stopping only when he realised that Alexander had positioned himself by the doorway, in case it proved necessary to prevent an attempt at a rapid exit.

"What can I do for you, Daniel?" he asked, breathing heavily from the exertion. "It's a busy morning."

"I need to ask you some questions about William Tench," I began.

"Who?"

"Come on, John. Don't be evasive," I insisted. "Tench was a tanner from Hospital Street. You were seen arguing with him in The White Swan on Saturday evening. Now he's dead – battered and strangled behind the tavern."

"Oh, him," conceded Davenport. "Serves the bastard right. Cheated me in a wager, he did."

"A wager?"

"A game of hazard. You can ask in The Angel. There were plenty of people that saw it. Those dice were loaded, I'll swear it."

"You mean you admit it?"

Davenport stopped what he was doing and leant on the barrow he had been manhandling. "Admit what?" he barked, giving me a shocked look. "You mean you think I killed him? I'm no murderer, Daniel. I didn't do it, but I expect he deserved what he got."

"What do you mean?"

"Someone would have got him sooner or later. He was well-known for asking awkward questions. There's those that think he's a royalist spy."

I thought about this for a moment and decided to change tack. "Tell me what your argument was about," I demanded. "And why go to The White Swan? Why meet in a tavern at the end of Welsh Row when there are two perfectly acceptable ones within a hundred yards of your wich house?"

"He said I owed him more than I do and asked me to meet him there. I expect he wanted to avoid discussing such things in taverns like The Angel and The Black Lion, because he knew he would be in the presence of friends of mine." What Davenport was saying made sense, but there was something in the tone of his voice that gave me the suspicion that something was not quite right.

"And the money you left at Comberbach's?" I continued.

"That was what I owed him. I didn't know he'd died until Saturday afternoon."

"That could just be a cover up to put us off the scent," I suggested.

"You think I did it?"

"I don't know, John," I admitted. "I've known you long enough to think you would not commit such a foul crime, but the circumstantial evidence is not good. Others around the town are beginning to talk, and that raises the possibility that Tench's relatives might come after you. For your own protection I should put you in jail until I get to the bottom of this whole affair. I have to do my duty. I can't be seen to be soft, just because I know you."

At this, Davenport's expression changed from one of stubborn resistance to one of abject horror.

"Daniel. If you do that I'll never get out. You know that," he pleaded. "I'll be hanging this time next week. I've also got the four days' walling to consider. How am I supposed to manage that in jail?"

I was on the point of offering to look after Davenport's affairs whilst I got the bottom of what had happened to Tench, when I felt an almighty blow in my guts and found myself sprawling on the floor, winded. Fortunately, the heavy barrow that Davenport had pushed into my midriff did not land directly on top of me, but had rolled away to the right, spilling salt all over the floor. Davenport, meanwhile, had sprinted for the doorway in a bid to surprise Alexander, but my friend was not so easily duped. He now held Davenport in a bear hug, the latter's legs kicking wildly in the air as he struggled frantically to get free.

"That was a mistake, John," I wheezed, fighting for breath. "Only a guilty man tries something like that. I will do everything I can to investigate this matter thoroughly and I will make sure this is done correctly. I'll also make sure Robinson is briefed to complete your kindling properly. But you are going to have to sit in jail."

With that, Alexander pinned Davenport's arms behind his back and marched him, moaning profusely, in the direction of the exit.

7

Nantwich – Monday, December 11, 1643

"It doesn't add up," I said to Alexander, after Davenport had safely been locked away in the cells and we had both returned to my house for lunch. "I could have sworn John Davenport was not the type of person to do this."

"You can never know the depths a man will sink to," said my friend, attacking with gusto the plate of mince and onions Mrs Padgett had placed in front of him.

"Yes, but there's more to this than meets the eye," I persisted. "Davenport seemed genuinely surprised we thought he was the murderer."

"That means nothing. He could just be a good actor."

"But what about the money that he delivered to the Comberbachs on Saturday morning and the note that he sent with it?"

"As you say, that could just be a ruse to make us think he didn't do it."

"Yes, but it's a bit obvious, isn't it?"

Alexander could do nothing but agree. We sat for a while in silence – silence that is, save for the sound of my friend eating. I considered the situation. Something just didn't make sense. Why have such a public row over a two pound gambling debt? Two pounds was a reasonable amount of money, but it was not enough to kill for. There was also something in the tone of Davenport's voice that suggested some other unknown factor was behind his behaviour. If I didn't know better, I would have said it seemed like fear. But fear of what? What could Davenport be afraid of? And why risk the hangman's noose by drawing attention to himself like that?

Then there was the question of the crimson sash. What was its importance? I could have sworn Randle Church recognised it when I produced it in his drawing-room the day before. And where did Tench and the rumours surrounding his clandestine spying activities fit in? I turned to Alexander and articulated what I had been thinking.

He squinted at me and belched onion breath in my direction. "You're right," he said. "It's a conundrum of the highest order, and, if I know you, you'll not rest until we get to the bottom of it. There is, however, a time and place for everything, and now is the time for Mrs Padgett's apple cake!" As if on cue, my housekeeper appeared in the doorway and placed a plate in front of each of us.

"It is remarkable how the world seems a much simpler place when apple cake is involved," I said, and tucked in heartily.

The Lamb was bustling with activity when I arrived there later in the afternoon. The impressive coaching house had always been among the more prestigious of the hostelries within the town, but since it had been commandeered by the garrison as its headquarters, it had effectively become an officers' residence. Unlike the common soldiers of the garrison, who, depending on their rank, were billeted in local houses, barns, and tents, Booth and his officers could rely on some degree of comfort during their stay in Nantwich. Having negotiated the two stone-faced halberdiers who stood guarding the entrance to the earthworks surrounding the hotel, I was led by another soldier into a drawing room in the rear of the building, which had been transformed into Booth's personal office.

The Colonel was sat at a table in the centre of the room with a drink in his hand. When I entered he rose and began to pour a second cup.

"Ah, Master Cheswis," he said, by way of welcome. "Thank you for coming. May I offer you some sack? It's very good." Without waiting for a reply, he handed me the newly-filled cup. I took a grateful swig of the sweet, fortified wine and, feeling somewhat uneasy, began to wonder what was behind the over-cordial welcome.

"Tell me," began the Colonel. "As one of the town constables, you are officially the King's representative in Nantwich. Do you not find this an odd state of affairs in a town that rebels against his Majesty?"

"The irony of this is something I think about every day," I replied, not liking the direction the conversation was heading.

"An irony indeed, but not necessarily a conflict," continued Booth, stroking his moustache thoughtfully. "This war is generally not a war of opposites. Wherever you go, the population has a mix of views. For example, in Nantwich, although most people support Parliament, it seems to me that many of the leading families are for the King. Are you for the King too, constable?"

"I'm for the King *and* Parliament," I answered guardedly.

The Colonel smiled. "Good. That's what my sources tell me. And you are aware, no doubt, that four thousand men have sailed from Ireland to join the King's party at Chester?"

"Everybody knows that, sir."

"Quite. Well let me give you a little more detail – a little more flesh on the bones, so to speak. When the first shipments of troops arrived in Mostyn and Anglesey just over three weeks ago, Sir William Brereton withdrew from his position in Flintshire. However, it seems that this might have been a mistake. Firstly, it appears there were relatively few Irish rebels among the troops. The King, I'm sure, would have loved to have accepted the aid of the rebels, but in the end he dared not accept the help of papists.

"Next, the soldiers that did land were weary and disaffected. They hadn't been paid and were practically walking around in rags. Our scouts tell us that if we had infiltrated their forces, we would have been able to convert many to our cause. As it was, Sir William wrote to them from Wrexham, offering to pay their arrears and stressing to them the need to fight for the true religion. However, it would appear that the message never reached the common soldier and their officers were made of sterner stuff. They simply replied that they'd gone to Ireland to fight the King's enemies and intended to do the same here. They then marched on to Chester to recuperate, where they were paid and reclothed. In addition, more reinforcements arrived from Ireland under the command of Sir Robert Byron, the nephew of Sir Nicholas Byron, the Governor of Chester."

"Ah. I heard that Byron had assumed command of the forces in Chester."

"Yes, but that was neither Robert nor Nicholas Byron. Rather, it is Lord John Byron, brother of Robert and nephew of Nicholas, who is now in command in Chester. Lord John was also sent by the King, arriving from Oxford with a thousand horse and three hundred foot."

I took another mouthful of sack and waited for the Colonel to stop speaking. This was all very interesting information, but I couldn't for the life of me fathom why Booth felt the need to entrust it to someone of my status.

"Colonel, why are you telling me all this?" I enquired.

Booth rose to his feet, brushing the front of his doublet where he had spilled some of his drink. "I'm merely trying to illustrate the fact that the royalist forces are gathering strength as we speak. You can be certain that once they are ready, Nantwich will be high on their list of priorities. When they arrive, we must be ready for them."

"And what if the town falls, sir?"

"The town will *not* fall, Master Cheswis," insisted the Colonel, with an edge to his voice. "However, Byron's reputation is, perhaps, a source of worry to the local townsfolk. I cannot imagine they will be well-treated if the town succumbs."

"So how do I fit into this?" I asked, still nonplussed, unsure what Booth was trying to achieve.

"I'm glad you asked me that," said the Colonel, somewhat mysteriously, whereupon he strode over to the door and whispered something, inaudibly, to the guard, who promptly disappeared, returning a few moments later with a dark-haired, clean-shaven officer in his mid-twenties.

"Good afternoon, Master Cheswis, I am Captain Draycott, sir," said the young officer, leaving me none the wiser as to what was going on.

The Colonel saw that I was confused and stepped in. "Draycott is the garrison quartermaster," he explained. "I understand that you have quite a thriving cheese business. Is that so?"

"That is correct, sir. It is my ambition to develop this

business once the war is over."

"Quite so. At this moment, however, there is every possibility that the King's forces may attempt to surround the town and cut off our supply lines."

"A siege?"

"Exactly. So we need to get as much in the way of supplies into the town as we possibly can. Cheese is one such staple supply item. I understand that much of your product is sourced from local farmers. Would you be able to help us build up stocks in the coming days?"

"What do you need?" I asked, turning to Draycott, who had taken a seat at the table and was poised with quill and ink pot, ready to take notes.

"As much cheese as you can lay your hands on, Master Cheswis. When do you collect produce from your suppliers?"

"On Fridays, generally," I replied. "In time for the market on Saturday."

"And how much cheese do you normally collect?"

"It depends on what the farmers can supply me with, but I usually bring back eight to ten cheeses for sale at the market and the same again for sale to regular customers during the week."

"And how much can your cart carry?"

"About twice that amount."

Draycott dipped the quill in his inkwell and made a few calculations, pausing to look at the Colonel before addressing me again. "Good," he said finally. "Please make sure the cart is full, and we'll take the whole cartload."

"I can't do that," I said. "I need to keep some back for the market. I can't let my customers down."

"Once Byron starts making his move on Nantwich, we'll be lucky to have a market," interjected the Colonel, with a wry smile.

"Very well," conceded the quartermaster, adjusting his figures accordingly. "Keep back eight cheeses for yourself and deliver the rest to our stores."

"Alright, Captain," I said, draining my cup of sack. "I'll try my best."

"And another thing. Can you go out on both Thursday and Friday next week? We believe the King's forces may well be not far off by that time, but if you stay to the east of the river you should be safe enough. We'll provide you with a guard to make sure, though. A couple of dragoons should be sufficient."

And so it continued. Ten minutes later, I was in possession of an order for the following three weeks that would see my sales double during that period and provide every prospect of further business afterwards.

"I am indebted to you, sir," I said to Booth, once the efficient Captain Draycott had packed up his writing implements and left the room, "but you did not bring me here to ply me with drink and to buy my cheese. What can I do for you?"

The Colonel narrowed his eyes and stared at me

inscrutably for a moment, but then he threw his head back and emitted a huge guffaw. "By Jesus, you are nobody's fool, Cheswis," he laughed. "My compliments, you are certainly astute." The Colonel hesitated a moment while he gathered his thoughts. "Alright," he added, "since you ask, here it is. I'm interested in what you can find out about William Tench."

"Why?"

"I am well aware that the King *does* have some support in this town," said the Colonel. "It is vital that I know which of these people is passive in their support and which are actively working against us. I am advised Tench may have been a royalist scout," he added." I would like to find out who could have wanted him dead and why."

"At this stage, I'm not sure-" I began, but Booth raised his hand to silence me.

"Take a look at this," he said, opening the drawer of his desk and producing three sheets of paper, which he laid out in front of me. I peered over the desk and realised I was being shown three handwritten documents, each containing a separate list of names.

"You will recall that last spring a remonstrance was circulated throughout Cheshire to ascertain who among the population of the county was in support of Parliament?" Without waiting for an answer, the Colonel jabbed a finger at the first sheet of paper. "This," he said, "is a list of people who signed the document."

I looked at the list and counted nearly seventy names, most of which I recognised as being those of Nantwich residents. "The second document," he continued, pointing to a much shorter list of names, "is a record of the Justices of the Peace and gentlemen who signed the remonstrance." The Colonel handed me the second list, and I counted a total of twenty-eight names.

"But these are all *supporters* of Parliament," I said. "What are you trying to say?"

"Patience, Master Cheswis," admonished the Colonel. "All will reveal itself. Now look at the third list. This is the most interesting of the three, because it lists those prominent gentlemen and town officials who were *not* prepared to sign the remonstrance." Booth pushed the third piece of paper across the table towards me and left me to read off ten names;

Thomas Wilbraham
Randle Church
Thomas Maisterson
Lady Margaret Norton
Alexander Walthall
William Allen
John Saring
William Leversage
Richard Wickstead
Hugh Wilbraham

"A most interesting list," I acknowledged, "but what does it signify?"

The Colonel reached out for the jug of sack and poured out two fresh cups. "This," he said, "is a list of ten of the King's most prominent supporters from among Nantwich's leading families. Thomas Wilbraham is now dead, but we believe his son Roger is of the same persuasion as his father. John Saring, the minister, is now locked away, thank the Lord, and the last three on the list actually signed the remonstrance, but our intelligence leads us to believe they have changed their minds and now support the King, if not actively, then at least passively. That leaves Church, Maisterson, Lady Norton, Walthall, and Allen, the first four of which are the heads of some of the town's most influential families, all capable of compromising the town's security should they feel so inclined. So you see, Master Cheswis, we have to be careful and keep a watchful eye over our enemies, in order to make sure we are able to foil any potential plots."

"And what is William Tench's role in this?" I asked.

"We're not quite sure," admitted Booth. "Of course, we know that his wife works for Randle Church, but that is the only connection we can find at the moment. Have you made any progress in the case?"

"We've made some headway," I admitted. "I've arrested John Davenport."

"Ah yes, the brine worker. Did he do it?"

"I'm not sure, but I don't think so."

"Do you have any ideas as to who might be responsible?"

"It's too early to tell," I said, wary of the probing nature of the Colonel's questions, "but I am making all the necessary enquiries."

"And you will keep me informed, should you make any progress?"

"I will provide you with whatever information I can freely give," I said, hoping that this was enough to satisfy him.

I took another look at the Colonel's list. One name which drew my attention was that of Richard Wickstead. It had not escaped my notice that Wickstead, the head of another of the town's leading merchant families, was one of the Rulers of Walling present at John Davenport's kindling that morning, and I wondered what possible significance there could be in that fact. Why were two Rulers in attendance when only one was necessary? I elected not to pass this information on to Booth until I knew more. The Colonel, for his part, had already moved on to his next question.

"The soldiers say Tench was found with an officer's crimson scarf around his neck," he ventured.

"That's correct."

"Most unusual – why use an object which so obviously suggests allegiance to the King, do you think?"

"I don't know," I replied, truthfully. "It may be relevant, but it may also be nothing more than a distraction."

Booth considered this for a moment, but must have decided he was not going to successfully extract any more information from me, because he suddenly rose to his feet and offered me his hand to shake.

"Master Cheswis, it's good to know I can rely on you to keep me informed about the progress of this case," he said.

"My first priority, sir, is to do my duty by the oaths I have taken as a constable, but you can rest assured that you will most certainly not be kept waiting, should any relevant information come to light."

Afterwards, I walked back to Pepper Street, my mind gripped by a feeling of confusion and uneasiness. Here was another person to add to the growing list of people showing a very specific interest in William Tench, a fact which filled me with foreboding. But if the mystery surrounding Tench was a conundrum for me, it was nothing compared to the sense of disquiet I felt about the manner in which my conversation with Colonel Booth had been conducted. Somehow, I had the feeling that, contrary to my intentions and wishes, I had been recruited for some unknown purpose and that I would not have to wait long before I found out what that purpose was.

Mrs Padgett was waiting for me, staring anxiously out of the window, when I arrived back in Pepper Street. She rose to her feet as I approached and hurried to the door in an agitated manner, flinging it open before I could reach it myself.

"I'm awful sorry, Mr Daniel," she flustered. "I told the lady you would be gone some time, but she insisted on waiting." I peered with curiosity past my housekeeper's shoulder and immediately saw the reason for her agitation. Sat in my armchair, cradling a cup of warm spiced ale and wearing an apologetic smile on her face, was Alice.

I must admit, I was rather shocked to find my former love presenting herself unannounced in my front room in this fashion, but I quickly recovered my composure and attempted to reassure my housekeeper.

"Calm yourself, Mrs Padgett," I said, stamping the snow from my boots as I stepped inside. "I will deal with this. Alice," I said, turning to my guest. "What a surprise. I did not anticipate that I would have the pleasure of your company again quite so soon."

Alice smiled sweetly at me. "Please accept my apologies for the intrusion, Daniel," she said. "I had not intended to disarm your housekeeper so. I will be brief and to the point."

"There is no need to apologise," I responded, shooting a disapproving look at Mrs Padgett, who, still wearing a flustered expression, was attempting to hide it by commencing to sweep the hearth. "You are always welcome here."

Alice inclined her head in acknowledgement. "I have received word from my husband that he will arrive in

Nantwich on Wednesday," she said. "He plans to hold a select reception in the Crown Hotel on Thursday to announce the introduction to Nantwich of his newsbook, *The Public Scout*. I would like to invite you to attend."

This was not what I was expecting, nor was it particularly welcome. Nevertheless, I accepted the invitation with good grace and was asked to present myself in the upper gallery of the Crown at 5 pm on the following Thursday afternoon, where, I was assured, I would be privy to the very latest in news and opinion from across the country.

Although I did not relish the prospect of spending any more time than was strictly necessary with Alice and her husband, I must confess I was intrigued at the prospect of a parliamentary newssheet becoming freely available within the town. Despite the fact that the influx of refugees from royalist strongholds had meant that the town was becoming religiously more extreme and politically more aware, Nantwich was still a relative backwater. Copies of the *Parliamentary Scout* or *Mercurius Britannicus* occasionally found their way into the town, but in no great numbers, whilst, of course, the royalist newssheets were nowhere to be seen.

"This newsletter," I began. "Will it be like a political and religious pamphlet or will there be local news too?"

"I'm sure Hugh will be able to answer your questions in more detail, but...although Hugh has gained a reputation as a political and religious campaigner, he does not just want to replicate the news from London. There are many local issues in Nantwich that are also of great interest. That is the main reason why he decided to come here. For example, I understand that there was a terrible murder here on Friday."

"Yes, a tanner called Tench from Hospital Street. The responsibility for investigating the death appears to have fallen to me."

"Really?" said Alice, with a surprised tone. "That must be an awful thing to have to deal with."

"It's my job," I responded, matter-of-factly.

"I heard the man had been struck over the head..."

"That is true."

"...and something about a crimson scarf."

"Yes, the victim was found with a red sash around his neck. It was similar to those worn by royalist officers. Why are you asking this, Alice?"

Alice cupped her hands around her drink and took a mouthful. "I'm sorry, Daniel. I'm just curious...I'm a bit of a gossip at heart, but I also know this is a case that Hugh will be interested in writing about."

"Well, it's certainly taking up plenty of my time at the moment," I said.

"Daniel, I'm sure you will find the perpetrator," said Alice, rising to her feet. "I don't want to outstay my welcome, so I will take my leave now, but Hugh and I will look forward to the pleasure of your company on Thursday."

"You want to watch that one," growled Mrs Padgett, when Alice had gone. "She's playing with your affections. You should be careful what you tell her."

I stared at Mrs Padgett, somewhat nonplussed at her attitude. "Nonsense," I said. "I've known Alice since I was a child, and furthermore," I added, "I'd thank you to mind your own business."

My housekeeper said nothing, but I could feel her eyes boring into my back as I stomped my way upstairs. I have to say, I was irritated at my housekeeper's behaviour. What right did she have to cast aspersions on a person she did not even know, and what grudge could she possibly hold against Alice? As I reached the top of the stairs, I turned to say as much, only to find her still staring meaningfully in my direction.

"Don't say I didn't warn you," she said, and disappeared into the kitchen.

8

Nantwich – Tuesday, December 12, 1643

It had become common knowledge that John Pym, the leader of our parliament, was gravely ill, so when news of his death reached Nantwich, it was of no great surprise to the populace. Few were taken in by the efforts of The Parliament Scout to have us believe that Master Pym was on the road to recovery, and so most townsfolk were well-prepared for the outbreak of mourning that would occur when the great man eventually succumbed to his illness. However, the manner in which I learned of Pym's demise *was* somewhat unexpected, and the bearer of that news was none other than Alexander Clowes.

I heard my friend coming long before he knocked on my door, for Tuesday the twelfth was to be the day of William Tench's burial. The metallic clang of Alexander's bell and his booming voice resonated loudly as he made his way up the street, bidding people to pay their respects to the tanner at his funeral, which was set to be held at St Mary's later that day.

"I have something you might find to be of interest," he announced, standing on the threshold of my front door.

Taking care to put his bell on the ground, he reached behind him and, putting his hand inside the rear of his breeches, extracted a crumpled collection of papers, which he thrust triumphantly in my direction.

Notwithstanding my natural reluctance to handle the contents of another man's breeches, I took what looked like a pamphlet from Alexander. "What is it?" I asked, not registering the importance of what I was being given.

"Read it," responded my friend. A certain urgency in his voice made me take a look at the writing on the first page.

Mercurius Aulicus

Communicating the Intelligence and Affaires of the Court to the Rest of the Kingdome

I realised with a start that I was holding a copy of the notorious royalist newssheet, famed throughout the kingdom for its scurrilous nature, but never before seen in a place like Nantwich.

"By the saints, man," I exclaimed, dragging my friend inside before any passer-by could see what I was holding. "Where in the name of God did you get hold of this?"

"In The Black Lion," he answered. "I was there yesterday evening when a young boy walked in, placed a pile of them on the bar and left without saying anything. He'd gone before anybody could see what he had brought. Turns out he left copies in three other taverns, including

The Crown. It didn't take long for Colonel Booth to find out what was happening, though, because, barely twenty minutes later, a group of soldiers came in and confiscated all remaining copies. Fortunately, I managed to secrete one out of the tavern under my shirt."

"I'm glad you did," I said, "but I'm amazed to see a copy of *Mercurius Aulicus* here. It's hard enough finding a copy of *The Parliamentary Scout* or *Mercurius Britannicus*. Why would anyone risk distributing a royalist newssheet here?"

"Take a look at the main story," said Alexander, jabbing a finger at the newssheet. "I think you'll find the reason is self-evident. King Pym is dead!"

I glanced at the headline and realised, with a start, that my friend was right. After thanking Alexander and leaving him to continue his duties as bellman, I sat down to read the report in more detail. According to the date on the cover, John Pym had died the previous Friday, which struck me as being odd, as Colonel Booth had shown no sign of knowing about this when I had seen him then. As I read, it occurred to me that *Mercurius Aulicus* had lost no time in trying to make the most of the news and understood why Booth had made sure that as many copies of the publication had been confiscated as possible. Pym was described as being '*a most loathsome and foul carcase*', having died, it was claimed, from the skin disease phthiriasis. Worse still, the report attempted to claim that his death was no less than divine retribution

– a just punishment for him being one of the five members of parliament accused of treason nearly two years ago.

The story was well-known. In January 1642, the King had entered the House of Commons in an attempt to arrest Pym, together with John Hampden, Sir Arthur Haselrig, Denzil Holles, and William Strode, as well as Viscount Mandeville (later to become the Earl of Manchester), under the belief that they had committed numerous treasonable acts, including inviting the Scots to invade England, colluding to turn Londoners against the King and planning to impeach the Queen. Forewarned, the five members and Mandeville had fled the House. The King, meanwhile, fearing for his family's safety, had left for Oxford and had not returned to London since.

Pym was the second of the five members to die, John Hampden having already met his end on the battlefield at Chalgrove. *Mercurius Aulicus* argued that these two deaths, together with the miserable fortunes of other leading parliamentarians, were a sign of God's judgement on their treacherous activities. Lord Brooke, pointed out the newssheet, had been shot dead from the roof of Lichfield Cathedral. The Hothams, who had refused to allow the King to enter Hull, had been arrested for treason, as had Nathaniel Fiennes, accused of surrendering Bristol without a fight. It seemed as though God was venting his wrath on those who had dared to question the King's divine right to rule his kingdom as he saw fit.

I, myself, gave no credence to such talk, but marvelled at the skill of the writer. I saw the danger presented by the argument and the reason why the King's men might have deemed it advantageous to distribute this particular issue of *Mercurius Aulicus* in Nantwich, when the King's army could mount an attack on the town at any time. From their point of view, anything that could be done to change the attitude of the townsfolk would be a good thing.

As I pulled on my boots, ready to face the day, I wondered who in the town could possibly have stood to gain from distributing such literature and prayed that the person responsible had been foiled in his intention, for the inference in the article was clear. Divine retribution, such as that meted out on John Pym and his followers, was not restricted to individual human beings. Such a fate could just as easily befall a town like Nantwich.

My first task that morning was one which I greeted with no small degree of trepidation. I did not anticipate a warm reception from Ann Davenport, for she was a formidable woman, who protected her interests with vehemence. She was more than capable of managing the wich house on her own if the fancy so took her, and so I had little concern about the effects of John Davenport's incarceration on the wellbeing of his business. However, the abuse which I knew was coming my way for having had the temerity to lock up her husband, was an entirely different matter.

Still, a promise is a promise, and I had given my word to John that I would keep an eye on his wife's welfare and make sure the kindling was completed without difficulties. So it was, therefore, that I headed across Town Bridge in the direction of Great Wood Street with a mind to spend a good part of the morning sweating amongst the salt pans. It was the least I could do, but it was also an opportunity to find out something of what Ann knew of her husband's dealings with William Tench.

The weather had continued to grow colder overnight, and as I crossed the bridge I noticed that ice had begun to form on the Weaver, creating a yard-wide ribbon of white along the length of the river bank. A lone figure stood by the brine pit, struggling to bind one of the theets, which had split in the cold. A kindling was clearly scheduled for somewhere in Snow Hill that morning.

I looked down Welsh Row and recognised two familiar figures approaching, rubbing their hands to maintain the circulation in their freezing fingers. Carter and Hughes, the two musketeers who had called me out to inspect Tench's body, were returning to their billets, having carried out sentry duty at the sconce at the end of the street. Carter greeted me with a nod as they approached.

"Good morrow," I replied. "What news of the Irish?"

"They'll be here soon enough, sir," said Carter. "Just in time for Christmas, I'll wager. But no point in wishing them here any sooner."

"They're on the march, then?" I enquired. "You have reports of their progress?"

"The scouts report they are closing in on Beeston Castle. Let us hope Captain Steele detains them awhile."

I nodded my assent.

"It is a secure place," I said, "but there will be some unhappy people in Nantwich if Beeston falls." I shuddered to think of the implications. Beeston Castle, situated about half-way between Nantwich and Chester, was a secure fortress whose inner ward was surrounded, on three sides, by impregnable cliffs. Many of Nantwich's richer townsfolk had moved the majority of their possessions to Beeston for safekeeping, in the belief that it would be more secure than Nantwich in the face of a royalist attack. Captain Thomas Steele, the parliamentary officer charged with defending the castle, had a heavy responsibility, which I did not envy. I thanked the soldiers and waved them on their way.

The Davenports' wich house, as I expected, was a hive of activity. Now in the middle of the kindling, women were busy scraping the salt out of the pans with their loots, and several barrows of wet salt stood by the wall, dripping leach brine onto the floor and waiting to be moved into the storeroom. I looked across to the team of women briners and recognised the Davenports' two eldest daughters, Margery and Martha, hard at work. I found Gilbert Robinson at the rear of the building, loading barrows onto a cart for delivery. James Skinner was helping him. Robinson acknowledged my presence with a raised hand and beckoned me over.

"You've proper pissed off her Majesty, Master Cheswis," he warned. "I wouldn't want to be in your shoes when she catches sight of you."

"Thanks for the warning," I said, "but John Davenport is better off where he is at the moment. Anyway, you saw what happened. I was left with no option."

"Try telling that to Mrs Davenport," he replied. I realised that Robinson was probably right, so I changed the subject.

"Tell me, you will be able to manage the rest of the kindling, right?"

"I will make sure it's done properly," said Robinson, "but there's no need really. Mrs Davenport has taken charge. You know how she is." Robinson slipped me a wry smile and indicated over in the direction of the ship, the hollowed out tree trunk used as a reservoir for the brine, from where Ann was directing operations. At that moment, she caught my eye and, pursing her lips in a grimace, she marched over to me purposefully.

"Shame on you, Daniel Cheswis," she hissed, her voice shaking with emotion. "My husband languishes in jail for a crime he did not commit, and it is you who put him there. I had thought you to be a friend."

"I am," I said, taking a step back, "and that's why he's not facing an assault charge. He nearly broke my leg."

"But you're holding him for murder. You know as well

as I do he's not a murderer."

"I have to do my duty," I replied, "and he's the only suspect at the moment."

"But you've got nothing on him."

"He was seen in an argument with the murder victim."

Ann waved her hands in the air and sighed with exasperation. "Is that all? That doesn't prove anything."

She was right of course. I looked Ann in the eye and tried a different tack. "Were you aware that John owed Tench money? He left over two pounds in a purse for him at Comberbachs' the morning the body was found."

Ann hesitated, clearly taken aback. "No," she said with suspicion. "Why would he do that?"

"That's what I'd like to know. He says he lost it in a bet, but two pounds is a fair amount of money."

"Well, if that's what he says, that's the truth of it. And why pay this money when Tench is already dead? That doesn't make sense. The truth is you haven't actually got anything at all. Why, if you have no proof, do you have to keep him locked in jail?" Despite her bravado, Ann's demeanour was one of puzzlement, and I could see she knew nothing about the money.

"Ann," I said, eventually. "For what it's worth, there is more to this than meets the eye, and I need to get to the bottom of it. John is safer where he is at the moment, and I would be in trouble if I let him go just yet. If the truth be told, I cannot see him being involved either. He's an idiot and a drunkard maybe, but not a murderer – at least to the best of my judgement. In the meantime, though, I need some time to complete my enquiries. I know this situation is difficult to bear, but I would ask you to please be patient. In the meantime, I have instructed Robinson to make sure you have the kindling under control, but, by the look of it, you have things well in hand."

Ann appeared somewhat pacified by my words and she grunted in resignation. "All right," she said, "but don't believe everything you hear. There are those around here that would cause us trouble."

"Trouble?" I said. "What do you mean?"

Ann hesitated, immediately aware that she had said too much. "Just that times are hard, and there are some who are jealous of how well we've done," she eventually confided, before hurriedly terminating the conversation and returning to her work at the ship.

I wiped the sweat from my brow, for it was stiflingly hot in the wich house, and considered Ann's words. I knew from experience that it was not the best time to be in the salt trade. It was certainly true that, if it were not for the additional income I enjoyed from my cheese business, I would have struggled to afford the cost of an apprentice. The Davenports, on the other hand, did not appear to be suffering such hardships, and it certainly seemed as though they picked up more than their fair share of contract work. I tried to shut the thought from my mind though, realising that this was yet another example of the conflicts inherent in holding public office.

As a constable, my duty was to be impartial, and yet there were many people in the town with whom I had relationships and who expected things of me.

Realising that a morning toiling in the Davenports' wich house was not the best way of displaying this impartiality, I decided to take my leave and stepped out once more into the icy air by the river bank. Deep in thought, I decided to take a stroll to the end of Great Wood Street, past the rows of wich houses all locked and silent. At the end of the street, near the earthworks that protected the northern edge of the town, I turned left over the bridge that crossed the common cistern, the brine-saturated water reservoir, which, I noticed, was ice-free, and turned left again down a pathway that led by the side of the cistern and behind the wich houses on Little Wood Street.

As I reached the southern end of the cistern and entered the area behind Welsh Row known as Strawberry Hill, I noticed a man approaching me in the opposite direction and recognised the thin, moustachioed features of Edward Yardley, the owner of the wich house opposite that of the Davenports.

I did not know Yardley well, but, for some irrational reason, he had always slightly irritated me, probably because he had the kind of face that always seemed to be carrying a slight smirk. Today, though, he greeted me with a beaming grin.

"Ha! Cheswis," he exclaimed. "Congratulations. It was

high time Davenport was locked away. Looks like you stuffed him good and proper – like a goose, I'd say!"

Taken aback by Yardley's demeanour, I bridled. "What do you mean?" I demanded. "Surely all salt men should stick together? Why rejoice in another man's misfortune?" I had known that John Davenport and Yardley had never been on good terms but did not know why. I wondered whether I was about to find out.

"It's best to look after yourself in this world," rejoined Yardley. "I must say, though, I was surprised to see you had arrested Davenport. I thought you and he were close."

"He's my friend," I said, "but he'll be treated fairly, for better or worse."

"Yes, but some people eventually get what's coming to them."

I had heard enough. "What on earth are you trying to insinuate?" I demanded. "Is there something you know? Were you in The White Swan on Friday?"

"The White Swan? No. I never go in that place. I don't mean what happened to William Tench. I've no idea about that, but there's plenty that would say anyone who cheats other brine workers deserves all he gets."

I have to say, I had no idea what Yardley was talking about. "What are you suggesting?" I said, amazed.

"Fraud, sir. You know Davenport was Ruler last year. You might want to have a look at how walling rights have been allocated in the past and how misdemeanours have been dealt with. That's all I'm saying. Still," he added. "It won't matter, will it? I dare say he'll swing for what he did to Tench, anyway."

"What evidence do you have of this?" I demanded. "If you have proof, speak now. Otherwise, I would be careful with my words, if I were you. What you say is tantamount to slander."

But Yardley was not going to venture any further information. He simply smiled and raised both his palms towards me. "I'm saying nothing more," he said, and, with a smirk playing at the corner of his mouth, he tipped his hat and headed straight for the rear door of his wich house.

9

Nantwich – Tuesday, December 12, 1643

Yardley's words bothered me for the rest of the morning. His accusations added a new dimension to my investigations and they were, I knew, something I would need to look into in due course. However, for the time being, I had more important matters to deal with.

I walked back to the jail in Pillory Street and found Davenport to be in a much more contrite frame of mind with regards to his unprovoked attack on me. However, a brief conversation allowed me to ascertain that he was not going to communicate anything beyond swearing that he had no hand in Tench's murder and begging for my help in proving his innocence.

I resolved that my best course of action was to investigate elsewhere, and so, scarcely able to conceal my impatience, I told Davenport I had no time to discuss the issue any further with him, and, unless he wanted to tell me something new, I would report back once I knew more.

Once out of sight, though, I summoned one of the bailiff's warders and slipped him a few coins.

"Don't be too tough on him," I said, "and if his wife turns up, allow her to bring in a few comforts." The warder gave me a withering look but pocketed the coins nonetheless and returned to his duties.

I spent the rest of the morning with Arthur Sawyer, allocating duties for the following week, one of which was maintenance work on the town's communal armour, which, we both realised, was likely to be required in the not-too-distant future.

I also needed to be present at Tench's funeral, so after a brief visit home for lunch, I made my way over to the church, taking care to keep myself in the background, where I could observe proceedings whilst remaining undisturbed.

As it turned out, the funeral was well-attended. The Comberbachs were there, as were one or two others, who I knew to be tanners. In addition to a number of Tench's friends, neighbours, and relatives, I also caught sight of the footman from Randle Church's house, as well as the hunched figure of Church himself, who, despite his age, had, to my surprise, braved the weather to offer his condolences to Mrs Tench. The footman, noticing my presence, ambled over to me and addressed me in a polite but insistent tone.

"Mr Church would like a word with you after the funeral," he said. "Please be sure to present yourself at his home at three this afternoon."

"And what would be the subject matter of this

discussion?" I asked, somewhat tersely, not taking too kindly to being ordered around.

"I am not privy to this information," replied the footman. "Just make sure that you're there."

The funeral service went on for some time, and it became clear that, if Tench was barely tolerated amongst strangers in the taverns of Nantwich, he was well-liked amongst his own community.

After the burial, I was approached by the portly figure of Gilbert Kinshaw, who I knew as a local merchant and one of the larger wich house owners. Kinshaw was a self-made man in his forties who had treated himself rather too well with the profits of his success. Clean-shaven, but with a mane of long curly hair shielding pallid features, he was grossly overweight and walked with a pronounced waddle. Still, he had influence in the town and was currently one of the Rulers of Walling. I was surprised to see him there but assumed there was a business connection between Kinshaw's salt works and the Comberbachs' tannery.

"It is a sad turn of events that takes a young man away from his wife like this," said Kinshaw. "What say you, Mr Cheswis?"

"Indeed it is, Mr Kinshaw," I replied, courteously. "Mr Tench's death was a particularly unpleasant one-"

"Which, no doubt, is taking up much of your resources as a constable," cut in Kinshaw, completing my sentence for me. I looked curiously at the corpulent merchant and wondered where the conversation was heading.

"The role of constable is a very time-consuming responsibility," he continued. "I find my duties as Ruler of Walling to be similarly burdensome."

"I'm sure they are," I concurred. "Was there something you wanted to say to me?"

Kinshaw raised his eyebrows at me and smiled. "People say that you make a good constable," he said. "That you have insight. I can see that they are right. I wanted to talk to you about corruption."

"Corruption?"

"Yes. Since I have become a Ruler of Walling, I have realised that the figures pertaining to walling allocations do not quite add up. Something appears to have been happening in the Great Wood Street area, and I wondered if you knew anything?"

"I have no idea about this," I said, "but I am curious to find out more. What do you mean, exactly?"

"I suspect there may have been some fraudulent activity with regards to the allocation of walling rights and accurate reporting of kindlings."

"This is something I was unaware of until today," I said, guardedly, "but I will be sure to look into it and will keep you informed should I find out anything of relevance."

"I should be most grateful," said Kinshaw, taking his leave with a slight bow of the head.

Afterwards, I considered Kinshaw's words and had to

admit I was in a greater state of confusion than before. I had never heard anything about anyone committing fraud over walling rights, and now two people had mentioned it within the space of a couple of hours. And if Davenport was involved, was there any connection with Tench? I realised with frustration that my task was becoming more and more complicated as time went on. My head reeling, I paid my respects to Mrs Tench and headed off down Hospital Street for my appointment with Randle Church.

The bells of St Mary's had already chimed three by the time I arrived at Church's Mansion. Randle Church's footman was waiting for me as I walked up the path to the front door, and he greeted me with a sardonic look as he held it open for me.

"You're late," he growled, as he ushered me once again into Church's drawing room. Saying nothing, I walked into the dimly-lit chamber and heard the door close behind me. Once my eyes grew accustomed to the light, I was able to pick out the white-haired figure of Church sat in his armchair. However, I realised with a start that we were not alone. Sat in adjacent chairs, arranged neatly around a low table, were two men I knew well.

Sat immediately to Church's left was a tall, immaculately-dressed gentleman in his late thirties, who I immediately recognised as Thomas Maisterson, head of one of the town's longest-standing families. Maisterson possessed an inordinately long face with a distinct hooked nose, down which he observed me through piercing grey eyes. For a moment, I thought he bore a disconcerting likeness to a sparrowhawk watching its prey.

Next to him was the shorter, stockier figure of Roger Wilbraham of Townsend House. Wilbraham was a young man, barely twenty years of age, but, with his father having died in October and his elder brother away in France, he had been forced to take on a leadership role within his family. Not that this was a burden to him. Despite his youth, he was already becoming known in the town for possessing a confidence and presence that belied his years.

None of the three gentlemen looked particularly pleased with me, and I realised with consternation that I was stood facing the heads of three of the main royalist families in the town. What was more, when I looked at the table, my eyes fell on a copy of *Mercurius Aulicus*, the very same issue that I had read that morning.

My agitation must have transmitted itself to my hosts, for when one of them spoke – and it was Thomas Maisterson who took the lead – I was addressed with a voice that had a distinct edge to it.

"Would you please take a seat, Master Cheswis," said Maisterson, gesturing towards an empty chair.

"I'll stand if it's all the same to you, sir," I replied.

"As you wish." An amused smile touched the corner of Maisterson's mouth.

I looked at the newssheet lying on the table and wondered whether any of the gentlemen had been behind its distribution that morning. Maisterson must have seen what I was thinking, for he was quick to quash any such thoughts.

"Ah," he said, "*Mercurius Aulicus*. The voice of the King's supporters in this land. It is refreshing to read something other than the bilious outpourings of rebel wordmongers, I assure you – but that is just between us. You are wondering, of course, whether we might have had something to do with the sudden appearance of this newssheet in our town."

"Such a scenario had occurred to me," I admitted.

"Then dismiss such thoughts from your mind. Everyone knows we are loyal to the King's cause. We can hardly deny it, but we would be foolhardy in the extreme to show active opposition to Parliament by overtly distributing royalist pamphlets. We have no wish to antagonise Colonel Booth."

"Then where have they come from?"

"We don't know," cut in Wilbraham, "but all three of us received a copy. My servants say a young boy delivered it last night but then made himself scarce before anyone could identify or question him."

"I see," I said, thoughtfully. "So you believe a third party is at work, promoting the royalist cause in Nantwich?"

"Precisely," said Maisterson, "but that is not why we

asked you here."

I stiffened slightly as a sudden sense of foreboding told me that my position was about to become more complicated. Maisterson rose to his feet and paced across the room. Seemingly lost in thought, he picked up a poker and stoked the fire that glowed in the hearth.

"Master Cheswis," he said, eventually. "In your office as a constable you are the King's representative. I don't know whether you are for the King or for Parliament but it's of no matter. This is a terrible conflict, which pits brother against brother – neighbour against neighbour. Two years ago, we would have thought it inconceivable that Englishmen would take up arms against each other in this way, but here we are. When this war is finished, I sincerely hope society won't be destroyed."

I was not sure whether Maisterson was expecting an answer, but I gave him one anyway. "I support the rights of Parliament, sir, but I believe that in the end there will be no winners in this conflict. There are good men and bad men on both sides, but the situation is barely helped by the chief protagonists. You have a king who thinks he's God and a parliament who wants to play at being king. That, in my view, can only be a recipe for disaster."

Maisterson raised an eyebrow and glanced at Church, who said nothing but nodded almost imperceptibly. "I'm not sure that was an entirely satisfactory riposte," he said. "I fear we may support different sides. Ultimately, however, we appear to be of the same mind."

"What are you trying to say, sir?" I ventured. Maisterson replaced the poker and gestured for me to sit. This time, I accepted his offer and perched on the edge of the remaining chair.

"The nub of the matter is this," said Maisterson. "You are charged with investigating the death of William Tench. The truth is, we have no idea why Tench was killed. We do not think it was a political act, but we cannot be sure. We would like to help you catch his killer, but there are some provisos."

"Provisos, sir?"

"Yes. Firstly, we are aware that you have been asking questions about William Tench's relationships, and the word is out that he might have been a scout for the King's party. It's no secret that we are for the King, but my friend Mr Church's connection to the Tench family is well known, so we don't want too much attention drawn to any clandestine activities that Mr Tench may or may not have been engaged in. We have land and interests here, and we have to protect them."

"But that would amount to a deliberate concealment of evidence," I protested.

A slight flicker of annoyance passed over Maisterson's face. "Very well," he said. "Let me put it this way. At present, there is no indication whether King or Parliament will prevail in this conflict. Even if Parliament *does* win, Colonel Booth will be back in his family estate in Dunham Massey as quickly as his legs will carry him. If the King prevails, as I believe he shall, Booth's head will be on a stake somewhere.

"Furthermore, if Byron's Irish army take over this town, it may be in your interests not to ask too many questions about Tench's activities, as you may need their support sooner than you think.

"And finally," he added, "and here's the most important thing – when all the soldiers have gone home, we will still be here. If the rebels win, we may well end up being sequestered, but we will still wield some influence in this town, and, as an inhabitant and businessman of Nantwich, you may wish to bear that in mind. You have a burgeoning cheese business, I understand. I'm sure we would wish to support someone who recognised our concerns and priorities during difficult times such as this."

Church and Wilbraham nodded their agreement sagely and looked at me expectantly. If the truth be told, I did not know how to react to this, and so I asked a question instead.

"Tell me," I said, addressing Randle Church, "if you have nothing to do with Tench's death, why are you so keen to avoid a murder investigation? Would the crimson scarf used to strangle him have anything to do with it?"

Church and Maisterson exchanged glances. "You'd better tell him, Randle," said Maisterson.

"Very well," conceded the old man. "You are right. The scarf belonged to my son. You know he was Sergeant-at-

Arms to the King?"

I nodded. "Please continue, sir," I said.

"Very well. The scarf was a ceremonial sash given to me as a keepsake. It was not for use in battle. I have no idea how it ended up around Tench's neck. As you will understand, I cannot allow it to become general knowledge that a symbol of royalism owned by me was used to murder the husband of one of my servants, especially one accused of being a royalist spy. I'm sure you can be relied upon to keep this matter quiet."

Afterwards, I sat on the wall by the churchyard and considered my situation.

I was well and truly caught between two stools. On the one hand, Colonel Booth wanted me to continue an active investigation into the affairs of William Tench, paying particular attention to those of a Royalist persuasion who might have connections with him. Maisterson, on the other hand, wanted me to turn a blind eye to Tench's activities. Worse still, both Booth and Maisterson had effectively bribed me with promises of additional business for doing their bidding.

In the meantime, my friend John Davenport, who I believed to be innocent, was sat in jail accused of murder, and I was no nearer solving the case than when I'd begun. I realised that Maisterson, Church, and Wilbraham wanted to stop me investigating too deeply into Tench's activities not because they were involved with Tench's murder, but because they knew he was a spy. Otherwise, why involve me at all? But, if Maisterson was not involved, then who? I had absolutely no idea.

Of course, I could not possibly ignore the whole issue, because if I were to do nothing, the pressure would mount to try Davenport for murder and he would likely hang.

And then there was the issue of the money left for Tench by Davenport at the Comberbachs and the strange suggestions by Yardley and Kinshaw regarding the fiddling of the walling records. How did all that fit in?

And to top it all, I had to cope with the return to my life of Alice Bickerton, now Furnival, and her husband, as well as the growing threat of the approaching royalist army.

With Byron's army on the march, there was no doubt that a tension was starting to build in Nantwich. Imperceptible at first, it was still akin to little more than a slight tightening in the gut, but I knew it would grow as the papists came nearer. Still, it was nothing compared to the mental siege I was under. I felt like I was being crushed by the demands of my role as constable and feared for my business as the war escalated. I picked up some small pebbles from behind the churchyard wall and started skimming them across the square, watching them skid across the surface of the frozen snow.

"A curse on this town," I seethed, as the stones flew. A beggarwoman, walking on her own twenty yards away, eyed me curiously, and I realised that I had spoken aloud.

Pulling myself to my feet, I shot the woman an angry look.

"Be off with you, you flea-bitten old crone, before I arrest you for vagrancy," I shouted, and the woman turned and shuffled off down the high street. I pulled myself to my feet, ashamed of myself for having abused the old woman, and trudged off home through the snow.

10

Beeston Castle, Cheshire – Wednesday,
December 13, 1643

*I*t was a cold, dark night in the upper ward of Beeston Castle. The thin sliver of the new moon had long since set and it would be three hours before the first light of dawn appeared tentatively on the eastern horizon. Nevertheless, the guest in the chamber at the top of the gatehouse stirred and slipped silently out of bed.

He carefully lit a candle-fired lamp, taking care that as little light as possible filtered down the staircase to where the Constable of the Keep was sleeping. Having slept fully-clothed, so as to make as little noise as possible upon waking, he quietly put on his boots, before reaching inside his baggage to extract a long length of rope which had been concealed under his clothes. He tied the rope around his waist with a secure knot and wound the rest over his shoulder. Finally, he stood and put on the cloak, which had been hanging over the chair at the foot of his bed. Finished. He was now ready for his night's work.

Creeping over to one of the arrow loops in the wall,

which provided the only natural light in his modest chamber, he cast his eyes across the expanse of the upper ward and assessed the weather. He noted with satisfaction that the oppressive leaden skies of the past few days had started to clear and winter constellations filled the moonless sky. It was ideal weather for what he had in mind.

Taking the lamp with him, he carefully opened the door to his chamber and descended the wooden staircase, which creaked in betrayal. The guest cursed to himself. It was not a loud noise, but it was enough to alert the Constable, who was a light sleeper.

"Is something amiss, sir?" enquired a voice from the shadows. "Are you having trouble sleeping?"

"There is no need to concern yourself, Constable," came the whispered reply. "I am not used to sleeping in a castle keep, that is all. I thought to take a brief stroll to get some fresh air and to settle my mind. I will return to my chamber presently."

"Then make sure you alert the guards to your presence and, for God's sake, don't fall down the well in the dark. I would not want to have to explain that to your brother-in-law." The guest grunted his assent and was relieved to see the Constable turn over and start to snore almost immediately.

Stepping out into the night, he scanned the upper ward and registered the presence of four sentries keeping watch at different corners of the ward. He waited until he was sure they had all seen him and then, taking his oil lamp with him, he made his way to his right and skirted around the ward, past the well, one of the deepest in the land, rumoured to be where King Richard II had once concealed treasure from his pursuing enemies. He approached a sentry at the foot of the south-eastern tower, who nodded a greeting.

"All's well?" asked the guest, in a low voice, looking around him.

"The guard in the tower is half-asleep," confided the sentry with a grin. "You won't have any trouble from that quarter."

The guest acknowledged this with satisfaction and walked round to the north-east corner of the ward, where another sentry was waiting. They exchanged a look of quiet recognition but no words were spoken.

The guest strained his eyes in the dark and noted that the point on the north-eastern corner of the ward where they stood was at least partially obscured from the view of both sentries patrolling the western part of the ward. He observed one sentry walk from the western gatehouse to halfway along the western wall, noting that he was hidden by the bulk of the gateways for half the time. The other sentry paced from the centre of the western wall to midway along the northern wall. A kink in the northern wall meant the sentry was not visible to the guest when he was walking along it.

The guest gave a thumbs-up to the sentry at the south-

eastern corner, who promptly walked past the well towards the gateway, where he engaged one of the other sentries in conversation, making sure they were both behind the gateway and therefore out of view.

Holding his breath in anticipation, the guest waited until the other sentry began his walk along the northern wall and sprang into action. He had to work fast, for he knew he had only a couple of minutes to complete his task. Thrusting his head between two crenellations, he looked over the wall. It was dark below, but he knew there were a couple of hundred feet of crags, trees, and steep slopes between him and the valley floor. Holding the lamp above the crenellations, so that it could be seen from the valley below, he counted to ten and then removed it from view. He then counted ten more and held the light up again. Time seemed to stop and the guest looked anxiously towards the north-western corner of the ward. There was still no sign of the sentry, so he lifted the lamp for a third time. From somewhere below, an owl hooted.

The guest then waited for the sentry to reappear and watched him for three minutes while he walked to the centre of the western wall and back. All this time, the steady murmur of conversation could be heard from behind the gateway.

As soon as the sentry disappeared along the northern wall again, the guest undid his coat and unravelled the rope from around his torso. He tied it securely around one of the crenellations and threw the end over the side of the castle walls. He then calmly picked up the lamp and walked back to his bedchamber in the western gatehouse.

Meanwhile, Captain Thomas Sandford had been standing down in the valley with eight of his firelocks, staring up at the castle walls, muskets slung over their backs. For the last thirty minutes, the men had been impatiently rubbing their hands and stamping their feet to keep warm. One of the soldiers had a rope wound over his shoulders, another a length of rope ladder. They were all battle-hardened veterans from the Irish campaign.

"By Jesu, it's cold," whispered one of them.

"You'll be warm soon enough," said Sandford in response.

Sandford was a tall, athletic, square-jawed soldier, who cut an air of authority as he waited with his men. He stared up at the dark mass of the castle, which rose like a spectre far above them, looming, black, and silent. Presently, he saw a light appear high above the castle walls. It illuminated one of the crenellations for a few seconds and then disappeared, only to reappear a few moments later. It did this for a third time and then disappeared again.

"That is the sign," said Sandford, and turned to his men. "Burroughs," he said, addressing the soldier with the length of rope. Burroughs stepped forward, cupped

his hands to his mouth and made a low hooting sound.

"Hear me well, my brave firelocks," said the Captain. "You all know exactly what to do. Let us show these rebel curs what the King's army is made of. Have courage, lads, and Cheshire will long talk of the day that Beeston Castle was taken for the King."

The soldiers murmured their assent.

"Begging your pardon, Captain Sandford, sir," said one of them. "There are but nine of us. What happens if they decide to fight?"

"Mister Maddocke, there will be less than ten men in the inner ward, of which three are with us. The majority of the force will either be guarding the outer walls or they will be asleep. They will never be expecting us to attack from this side of the castle. What's more, the captain in charge of this place is but a Chester cheese vendor. He is here only reluctantly. If we show discipline and courage, they will yield quickly, mark my words." Sandford faced his men and put his hands out in front of him, one on top of the other. One by one the soldiers laid their hands on top of his.

"For God and the King," he said. The soldiers repeated his words in unison, eager at the prospect of action.

Sandford turned again to the soldier with the rope. "March on, Burroughs," he said. "You lead the way. Sergeant Wright - You take the rear."

The line of soldiers marched silently up the steep grass slope leading to the crags below the castle walls, through a group of trees, until they reached the base of the crags.

"How the fuck do we get up that?" whispered Maddocke, who was the second-last man.

"Silence," whispered the sergeant behind him. "You'll alert the whole fucking castle."

Sandford gestured to Burroughs, who skirted to the left around the base of the rock face to reveal a possible route up a groove in the rock. Demonstrating why he had been chosen to carry the rope, Burroughs sprang athletically up the rock face and emerged five minutes later on a ledge underneath the walls. He felt his way a couple of feet to his right and located a length of rope hanging from the walls above. Positioning himself below the rope, with his back against the wall and his feet against a large boulder, he then tied his own rope securely round his waist and let it fall to the men below.

A few minutes later, the soldier with the rope ladder appeared next to him. This soldier tied the top rung of the rope ladder securely to the rope hanging from the castle. Once secure, he gave it three sharp tugs and a face peered over the wall. Suddenly, the rope ladder was being dragged up the side of the castle ramparts, unravelling as it did so. A few seconds later, the face appeared again and nodded at the man below. The soldier then climbed the thirty feet up the ladder and was helped over the castle wall. He dropped noiselessly to the floor and remained motionless for a few seconds.

At the appearance of the firelock, the sentry at the

south-eastern tower walked back to the gatehouse and recommenced his conversation with the other sentry.

Having watched this, his co-conspirator whispered to the firelock. "March round to the south-east tower and wait in the garderobe until everyone is over the wall. You can walk normally. It's too dark for the sentries on the other side to see you properly."

Sandford was the next soldier to emerge above the parapet, followed quickly by the rest of the men. Three of these waited for a sign from the garderobe that the sentry on the northern wall was facing the other way before scuttling quickly along the eastern wall to join their colleague.

The final four firelocks, including Sergeant Wright, Maddocke, and Burroughs, waited by the northern wall.

What happened next passed in a blur. Sandford's troops emerged from the south-eastern tower with two sentries at gun point, one of whom looked a little unsteady on his feet and was holding the back of his head. Cursing, they were made to lie face down while one of the intruders guarded them, a musket trained on their backs. Sandford and the other three firelocks manoeuvred their way through the shadows towards the gatehouse, where the two sentries on duty were still talking. The sentry who had been guarding the south-eastern corner of the ward had positioned himself so he could see his colleague and the four remaining soldiers in the north-eastern corner. At a sign from them, he threw his hands in the air, leaving Sandford and his men to overpower the other sentry. The remaining sentry on the northern wall saw what was happening, but had no time to react, for three of the remaining four firelocks sprinted into view with their muskets raised. In shock, he immediately dropped his weapon and raised his hands, but he was too slow. A musket butt crashed into his temple, and he sank to the ground, unconscious.

Within two minutes, the remaining guards in the gatehouse were rounded up and the Constable was dragged unceremoniously from his bed. All the prisoners were made to sit with their backs to the gatehouse wall. Sandford counted them. Nine men in total.

Sandford grimaced at the bleary-eyed constable. "Who's in charge here?" he barked.

"I am the Constable of the Keep. There is also Sergeant Wilkes." The Constable indicated one of the guards, who had emerged from the gatehouse.

"Is there anyone else here?"

"There is a guest asleep in the bedchamber at the top of the gatehouse, but he is a civilian guest. He is Captain Steele's brother-in-law."

"Then we'd better raise him," said Sandford. Burroughs and another soldier were despatched and emerged a couple of minutes later with a groggy-looking guest.

Sandford addressed the sergeant. "Sergeant Wilkes. You are to send one of your men to Captain Steele's quarters to advise him of our presence. Have him present himself at the gates without delay. I would parley with him."

Twenty minutes later, Captain Thomas Steele and fifteen of his men were positioned on the grass at the foot of the gateway opposite the raised drawbridge. Sandford, meanwhile, had placed himself at the top of eastern gateway tower.

"Good morning, Captain Steele. I trust we didn't wake you too early," he said.

"Who the blazes are you?" demanded Steele, "and what is your purpose?"

"I am Captain Thomas Sandford of his Majesty's firelocks. I come to request that you surrender this castle to my Lord Byron for the King's use."

"And why, sirrah, do you suppose, I would submit to this request without resistance?"

"Come, Captain Steele," said Sandford. "We have gained control of the inner ward, and more of our men are entering as we speak. We also have your brother-in-law captive. Furthermore, his Majesty's army is within striking distance of your outer walls and you are but sixty strong. Do you seriously consider that you can resist us?"

"It is my duty to do exactly that."

"Then let me be clear, Captain Steele. I will tell you the same as I told the inhabitants of Hawarden Castle a few days ago. We are loyal to his Majesty and will not shrink

from correcting rebels such as yourselves. However, as I am loath to spill the blood of my own countrymen, you will be received into mercy if you surrender this place together with its provisions, and you will be permitted to leave with your arms and your colours flying. Your brother-in-law will be freed once you have left. However, if you put us to the least trouble, or if any of my men are harmed, you can expect no quarter."

Steele considered this for a moment. "Captain," he said, eventually. "You have a nerve, I'll grant you that. Let us discuss terms like the gentlemen that we are. Bring one of your men and we will discuss this over breakfast in my quarters. I will receive you in half an hour. In the meantime, I will have bread and ale sent up for your men."

The guest, who had been listening to this exchange with interest, had been separated from the others and was sitting on his own by the well, with only one firelock guarding him. Sandford approached him and gave him a wry smile.

"That was easier than I thought," he breathed. "If this is the quality of the men that defends Parliament's cause, we shall carve our way through Cheshire like a knife through butter."

"My brother-in-law's a good man," said the guest, "but he's far too easily manipulated."

Sandford nodded. "Let's hope the townsfolk of Nantwich treat him as well as we are doing. Somehow, I doubt that will be the case."

11

The first indication that Byron's troops were getting close was on the Wednesday evening. Skinner and I had just returned to Nantwich with a cart fully-laden with cheese and, ironically, having spent the day in the countryside to the east of the town, where the chance of running into a royalist patrol was negligible, we had both felt further removed from the tension pervading the garrison than we had for some time.

We had taken the horse and cart and paid a visit to my parents' farm in Barthomley, visiting, on the way back, other farms in the hamlets of Englesea Brook, Weston, Shavington-cum-Gresty, and Willaston with which I had developed a relationship. It had been another bitterly cold day, but the weather, which had been bright and sunny with cloudless skies, lifted our spirits and lightened our mood. The only downside to this was that I was forced to put up with Skinner's incessant singing, which, I had discovered, he was wont to do when in the right mood – or wrong mood, depending on how you looked at it. As we manoeuvred the cart down Hospital Street, Skinner again broke into song, drawing the attention of the passers-by.

"The Lord Capell with a thousand and a half,
Came to Bartons Crosse and there they kill'd a calf,
And staying there until the break of day,
They took their heels and fast they ran away."

Several people smiled as they heard the melody, not because of Skinner's singing voice, which was tuneful enough, but because they recognised the ditty, which had become all the rage in Nantwich during the past six months.

The song told of events in May, when Arthur, Lord Capel, who was in charge of the King's forces in Shropshire, had ridden to Nantwich with near enough fifteen hundred men and tried to attack the town. However, the ordnance that he had brought with him had been placed on ground that was too high, and, despite the strength of his forces, all they managed to achieve was to damage some barns and kill a calf belonging to Mr Thomas Mainwaring. The royalists were forced to return in shame to Whitchurch, the town's ridicule which nipped at their heels being reflected in the words of the rhyme.

A small group of soldiers by the sconce near Church's Mansion cheered in approval as we passed.

"That's right, lad. A bunch of useless Irish piss-pots is

what they are," shouted one of them. "Couldn't shoot a barn wall from the inside and that's the truth of it."

"Aye, we'll send the whoreson papist bastards back where they came from," agreed another.

Despite the confidence, I couldn't help feeling that the army that was heading our way might be a different proposition to the Shropshire forces that had attacked the town before; a view which I knew was held by many. Indeed, the apprehension in Nantwich at the prospect of being overrun by Byron's forces was palpable. It was not without justification, for the townsfolk had, in fact, already suffered an invasion of their streets by royalist soldiers. The experience had not been a pleasant one.

In September 1642, before the earthworks had been built, the royalist commander, Lord Grandison, the brother of the Duke of Buckingham, had approached the town with around seven hundred horse, including troopers and dragooners. A number of townsfolk had drawn chains across the end of Hospital Street and were ready to mount a defence. However, partly in recognition of the fact that the King, at that time, was in Shrewsbury and would have been able to call on a much larger force, but mainly because Lord Grandison gave an undertaking not to do them or the town any harm, the chain was withdrawn and the cavaliers given access to the town.

To our dismay, Grandison had promptly reneged on his word and disarmed every man in Nantwich, taking his arms and armour and taking whatever else they could find from both the town and the countryside thereabouts, before high-tailing it back to Shrewsbury. Grandison's men took a week's supply of my cheese with them and would have taken my horse, Demeter, too, had I not taken the precaution of stabling him temporarily in my wich house. Trusting royalist promises was a mistake that the townspeople had no intention of making again, particularly now that Nantwich was defended by the garrison.

After delivering half the stock of cheese to Captain Draycott and storing the remainder at home for Saturday's market, I became aware of a commotion taking place on the other side of the buildings between my house and the Crown Hotel. I unsaddled the horse and put the cart in the yard, before walking down to the square and turning right to see a most unusual scene unfolding in front of The Crown. A middle-aged officer was being roughly handled by some of the townsfolk and was being forced towards the entrance of the hotel. I noticed with surprise that the commotion seemed to be being led by several gentlemen, whose faces were lined with animosity, but the disturbance had spread to include most of the men in the street at that time. Of greater concern was the fact that none of the soldiers thereabouts seemed prepared to lift a finger to help the officer, who was on the point of being overwhelmed in the melee. Over the rumpus I heard shouts of "traitor" and "coward" ring through the air, whilst, in the distance, a small company of about sixty men waited in formation in the Swine Market.

I was just about to try to break up the disturbance when, out of the corner of my eye, I caught sight of my brother, Simon, lingering on the edge of the crowd, so I went over to him.

"Is something amiss?" I asked.

"Beeston Castle has fallen," replied my brother. "It appears the garrison there was attacked last night. Captain Steele has surrendered the castle and all its contents without a fight."

"Beeston, fallen? It can't be," I said, with incredulity. "I thought that place was nigh-on impregnable. How strong was the attacking force?"

"That, brother, would appear to be the problem. The soldiers standing in the market are suggesting that fewer than ten men actually got into the castle. Some of the people here had moved livestock and valuables up to Beeston for safekeeping. You can see why they are not best pleased."

"And the soldiers? Why are they not helping?"

"They are angry too. The castle had ammunition and provisions for half a year at least – all now in the King's possession."

I whistled in surprise and peered again into the crowd. "And that, I presume, is Captain Steele," I speculated, nodding towards the unfortunate officer, who was in the process of being felled by a clubbing fist from one of the angry mob.

At that moment, a column of perhaps a dozen soldiers approaching from the square cut a swathe through the seething mob and grabbed Steele by the scruff of the neck, extracting him from the crowd. At the same time, a pistol shot rang out, and some of the people attacking the officer were barged out of the way and sent sprawling on the floor. Out of the confusion, the lithe figure of Major Lothian appeared.

"I will no' permit the assault of parliamentary soldiers by a stinking mob of townspeople – d'ye hear?" shouted Lothian, his scots accent being accentuated as a result of his raised voice. "If there is military justice to be dispensed in this town, it will be carried out in the proper manner, not in a free-for-all."

Lothian's voice was enough to stop the disturbance momentarily, and, despite some discontented grumblings, the noise began to die down. Those who had been foremost in assaulting the Captain melted magically into the mass of the crowd, and Steele was allowed to get gingerly to his feet. "Thank you, Major," he said, straightening his collar.

"You have got nothing to be thankful for yet, Captain," barked Lothian, his face like thunder. "You have got some explaining to do." With that, Steele was grabbed by the arms and led away towards the Lamb, leaving one of the other officers, Captain Sadler, to take charge of Steele's men.

When order had been restored and the crowd

dispersed, I invited Simon to join me in a tankard of ale. A full day on the road had left me with a rare thirst, and so we headed straight for The Crown and ordered two pints of strong ale. The air was heavy in the tavern, a sweet tobacco smell mixed with male sweat and beer dominating the fug of the taproom. Many soldiers from the garrison were billeted in The Crown, and so the tavern was full of them. We took our ale over to a table by a window and sat down.

"I've not seen you these past three days," I said, slaking my thirst with a huge gulp of beer. Simon smiled and ran his fingers through his hair, brushing the long, straight strands from his face.

"We've been busy in the workshop," he revealed, "but you will probably be seeing much more of me soon. It is too risky to go to Manchester at the moment, but there is plenty of business locally. It is surprising how many boots are required for the soldiers and other hangers-on."

"These are difficult times," I reflected, "but it's true that having over a thousand soldiers in the town does have its advantages."

"Thank God they are here," said my brother. "We need both them and the efforts of the townsfolk if we are not to be overrun by the Irish and sacked. It seems Nantwich has become the only haven in Cheshire for right-thinking people of the true faith. We need to stand against supporters of this romish King of ours. We must act against those who would ally themselves with papists."

I have to admit, I was somewhat taken aback by the strength of feeling in Simon's words. I had no idea he felt this strongly and realised with a pang that I no longer knew my own brother the way I should. I gave him a penetrating look.

"Do you really believe all these stories about barbarity?" I said. "Are we really to believe the Irish boil the heads of children in front of their mothers and murder babies as soon as they are born? These are surely stories created for political expediency. What I hear is that these people are mostly not Irishmen. They are Cheshire men like you and I. Anyway, I didn't think you were such a hot protestant, Simon."

"I'm not. I'm all for tolerance, but, over the years, it's been difficult for anyone with puritan views to worship in this area."

"And you believe it will be better if the place were run by puritans of the likes of William Prynne or John Bastwick? They'll be banning Christmas before long, I'll wager. Surely the best road is a middle road?"

"You're right, brother," said Simon. "But it's not religion that is my main concern. It is opportunity that is the most important factor for me. The opportunity to act against a King who thinks it's his divine right to rule as he sees fit. The opportunity for ordinary people in Parliament to run the country. Equal opportunities for all. We have to fight for this. You say we will run a cheese business when this is all over, Daniel, but we need to fight to make sure we can."

"Protecting Nantwich won't be easy," I said.

"I know. Booth's forces are only a thousand strong, and they say five thousand of the King's men are on their way here. Even within this town, there are still forces which would have Byron running the place. The main families are mostly for the King, and, until recently, even the vicar was a royalist. And there are other forces at play too. Who do you suppose is responsible for distributing the poisonous literature from Oxford that turned up yesterday?"

"I don't know," I admitted, intrigued at Simon's show of passion for this subject too. "One thing is certain, though," I added. The puritan pamphlets coming out of Shrewsbury recently bear no more proximity to the truth than *Mercurius Aulicus*. If you believe them, the King's soldiers have crucifixes hanging around their necks and openly drink to the health of Phelim O'Neale."

"The very devil and a murderer of good Irish Protestants," said Simon.

"I'd no idea you were such a firebrand," I said. "Perhaps you would benefit from a meeting with the printer of these pamphlets."

"You can arrange this?" he asked, his eyes widening. "I heard the publisher Hugh Furnival plans to be in town and will be presenting his new newssheet in The Crown, tomorrow." I realised with a start that Simon did not realise that Furnival was married to Alice – and why should he? Simon was only eleven when I had left home and fourteen when Alice had left me for Furnival. At that time, nobody had dared speak of what had happened between Alice and me, and I certainly had not mentioned it to Simon.

I smiled. "For you, brother, anything," I said. "I have an invitation to Furnival's reception. I suggest you join me."

12

Nantwich – Thursday, December 14, 1643

The weather had changed again overnight, bringing with it a fresh fall of snow and a bitter wind that cut through my coat like a knife, blowing fresh powder snow like a fine mist in swirls around the streets. The snow had stopped falling by the time I ventured out onto Pepper Street, but the sky remained heavy and oppressive.

However, the weather was not the only thing that was closing in. The previous night had brought with it clear evidence that royalist forces were beginning to amass in the surrounding countryside. There had been several alarms in the town during the hours of darkness, the night being punctuated by the sound of occasional musket-fire as opportunists hiding in the fields and hedgerows took occasional pot-shots at anyone from the garrison who stuck their heads too far over the earthen walls.

One of the first signs that things were about to change was the appearance of Major Lothian at my front door as soon as it was light. I was surprised to see him but pleased at the same time, for he was able to update me on what had happened during the night. One soldier had apparently received a musket ball in the arm, and sentries were reporting that the fires of groups of royalists could now be seen in the neighbouring hamlets. The only consolation was that they were camping out in the open air or in isolated barns. Captain Steele, meanwhile, had been locked up in the town jail alongside Davenport. I felt sorry for the Captain, but at least he was indoors, out of the biting cold.

Lothian had approached me because as constables, Arthur Sawyer and I were in charge of musters. The Scotsman, meanwhile, was responsible for training the garrison, and it had occurred to him that, in the likelihood of the town being stormed or placed under siege, it would be worthwhile training some of the townsfolk to defend themselves, given that Colonel Booth would, as likely as not, conscript all able-bodied men, should such an eventuality come to pass. Lothian, apparently, had thirty spare muskets, with which he proposed to arm an equal number of suitable townsfolk.

"Make sure you and Sawyer get together thirty able-bodied men and present yourselves for training at Tinkers Croft tomorrow morning at ten," he said, before leaving me to contemplate having to rely on the good nature of Alexander to help me with my ever-increasing workload.

I realised that this time it might take a little more than my persuasive skills to convince Margery Clowes that her husband should give up part of his day to help me, so, once I had breakfasted, I made sure I wrapped up a good portion of my father's best cream cheese and took it with me.

It was Margery herself who opened the door, and she eyed me with suspicion when she saw what I was carrying.

"Is that a peace offering or a bribe, Daniel?" she asked, opening the package and taking in the rich aroma of the cheese. "Only we cannot live on cheese alone. We need bread too and we can't buy that unless Alexander works to put pennies in our pocket."

I glanced behind Margery at Alexander, who was wearing a sheepish look on his face.

"I know, Margery," I said. "I'm truly sorry, but we may all have difficulties putting bread on the table if Lord Byron attacks. What I need Alexander for today is vital for the safety of the town."

"And what would that be exactly?"

I was about to tell Margery the truth, but before I could put my foot in it, Alexander slipped by his wife and grabbed me by the arm.

"I will be back by lunchtime," he called over his shoulder, leading me swiftly down the street. "If you were a married man, Daniel," he said to me once we were out of earshot, "you would know there is no winning arguments of this kind."

Alexander and I first walked over to the Davenport's wich house to make sure Skinner had been sent over to work the final day's walling. We then hurried over to the jail where the talk was all about Beeston Castle and the near riot that had been avoided the previous day. Hopwood and Sawyer were both there, discussing the rising tension in the town and the concern many felt that the size of Booth's garrison would not be large enough to repel Lord Byron's forces. Until Sir William Brereton returned to Nantwich with reinforcements, the consensus was that the next few weeks would not be pleasant.

Sawyer and I quickly arranged to split up the task of recruiting trainee musketeers for Lothian by finding fifteen people each, so Alexander and I spent the next two hours accosting people in the street and knocking on tradesmen's doors. Walking down Barker Street, having recruited Roger and John Comberbach, we noticed an altercation by one of the tanners' yards.

A young Beeston musketeer, tall and spindly but no older than eighteen or nineteen, was being pushed around by three burly-looking soldiers, who I recognised from the disturbance the day before. The youth's nose was bleeding and his musket had been knocked to the ground.

"Just as I thought, a proper soft bastard," sneered one of the soldiers, a short, stocky man with the beginnings of a paunch, who seemed to be the ringleader of the group.

"Aye, no more than you'd expect from one of those milk-livered arseholes from Beeston," said another, a taller man with a short red beard.

"Milk-livered? What do you mean?" shot back the

youth. "What do you want from me?"

"Just some sport," grinned Paunch. "You beetle-headed cowards didn't even have it within you to face up to a few high-born cavaliers. Now you're going to pay for it."

"Aye," added Red Beard. "I've been to Beeston. It's built on a fucking cliff. How can you not defend such a place?"

At that, the third man, a balding man in his thirties with a black-toothed grin, stepped forward and started pushing the youth up against the tannery wall. The youngster, to his credit, was not cowed and aimed a kick at Black Tooth's shins, sending the man howling backwards, where he slipped and fell into the snow.

"Go fuck yourself, maggot-pie," spat the youth. "The surrender of Beeston has nothing to do with me. That was Captain Steele's doing, as you well know, and he awaits judgement on his actions."

Although the youth was giving an impressive account of himself, it was evident that he was in for a beating, so I stepped forward.

"Hold!" I shouted. "I'd leave the lad alone if I were you."

Paunch turned round and stared at me with curiosity. "And who are you to order us about?" he snarled.

"My name is Cheswis," I said, observing Alexander pick up the youth's musket out of the corner of my eye. "I'm one of the elected constables here."

"Get lost, bum-bailey," snarled Paunch. "Go concern

yourself with your own affairs. This is military business. And tell that lackey of yours to put that musket down before he gets hurt. He looks like he doesn't know one end of it from the other."

Red Beard and Black Tooth both sniggered at this and took Paunch's comments as the signal to step forward and grab hold of the youth again.

"This is no military business," I insisted. "This is common assault." Paunch scowled and made to grab for my collar, but he was too slow. Alexander had taken hold of the musket by the barrel and swung it, catching Paunch full in the face with the butt, sending him sprawling on his back, spitting blood and teeth into the snow. Red Beard and Black Tooth froze as they took in the scene.

"There's more than one way to use a musket," said Alexander.

"I suggest you pick up your friend and move it," I said, "unless you wish to be arrested for assault, that is."

Red Beard and Black Tooth said nothing, but helped their groaning colleague to his feet and scuttled off down the street in defeat, whilst the youth watched in disbelief.

"You have a way with that musket, sir," he said, addressing Alexander. "I owe you my thanks."

"It was nothing," acknowledged my friend. "You looked like you were managing well enough without our help."

The youth, I noticed, spoke with the flat monotone of one born in the town of Birmingham.

"You are some way from home, young man," I said. "What do they call you?"

"My name is Jack Wade, sir," he replied. "I was among the garrison that arrived from Beeston yesterday. Many of our men are being treated in this manner. I shouldn't really be walking around on my own."

I offered my hand to Wade and introduced myself, as did Alexander. "Tell me," I asked, "How is it a Birmingham man ends up in Beeston Castle? Don't tell me you were at home when it was attacked by Prince Rupert in April?"

"I was, sir. It is quite a story but one worth telling. My father was a blacksmith, a profitable trade in Birmingham, for the town made thousands of swords for the parliamentary army. Birmingham is a puritan town and stood firmly against the King, and although we made the best swords in the land, many refused to sell to the royalists. Then, last October, the King happened to march through Birmingham on the way from Shrewsbury to Edgehill. On his way through, a group of townsfolk seized some of the King's carriages, taking some of his plate and furniture. We knew then we would pay for this action, for the King could not allow such a humiliation."

"So he sent his nephew to teach you a lesson," I said.

"Yes, Prince Rupert came with twelve hundred troopers and dragoons and seven hundred foot. Our defence under Sir Richard Greaves was no more than three hundred strong. We never stood a chance, and yet

Sir Richard's brave men repelled the Prince twice from their earthworks. However, the Prince then attacked from the rear, and our men were forced to retreat into the town, where they shot at the enemy from the houses. It was a terrible sight. The cavaliers set fire to our houses, scattering those men that were left. And yet Sir Richard still did not give up. He gathered up all his horse, retreated to the far end of the town and then charged the cavaliers, causing them to retreat themselves."

"And then what happened?"

"It was a disaster. Sir Richard knew he could not win, and it soon became clear that the last charge was only to give him enough time to save his men. He drew his forces together and set off for Lichfield, leaving us to our fate."

I didn't need to ask Wade what happened next, for I knew the story. Prince Rupert had exacted revenge in the most savage manner, his men raping, killing, and burning indiscriminately. Many houses were razed to the ground, and there were even tales that a minister of the church had been cut down and murdered.

"And what of your family?" I asked.

"I saw my father butchered in his own workshop. I was with him at the time and managed to escape through the back door. I hid for four hours under some sheets and a pile of firewood in one of the outhouses belonging to our neighbours and then escaped under darkness into the woods nearby. I have no idea what horrors my mother was forced to endure, but I found her body in our yard when I returned the following day once the royalists had left. The bastards had slit her throat. My father's workshop, meanwhile, was little more than a pile of ashes. They had burned it to the ground."

Wade's story was a terrible one, and I did not know what to say in terms of offering sympathy to the lad, so I simply asked him what he did next.

"I had no reason to stay in Birmingham," he said. "I had no family and no business, so I walked north until I happened upon Sir William Brereton's forces near Whitchurch. There was nothing that I would have rather done than kill some of the bastards who had murdered my family, so I joined Sir William's forces. I was with them when Whitchurch was taken at the end of May, but, shortly after that, I was sent north as a secondment to the garrison at Beeston."

"You have lived a lot in a short space of time," I said. "Tell me, what happened yesterday in Beeston?"

"I don't know, sir. I was in the lower ward at the time, but I can't understand how they got in. I suspect treachery is the answer."

"And Captain Steele?"

"He was trying to save our lives, sir, and he is to be commended for that. The problem is that he sent food and ale up to the invaders and entertained the firelock captain to a meal. He will pay for that, I'm sure, but at least we live to fight another day."

"I wouldn't be so sure that you have got the best of it," I said. "Given the choice of attacking less than ten firelocks or being besieged by five thousand Irish veterans, I know what I would prefer."

The gallery on the top floor of the Crown Hotel was a swarming throng of people when Simon and I arrived later that afternoon for the unveiling of *The Public Scout*. Far from the "select reception" described by Alice, the gathering was more closely akin to a public meeting. Although the gallery was usually light and airy, benefiting from a continuous range of windows which overlooked the High Street and ran along the whole length of the building, the midwinter dusk meant that it was illuminated by a row of candles affixed in sconces along the walls. The room, which filled the whole of the top storey of the inn, contained over a hundred people, who milled around, engaging in animated conversation. Many held copies of the newssheet, which, together with some modest refreshments, had been laid out for the guests on a large oak table in the centre of the room.

I had to admit that attendance at the meeting had been exceptional, for nearly every townsperson of importance seemed to be in the room. Unsurprisingly, most of the gentlemen who had signed the "*Remonstrance of the Inhabitants of the County Palatine of Chester*" were present, including Roger Wright, Thomas Walthall, and the ageing lawyer Thomas Malbon, but so were Thomas

Maisterson, Roger Wilbraham and several others known to have been sympathetic to the King's cause.

There were a number of local clergymen, and Colonel Booth was there with several of his officers, including Major Lothian.

Looking around the room, I realised that nearly all the town's public officials had put in an appearance – all four Rulers of Walling, including Gilbert Kinshaw, Welch, the new minister, leave-lookers, ale-tasters, fire-lookers and channel-lookers – even Arthur Sawyer was to be seen deep in conversation with Hopwood the bailiff. With a pang of disappointment, I realised that there was nothing special about Alice's invitation to me – the Furnivals had simply invited anyone they considered to be of influence.

Simon and I had been ten minutes late, and it quickly became apparent that Hugh Furnival had already spoken to the assembled crowd before our arrival, as both he and Alice were busy making sure they mingled with everyone who had made the effort to attend.

Alice was dressed elegantly, but in the sober colours that were to be expected of the wife of a prominent puritan. She wore a pointed stomacher under her high-waisted black dress with lace-trimmed collar and cuffs, accompanied by a high-necked white chemise. Despite the restrained style of her garb, I still felt the same pangs of anguish as before.

I turned away, knowing that such thoughts needed to

be suppressed, and turned my attention to Furnival in the other corner of the room. I had not seen Hugh Furnival for years, but I recognised him immediately. Slim and slightly shorter than Alice, he had grown a short pointed beard, and his jet black hair, now greying slightly around the temples, was cut short. He, too, was dressed soberly in the Dutch fashion, with a black, unstiffened jacket and wide breeches.

He had been in conversation with the lawyer Malbon, but, when he saw me looking his way, he smiled and weaved his way through the room towards us.

"Mr Cheswis, I am indebted to you for attending the launch of *The Public Scout*. I understand you know my wife well."

"That was many years ago," I said, caught off-guard by Furnival's directness.

"Quite so. And you, sir," he said, addressing Simon. "I don't believe I've had the pleasure of your acquaintance." My brother stepped forward and shook Furnival's hand.

"My name is Simon Cheswis," he said. "Daniel is my elder brother."

"Then you cannot have been more than a child the last time I was in Barthomley."

"That is true, sir. I don't remember you, but I am aware of your achievements."

Furnival bowed his head slightly at the compliment.

"Tell me, sir," continued Simon, who seemed curiously awestruck in Furnival's presence, "how does a Barthomley man become involved in printing political pamphlets? The subject fascinates me."

Furnival smiled indulgently and embarked on what was clearly one of his favourite subjects.

"It was largely a matter of good fortune," he replied. "I was sent to London at the age of sixteen, apprenticed to a printer. I learned my trade and became a journeyman printer. By the time I got married in sixteen-thirty-four, I had already been in the business seventeen years and had become a partner in a small print workshop publishing textbooks. That was a particularly difficult time for my trade and one of no little danger. All printing was controlled by the Stationers Company, but there was a thriving trade in publishing unlicensed books and newssheets."

"But that must have been a time of opportunity for the printers of such material," I interjected.

"Not at first. Things became very difficult, especially after sixteen-thirty-seven, when the Star Chamber issued a decree which sought to suppress publications deemed to be seditious, especially those of a religious nature which did not agree with Archbishop Laud's religious views. They were times of great hazard, especially if you were caught in possession of such material. They were exciting times, though, as they brought me into contact with pamphleteers like Lilburne, Bastwick, and Prynne. Of course, since the Star Chamber was abolished in sixteen-forty-one, there have been massive opportunities for printers like me."

"You know John Lilburne?" asked Simon, with surprise.

"Yes," said Furnival. "Do you know his work?"

"I do. I've read *The Work of the Beast*. His description of the punishments and imprisonment he had to endure for printing and distributing unlicensed books is inspirational. He is a brave man."

"Brave, maybe," countered Furnival, "but foolish nonetheless. If he'd been a little less confrontational, he may have managed to stay out of jail."

I stared at Simon in amazement. He was a veritable box of surprises. My brother had never been the studious type, and yet here he was, displaying knowledge of the very latest in political and religious writings. Where on Earth had he learned such things? I watched Simon's face, which registered disappointment at Furnival's casual assessment of Lilburne. Furnival, obviously, noticed this too, because he quickly stepped in to temper the effect of his words.

"To be frank," he interjected, "my partner and I were not directly involved with the likes of Prynne and Bastwick, who, as you know, had their ears cropped for their troubles, nor were we involved in the illegal import of books from Holland like Lilburne, but we *did* publish our fair share of pamphlets and books, and we were well-acquainted with John Wharton, the bookseller who persuaded Bastwick to have *The Letany* published.

Through him we knew these men."

"I see."

"You realise, of course," said Furvival, "that Lilburne, like Bastwick and Prynne, was strongly critical of the Laudian church. You have read *Come out of her my People*?"

"No, but I am aware of his arguments."

"So, it is the anti-Laudianism that attracts you to Lilburne?"

"Not particularly. I am for freedom, religious tolerance, and equality. If I am against Arminianism and Laudianism, it is because their followers are religiously *intolerant*."

Furnival looked closely at Simon, and a flicker of a smile came over his face. "I think you would get on well with Lilburne," he said, at length.

"I must apologise for my brother," I said, hurriedly. "He has strong views."

"Not at all, Mr Cheswis. My business is founded on strong views. The proof is herein." With that, Furnival offered us both a copy of *The Public Scout* and passed onto his next group of guests.

I was about to admonish Simon for his impertinence, but was beaten to it by a quiet but insistent voice to my left. "Pardon my intrusion, gentlemen, but I could not help but overhear your comments on religious tolerance."

I turned and recognised the short, slightly overweight figure of Edward Burghall, the headmaster of the school in the nearby village of Bunbury. I would normally have been surprised at the presence of a village schoolmaster at such a gathering, but Burghall was a controversial figure around Nantwich. A strict Presbyterian, he had developed a reputation as a firebrand minister, stridently preaching in favour of a sober, hardworking lifestyle and intolerance of sins such as games, drunkenness, and profaning the Sabbath. He was well-respected but considered by many to be dogmatic and possessing a godly righteousness which bordered on arrogance. I sensed that Simon had talked his way into a longer debate than he had bargained for.

"If you are in favour of tolerance," demanded Burghall, "does that mean you would tolerate Arminians and papists in our church?"

Simon looked at the schoolmaster and rose to the bait. "I am no Arminian," he replied. "I would not want to force popery into our church as has been the case these past years, thanks to the efforts of the King and Archbishop Laud, but I would not wish to persecute them. I would leave them to worship in peace. You, sir, I take it, would not?"

"I would consider it my duty not to do so," said Burghall. "It is incumbent upon all godly ministers to guide their brethren on the right path, for God is working actively against the powers of evil. Our King, married to a papist, has promoted popery in our church for years and subjected this land to the tyranny of Laud and Strafford.

Now, one of these traitors languishes in jail waiting to stand trial for his life, whilst the other has already met his end on the executioner's block. Meanwhile, the King rules over a kingdom that is split from head to toe. Is that not divine providence?"

"I don't think so. I think that is just a King who will not listen to his people. In any case, the King's side use exactly the same argument. If *Mercurius Aulicus* is to be believed, John Pym's death is also due to divine providence."

"No, I have studied this in some detail," insisted Burghall, who was now in full flow. "God's judgement is to be seen every day. Those who would live a godless life, indulging in drunkenness, dancing, and forbidden sports, and those who take part in wakes, popish festivals as they are; they all stand to be judged. I remember, many years ago at Bunbury, a bear-ward was torn apart at a bear baiting by the animal he was in charge of. That is an illegal calling, sir. Was it not providence that he paid with his life?"

I saw that Simon had his hands full, and so I left him to it. Instead, my attention was drawn to the copy of *The Public Scout* that I was holding. I started reading the main article, a long elegy to John Pym. I had barely been reading five minutes when Furnival appeared at my shoulder again.

"These must be profitable times for printers like you, Mr Furnival," I said, turning the page to reveal a series of local news items from Shrewsbury.

"You are right," replied Furnival. "There is a thirst for public debate of the issues of the day, especially in a garrison town like Nantwich. This town has become a melting pot for all manner of political and religious debate. There are rich pickings to be had for a wordsmith like me."

"Why would that be so?" I asked.

"With Chester being controlled by the royalists, Nantwich has become a magnet for all kinds of diverse groups. There are puritans of the more extreme kind, including ministers who were persecuted under Laud, and there is a sizeable parliamentary force, and yet Nantwich also has more wealthy merchants and gentlemen than any other town in Cheshire. Even amongst the general population it is clear that the town has been torn asunder by this conflict. Despite the fact that most people here are for Parliament, it is clear that this town still has many people who are not of that persuasion. It is this aspect that I find most interesting."

"I see."

"For instance," he said. "Take the murder that took place at Welsh Row End on Saturday, which I understand you are investigating."

"That is correct," I acknowledged.

"On the face of it, it appears that it may have been politically motivated."

"Politically motivated?"

"Yes. I understand the victim was found with a crimson sash around his neck."

"He was. I still have the scarf, but that is no proof that he was killed for his political allegiance."

"No, but nonetheless, the simple act of using the scarf is symptomatic of the type of conflict we have. Matters such as this are of great interest to me. Perhaps you could spare some time to discuss this with me, perhaps over lunch tomorrow? *The Public Scout* needs to maintain a local flavour, and so I would like to find out more about this case."

"I suppose I could do that," I conceded.

"Good, then I will see you here at midday tomorrow – and bring the scarf with you. As you know, I spent some time in Shrewsbury, when the King was there. I may be able to help identify it."

Of course, I had no need to show Furnival the scarf, as Randle Church had already told me it had belonged to him. Nevertheless, I was hardly going to admit this to Furnival. Intrigued at his interest, I turned my attention to rescuing my brother from the attentions of Edward Burghall.

13

Nantwich – Friday, December 15, 1643

Tinkers Croft was wreathed in an unsettling, spectral atmosphere as Sawyer, myself, and twenty-eight other reluctant townsfolk stood shivering in the morning mist, awaiting our prescribed musket training. A row of white tents, which ran alongside the southern edge of the field, appeared like ghostly apparitions in the icy mist. Behind us, St Mary's rose forbiddingly, in a manner which belied the fact that it was God's house.

As I peered through the murk, I became aware of three figures loitering a hundred yards away, barely visible in the fog, but as I continued to stare, I realised that I was looking at three large hay bales, which had been erected as targets. Affixed to the front of each of them was a metal breastplate.

As we waited, men began to emerge from the tents and started to gather in small groups, murmuring their interest at the sudden appearance of thirty civilians in their midst. These, I knew, were some of the unfortunate soldiers who had failed to find quarter within the town. I recognised Jack Wade amongst them and realised many of those camping must have been the remnants of the garrison from Beeston. Wade acknowledged my presence with a raised hand as I surveyed our small group, a mixed bag of local tradesmen, servants, apprentices and youths, most of whom had never handled a musket before. Alexander and my brother Simon had joined us, as had Will Butters and several other servants from Townsend House. Also present were James Skinner and his two brothers, who stood huddled together, talking to each other in low voices.

Eventually, Major Lothian appeared with a lean-looking sergeant, who he introduced as Sergeant Bradshaw. Behind him came two more soldiers, who led a horse and cart, on which were loaded crates containing muskets, bandoliers, and other equipment. Once he had our attention, Lothian strode over to the cart and helped himself to one of the muskets.

"You may be wondering," he said, "why you have been dragged out onto a freezing field in the depths of winter. Well, Lord Byron and his Irish army are nearly at our gates and they are getting closer. This town will need to be defended and we need as many able-bodied men as possible to help us do that. The purpose of today is to teach you how to use one of these muskets and give you half a chance of hitting something. Sergeant Bradshaw will demonstrate."

"This," said Bradshaw, taking the musket from Lothian and holding it in the air, "is a matchlock musket. The first thing you need to know is that it's useless in the wet and the wind, and if you're using it in the dark, your enemy will know exactly where you are. However, if you hit somebody with a ball from this, if he's within a hundred yards, he isn't going to get up. That means these things are dangerous buggers. So, if you want to avoid shooting a hole in your foot, pay attention."

Satisfied that all eyes were on him, Bradshaw then held the musket in front of himself in both hands.

"Hold your weapon like this," he said. "Open the priming pan and put some powder into it. Not too much – just enough. Now close the pan and blow the excess powder away." Bradshaw demonstrated the procedure.

"Next, place your musket with the butt on the ground and the trigger facing backwards, but keep your eye on your burning match cord. You don't want to set off a charge. Now put in one of the charges from your bandolier." Bradshaw paused for a moment to make sure everyone was still watching before continuing.

"Now put a ball in the barrel and some wadding and seat the charge using the ramrod." The sergeant removed the ramrod from its holder and thrust it into the barrel.

"Now you can reseat the ramrod - but be careful. Only use your little finger. You don't want to blow your hand off." Bradshaw then picked up the musket, holding it in his right hand.

"Now you're ready," he said. "Get your matchcord, blow on it, and fix it into the serpent. Test it by moving it towards the closed pan. Cover the pan and blow on the match again. If everything is all right, you can now open the pan and take aim – but make sure you hold the gun tightly to your body. Then... fire." Bradshaw fired the musket and a metallic clunk sounded from one of the hay bales in the distance. Those watching emitted a low murmur of approval.

"And that's all there is to it," said Bradshaw, with a wry grin. "And now it's your turn. Who would like to go first?" When nobody moved, Lothian stepped forward and smiled.

"What about you, Mr Cheswis?" he said. "Show them how it's done".

Cursing, I stepped forward and began the procedure. I had got as far as putting the ramrod back, when my concentration was broken by Bradshaw's scream.

"Not like that! You'll blow your fucking hand off! – Beggin' your pardon, sir."

The group broke out into nervous laughter, but Lothian said nothing. Replacing the ramrod as instructed, I completed the procedure, aimed, and fired. In the distance, the musket ball buried itself in the hay bale with a dull thud. Bradshaw peered into the mist and then turned to me, his face betraying nothing.

"Not a bad shot, sir," he said. "You just missed the breastplate. Problem is you've shot the fucking scouring rod halfway across the field too, so now you can't reload."

The group of soldiers standing by their tents erupted

in mirth as I traipsed across the field to retrieve the rod.

Next in line was Sawyer, who was biting his lip nervously. Taking the musket from Bradshaw, he surprisingly managed the loading process correctly but then spoiled it all by missing the target completely. Several other recruits followed with similar results. Two or three hit the bale, but most missed. Worst of all was Will Butters, who dropped the musket completely, scattering all and sundry as everyone dived for cover.

Next, it was James Skinner's turn. My apprentice, his demeanour seemingly transformed, stepped forward confidently and, to our amazement, hit the breastplate squarely in the middle.

"Well done, young man," said the sergeant, as Skinner returned, beaming, to the ranks. "That's the way it should be done."

After that, things began to improve. One of Skinner's brothers also hit the breastplate, as did Simon. We then split into three groups, and, after an hour of practice, most of us had hit the breastplate at least once and those that hadn't had at least managed to hit the bale.

Once the session had ended, each of us was allocated a musket and advised of the procedures for getting hold of powder, charges, and ammunition, should we be required to report for duty. As we filed from the field, I was approached by Jack Wade, who stepped forward from the group of soldiers from Beeston, who had been watching the whole procedure with some degree of amusement.

"Good shooting," he said, with a grin, addressing Alexander and myself. "You did alright in the end, but I would say you still have some work to do."

"Some work?" came a voice from behind Wade, heavy with sarcasm. "It will take more than a bit of work to train these useless bastards."

I looked over Wade's shoulder and my eyes fell on a tall, dark-skinned man with angular features, jet-black hair and a close-cropped beard. I was about to object to the man's comments, but I was beaten to it by one of the Skinner brothers, who had been following close behind me.

"From what I hear, if you bunch of arseholes had known how to use your muskets properly, you'd still be in Beeston instead of being stuck in this field with your captain in jail for cowardice."

I have to admit, I was impressed at the speed of the reactions of Wade and his colleagues, for the soldier had barely taken two steps towards Skinner's brother before his arms had been pinned behind him. Alexander and I were a little slower, though, and Skinner's brother had managed to land a glancing blow on the soldier's cheek before we managed to restrain him.

"Leave it, Jem," barked Wade, as the soldier was hustled away to his tent to cool down.

"I thought we were supposed to be on the same side," I said, five minutes later, to Sergeant Bradshaw, who had been supervising the removal of the horse and cart and had returned to the scene just in time to see the aftermath of the incident.

"We are," he replied. "Take no notice of Jem Bressy. He causes more trouble than most. But if I were you, I'd tell those three brothers to watch out for themselves. Bressy's not just a hothead; he's also a vindictive bastard. He'll be looking to get his own back. You can be sure of that."

Having made no progress whatsoever with my investigations into William Tench's murder, I decided my time would be best spent looking into the fraud accusations against John Davenport. My first line of enquiry was to gain access to the Court Rolls, so later that morning I walked over to the Court House in the High Street, otherwise known as the Booth Hall, and sought out the bailiff's clerk, a studious young man by the name of Ezekiel Green, who turned out to be most accommodating.

I was well-aware of the dogmatic nature of the rules of walling, but I had not seen documents like the Court Rolls before. The papers, which Green placed before me, went back ten years and contained surprisingly long lists of petty contraventions of the rules of walling, carried out by briners and wich house owners over that period of time. Men had been fined for offences such as making salt less than measure and not allowing the leave-lookers to check the barrows to ascertain they carried the correct measures, even for not carrying out walling at all, despite having sufficient wood. It seemed that several cases had been heard at every court session, most of which I had not been aware of, despite being in the business myself.

Also made available to me were a number of old walling books, which showed the walling allocations set according to right, as well as any amendments made during making meet sessions.

I was not sure exactly what I was looking for, but, going through the old court records, I did make several interesting discoveries. Firstly, it struck me that in 1642, the last year that Davenport was a Ruler of Walling, the number of misdemeanours finding their way before the court fell substantially. I also noticed with interest that Edward Yardley had been fined during that year for carrying out a night and day's walling from a previous year's book, despite having no right to do so. This, I mused, may have gone some way towards explaining the continuing antipathy between Davenport and Yardley.

Next, I picked up the old walling books and discovered two or three further anomalies during Davenport's period of office. It appeared that Davenport had carried out four extra days walling that had not been picked up on and a further two days brought forward as old days but mis-accounted for. In addition, there was an instance where a wich house owner called Henry Ellcock had failed to claim two extra days walling, which should have been included as old days. These two days, it appeared, had been carried out on Ellcock's behalf by Davenport. I couldn't prove anything, but I wondered whether Ellcock actually knew about this. I was unwilling to condemn my friend without proof, but the irregularities in the accounts did appear somewhat suspicious, and it seemed, on analysis, that Davenport had, at best, miscalculated and broken several rules; offences which would result in quite a fine, in addition to loss of face.

I also wondered why it was that, if these misdemeanours had been so easy to spot, they had not been followed up by Kinshaw and the rest of the new Rulers months ago. My findings seemed to provide more questions than answers, but, noticing that I was late for my appointment with Hugh Furnival, I realised I had no time to look into the matter any further. Gathering together my papers, I resolved to take the matter up with Davenport at the earliest possible opportunity.

Furnival, it turned out, was a skilled conversationalist and a most agreeable companion, as indeed was the lunch – rabbit stew, one of The Crown's specialities. We talked for nearly an hour about the politics of the day, by which time I could have almost forgotten that this was the man who was married to Alice.

Eventually, though, the subject turned to the purpose of our meeting, so I took the initiative and asked Furnival why he was so interested in the murder of William Tench.

"*The Public Scout* is primarily a political newssheet," he answered, after a moment's consideration. "Our aim is to represent a variety of views, supported by stories of local interest. However, the circumstances surrounding Mr Tench's demise suggest that there is more to the story than just a locally-motivated murder, don't you think?"

I took a mouthful of ale and considered Furnival's comment for a moment before saying; "What do you mean?"

"Come on, man," said Furnival, his eyebrows raised in mock disbelief. "I don't need to spell it out, do I? Tench is found murdered by the earthworks around a town which is most likely to become the focus of the war in Cheshire. The dead man, it appears, is suspected of being a royalist scout, even though, strangely, none of his acquaintances had thought it necessary to bring these suspicions to anyone's attention. The Good Lord knows how that was kept quiet. And what's more, the victim is found to have been throttled with a crimson scarf, identical to those worn by officers in the King's army. Did you bring the scarf?"

I extracted the scarf from a pocket inside my cloak and laid it on the table. Furnival picked it up and inspected it closely, fingering the gold embroidery.

"This material is of high quality," he said. "Not the sort of thing worn by every officer in the King's army. This must have come from someone of high standing."

"That is what I had assumed."

"William Tench's wife is employed by Randle Church, who has connections in high places. Could this scarf possibly belong to him, do you think?"

I gave Furnival a sharp look, but he merely smiled at me inscrutably and took another mouthful of rabbit stew.

"You seem to know a lot about this murder, Mr Furnival," I observed.

"I make it my business to know such things," he replied, breaking off a piece of bread. "The public wants information and I try to give it to them."

"Information? You mean second-hand rumours about the Irish, designed to scare and manipulate your readers? Tell me, why is this murder so significant for you? Why is a little local affair like this of such importance to a political newssheet?"

Furnival wiped up the juices around the edge of his plate with his bread. "So many questions," he said. "Let me try to answer you. The mystery and hubbub surrounding the death of William Tench is symptomatic of this whole conflict. He was, on the face of it, a royalist in a parliamentarian town. But there is no black and white in defining the loyalties of individual towns in this war – only shades of grey.

"Think about it. Nantwich is, in principal, supportive of Parliament. Sir William Brereton is a radical leader, and his way of thinking has attracted many like-minded people, not only politically-motivated activists such as your brother, but also the radical preachers and hot protestants who are so prevalent in these parts. However, it is not the aim of all parliamentarians to create upheaval and change the world. There are just as many moderates like Colonel Booth and Roger Wilbraham at Dorfold, who would not want to change the established way of things and who would oppose much of what the likes of Brereton stand for.

"Then again," he continued, "Nantwich is like any other town in England. The King has his supporters too. For every Dorfold Wilbraham there is a Townsend Wilbraham. Men who are loyal to the King but dare not come out in open support. It's the same in Oxford. The university colleges support the King, but many of the townsfolk are for Parliament, and yet Oxford has become the King's headquarters. Tell me, were you aware of the tangled web of relationships that link the main families of this town to serving the Crown in Ireland?"

"No," I admitted. "Pray educate me."

"Very well. Let us start with Lady Margaret Norton, whose husband was Secretary of State for Ireland under King James. That connection is clear, but he was not Lady Margaret's first husband. That was Roger Mainwaring, head of one of Nantwich's other leading families. Mainwaring also held high office in Ireland. He was Auditor for Ireland in the fifteen-eighties."

"Alright, but where does everyone else fit in?"

"Patience," said Furnival, with a touch of irritation. "I'm getting to that. The interesting thing is that Lady Norton was born Margaret Maisterson. Both her brother and her father held the position of Seneschal of Wexford, and her father was the younger brother of Thomas Maisterson's great-grandfather. There are other connections too. Thomas Maisterson is also married to a Mainwaring, and if you want to find out where the Wilbrahams fit in then you need look no further than Roger Wilbraham's great-uncle, who was Solicitor General for Ireland in the fifteen-eighties and therefore a contemporary of both Roger Mainwaring and Lady Norton's father."

I whistled quietly to myself as I took in what Furnival was saying.

"And that's not all," he continued. "There are connections everywhere. Tench's wife works for one of the key merchants in the town, whose son has been a personal assistant to the King. Lord Cholmondeley is for the King, and even the minister at the church was for him until he was removed from office. This war pits brother against brother, and it's this that I want to get across."

"I see," I said. I had not seen things in this way before, but I had to admit my companion was right. It was then that a thought suddenly struck me.

"One thing I'd like to know," I said. "Your newssheet. What happens if the King wins this conflict?"

"Then we'll adapt and change our stance to reflect prevailing public opinion. Our job is to report and stimulate debate. We are publishers, and publishing is a business after all. I am not averse to changing my words according to demand."

"So you're like a mercenary – a wordmonger – tailoring your words for public consumption? Changing them according to which way the wind is blowing?"

"If you like."

As I observed Furnival's self-satisfied manner, I realised what it was that Furnival sought to achieve with *The Public Scout*. It wasn't the truth, or even business success. It was power, and I knew that men with such aims could be dangerous people indeed.

14

Nantwich – Saturday, December 16, 1643

As the week progressed, the proximity of Lord Byron's army had become increasingly apparent, and, by Saturday morning, a tangible blanket of fear and apprehension had begun to settle over Nantwich. Barely an hour went by, day or night, without an alarm being raised. Soldiers guarding the earthen walls surrounding the town dared not lift their heads above the wooden parapet for fear of attracting a musket shot from the frozen hedgerows or from the shattered ruins of barns and cottages flattened by the townsfolk in an attempt to minimise cover for potential aggressors. Attempts were made to damage the earthworks at night, and stories began to emerge of plundering in the nearby villages of Stoke, Hurleston, Wrenbury, and Brindley – all settlements on the west side of the river.

Not surprisingly, these developments had a marked effect on the regular Saturday market. Farmers and visitors coming from the west could not approach the town without risk of being attacked and having their goods and livestock stolen by marauding royalists.

As Skinner and I set up our stall in the cold and the mist, it quickly became clear that a number of regular stallholders had not risked the trip, and the market began to take on a distinctly forlorn and empty look. In the light of the poor turnout, I was beginning to contemplate ways of disposing of the stocks of cheese I had bought, when my attention was diverted by the sight of my brother striding purposefully up the road from the direction of Beam Street.

I was about to give Simon a hearty welcome but stopped myself abruptly when I saw his demeanour. Instead of wearing his customary affable grin, my brother wrung his hands in agitation, his face pinched and as white as a sheet.

"What is it, brother?" I said, laying down the cheese I had been preparing to cut and wiping my knife on my apron. "You look like you've seen a ghost."

"Daniel, you must come immediately," he replied, his voice quivering slightly as he fought to control the symptoms of shock. "There has been another murder, at the end of Beam Street by Lady Norton's house, and this time it's someone I know."

"Someone you know?" I exclaimed, registering the level to which my brother had been affected by this new occurrence. "What do you mean?"

"I'll explain on the way," said Simon, "but you need to come right now. The body has been found by the earthworks, and Major Lothian is already there."

Removing my apron and throwing it on the table, I gave Skinner brief instructions to take over the stall, warning him not to leave his post until I returned, and then set off at a jog after Simon, who was already halfway down Pepper Street, marching like a man possessed. This was quite unlike Simon, who was normally an unflappable, easygoing character, but his state of unease had begun to be noticed by the street traders lining the sides of Pepper Street, and several of them laid down their tools and began to watch us with interest.

"Calm down," I breathed, as I reached Simon's shoulder. "You are drawing attention to yourself. Tell me. Who is the victim?"

"His name is Ralph Brett," answered my brother, taking a deep breath.

"You mean the mercer?"

Simon nodded. "The very same," he said.

I considered this for a moment. Brett was a well-known trader in fabrics, but I did not know him personally. He was, if I remembered correctly, in his mid-thirties. "How is it that you're acquainted with him?" I asked.

"He is...was a neighbour of mine," said Simon. "I got to know him quite well. We discussed politics together. He was an interesting man and made for a good conversation partner."

"I see," I said. "Good enough to get him murdered, do you think?"

Simon gave me a strange look, which made me wonder

whether I had hit the nail exactly on the head, but he said nothing, and we walked on in silence.

Once we had reached the junction with Beam Street, Simon and I turned right and walked a couple of hundred yards towards the row of tenements and cottages on the left-hand side of the street, where my brother had his lodging. Just before these stood a medium-sized brick residence, which Simon explained was inhabited by Brett, together with his wife and young son. On the opposite side of the road stood the substantial house and gardens belonging to Lady Margaret Norton, beyond which lay the imposing bulk of the earthworks and the sconce at Beam Street End. As the mist cleared, I caught sight of the equally imposing figure of Major Lothian, who appeared to be trying to keep curious onlookers away from the area around the sconce, in order to allow traders and other visitors to the market to pass unhindered through the gates.

"Looks like you may have locked the wrong man up, Mr Cheswis," said the Scotsman, in a voice which seemed to me to convey a tone of greater satisfaction than it needed to. Lothian gestured towards the little side lane, which ran alongside the wall to Lady Norton's garden, fifty yards or so from the earthworks, which led eventually to Churchyardside and Tinkers Croft. Gathered by the wall, a couple of yards from the gate to Lady Norton's garden, stood a small group of soldiers guarding what looked like a bundle of rags.

As I walked up to the group, the soldiers stepped aside, allowing me to see that what they were guarding was, in fact, the body of a man lying face down in the mud and snow, a mass of golden curls emanating from a gory mess. Fighting back the urge to retch, I forced myself to look closely at the victim. The man had obviously been hit several times on the back of his head, which was heavily misshapen. Reaching over, I turned the body onto its back and was met with the vacant expression of a once-handsome man in his thirties with strong, craggy features.

"A well-lived-in face," I said.

"He had been a professional soldier," replied Simon. "He told me he had served under the Duke of Hamilton during the Great War."

"That's interesting," I mused, inspecting the wound on the back of Brett's skull. "Most ex-soldiers with experience in Europe have taken up commissions with either the King or Parliament. That kind of experience is much sought after. Why wasn't he fighting, do you suppose?"

"He told me he wanted to settle down with his family business and take care of his wife and child. He was strong for Parliament but didn't want to take up arms against the King."

"Clearly not," I said, as I pulled the victim's cloak open. Tied around Brett's waist was a crimson silk sash with gold borders. "Do we have another of the King's supporters here?" I asked. Simon reddened and said nothing, clearly deciding that his interests were best served by remaining silent. I fingered the soft fabric of the scarf, which, I noticed, was less ornate than the one found on Tench's body but recognisable nonetheless for what it was.

"How was he found?" I asked, turning my attention to Lothian.

"Hulse and Bressy found him," said the Major, pointing to two soldiers sat on the earthworks, the taller of the pair nursing a cut on his cheek and the beginnings of a black eye. He was a bearded, dark-skinned individual, muscular in build, with jet black hair cut only as far as the collar of his shirt. The other, three or four inches shorter, had a hooked nose and curly hair the colour of straw. With a start, I realised that it was the taller of the men, Bressy, who had started the argument with the Skinners the morning before. Clearly not recognising me, he rose to his feet and acknowledged me with a smile.

"Jem Bressy, sir," he said, "and this is my pal, Nathaniel Hulse."

"Nat, sir," added the other man.

"I know you," I said to Bressy. "You were at Beeston. You picked a fight with my apprentice and his brothers yesterday."

The smile disappeared instantaneously from Bressy's face and his eyes narrowed to slits as he surveyed me.

"You were amongst that shower having musket

practice?" he said, eventually. "Well, I'm not going to apologise for the comments I made. You were fucking useless."

Hulse spluttered as he tried to hold in his laughter, but I wasn't in the mood for humour. Neither, it appeared, was Lothian, who maintained an inscrutable demeanour through all this.

"So you two found the body?" I asked, ignoring Bressy's barb.

"Yes," replied Hulse, making an effort to be more agreeable than his friend. "We nearly caught the bastard who did it, too. Would have, if he hadn't clubbed Jem here with his staff." Hulse indicated the lump and cuts on Bressy's face.

"When did this happen?"

"About seven o'clock," said Hulse. "It was still dark. Jem and I were keeping watch on the walkway when we heard a commotion – shouting and the like. It seemed to be coming from the garden at the back of Lady Norton's, so Jem here says we should go to investigate."

"And what happened next?"

"We'd just got down from the earthworks when a body fell forward out of the gate, followed by a man in a dark cloak."

"And then?"

"The man was holding a large stone – more like a rock – and he smashed it on the back of this poor bastard's head. He didn't move after that. Jem and I ran down the side of the earthworks and grabbed the man, but he was a right slippery bugger. There was a bit of a struggle. We nearly had him, but he clubbed Jem and ran off back through the garden."

"Is that how you saw it?" I asked Bressy, who had sat back down at the foot of the earthworks and was dabbing the cut on his face.

"Aye, that's about it," he grunted. "Nat speaks the truth."

Bidding Hulse to follow me, I walked back over to inspect the gate, which was swinging on its hinges. Behind it was a large stone smeared in blood, which I lifted carefully with both hands, the group of soldiers stepping backwards to allow me to lay it in front of the gate.

"This would appear to be our murder weapon," I said to Hulse. "Now tell me what happened next."

"Well, sir, several other soldiers saw what was happening and came running, but he ran pretty quickly and we lost him in the mist." I looked round at the group of soldiers who had been standing by the gate and who, up to now, had said nothing.

"Who else saw this?" I asked.

"I did, sir," volunteered a young corporal, who gave his name as Cotton. "Me and three of the lads further round the wall heard a shout and saw Hulse and Bressy wrestling with the murderer. We shouted a warning, but we were too late. He clubbed Bressy and ran off. We were there in a second, but he was too quick, sir."

"Would you recognise him again?" I asked, more in hope than expectation.

"No chance, sir. It was too misty and happened too quickly. He also wore a cloak with a hood so as you couldn't see his face properly."

I sighed in exasperation. Once again, it appeared that I had precious little to work on. I took my leave from the soldiers and, deep in thought, climbed the ladder to the walkway at the top of the earthworks, from where I could look out towards Beam Heath, the area used in quieter times by the townsfolk as common pasture. Now, the landscape, shrouded in mist, looked like an eerie wasteland. All around the town outside the walls, houses and barns had been pulled down or set fire to so the enemy could not hide in them. I looked at the desolation, and knew that this was what the town would look like if Byron's army were to prevail.

From my elevated viewpoint I turned round towards Lady Norton's house but couldn't see far beyond the wall, which was itself half-covered in mist. Descending from my vantage point, I walked into Lady Norton's garden and saw another gate open, leading into a pathway on the far side of the lawn. It appeared as though the perpetrator had escaped through here into the fields behind the house across to Monks Lane and Churchyardside. Returning to the body, I gave Major Lothian leave to get some attention to Bressy's wound and turned my own attention to Simon, who, during all my questions, had remained quiet, listening attentively.

"You say you know this man?" I said, gesturing towards the dead body.

"Yes, his wife will need to be informed," said my brother. At this point, as if on cue, a terrible screaming noise began to emanate from the direction of the cottages, and a few seconds later a young woman emerged, hysterical with grief, closely followed by a sandy-haired young man around Simon's age. Holding her skirts to avoid tripping over, she ran up to the sconce and then, noticing the congregation of people around the gate, screamed again and made to come over.

"Ralph, Ralph, they've killed my Ralph," she howled. Before she could get close to the body, though, Simon stepped in front of her and grabbed her tightly, dislodging her coif.

"You mustn't go there, Elizabeth," he said, holding her fast.

"But he's my husband," she sobbed, and, breaking free from Simon's grasp, she ran over to the body and wailed, holding it close. The soldiers, clearly embarrassed, began to disperse. I looked at Lothian, who nodded at me and stepped over to the woman, putting a cloak round her shoulders and helping her to her feet. He then whispered something into her ear and began to lead her slowly away. Simon, however, suddenly stepped in, closely followed by the sandy-haired youth.

"It's alright, Major. We'll take care of her. She's a friend of ours," he said.

As the two of them led the sobbing woman away, Simon turned to me and beckoned me to follow. As he did so, I thought I saw something in Simon's eyes which I had not seen before. If I didn't know any better, I could have sworn it was fear.

Quickly making my excuses to Lothian and leaving him to arrange for the body to be moved, I followed Simon, somewhat perplexed, towards the cottages.

Simon led the way slowly back to the medium-sized brick house near his lodgings, steering the sobbing woman through the front door and into the hall. The sandy-haired young man, who had introduced himself as James Nuttall, a footman in Lady Norton's household, pulled out a chair from under the drawing table and ushered her gently towards it. Entering discreetly behind them, I noticed that two people were already in the room. A middle-aged woman, wearing a white shirt and a blue bodice, sat at the table, dabbing her eyes with a handkerchief, whilst a young boy of no more than five stood cowering by the fire, half-hidden behind a large oak court cupboard.

"Is it true?" asked the woman in the blue bodice, rising to her feet. The young widow nodded and burst into a fresh deluge of tears as the child ran over to her and buried its head in her lap.

"Your father has been taken from us, Ralph," she sobbed. "It's you and me now. A curse on this war."

"May the Lord have mercy," whispered the older woman, "and may he bring his judgement upon those who have done this."

"We were trying to live a quiet life," said the young widow, addressing me directly. "We wanted to forget the past – and now this happens."

I noticed Simon and Nuttall exchange a quick glance, and my brother stepped forward.

"Elizabeth," he said, "perhaps Mistress Johnson should take care of young Ralph awhile. My brother Daniel, as you can see, is one of the town constables. If you can face up to it, I imagine he has a few questions he would like to ask." That was the cue for the middle-aged woman to scoop up the young boy and take him to one of the nearby cottages with the promise of a slice of apple pudding. Once they had left, I turned and surveyed the young woman sat at the table.

Through the red eyes and tear-stained face, I could see that Elizabeth Brett was an attractive woman in her late twenties, with thick locks of straight, lustrous honey-blond hair that fell from underneath her coif down both sides of her face to her shoulders. She had a round face with large, almond-shaped eyes and a curious, pale half-inch scar above her right eye, which in no way detracted from her charm. I must say, I envied Simon's job of comforting her. With a pang of shame, I banished this thought from my mind and focused on the matter in hand.

"Mistress Brett," I began, "I realise that this may be difficult for you, but I *do* need to ask a few questions that might aid me in my task of apprehending the person or persons who did this to your husband. Would that be acceptable?"

Elizabeth Brett cast a quick glance at Simon and Nuttall, swallowed back a sob, and nodded her assent.

"Thank you," I said. "Could you begin by telling me what time your husband left home this morning?"

"About six o'clock," replied Mrs Brett.

"Isn't that rather early?"

"Earlier than usual, certainly, although today is market day. Ralph said he had some business to attend to before setting up his market stall. He didn't come back because his cart is unladen and still stands where it was last night."

"Any idea what business?"

"I don't pry in my husband's business, but he said he was asked to meet a client for payment."

"Isn't that unusual? At six in the morning?"

"Perhaps. I don't know," said the young widow, somewhat flustered. "Perhaps he was concerned he might not get paid."

"Yes, maybe," I agreed, "but why would he be in Lady Norton's garden, do you suppose?"

Nuttall stepped in. "I can answer that, sir," he interjected. "It's the quickest way to Churchyardside.

The path behind the house leads across the field directly to Monks Lane and then down towards the church. Mr Brett was known to Lady Norton, and she allowed him to use the path through her property."

"I see. You say he was carrying out a business transaction," I continued, addressing Mrs Brett again. "Has there been any indication recently of a disagreement with a customer?"

"I couldn't say. There are a lot of customers." It was clear that Elizabeth Brett either didn't know what her husband was doing that morning or wouldn't say, so I decided to try a different tack.

"Your husband's body had a crimson sash tied round his waist," I began, "a symbol of royalist support. My brother tells me your husband has a long history in the European wars and served under Lord Hamilton, the King's man in Scotland. Bearing in mind the current upheaval in our land, was there any connection remaining with him?"

I noticed Elizabeth Brett glance quickly at Simon and thought I caught a flash of anger in her eye, but it disappeared in an instant.

"No, my husband was not in regular contact with Lord Hamilton or any of his old colleagues. My husband was a dedicated servant of his Lordship, but he was no royalist."

"What about Lady Norton?" I continued. "Her husband was Secretary of State for Ireland under King James. She is a known supporter of the King. Your husband seems to have been on particularly good terms with her."

"Sir Dudley Norton is long since dead, and Lady Norton is, after all, our neighbour," replied Mrs Brett, a degree of irritation now entering her voice.

"Of course," I said, bowing slightly, "I apologise. Tell me," I continued, "your husband was a mercer. Did he travel much?"

"He travelled regularly to London, and in October he was in Edinburgh. However, he didn't confide in me the closer details of business."

"I see," I said. I considered this for a moment, and a thought suddenly struck me. "Tell me," I said, holding up the scarf I had removed from Ralph Brett's waist. "Your husband supplied silk like this. The material didn't come from him, did it?"

"I've no idea," said Elizabeth Brett, her voice now beginning to shake with anger. "What are you suggesting, sir?"

"Nothing, at the moment, mistress. I'm just trying to establish the facts."

At this point, Simon saw that I had gone too far and stepped in to avoid me embarrassing myself any further. "I'm sorry for my brother's persistence," he said, glaring at me, "but Daniel is just trying to be thorough. I'm sure he will be happy to postpone any more questions until tomorrow."

After agreeing that I would return the following day to check on her wellbeing, I took my leave, but once outside the front door, Simon grabbed me by the sleeve and stopped me from heading off back down Beam Street towards the market.

"What in the name of Jesus are you doing?" he exclaimed, his eyes flashing dangerously. "The poor woman has just lost her husband, and you are questioning her as though she is a royalist spy. That is not your job. Yours is to catch the murderer."

"I'm sorry, Simon," I said, shrugging him off. "I have no wish to upset Mrs Brett, but I need to find out what is behind these murders. There are a lot of strange things going on in Nantwich, and nobody is being straight with me. I'd think on that if I were you. I will see you tomorrow, and, in the meantime, perhaps you'd like to consider whether there are a few things you'd like to tell me."

15

Nantwich – Saturday, December 16, 1643

Candles flickered in the windows of the houses on Beam Street as I negotiated my way home through the uncommonly sparse crowds of market-goers. In the short time I had spent in Elizabeth Brett's parlour, the wintery mist had thickened into a freezing fog, casting a pall over the town and reducing vision to no more than fifty yards. The oppressive gloom seemed to subdue the townsfolk as they went about their business, and even the clatter of carts and horses, as traders dragged their wares to market, seemed quieter than usual. Never before, I mused, had our world seemed so constricted, so threatened as now.

Despite the malaise pervading the town, I was gratified to see Skinner still at his post. The lack of customers seemed not to have affected him, for people were still buying up our cheese; an unexpected blessing for which I was thankful. Like the garrison quartermaster, many townsfolk, it appeared, had begun to increase their stocks of food while they could, uncertain of what might be available once the royalists got closer.

Realising that Skinner had the stall well under control, I sat down on my doorstep and tried to take in the significance of what had just happened.

The inescapable fact was that I was now faced with two murders connected by a single common thread – namely that both victims' bodies had been found adorned with a crimson scarf, a symbol of royalist support. Despite this, there was no apparent connection between William Tench and Ralph Brett and no definitive proof that either was actually a royalist. The idea that Tench was a royalist scout was, on analysis, mere hearsay, and the relevance of Brett's supposed connection with the royalist cause, that he was an acquaintance of the Duke of Hamilton, was even more tenuous.

Nevertheless, there were a number of things which didn't add up. Take the curious cabal of prominent townspeople and their leader, Thomas Maisterson. None denied their support for the King, and most had close family connections with the monarch. Roger Wilbraham's father had played host to King James, Randle Church's son had been Sergeant-at-Arms to King Charles and Lady Norton's husband had been Secretary of State to Ireland under the previous king.

Despite Maisterson's protestations that his group were merely passive supporters of the King, there were clear connections between both victims and the households of different members of the group. Marion Tench was employed by Randle Church whilst Ralph Brett's young friend, James Nuttall, worked for Lady Norton.

On top of all this, there was also the mysterious appearance of *Mercurius Aulicus* in the town. Who was responsible for that, I wondered?

I was beginning to get the distinct impression that the key to solving the mystery of the two murders lay in understanding the connection between all these people. And yet, how to do that when my overriding conviction was that nobody I spoke to was being entirely straight with me? That everyone from Randle Church, Marion Tench, and Thomas Maisterson, to John Davenport, Colonel Booth, and my own brother, Simon, were each withholding a small piece of the jigsaw that would help me solve the whole conundrum?

Typical of this was the young widow, Elizabeth Brett. I simply did not believe that she knew nothing about her husband's business. I thought I'd perceived something in her demeanour, a sense of disquiet perhaps, a tension over something she was holding back. I was also concerned about the strange familiarity between her, Nuttall, and Simon. I was not sure where that came from and resolved to get to the bottom of it.

My first task, though, was to free John Davenport. If one thing had emerged from the morning's events, it was the knowledge that my friend had nothing to do with the murders, as he had been safely locked in jail when Brett was attacked. The argument with Tench had obviously been a coincidence, and, although the payment left at the Comberbachs' and the accusations of fraud needed looking into, they could wait awhile or perhaps even be left in the hands of the Rulers of Walling.

When the jailer let me into Davenport's cell, it took my eyes a few seconds to adjust to the light, for the room, which reeked of human sweat and urine, was illuminated only by a single barred window. Catching my breath as I inhaled the foul atmosphere, I saw Davenport slumped up against the wall, lying on a dirty pile of straw, his left ankle clamped in chains. Sat in the shadows on the other side of the cell was another prisoner, who nodded to me as I entered.

I found Davenport, understandably, to be less than enamoured with the fact that he had been left to rot for four days. However, I noticed with gratification that the experience seemed to have loosened his tongue somewhat. I was about to release him from his irons but quickly realised that my interests would be best served by simply letting my friend talk.

"Daniel. You believe me when I say I had no hand in the murder of William Tench, don't you?" he said, rubbing his ankle where the chains had chafed against his skin.

"Of course," I said, truthfully. Although I'd always believed my friend to be no murderer, I decided not to confide what I knew about this morning's events just yet. "John," I said. "I have known you some time, and when I look at you, I do not see a murderer before me.

I have assumed that my job this week was to prove you innocent of this crime."

"Good," said Davenport. "I am grateful for your faith in me. However, that faith does not necessarily extend to others in this town, and, as I have no wish to hang for something I didn't do, I must confide in you."

"Go on."

Davenport lowered his voice to a whisper so the other prisoner could not hear. "You wanted to know what I was arguing with Tench about."

I nodded.

"He was blackmailing me, Daniel. It is about something for which I will be forever ashamed, but it relates to my period of service last year as one of the Rulers of Walling."

"We are talking about manipulating the making meet and defrauding your fellow wallers by walling more than your allocation, I believe. Am I correct?"

Davenport's eyes opened wide. "You know about this?"

"Just what I've gleaned from looking at old court records and the walling records. I've noticed a number of anomalies in the accounts, particularly the mis-accounting of old days walling for various people, which you appear to have done yourself. I also noticed a big fall in recorded misdemeanours during your time in office. I dread to think what the significance of that is."

"It's true, there have been a couple of occasions when

I've done a day's walling that I shouldn't have."

"And maybe you received the occasional incentive from certain wallers not to report misdemeanours?"

Davenport bowed his head. "I was short of money, Daniel," he said. "But how did you find out?"

"Gilbert Kinshaw said he was investigating it."

"Then I'm done for."

"And, strangely enough," I added, "Edward Yardley."

Davenport stared open-mouthed at me. "Yardley? That bastard?"

"I notice that Edward Yardley was fined last year for carrying out a night and day's walling from a previous year's book. That wouldn't have had anything to do with you, would it? Am I right in thinking you asked for a payment to overlook his misdemeanour and he refused?"

Davenport looked up. "No, you're wrong there. He suggested it, actually, but I refused to take his money. I didn't trust him to keep his mouth shut. He deserves everything he gets, that one. He's just like his father was in that respect."

"And what of William Tench, where does he fit in?"

Davenport sucked his teeth and shrugged. "I've no idea how he found out, but he threatened to spill the beans if I didn't pay him off. That's what I was arguing about in The White Swan. I had to pay him off, Daniel. I stood to lose my wich house and my living. I didn't murder him though, I swear."

"I know that now," I admitted, "because there has been

a second murder." I explained briefly about the discovery of Ralph Brett's body that morning.

Davenport was silent for a moment while the significance of what I had said sank in. "You mean you've let me tell you all this in full knowledge that I'm innocent?" he snapped, anger spreading across his face.

"Yes," I conceded, "but you should be glad I did. Look on the bright side. You're free to go back home.

"Look, John," I added, "I'm not going to start chasing you for fraud at this stage. It's a matter for the Rulers of Walling in the first instance, and, to be honest, I'm not sure why Kinshaw and the others have not approached you about it before. If they decide to follow this up, there's nothing I can do about it. You'll just have to face up to your misdemeanours, but at least you won't have to sit here in your own piss, waiting to hang."

Davenport knew I was right. He grunted begrudgingly in acquiescence and rose to his feet as I called the jailer into the cell to unlock the chains around his ankle. Then, after stretching his leg once or twice, he walked over to the other prisoner.

"I wish you good fortune, Captain," he said, shaking the other man's hand. "I must take my leave before the Constable changes his mind, but I will pray that Colonel Booth treats you with respect and mercy."

"I thank you for your thoughts, Master Davenport," replied the prisoner. "However, I fear my fate may already be sealed. Many men in Nantwich have lost their possessions, and Colonel Booth has already decided I'm to blame."

I had not paid much attention to the sorry-looking figure sat in the shadows at the opposite end of the cell, but now I looked closer and saw a man in his forties with greying, balding hair. Stripped to his shirt and breeches, he was now covered in filth, but he spoke with an educated voice and still wore the high-quality boots of an infantry officer. I realised that I was looking at Captain Steele, the officer who had been in charge of Beeston Castle.

"I hear some of your men suspect treachery," I ventured.

Steele inspected me through weary eyes. "Aye, so it would seem, constable," he acknowledged. "I have no idea how Captain Sandford and his men got into the upper ward. But that's irrelevant now. They managed to persuade me we had no chance of defending the castle, and I chose to save my men rather than the townsmen's goods. Perhaps I am just unsuited to the military office that has been thrust upon me."

"This war has forced many gentlemen into a position such as yours," I pointed out. "Many officers had no experience of war before this conflict started."

"True. This war has found many wanting, and I am certainly one of them. I would perhaps have been wiser supporting Parliament in other ways and staying in Chester."

"I understand you are a cheese merchant, sir," I said,

changing the subject. "I am a cheesemonger myself. When the war is over, it is my aim to introduce Cheshire cheese to Londoners. I have it on good authority that the best cheese from Cheshire is far superior to the Suffolk cheeses that are eaten in those parts."

"That's true. I too have heard this," said the Captain, his eyes lighting up as he warmed to the subject. "The difficulty, though, is transportation. At the moment, the London cheesemongers do not believe Londoners will pay the premium to buy our superior cheese in sufficient quantities to make shipping by sea freight worthwhile."

"Yes," I agreed, "and transporting by cart is too expensive. Of course, it's possible to minimise the cost by shipping down the Severn then across land to the Thames, but that is no real solution."

"One day, the situation will change, and the opportunity will be there," said Steele. "I don't think I will live to see that day though. I wish you well, Constable....?"

"Cheswis, sir."

"Cheswis Cheshire Cheese," said Steele, slowly, accentuating the start of each word. "That has a good ring to it."

With a smile, I realised that, if only for a brief moment, I had made Captain Steele's day a little more bearable. Once I had begun talking about the mundane world of cheese, he had become animated and his face had lost the preoccupied look he had worn since I entered the cell. However, as I led Davenport away and prepared to send him home to his wife and family, I looked over my shoulder and saw that the Captain had already returned to his hunched position in the corner of the cell and was staring absent-mindedly towards the barred window. I put my hands in my pockets and, with a sigh, followed Davenport down the street.

16

Nantwich – Sunday, December 17, 1643

The next morning, Mrs Padgett, Amy, and I walked to church with Alexander and his family. The three children were lively enough, running up and down Pepper Street, kicking snow at each other. The rest of us, however, were in a much more subdued frame of mind, not least because all of us were suffering from lack of sleep. There had been constant alarms throughout the night, raucous shouts from the soldiers on watch punctuated by intermittent musket fire. Mercifully, there had been no sign of any artillery as yet, but that, I realised, was only a matter of time. I had tossed and turned all night and eventually gave up shortly after the four o'clock bells, when a brief period of quiet was broken by the noise of thirty foot soldiers clattering their way down Pepper Street on their way to man the walls on the other side of the bridge.

The tension amongst the congregation was palpable as they gathered in the square outside the church, worry etched on the faces of each and every one of those present. As we waited, Hugh Furnival walked by, dressed soberly as usual, with Alice on his arm. I received a nod and a flicker of a smile from Furnival, but Alice greeted me more effusively and thanked me again for attending the launch of *The Public Scout*. I cursed Furnival again under my breath. Every time I saw Alice, it seemed to bring back unwelcome memories.

"You should watch out for her," warned Alexander, who had been observing me closely. "She's dangerous. You're smitten by her and she knows it."

I was just ruminating on this when I was awoken from my reverie by a familiar voice, and turned to see the towering presence of Thomas Maisterson looking down at me.

"Good morning, Master Cheswis," he said. "Word has reached me that another townsman has been murdered, this time near Lady Norton's house."

"That's correct, sir," I said, and filled Maisterson in on the gory details.

"As your previous suspect was languishing in jail at the time," he said. "I presume this means you are looking for a new murderer?"

"You presume correctly, Mr Maisterson," I said. "John Davenport was in jail at the time of the second murder. He is no longer under suspicion. Consequently, he was released last night." Maisterson pursed his lips and reached into the pocket of his doublet, extracting a pocket watch which he checked before looking up at the church clock and returning the watch to his pocket.

"Forgive me, a matter of habit," he said, noticing me watching him. "I expect you will want to speak to Lady Norton about this matter?" he added. "As you know, Lady Norton is now old and infirm, and consequently she has requested that I be present when you interview her. I trust you would have no objection to an arrangement of this kind?"

In truth, I found the request a little unusual but, on reflection, saw no reason not to acquiesce to her Ladyship's wishes.

"That is acceptable to me," I said.

"Splendid, then shall we say tomorrow at eleven am?"

Maisterson, it appeared, was not the only person interested in talking to me, for no sooner had he melted back into the crowd, if indeed a six-foot-four man can do such a thing, than I was accosted by Colonel Booth.

"Good morning, constable," he said, brusquely. "A word with you after the service if I may. I'm sure you know what about."

I nodded curtly and began once again to wonder why my activities of late were the source of so much interest from key people within the town.

Unfortunately for me, as it turned out, the discussion with Booth did not materialise as quickly as was intended, as subsequent events intervened to make sure that more immediate concerns were dealt with.

St Mary's was full, in anticipation of a lengthy elegy in memory of John Pym from the puritan minister Mr

Welch, but his sermon was no longer than ten minutes old when a piercing shout was heard from outside the church. A few seconds later, the door in the south side of the nave was flung open, and a young cavalry officer tumbled into one of the aisles. Frantically, the newcomer scanned the congregation until he spotted Booth, who by now had risen to his feet, a quizzical look on his face.

"Cornet Dunning," said the Colonel, evenly, "I trust you have good reason for causing such a disturbance in the Lord's house?"

"Beg pardon, sir," replied Dunning, breathlessly, his hand scraping nervously through his hair. "And beg pardon to you too, Mr Welch," he added, turning momentarily to the minister, whose countenance bore a look of barely suppressed outrage. "A message from Captain Sadler, sir. He asks you come immediately. It's Lord Byron. He marches on Nantwich. The scouts are reporting soldiers – lots of them – approaching from the direction of Acton."

This was the cue for immediate pandemonium. Major Lothian and those captains present immediately stood up and rushed wordlessly from the church with Booth to gather their forces together. The rest of the congregation, however, erupted into a general hubbub of chattering, crying, and praying, and it took some considerable effort from the minister to quieten everyone down. In deference to the general mood and in obvious irritation at not being able to deliver his sermon, Welch quickly wound up the service with a hymn and some prayers before dismissing the congregation to prepare for the inevitable attack.

When I emerged from the church, a brisk walk down the high street revealed that columns of horse and foot were already streaming across the bridge into Welsh Row as they made their way towards Acton. Those women still on the streets were scuttling home, dragging uncomprehending children in their wakes. The sight of the lean, energetic figure of Sergeant Bradshaw striding through the crowds of men across the street reminded me that those of us who had trained the day before were meant to ready themselves to head for the earthworks with muskets if required. Meanwhile, men coming back across the bridge from the direction of Welsh Row were shouting excitedly, and there were reports of musket fire in the distance. Making haste to return home and grab my weapon before I was told to, I realised with trepidation that the townsfolk of Nantwich were in for a Sunday filled with fear and uncertainty.

As it happened, I spent most of it perched in the freezing cold on the wooden walkway at the top of the earthworks at Welsh Row End, peering in vain across the snow-covered fields for a sight of the enemy. It was a still day, and we could hear the sounds of shouting and gunfire echoing from somewhere in the direction of the trees to the right of Acton's church, but it was too far away and too misty to make out what was happening. It was the middle of the afternoon before the soldiers returned, and, although there was no sight of the royalist army, the news was not good.

Major Lothian's group of horse, it transpired, had advanced quickly to the hamlet of Burford, just north of Acton, with a view to heading off a large group of royalists, the cause of the alarm on the town. However, Lothian's men, keen to teach Byron a lesson, attacked some of the royalist horse before the foot soldiers from the garrison had time to reach them to offer support. Although the Scotsman and his men fought bravely, killing and capturing a number of the King's men, Lothian himself made the uncharacteristic mistake of venturing too far and was taken prisoner. When the Nantwich foot eventually arrived, it was too late. The royalists had fled, and Lothian had been spirited away into captivity. What had seemed ready to become a victory had been turned into a defeat. The cavaliers had been chased away into the Cheshire countryside, at least for the time being, but Colonel Booth had lost his most important military advisor. The dour Scotsman was seen by most Nantwich people as an outsider, but he was recognised by all as a discreet and valiant soldier, whose influence on the Colonel would be greatly missed.

I sighed and watched the last stragglers from the skirmish return through the gates into Welsh Row, a group of pikemen marching at the head of a small group of half a dozen royalist prisoners, one of whom was clutching a wound on his arm, a cart carrying back two injured cavalrymen, and, finally, the last of the musketeers, amongst whose number I spotted Carter and Hughes. Carter looked up and saluted me as he passed, but the whole group wore a downcast look. The people of Nantwich would feel a little less secure that night in the knowledge that James Lothian was no longer in charge.

It was about seven o'clock that evening before I was able to find the time to fulfil my obligation to Elizabeth Brett. Two hours after the return of the last of the men from Burford, I was finally relieved of my post on the walkway at Welsh Row End by a reluctant-looking tanner's apprentice and allowed to return, shivering, to the warmth of my front room. It had been a long day. However, once warmed and fortified with a bellyful of Mrs Padgett's mutton stew, I felt somewhat re-invigorated and was able to pull my coat around my shoulders and set out with Alexander towards the Bretts' house on Beam Street, with a view to checking on the widow's well-being.

The mist from earlier in the day had cleared, and it was a bright albeit bitterly cold evening in Nantwich. An icy sheen covered the almost full moon, whose now-waning orb cast a magical, almost other-wordly light on the frost-covered trees lining the road where the buildings thinned out towards the edge of town. The luminescent glow of the moonlight reflected off the cobbles and contrasted eerily with the shadows, which seemed to move in the corner of my eye and disappear down alleyways to the side of houses. The air was perfectly still, allowing the sound of the guards manning the earthworks to carry from behind the houses to the left of the street. Intermittent shouts of alarm and the occasional musket shot echoed through the air. The town was still on high alert, and, although the royalists had initially been chased away from Acton by the men from the garrison, it had not been long before they had returned and begun to harass the town once more. This activity became more evident as Alexander and I walked up Beam Street towards the sconce at the end of the street. I thanked God that I lived in the middle of the town and not close to the earthworks.

We were able to see the Bretts' brick house clearly in the moonlight, shadows playing off the side of the building. Candlelight emanated from the cottages behind, a lantern hanging from the front door of one. However, the Bretts' house was curiously in darkness.

Alexander and I knocked loudly on the door and waited a few moments, but there was no answer. Shrugging, I knocked a second time and, this time, called Mrs Brett's name. This attracted a few curious looks from passers-by, but there was still no answer.

I was just about to turn away when I heard a strange noise from somewhere inside the house, like the sound of earthenware smashing. Casting a quick glance at Alexander, I noticed he was ready to break down the front door, but I motioned for him to calm down.

"Wait here," I whispered. "I'll go round the back."

Drawing my club from my belt, I crept stealthily towards the alleyway down the left side of the house, which led to the rear of the property. It still felt strange wielding the wooden cudgel I was required to carry by the manorial court. I had owned mine for a while, as all households in Nantwich were expected to carry a suitable club in order to assist the constable with his work, but it still gave me an uncomfortable feeling to use it as a tool of the trade.

Fortunately, the moonlight was shining directly into the alley, so I walked straight down it, into the back yard. It was a large yard, with a stable block on the left, a pigsty down the bottom of garden, and housing for other livestock next to it. A horse whickered as I approached the stables and peered down towards the back fence for any sign of movement, but there was nothing there. I noticed, however, that the rear door to the house had been forced and stood slightly ajar.

I pushed the door open gingerly and walked into what appeared to be the kitchen. As my eyes grew accustomed to the light, I noticed a table in the middle of the room and a row of cooking implements hanging on the wall. Next to them was a shelf, with food jars on it and an unlit candle at one end. I made a move towards the candle with a view to lighting it, but, just as I did so, I heard the sound of footsteps on the floorboards upstairs.

"Mrs Brett, it's Constable Cheswis here. Are you

there?" I called. The footsteps ceased immediately, but there was no response. My mouth went dry as I strained my ears to try and pick out any sound. There was nothing but silence and a growing feeling that I was in the presence of somebody else. I waited a moment before edging my way towards a door in the far wall. Going through it, I found myself in the hall I was in the day before. There was no sign of recent occupation, but the cupboards were open and had been ransacked. Papers lay strewn across the floor.

With a start, I began to wonder what had happened to Elizabeth Brett. My eyes focused on the stairs leading to the bedchambers, and I was just about to head over to them when I caught a swift movement out of the corner of my eye. Suddenly, a huge weight crashed into me from the side, sending me sprawling into a chair, which snapped under me as I fell, sending splinters flying across the room. I struggled to get up and turn round to catch sight of my assailant, but I was too slow. A heavy leather boot caught me full in the gut, and, as I doubled up in pain, I felt a sharp blow on the side of my head, and my world descended into blackness.

When I regained consciousness, I was surprised to find myself staring into the face of Elizabeth Brett, who had just thrown a bowl of ice cold water into my face. At first, I thought I must be dreaming. However, I was soon brought to my senses by the sound of Simon from somewhere behind me, saying "Thank the Lord – he's coming round."

I tried to sit up but was forced to lie straight back down again as a bolt of pain shot through my skull.

"What happened?" I asked, weakly, running my fingers across my cranium and finding a lump the size of an egg just above my temple. Alexander stepped forward and looked at me with concerned eyes over Elizabeth Brett's shoulder.

"I heard the noise from inside the building," he said. "I shouted and tried to break down the door. Fortunately, Mrs Brett was at your brother's house and they both came running when they were alerted by the noise."

"Aye. We found you on the floor like this," added Simon. "It's a blessing that you were wearing your hat, because whoever did this gave you a fearsome crack on the skull."

I couldn't disagree. I picked up my wide-brimmed hat, which was lying by my side, and inspected it.

"Did you see who did this?" I asked, eventually.

"No," said Alexander. "He escaped over the back fence, through the trees and across the meadow behind the house. He probably doubled left when he reached the earthworks and ended up in Snow Hill."

"Was he alone?"

"I don't know – I couldn't say. I lost sight of him in the trees." At that moment, a figure appeared at the foot of the stairs, and I frowned as I recognised the youthful features of James Nuttall.

"Nothing seems to have been taken," he said, "but he's left a fearful mess."

I squinted uncomfortably at the sandy-haired youth as he descended the stairs, and I realised that he must also have arrived with Simon. As my head cleared, the truth began to dawn on me. Whoever had broken into Mrs Brett's house knew exactly what they were looking for. What was more, Nuttall, Simon, and the young widow were all in the know too. I pursed my lips and glared at Elizabeth Brett. I was beginning to lose my patience.

"Why would somebody want to break into your house, Mrs Brett, no more than twenty-four hours after your husband has been murdered? What was he looking for? I think it's about time you all explained what's going on."

I pulled myself into a sitting position and groaned as I felt the imprint of my assailant's boot on my belly. I lifted up my shirt and inspected the bright red mark underneath my ribs. I watched Nuttall shoot a furtive glance at Simon, who gave him an almost imperceptible nod.

"We'll explain to you tomorrow," said Simon. "Right now, we need to get you back home for some rest." Turning to Mrs Brett, he added, "We'll sort this mess out in the morning when it's light."

I tried to protest, but Simon and Alexander hoisted me to my feet and helped me walk groggily back down Beam Street, making me hold a ball of snow to my head to reduce the swelling. They led me back down Pepper Street to my house, where Mrs Padgett made a terrible fuss and insisted I was put straight to bed, where, thankful for the rest, I fell into a deep sleep.

17

Nantwich – Monday, December 18, 1643

I dreamt I was in Tinkers Croft. It was summertime, and the meadow was being used for a fair. At the edge of the field, hawkers were selling all kinds of food and drink to the townsfolk, who were milling across the field, all in good humour. Music was playing, and in the middle distance, two teams of men were preparing to take part in a tug-of-war contest. They were already beginning to line up and take the strain when I realised that the flag in the middle of the rope was, in fact, the crimson scarf that was found around William Tench's neck.

I looked around in consternation and realised that I recognised all the participants. On one side, his long brown curls waving madly from side to side, was Colonel Booth. Behind him was Major Lothian, followed, bizarrely, by the sober figures of Hugh Furnival and the puritan schoolmaster Edward Burghall. At the other end of the rope was the steely grin of Thomas Maisterson, followed by young Roger Wilbraham of Townsend House, Randle Church, and, again rather oddly, John Saring, the recently removed minister of St Mary's.

I walked over to inspect the scarf in the middle of the rope. Then, suddenly, it was no longer the rope that was being tugged but my arms. I looked up in shock to see that the referee was none other than Alice, who was encouraging both sides to heave and laughing hysterically, banging her hands on a drum. I struggled to get free but couldn't move. My arms were burning, and I felt as though they were about to be ripped from their sockets. Just when I felt I could hold on no longer, I awoke with a start, my body bathed in sweat, to find that I had been lying on my arm. Downstairs, someone was shouting and banging heavily on the front door.

Cursing silently, I stumbled downstairs to find that Mrs Padgett had already opened the door to reveal two soldiers.

"Sorry to disturb you so early, mistress," said one, "but I have a message from Colonel Booth. He would speak to Master Cheswis. We are to fetch him to The Lamb."

Mrs Padgett gave them a scornful look. "You'll do no such thing," she growled, making to shut the door in their faces. "Master Cheswis was brought here last night with a head wound, and he needs to rest. It's only seven o' clock in the morning. Come back after lunch."

"I'm sorry, mistress, but we have our orders," insisted the soldier.

"It's alright, Mrs Padgett," I said, rubbing my hand across my skull, "I've slept well and my head is not as bad as yesterday. I will go with them. Please let them in out of the cold and give them some ale whilst I get ready."

Mrs Padgett mumbled something about my job being the death of me and that nobody ever listened to her, but she let the men in nonetheless. Meanwhile, I returned to my chamber and pulled on some breeches, a doublet, my winter cloak, and some boots and grabbed my hat, fingering the area that had saved me the night before.

The weather had taken a turn for the worse again, and a light snow was falling from leaden skies as I made my way up Pepper Street, past the church, and through the protective earthworks around The Lamb. My two escorts led me into the building and directly into Booth's drawing room, where I found the Colonel at the breakfast table, spearing a slice of ham. Waving his fork at me by way of greeting, he motioned for me to sit down.

"How are you faring, Master Cheswis?" he asked, between mouthfuls. "I understand you took a nasty bang to the head yesterday."

I studied the Colonel carefully, surprised at the extent of his knowledge. "I've been better, but thanks to the quality of my hat, I am still in the land of the living. News travels fast," I added. "How did you know?"

"It's my job to be aware of such things. You are feeling somewhat recovered?"

"A little. It will take more than a crack on the skull to prevent me doing my duty."

"That is certainly my impression of you. You have a persistence that is to be admired."

I nodded my thanks. "But yesterday was not a good day for either of us," I ventured.

"That is an understatement," said Booth, grimly. "Not only has it become patently clear that Byron and his hoards of Irishmen have set their sights on removing us from this town, but I have also lost my best man. I have to be grateful that Major Lothian was not killed, but the absence of his particular skills will be a great loss to me."

"So how do you view our prospects of defending the town, Colonel?"

"We have but a thousand men to repel Byron and his troops. Make no mistake, we have motivated, experienced soldiers, but so do they. We cannot hope to engage four thousand men outside of the town. We will need reinforcements from Sir William Brereton if we are to do this and avoid a siege. Hopefully, help is on its way, but, in the meantime, there is little we can do but sit tight. One thing in our favour is that the town is well-fortified, and the people here are largely for Parliament. The townsfolk are also very well-aware of the implications for this place if the town falls. Nantwich has become one of the last bastions of Parliament in this area, and the town will not be treated well if it falls, so there is great motivation to defend the town. We are also nice and warm in our billets. The enemy cannot find it pleasant camping out in the countryside in such weather."

"So a reckoning is coming one way or the other?"

"Aye, we must hope our lads stand fast and defend this

place."

There were a few moments of silence whilst I took in Booth's honest assessment of the situation and studied his demeanour. For the first time since I had known him, the Colonel appeared preoccupied, his countenance lined with worry. It was not hard to see why.

"I presume there was a particular reason you wished to see me this morning?" I said, eventually. "And that this is connected in some way with the body discovered by Lady Norton's house yesterday?"

"As I showed a distinct interest in the death of William Tench, I would have thought that would have been self-evident," said Booth, evenly.

"The dead man's name is Ralph Brett," I said. "He was a mercer and lived in the house in Beam Street where I was attacked yesterday, but I'm sure you know this already."

Booth gave a half smile and inclined his head in acknowledgement.

"It appears that Brett has a military past," I continued. "He fought in the wars in Europe as a captain under Lord Hamilton, who, as you know, is the King's personal representative in Scotland. However, Brett has not been active for a number of years and preferred to stay in Nantwich with his wife and family rather than join with a regiment on either side in this conflict. As both Tench and Brett were found with crimson sashes on their bodies, my initial assumption has been that both men had royalist sympathies, particularly bearing in mind Brett's aforementioned connections."

Booth harrumphed loudly and sat forward in his seat, lowering his voice. "Master Cheswis. I am advised that you are loyal to Parliament's cause and that you are worthy of trust," he said. "The time has come when I must put that trust to the test and confide in you to some degree. Can I put my faith in your allegiance?"

"Of course, Colonel," I replied, somewhat confused. "But what do you mean?"

"The assumption that Ralph Brett's sympathies lie with the royal cause is incorrect. He may have served with people who now side with the King, but he was most certainly not of their current persuasion. Brett was a loyal parliamentarian."

I looked askance at him, wondering where Booth was leading. "How do you know this, sir?" I asked.

"Because he was working in our interests, protecting information that is vital to the war effort."

"You mean he was a spy?"

"Not exactly, but I would not be exaggerating if I were to tell you that the retention of this information in parliamentary hands has the potential to alter the course of this war."

"And I presume you are not going to confide in me as to the nature of this information?"

"You presume rightly. You do not need to know the precise details, but I do need your help as one of the town's constables in getting to the bottom of the connection between Tench and Brett."

I considered this for a moment and then the full horror of what Colonel Booth was saying hit me. With a start, I realised how he had come to know so quickly about my altercation with the intruder at Elizabeth Brett's house and, indeed, why he was ransacking the place. Something in my face must have given my thought processes away, for Booth interjected before I could say anything else;

"That's right. Your brother and others are not unconnected to this affair, and their safety is also at risk. This is one reason why I know this information will not go beyond the two of us."

My mind started to spin. What manner of business had Simon involved himself in? "You say that Brett was for Parliament. Does that mean that Tench was a parliamentarian too? And why the crimson scarf?"

Booth cut himself another slice of bread and shrugged. "That is what we don't know. We were not aware of Tench at all until he was murdered. I was interested in him because rumours surfaced that he may have been a royalist scout. I'm always interested in making sure informants are identified and dealt with appropriately. However, the similarity of his death to Brett's puts a different complexion on things. I can't say for certain whether Tench was a scout or not, but he certainly had dealings with some leading townsfolk who have close connections with the King."

"Like Randle Church's family, for example."

"Precisely, but not only him. The Maistersons, the Wilbrahams of Townsend, and Lady Norton all have close connections with the King. I don't think there can be a town anywhere in England where there are so many prosperous merchants and gentry. They will all be looking for assurances that their property will not be damaged if Byron marches in here."

"And you believe Maisterson and his ilk are plotting to betray the town in exchange for assurances regarding their personal property?"

"Perhaps. To be honest, Master Cheswis, I just don't know. Whoever murdered Brett knew exactly what he was looking for. However, that person has a connection with Tench and through him, in some way, to Church, Maisterson, and the others. I need to find out what that connection is. I think you are in the best position to find out."

I considered the Colonel's words carefully and a thought struck me. "What about Brett's friend, Nuttall?" I asked. "I presume he's involved too? He works in Lady Norton's household. Surely he will have been able to find out?"

The Colonel shook his head. "I'm afraid not. Nuttall can only do so much without raising suspicion. Furthermore, if something is going on, you can be sure that Lady Norton is not at the centre of it. She's an old lady. She will only be a passive supporter."

Booth was right, of course, but this didn't make the matter easier to understand. It seemed to me that the more I found out about Tench and Brett, the more complicated the whole matter became – a veritable Pandora's Box of unforeseen troubles. I was ruminating on this when Booth changed the subject.

"What about your friend Davenport?" he asked. "I understand he has been freed. Does he have any involvement in this, do you think?"

"I think not, Colonel," I replied, taking care to avoid any mention of what I knew about Davenport's abuse of walling rights. "He cannot have murdered Brett as he was in jail at the time, and he was probably just in the wrong place at the wrong time in terms of Tench's murder." To my relief, Booth did not press me any further on this issue and simply asked me to keep him informed of any future developments, which I gladly agreed to do.

"One more question," I asked, before taking my leave. "Do you still require me to source cheese for you this week? Things are getting dangerous for travellers."

"Indeed I do, Master Cheswis," replied the Colonel. "It may be our last chance. You should be safe if you stay on the east side of the river. Nevertheless, if you present yourself here on Friday morning, I will see to it that an armed escort is made available for you."

Snow continued to fall throughout the morning, and, by the time I arrived at Lady Norton's house at 11 o'clock for my appointment with Thomas Maisterson, a fresh layer of pristine white powder covered the front lawn. There was no wind, and, as the large flakes fell silently onto the frozen ground, the scene I observed was one of perfect serenity. It was hard to imagine that a gruesome murder had taken place here only two days before.

When I knocked on the front door, I was shown into a drawing room by a servant, who announced my presence to Lady Norton. The lady of the house was, I realised, quite possibly the smallest person I had seen in my life. No taller than four foot six, she possessed white hair and sharp features, which betrayed the fact that she would have had a striking appearance when younger. Now, however, she was a frail old lady. I realised that, even if there had been something to see when Brett was murdered on Saturday morning, she would have had difficulty doing so.

Thomas Maisterson was already present and rose to his feet on my arrival, beckoning me towards an upholstered chair placed next to an exquisite draw-leaf table, behind which sat the only other person in the room, the youthful Roger Wilbraham of Townsend House. I took my seat and began by explaining my presence to Lady Norton and asking her if she knew Ralph Brett.

"I did," she replied, in a firm voice I was not expecting. "He was a neighbour of mine and his family's drapery business has supplied me for years. I allowed him to cut through my garden should he need to."

"I see," I said. "It would appear he did exactly that on Saturday morning. Did you see or hear anything at that time?"

"I was in bed," replied Lady Norton. "My chamber overlooks the lawn and the path which Mr Brett would have walked. I was woken by the sound of shouting outside my window."

"And what time was that?"

"Just before seven. I was concerned it might be intruders, so I called for one of my maidservants, who came running. She said she could not be sure who was making the noise."

"Could I speak to the girl in question?"

"Certainly," Maisterson interjected, as though he were in his own house. "I'll have her brought in."

Presently, a short and slightly plump girl of about eighteen appeared with a worried look on her face. Her eyes darted to and fro between Lady Norton and Maisterson as if looking for guidance. She was introduced as Mary Wright.

"You may tell the Constable what you saw, Mary," said Lady Norton, gently.

"I saw very little, sir," said the girl, hesitantly. "When the Mistress called me, she said there was shouting outside. I was in the kitchen, so I heard nothing at first."

"But you looked through the window to see what the noise was about?"

"Yes, it was very dark and misty so I couldn't see

much. The noise had stopped by this time. All I could see were three figures in the mist. It looked like they had their arms around each other, but I can't be sure."

"Which direction were they going?"

"Towards the gate near the earthworks."

I realised that the maidservant had seen the murderer dragging Brett's body across the lawn, but something didn't ring true. Why were there three figures and not two? Bressy and Hulse had only talked about one assailant.

"Are you sure it was three people that you saw and not just two?" I asked." After all, it was misty, as you say."

"No, sir," insisted Mary. "I'm quite sure. It was at least three."

"Could you say what they looked like?"

"I'm sorry, sir, they were already some way away at this time, and all I could make out were dark figures – shadows in the mist." I considered this for a moment and exhaled loudly with frustration. Who on earth was the extra man, let alone the first one?

"And after that?" I continued. "What happened next?"

"Nothing, sir. Once I was sure they had gone, I returned to my duties, although my mistress tells me she heard noises again a while later."

"Is that true, Lady Norton?"

"Yes, I heard some shouting about ten minutes later, but it only lasted a few seconds."

I realised this must have been the soldiers chasing after

the murderer. Deep in thought, I got to my feet and strode over to the window, looking at the route the murderer must have taken to get from one gate to the other. The silence was broken by Wilbraham, who, up until now, had remained silent.

"Have you finished with Mary?" he asked, in a tone which suggested his time was being wasted.

"Yes, thank you," I said, turning to the girl. "You've been most helpful."

With that, Mary Wright gave me a beaming smile and went back to her work.

"I'm sorry that we can't be more helpful," said Lady Norton.

"On the contrary," I said, as politely as I could, "the information is most useful."

"But has it given you any idea who might be responsible for this foul act?" asked Wilbraham, pointedly. "I see you have managed to solve precious little so far."

I looked at the young gentleman with no little degree of exasperation. His attitude was beginning to rankle, particularly as I had been placed in a position where I was expected to identify a murderer without any information about Tench at all.

"Mr Wilbraham, I would be grateful if you would refrain from abrading me in such a manner. My Lady Norton's information is most interesting, but I'm afraid in itself it does not help me a great deal. The last time we spoke, you were very explicit in warning me away from asking questions about William Tench. However, forming a connection between the two murders is crucial to solving these crimes. It seems to me you are more interested in avoiding questions about Tench than in locating the murderer. Is the same true with Brett? Is there something here you're not telling me, too?"

Wilbraham stood up, his face turning crimson. "Master Cheswis, you have no right-" Maisterson put his hand up to silence Wilbraham.

"You must excuse Roger," he cut in. "With the passing of his father, he is forced to represent his family here. As you see, he takes on considerable responsibility at a young age, and one day he will do great things in this town, I'm sure. For now, he's still young."

Wilbraham glared at Maisterson, but the older man continued. "Our concern in revealing more to you is that we are not aware of your allegiance in this conflict. We suspect, like most people of this town, that you support the rebel cause, and we are hesitant to confide any more. The majority of people in Nantwich are aware of our families' sympathies, but we do not want to advertise the fact any more than is necessary. As it stands, if Parliament wins the conflict, we are likely to have our property sequestered or to be fined at the very least. As I previously mentioned, it is also in our interests to make sure that, if the King does prevail, damage to our property is minimised."

"Fine," I said. "If it helps, this is where I stand. I'm

not against the King, but I *do* support the rights of Parliament. My view, like many, is that if the King were a little less stubborn, much of this conflict could have been avoided, and for that he bears some responsibility. So, in that sense, you are right about where my sympathies lie. However, my duty in this case is only to capture the person who committed these crimes. In this, I support the same aims as you, and, as you took great pains to point out, it is in my interest that I do not abuse your trust."

Maisterson cast a glance at Lady Norton, who smiled thinly and nodded.

"Very well," said Maisterson. "This is what we know. Brett was known to Lady Norton as a neighbour, whereas Tench was married to a servant of Randle Church. Both Lady Norton and Mr Church, like Roger and I, are known to be passive supporters of the King, but there doesn't seem to be any obvious reason why the murderer should want to kill both Tench and Brett. As I've said before, we are concerned that some agent is at play here that we are not aware of. We're not even aware whose side he's on."

"And what of Tench?"

"It's true that Tench has been an informer to the Royalist cause, but as you will be aware, there have been several of these in Nantwich. You will remember the raid carried out by the Nantwich garrison on Cholmondeley House in April."

I cast my mind back and recalled the events that

culminated in the arrest of Saring, the town minister, as well as Dudley, Lady Norton's son, and several others. On that day, at the start of April, most of the Nantwich forces had marched to nearby Cholmondeley House after being informed that four hundred of the King's men were holed up in the garrison there. However, when they arrived, they found the royalists ready and waiting for them. Despite killing a number of the King's party, the Nantwich soldiers were unable to storm the house and were eventually obliged to return whence they had come. Accusations of treachery followed, and those arrested had been charged with malignancy and betraying the plans to attack Cholmondeley to the royalist command.

"I recall it as if it were yesterday," I said.

"Well, William Tench was involved in that, but was neither identified nor arrested, although Randle Church tells me his wife was very fearful that he would be. Of course, since then I had heard, as you did, that he was scouting for Lord Byron, but beyond this, I do not know. We prefer to stay clear of this kind of activity."

I was not sure how far to believe Maisterson but acknowledged that at least this identified a motive for someone to kill Tench. "But there must be a connection between Tench and Brett," I asserted.

"Evidently," agreed Maisterson, "but we don't know what that is. We are aware of his military background and his connection with the Duke of Hamilton, but nothing beyond that."

I decided that my enquiries were not going to yield any further results and was just about to take my leave when a thought struck me.

"One last thing, Lady Norton," I said. "Your footman, James Nuttall, appears to have been a close acquaintance of Brett. Would you say he had been behaving strangely recently?"

"Nuttall?" answered Lady Norton, a puzzled look on her face. "Not at all. He is a good servant. I have never had cause to complain. However," she added, almost as an afterthought, "now that you mention it, he has not reported for work today. Would you like me to enquire as to his whereabouts?"

Despite my suspicions regarding Nuttall, I would have thought little more of his absence from work that morning, were it not for my decision to make a brief visit to the shoemaker's workshop just off Beam Street where Simon was apprenticed. There I found my brother's employer George Simkins entirely on his own, cursing silently amongst a pile of unfinished boots. Simon, it transpired, had also disappeared without a trace.

"He's nought but a worthless lossell, that brother of yours, a lazy ne'er do well," growled Simkins, as he recognised me standing in the doorway. "He deserves a proper kick up the arse, and he'll get one when he shows up, believe me. He takes half Saturday off comforting the woman who lost her husband. I says, if you're sweet on her, that's alright by me, but don't let me down on Monday. So he promises me faithfully he'll be here early today to clear the backlog, but now he's nowhere to be found. He's all flam, I tell you."

Simkins' words did little to alleviate the nagging feeling I had that the disappearance of Simon and his friend was more than a simple coincidence, so, more in hope than expectation, I walked the few yards to Elizabeth Brett's house and banged loudly on the front door. I must confess, I was half-expecting to find an empty house and was somewhat surprised to see Mrs Brett herself open the door, her young boy holding onto her skirts like a limpet. I was pleased to observe that this time there was a pleasant smile for me and nothing of the evasiveness of the day before.

"Good morning, Master Cheswis," she said. "It's good to see you out and about. I trust your headache is somewhat better?"

"I still have a lump on my head," I replied, "but it's bearable. All the better for seeing that you are also up and well. And this is your son?" I nodded in the direction of the child, who stared at me, wide-eyed, from behind his mother's legs.

"This is Ralph. He's a little shy and does not really understand what has happened to his father."

"It will be difficult for him – and for you," I said, "but I see you have good friends here. God willing, they will provide you with some comfort and support."

"I am grateful to Mistress Johnson and to people like James and your brother. They are helping me to cope." I looked over her shoulder, into the house, to see Mistress Johnson, today wearing a bright red bodice, sweeping and tidying up the hall in the background. The smell of food lingered in the air, and I thought I caught the sight of a huge container of pottage hanging from the chimneypiece as I looked through the open kitchen door.

"Talking of my brother and Nuttall," I ventured, "have you seen either of them this morning? Neither has reported for work."

Mrs Brett appeared somewhat surprised at this and looked furtively past me towards Lady Norton's house. "No. Like you, I have not seen them since yesterday. They have their own lives to lead. I would not expect it to be any other way."

"I'm sorry, I didn't mean anything by that. I merely-"

"Where are your manners, Elizabeth?" piped up Mistress Johnson, from behind Mrs Brett. "Ask the young man in out of the snow. He'll catch his death in this weather." Mrs Brett reddened and stepped aside to let me enter.

"I'm sorry, Master Cheswis," she said apologetically. "I'm not offended by your words, and I'm being most inhospitable, please come in out of the snow."

I sat down at the table and was given a bowl of pottage and some bread, which started to take some of the coldness out of my bones. After a while, I addressed

Mrs Brett, offering her once more my sympathies for the loss of her husband and asking her how she had been coping. This was the kind of conversation I usually found difficult to deal with, but I found Elizabeth Brett curiously easy to talk to.

"Thank you for asking," she replied. "Ralph's death was a great shock to me. We had been married only five years, and now I am left on my own. I did not expect to be a widow so soon. I have honestly not yet considered how my life will be without him."

"Your husband made good provision for you, I hope?"

"Fortunately, I will inherit the house and then there is the matter of Ralph's mercer's business."

"What will happen to that?" I asked.

"That will have to be sold. It will make good money, and there will be no shortage of buyers. In fact, they are already starting to emerge from the woodwork. The sale of the business will make me secure, but I will need to use some of the money as capital for a business of my own." She hesitated. "But it's too early to talk of this. Ralph is not even buried yet."

I lowered my head in deference to Mrs Brett's wishes and changed the subject.

"You have a local accent," I said. "You are originally from Nantwich, I think?"

"From Wrenbury, I moved here when I was married."

"Your husband was also a local man, I believe. But he was somewhat older than you?"

"Yes, that's true. His family have been here for generations. As you know, he left here as a young man to fight in the wars but came back six years ago. He wanted to change his life and swore he would not take up the sword again, so we could forge a better life for ourselves."

"And he was true to his word?"

"I had no reason to doubt he would ever go back on it."

"Where did he travel?" I asked, curious to know more about this soldier of fortune, who had traded a life of adventure for married life with this young woman. Why had this man, with all his military experience, not joined the war on one side or the other? Was there more to him than met the eye?

"All over the Kingdom," replied his widow. "London, Edinburgh. Also to Chester, although not since it was taken by the King."

"I see. And why, do you suppose, would anyone want to ransack your house? The people who broke in were clearly looking for something. Would this have had something to do with your husband's past connections, perhaps?"

"I really have no idea, constable. I don't know what they would be looking for. As I told you, my husband did not confide in me in business matters such as this. Perhaps they found what they were looking for."

"I think that is unlikely, Mistress Brett," I said. "What about the red scarf? Did your husband have any connections with any of the leading royalist families in this town? The Maistersons, the Wilbrahams, the Churches?"

"I'm sorry, I can't help," said Mrs Brett, evenly, her face betraying nothing. I did not believe that Elizabeth Brett was completely devoid of knowledge about her husband's activities, but I could not prove any of my suspicions and so decided not to press her any further. Instead, I asked her if she minded if I checked on her wellbeing from time to time, especially considering the possibility that she might still be in danger.

"Not at all," she said. "You are most welcome here."

"Good," I replied. "In the meantime, if you see my brother, please tell him I would like a word with him."

I was just about to leave, but there was something in Elizabeth Brett's demeanour that stopped me from doing so; a slight hesitation, perhaps, a flicker of concern in her eyes that aroused my suspicions.

"Master Cheswis," she said. "You seem like a good man, and your concern for your brother is admirable, but believe me, there are some things which are better not to know. I do not know exactly where Simon and James have gone, and that is probably also for the best, but I am aware of the importance of their work. They will return when they are ready, but for their safety and yours, I beg you not to dig too deep into this matter. It may put us all in grave danger."

And with that, Elizabeth Brett left me standing, open-mouthed, in her hallway and walked into her kitchen, leaving an apologetic Mistress Johnson to show me out.

18

Nantwich, Hankelow and Hunsterson – Friday, December 22, 1643

The next few days did nothing to ease my state of mind, and I lapsed into a mood every bit as grey as the freezing mist which cloaked the Cheshire countryside. The wich house and my constabulary duties kept me busy for much of the day, but my leisure time was spent moping around the house and driving Mrs Padgett to distraction by constantly rearranging the contents of her kitchen, so much so that by the Wednesday evening she was threatening to pack her bags unless I took myself off to a tavern to cure the malaise that had taken hold of me.

The gnawing cold was beginning to prey on the minds of the people of Nantwich too. The snow had stopped again, but there was a certain depression in the demeanour of the townsfolk as they went about their business. Everybody seemed to be moving a little slower than normal, and the streets seemed unusually quiet. There was something else too, an intangible feeling of tension in the air like the calm before a storm. We all knew it was coming, and the colour of that storm was crimson.

The biggest concern for me was the continued absence of Simon. By the Friday morning, neither he nor Nuttall had been seen for four days. Enquiries made at Lady Norton's house and Simkins' workshop revealed that neither had reported for work and none of Simon's friends or acquaintances had seen him anywhere near the town. He had certainly not slept at his home since Sunday night. I even paid a visit to the home of his flame-haired fiancée, Rose Bailey, who was frantic with worry. There had not been so much as a word to her either.

Of course, I was concerned for Simon's safety, but far more worried about what he and Nuttall were up to. It began to dawn on me after a couple of days that Simon had deliberately avoided telling me about their activities on the Sunday evening, in the knowledge that he and Nuttall would be gone the next day. I felt helpless knowing that there was at least one murderer on the loose, perhaps more.

My mind turned to the enigmatic Elizabeth Brett. What did she know about the activities of her husband and of his protégés? What was it that she would not tell me? Surely it could not be feasible that she knew absolutely nothing of their whereabouts?

Then there was the issue of John Davenport, whose connection with the whole affair continued to perplex me. My friend had returned home to his family and, to all intents and purposes, was resuming his normal life, although he seemed to be displaying the common sense to keep his head low. A visit to Davenport's to check up on his family's welfare had revealed nothing, although Edward Yardley had seen me coming and berated me on the street for not putting Davenport on trial both for fraud and for the murder of Tench. Knowing the history of antipathy between Yardley and Davenport, I was not particularly surprised by this. What was odd, though, given Yardley's stance, was the fact that the Rulers of Walling had made no move at all to approach Davenport about his misdemeanours. Perhaps, with Byron's men beginning to grow in numbers around the town, they, like everyone else in Nantwich, had more on their minds to deal with than such trivial matters.

And finally, there was the issue of Alice. There was always Alice. I had seen her around the town on a couple of occasions since Sunday, and each time she had greeted me with the sweet smile I had remembered from my youth, designed, it seemed, to twist my heart in knots. The second time I saw her she revealed that her husband had left Nantwich on business again, although she didn't reveal where. He would be back in a few days, she said.

Although I had tried hard not to reveal my continuing feelings for Alice to those I knew well, I had failed miserably. Alexander and Mrs Padgett in particular had noticed and were both of the opinion that Alice's continued presence did not bode well for me. I brushed this away with a nonchalant wave, of course, but one day

I came back home to lunch to find the two of them deep in conversation in my hall. They pretended they were talking about something else, but I knew this was not the case. I was forced to grab my food in silence and to maintain a haughty distance from the two of them. My relationship with Alice was none of their business.

The one ray of light on the horizon was that Skinner had started to show a little more interest in his work since his success on the shooting range. His hangdog, surly mood seemed to have disappeared and he busied himself cheerfully with our cheese customers and down at the wich house. It came to something when I preferred the company of my apprentice to that of my best friend and housekeeper.

It was, therefore, a welcome change on Friday morning to be faced with the prospect of a cart ride to collect cheese for the market and for the garrison's quartermaster. I rose early to ready my horse, a bay gelding called Goodwyn. I harnessed him to the cart to be driven by Skinner and by 9 o'clock we were heading across the river at Shrewbridge and heading down the road towards Audlem.

Both Skinner and I had armed ourselves with our newly-acquired muskets and were kitted out with bandoliers, waist belts with bullets and flasks of priming powder. As promised, Colonel Booth had provided us with some protection in the form of two dragoons, one a sergeant, a taciturn Mancunian called Prescott, and the other a younger man in his twenties called Cowper.

My intention was to ride a circular route to visit farms in the villages of Hatherton, Hankelow, Hunsterson, and Wybunbury. Although the King's forces had robbed and plundered Wrenbury, Stoke, Hurleston, and the like, they had stayed on the west side of the Weaver and our hope was that they might remain there. It was still a risk but much safer than visiting farmers on the other side of the river, several of whose farms had already been plundered by marauding bands of royalists.

The frozen ground and relatively thin layer of snow meant that it was easy to drive the cart along the narrow road leading towards the village of Audlem, which, in times of thaw after so much snow, would have otherwise been little more than a quagmire. From Nantwich, the normally muddy track travels in a south-easterly direction through farming land, holding a line about a quarter of a mile from the river until, after four miles or so, it reaches the hamlet of Hatherton. From there, the road veers to the right, heading south-west into Hankelow and eventually into Audlem. We made good time on the frozen surface, the two dragoons riding by the side of the cart, their swords clinking at their sides. Cowper turned out to be a jolly companion, entertaining us with a selection of bawdy songs along the way, quite a relief from the heavy mixture of psalms and anti-episcopal rants I was used to hearing from the soldiers of the garrison. Skinner, meanwhile, sat bright-eyed at the front of the cart with his musket by his side.

"You are a different person doing this kind of work," I observed, as we rode towards the first farm on our list.

"Aye, sir," he replied. "Don't think me ungrateful an' all that, Master Cheswis. I'm thankful for the opportunity you gave me, but I'm an apprentice salt worker because I need to be. I much prefer soldiering, if the truth be told."

"I can see that," I said. "One thing's for certain. There's no shortage of opportunity in that line of work at times like these."

As we travelled southwards, it became clear that word had already travelled widely regarding the plundering that had taken place on the other side of the river, so it did not prove difficult to persuade farmers to sell their produce to us. It was better to sell the cheese to us at wholesale prices than have it stolen by the King's forces. By the time we were ready to leave our second farm of the day, near Hankelow, the cart was almost half full.

While we were loading, a rider cantered into the farmyard and drew up alongside us.

"No need for alarm," said the farmer to the two dragoons, who were ready to draw their weapons. "It's my brother, come from Audlem." The look on the brother's face, however, told a different story.

"I bring bad tidings," he said, breathlessly. "The cavaliers have crossed the bridge in the village and are plundering the houses and nearby farms. John Bithell's farm at Buerton has already been raided, and his cattle and horses have been stolen. It looks like they are heading for Nantwich. I suggest you lock up your livestock. And you, sir," he added, addressing me, "you should make haste back to Nantwich. A cartload of cheese would make fine plunder for a troop of hungry Irishmen."

I thanked the farmer and his brother, and we finished loading the cart as quickly as we could. It was clear that we needed to head back home with all possible speed. However, we decided to return via our originally planned route through the back lanes on the assumption that the royalists were more likely to prefer the main route to Nantwich. Clearly, if they could cross the river at Audlem, they could cross it again at Shrewbridge. Just before we reached Hatherton, therefore, we branched off to the right and headed off down one of the small lanes to the hamlet of Hunsterson, where we planned to visit one last farm, in order to make sure we returned to Nantwich with a fully-laden cart.

The farmhouse in question was just north of Hunsterson, a couple of hundred yards down a narrow track, which branched off the lane to Heathfield and Walgherton. Bordering the track on one side was Chapel Wood, an area of thick woodland containing a small lake known as Ridley's Pool. There were trees lining the other side of the track too, though not as thick. Eventually, the path opened up into a clearing where the farm stood, surrounded by fields to the south and east.

We did not linger at the farm, staying only long enough to buy the cheese we needed and to take some brief refreshment before heading off again towards the Hunsterson road. Prescott was at the head of our convoy, with Cowper on the left and myself sat next to Skinner on the right-hand side of the cart. I remember feeling a sense of relief that we could now concentrate on making our way back to the safety of Nantwich, but just as we reached the trees, things started to happen very quickly.

Firstly, I heard two sharp cracks from somewhere up ahead and a dull thud from the other side of the cart. I glanced to my left just in time to see Cowper's neck explode in a mass of red, his song halted in mid-verse. The dragoon did not make a sound but fell first backwards and then sideways from his horse, landing in a crumpled heap on the ground. Time stood still for a second as I took in the horror of what had just happened. At first, it seemed that the second shot has missed, but then the horse, Goodwyn, suddenly stumbled and sank to his knees, his weight tipping the cart over. The cheeses we had bought landed on the ground with a thump, followed by Skinner, who banged his head on a stone by the roadside and remained motionless in the snow. Looking ahead, I saw two people dive back quickly into the woods, one either side of the road. I grabbed my musket and fired a shot in their direction but missed, the musket ball burying itself in a tree.

"Get under cover, quickly, before they reload," yelled Prescott. Dismounting rapidly, we tied the horses to the upturned cart and dived for cover. I took another look across to where the shots had come from and a musket ball flew over my head.

"Keep your head down and reload your musket," shouted Prescott. "One of them's over there," he said, pointing to where the shot had come from. "Where the fuck's the other one?"

At that moment, a second bang reverberated from the midst of the woods, and a musket ball caught Prescott in the shoulder. I realised with alarm that the second man had doubled back through the undergrowth, re-emerging to Prescott's right. With a shout, the enemy soldier charged directly at Sergeant Prescott and kicked his musket firmly out of reach. Prescott fell back with a groan, holding his shoulder, blood seeping from between his fingers. I realised I had no time to finish reloading my musket, so I reached for my dagger instead. It was too late. My assailant knocked the weapon away with his musket butt and drew a pistol, which he pointed at my head. I looked into the soldier's face and realised with surprise and horror that, far from the royalist soldier I had been expecting, I was looking at the features of Nathaniel Hulse. With resignation, I laid back, closed my eyes and waited for the release that death would bring.

19

Barthomley, Cheshire – Saturday,
December 23, 1643

*M*ajor John Connaught stood on the road outside
the village of Barthomley and surveyed the scene
before him. It was late afternoon and dusk was fast
approaching. Two hundred yards away, he could see
the snow-covered roofs of the small cluster of thatched
cottages that were crowded closely around the red
sandstone tower of St Bertoline's church. In front of
the buildings, lined across the road, was a makeshift
barricade made of barrels, bales, fencing – anything
that could be gathered together. Behind it stood twenty
men, some with muskets, others with pikes and other
weaponry. The muskets were pointed towards Connaught
and the band of men who accompanied him.

Connaught was an Ulsterman bent on revenge. He
fought alongside the royalists, but not for the King.
He was fighting for his own people, whose lands in
the North of Ireland had been captured and ravaged
by the Presbyterian covenanter leader Robert Monro.
Originally part of a group of forces commissioned by

the Earl of Antrim to resist Monro, Connaught now led a company of his own countrymen, seconded to the command of Colonel Ralph Sneyd, the Staffordshire landowner. His orders were to march to Crewe Hall and take the small garrison there. Since leaving Chester, his company had cut a swathe of terror through Cheshire, burning, looting, and plundering its way through Audlem, Hankelow, Hatherton, Wybunbury, and Weston, before emerging on the road to Barthomley.

Connaught and his men had hitherto met with little resistance, so they were surprised to see the barricades outside Barthomley, especially as there were fields either side of the road, which would make it impossible for defenders to keep the advancing Irishmen out.

The Major scratched his head and turned to one of his lieutenants. "What do you make of this, Curran?" he asked.

Curran grinned and deposited a mouthful of spittle on the roadside. "I think it's very decent of them to give us the opportunity for some sport, sir," he replied.

"My thinking exactly," said Connaught. "My guess is that these people are not just simple villagers. Puritan rabble, that's what they are. They deserve everything that's coming to them."

Meanwhile, behind the barricades, brothers John and Henry Fowler crouched behind the barrels and trained the sights of their muskets on the approaching soldiers. John Fowler was the schoolmaster and curate of Barthomley and son of the rector. He was only twenty years of age, but being the most educated of the villagers, he was accepted as their leader.

"What do we do, brother?" breathed Henry Fowler, the younger of the two siblings. "We cannot possibly resist a whole company of trained soldiers."

"We must," said John. "The Irish are little more than animals. They will rape our women and steal our belongings. They have pillaged every village from Audlem to here. We must try and divert them." With that, he stood up and called to the soldiers.

"What do you want? There's no passage for you here."

There was a moment of hesitation before Major Connaught stepped forward. "In the name of the King, we demand passage and sustenance. Let us through and you will not be harmed."

"Go away, Irishman," responded Fowler. "We hear what you have perpetrated in the villages around these parts. Leave us in peace. If you are heading for Crewe, take the road behind you to your left."

Connaught said nothing but motioned his men forward with a wave of his hand. Twenty of them moved across the field to the right whilst another group crossed the narrow stream called the Wulvarn, which runs along the side of the road. This group headed to the left to encircle the village, whilst the rest headed straight for the barricades, walking slowly. The villagers looked at each other and shuffled nervously, not knowing whether to shoot or run.

"We can't hold this many men here," said one. "What do we do?"

Fowler looked round in desperation. Building a defence around the half-timbered houses in the village was not an option. Apart from the fact that this would expose the women and children hiding inside the houses to immediate danger, they would be overrun by a group of soldiers as large as this in a matter of minutes. St Bertoline's, however, had been built on an ancient drumlin and burial mound and, with its crenellated roof, could have passed for a fortress in the half-light of dusk.

"Withdraw," shouted Fowler, "to the church. We can hold them from the tower."

Dragging their weapons with them, the villagers scuttled back down the street, musket shots flying above their heads. Entering the church, they climbed the turret stair of the western tower, several of them, including John Fowler, emerging at the top, whilst the remainder guarded the stairs. The Irish soldiers quickly surrounded the church and positioned themselves behind walls and gravestones.

"Don't be fools," shouted Connaught, stepping out to where the villagers could see him. "Surrender now and in the name of the King, quarter will be given to all."

"Fuck off back to Ireland, you papist scum," screamed Fowler, from the top of the tower, and aimed a shot at Connaught. The musket ball fizzed past the Major's head

and hit the soldier behind him, who screamed and fell to the ground. *Connaught dived back behind a gravestone to loud jeers from the villagers.*

"O'Quig's been shot, Major," said a voice behind him. Connaught turned round to see the stricken soldier lying on the ground with a hole the size of a fist in his belly. His face was as grey as the sky.

"I can see that, Mallon. By all that is holy, these bastards will pay for this." With an effort, Connaught swivelled himself round with his back to the gravestone. To his right, he noticed the hats of some of his men protruding from behind the churchyard wall, where they were crouching, waiting for his instructions. A steely, determined look entered his eyes and he called over to them.

"You men, behind the wall," he barked. "Cover us." The response was instant. A volley of shots was fired, the musket balls sending chips of stone flying from the wall near the top of the tower. The heads of the villagers disappeared momentarily and Connaught was up and sprinting for the church door, followed by five others. This process was repeated until thirty Irishmen stood inside the church, inspecting the locked door to the turret stairs.

Inside the church, Connaught took in the nave with its oak ceiling and carved altar. A private chapel stood on the south side of the chancel.

"What are we to do, sir?" asked Mallon. "They're not

coming down and we can't stay here all night."

Connaught considered the question for a moment and then grinned. "Rip out the pews," he said.

Curran looked horrified. "Sir, surely you're not going to destroy a church?"

"This is a not a church loyal to Rome, Curran. God will forgive us. These people are nought but a bunch of calvinists. To put them on the right path will be a mercy."

Some of the soldiers crossed themselves, but, nevertheless, they started to gather up the sweet-smelling rushes lining the floor and break up the pews, piling everything up against the door to the turret stairs. One soldier brought a book over and showed it to Connaught.

"Yes – the parish registers too," he said.

Within a few minutes, a roaring furnace was burning with smoke, which billowed up the stairs in great clouds. Angry shouts and coughing were heard from behind the door to the tower.

Eventually, a cry rang out from the rooftop. "Quarter!"

Connaught smiled to himself in satisfaction and issued the order for the villagers to throw their guns from the roof and to descend one by one. Wood and rushes were brushed to one side at the foot of the stairs, and the door opened. One by one the men emerged and were lined up and made to strip naked. Any who resisted were hacked and stabbed and had their throats cut. Two men suffered this fate and collapsed against the wall, gurgling as they fought for breath. Most, though, had the sense to stand stock still and were unharmed.

John Fowler was the last to emerge from the smoke-filled staircase. When he did so, he stared in horror at the scene in front of him.

"You murdering animal," he seethed, taking a step forward. "You would commit such a foul atrocity in the house of God? May the Lord have mercy-" It is as far as he got. Connaught, his face contorted with rage, grabbed hold of Fowler and felled him with a single axle blow to the left temple. The wound was only small, but the blow was instantly fatal, and Fowler slumped to the ground in a heap.

In the frenzy that ensued, nine more men were killed, five were injured, and only three escaped unhurt. In addition to John Fowler, among the dead were Henry Fowler, Richard Steele, and his two sons, Richard, William, and Randall Hassall, whose wife, as well as the younger Richard Steele's wife, would give birth to sons the following summer, both named after their dead fathers. The men who were unhurt, and those of the injured who could still walk, staggered out of the church into the trees to fend for themselves in the cold of the winter's dusk.

"Right, my friends," said Connaught. "God's work is done for today. I know where I'm going now." The major strode off towards the village's only inn, The White Lion. Curran stared in disbelief, but he and the remaining soldiers followed Connaught, leaving the bodies of the

dead piled up against the wall and the door to the turret stairs.

Meanwhile, from the safety of the trees, two shadowy figures had been watching the proceedings with interest. They waited an hour until darkness began to set in and they were sure no-one else was about, before dragging a further body out of the undergrowth and into the church. They surveyed the scene with a mixture of horror and admiration.

"God's teeth," said the elder of the two men. "It has come to this. May God preserve us. One day someone will pay dearly for this. Let us hope that it is not the King." The two men did not linger, but before they took their leave, the dead body they had been dragging behind them was propped up against the wall in the same manner as the rest of the corpses. The only difference was that the body had a crimson sash covering the gaping wound in its throat.

20

Nantwich – Tuesday, December 26, 1643

News that something was amiss at Barthomley had begun to filter through to the town by Christmas Day, but it was not until Saint Stephen's Day that a first-hand account of the true horror of the terrible events in my home village reached my household, and it was a familiar face that brought it. I was still in my chamber, having just about recovered from my ordeal of five days earlier, when I heard a terrible clattering on the front door and shouting from outside. When I opened the door, Gabriel Broomhall, the young farm-hand from my parents' farm in Barthomley, stumbled across the threshold. He was shaking uncontrollably from head to toe, which was unsurprising as he was not dressed in a winter cloak. Before I had the chance to ask him why he was abroad in such weather and so lightly-dressed, Mrs Padgett, who, as usual, was already up and pottering around the kitchen, ushered him over to the fireplace to warm up and plied him with a cup of warmed spiced ale. Clearly in shock, Gabriel was scarcely able to speak, so I left him to recover his senses by the heat of the fire whilst

I returned to my chamber to dress myself.

Although it was a shock to see Gabriel, who I had known for years, in such a state, I had barely fared much better myself over the past few days. Shocked to my core after my experience in Chapel Wood, it had taken me a couple of days to fully recover my composure, and I had only now begun to realise how close I had come to death.

Staring at the manic grin on Hulse's face, I had already given up hope and mentally begun to commit myself to my maker. However, just as the musketeer cocked his pistol, I heard a crack from the road behind him and Hulse pitched forward, landing across my chest, the pistol spinning away into the grass. I screamed in shock and pushed Hulse away onto his back. As I did so, I saw the huge gaping wound in Hulse's chest where the fragments of musket ball had entered him. I looked at my shirt and realised that it was covered in blood and bits of Hulse's innards. I leaned over to my right and vomited into the grass as Hulse's body twitched in its final death throes. Seconds later, Skinner was at my side, having sprinted the few yards across the grass.

"That was a close one, Master Cheswis," he breathed, as he threw himself on the ground and proceeded to reload his musket. "Quick, get your weapon, sir," he added. "The other bastard is still out there on the road."

I struggled to regain my senses and grabbed the musket that Hulse had kicked away. Fortunately, the match had not extinguished in the snow, so I was able to quickly reload it.

Prescott, meanwhile, had sat up and regained the carbine he had been using. The shot from Hulse had scraped his shoulder, and, although there was plenty of blood, it was clearly not a life-threatening wound. The three of us lay side-by-side in the undergrowth and stared at the other assailant who had retreated to where he and Hulse had left their horses, just out of range. I focused my vision and confirmed what I already knew, that the other man was Bressy, Hulse's friend.

"That was impressive, lad," grunted Prescott, as he tried to stem the flow of blood from his shoulder. "I'll wager you'll make a fine soldier one day soon." Skinner beamed from ear to ear at the compliment, but Prescott was right. Skinner had surpassed all possible expectations of a youth of his age. He had shown no panic in the heat of battle – just ruthless efficiency.

"Right, lads. Here's what we do," whispered Prescott, under his breath. "We've all reloaded, right?... Good. Skinner, you take a shot at him to let him know we're here. Then, if he comes any nearer, we take alternate shots at twenty second intervals, allowing us to reload, but not him. Do you understand?"

Skinner nodded and aimed his musket at Bressy, who was stood watching. The musket ball whistled harmlessly into the grass some yards short of where he was standing. Bressy did not move a muscle at first, but then he calmly untied the horses, mounted up, and rode away in the direction of Hunsterson.

"He's no fool, that one," said Prescott. "He knows he's on a hiding to nothing. He's better off withdrawing and living to fight another day."

With Skinner quickly reloading and making sure that Bressy continued to retreat, I turned my attention to the body of Hulse, removing the dead musketeer's coat and then his shirt, which I tore into strips and used as a makeshift bandage for Prescott, to ensure his wound didn't bleed any more until I could get him to a physician. I then inspected the cart, which lay on its side. Unfortunately, the front axle had buckled and one of the wheels was broken beyond repair. It was clear that it would not be possible to get it back to Nantwich that evening, so I sent Skinner to find the farmer, who he eventually discovered cowering in a barn. After some persuasion, he agreed to help us get the cart and the cheese back to the farm and to store both until we could get a blacksmith out to mend the cart.

We then retrieved Cowper's horse but unfortunately had to leave Cowper and Hulse's bodies, with a promise that some soldiers would be sent out to bury them the next day.

Prescott rode his own horse back to Nantwich, whilst Skinner and I followed on behind on Cowper's. Skinner was feted as a hero when we returned to the safety of the town and was still basking in the glory of his newly-found status several days later. I, however, apart from spending three days in bed with a fever, clearly brought on by the shock of the incident, was deeply disturbed by the involvement of Hulse and Bressy. It was clear to me that the two soldiers were involved in the murder of Ralph Brett and that the encounter in Hunsterson had been no chance meeting. They had come specifically for me. But why? What did they think I knew?

In the meantime, we had also heard that the royalist soldiers that passed through Audlem, a band of Irishmen, had carved a swathe of destruction through the countryside, raiding farms throughout the villages in the area, burning and looting without mercy. Victims had been stripped naked and robbed of all their possessions, women were raped, and any man who resisted murdered. I prayed that the farm in Hunsterson where I had left my goods would be spared. I dared not think what had happened in Barthomley.

It was with feelings of deep apprehension, therefore, that I returned to my fireside to receive Gabriel Broomhall.

My fears were not unfounded. Gabriel struggled to tell his tale, and, as he did so, I could scarcely believe what I was being told. What depths of depravity could this band of heathens sink to? The company of Irishmen had chased twenty of my friends and acquaintances into St Bertoline's, desecrated the church by ripping out the pews and setting fire to them. They had then smoked the young men of Barthomley out of the tower, stripped them, and killed them in cold blood. I recoiled in shock as Gabriel recounted the names of some of those who had been lost: the Fowler brothers, my childhood friends James Boughey and Richard Cawell, Thomas Elcocke, the son of the previous rector of Barthomley, Richard Steele, and two of his sons. It brought tears to my eyes – friends of my youth cut down mercilessly by these barbarians, and in the House of God, too.

Gabriel was one of the lucky ones who'd escaped. He was among the last down the stairs and would surely have had his throat cut too, if the frenzy catalysed by Connaught's slaying of John Fowler had not caused such confusion that he was able to slide out of the church door unnoticed. I had wondered how it had taken two days for details to travel the ten miles from Barthomley, but this was now patently obvious. The villagers had clearly been too terrified to leave their homes.

Gabriel related how he had managed to get out of the church and into my parents' house nearby, where he was supplied with clean clothes. However, he had to leave almost immediately to avoid the rampaging troops. He would certainly have been killed, had he stayed. He had run across the road into Domville's Wood, where he had hidden amongst the trees in the freezing cold for two days. On Christmas Day, he had managed to return to my parents' house to find my parents and brother George terrified but alive, albeit with many of their belongings stolen.

The rest of the village had fared little better. The soldiers had billeted themselves in the houses of the villagers for nearly three days, even in the houses of those whose men had been murdered, and proceeded to rampage around the surrounding countryside. My parents had said there was talk of attacking Crewe Hall. Seeing the state of my parents and knowing the soldiers would be back later that day, Gabriel had decided he had to seek help. For fear of being caught by any remaining soldiers, he had walked behind the farm due South to Balterley and then marched through the night to Nantwich, staying to fields and woods and avoiding settlements, in order to avoid any other royalist soldiers that were out and about. As my parents' winter clothes had been stolen, Gabriel had, rather foolishly some might say, left his own heavy winter's cloak for my father. Although he wore two shirts and a jacket and had moved quickly to keep as warm as possible, it was clear that he could not have survived much longer so inadequately dressed for the bitter winter's night.

"We must return to Barthomley with all haste," I said to Gabriel, "but first you must eat and warm yourself. I will give you my spare coat."

"And what of Master Simon?" asked Gabriel. "Will he come too?"

"I'm afraid not," I said, explaining about Simon's disappearance the week before. "I haven't seen my brother in over a week. I was hoping you might be able to shed some light on his disappearance." As I spoke, I saw Gabriel's features take on a troubled look.

"I can," he said, hesitantly. "Simon arrived in Barthomley last Monday evening. He had a companion with him. A man called Nuttall, but we haven't seen either of them since Saturday morning. We assumed they'd returned to Nantwich."

I looked at Gabriel, and, as I realised the implications of what he was saying, a dark sense of foreboding began to overwhelm me.

Whilst Gabriel was being revitalised by the magical skills of Mrs Padgett, I put on my cloak and walked down to the Beast Market to hire two horses. I thought about taking my own bay mare, Demeter, to Barthomley, but having lost my cart horse already that week, I did not wish to risk Demeter, to whom I was greatly attached.

It being St Stephen's day morning, Edward Shenton, the owner of the stables I usually patronised when I needed to rent a horse, was not expecting much business, and he was still in his chamber when I knocked on his door. It took some time to persuade him to come down, but he eventually emerged, grumbling, and led me to his stables where I hired a chestnut mare for myself, which I had ridden once before, and a black gelding for Gabriel.

By the time I returned home, Gabriel was ready to move, so I lent him a spare cloak and we set off down Hospital Street. I was glad I had hired the horses, as we could move much quicker than on foot and, despite the restorative effects of Mrs Padgett's breakfast, Gabriel didn't look like he would appreciate a walk back to Barthomley in the biting cold of the December morning.

When we arrived at the sconce at the end of Hospital Street, the soldiers told us to be careful and keep off the main roads. However, they had received no reported sightings of royalist soldiers that morning. It appeared the marauding band of Irishmen was on the move elsewhere, possibly to Sandbach or Middlewich. Nevertheless, we decided to take the soldiers' advice and keep to the fields and side roads.

As we made our way through the fields, everything was silent, save the soft crunch of our horses' hooves as they penetrated the frozen crust of the snow. No-one, it appeared, dared to venture forth from their houses that morning. We headed first towards Butt Green and across pristine white meadows to Wybunbury, skirting the woods to the North of the village. From the trees, we were able to look over into the village, but there were no signs of any royalist soldiers. It began to look as if they had, indeed, moved north. We therefore rode across the fields south of Hough, then due east to Balterley, where we turned north, through Basford Coppice, approaching Barthomley Church from behind. The ride was tense, and Gabriel and I barely spoke to each other. But we need not have worried. Not a soul disturbed our eerie solitude.

As we approached St Bertoline's Church, though, I

realised that there was some activity in and around the churchyard. As we drew nearer, a shout echoed across the fields, and a number of men with muskets appeared behind the church wall, their weapons pointed firmly in our direction. As we came within musket range, however, someone else shouted; "Stand easy, lads. It's Gabriel Broomhall and Daniel Cheswis."

The musket barrels gradually disappeared from behind the wall, and men began to file out into the field to help us from our horses and to tether them to one of the trees lining the churchyard. A middle-aged man with a balding head and a florid complexion stepped out from the group.

"Praise the Lord, Gabriel, we thought you were dead too." The village rector, Richard Fowler, stood leaning on a spade. He wore an expression of desperation and stoic resilience, and I realised the sad duty that he and the other men were in the midst of performing.

"I nearly froze to death in the woods," said Gabriel, briefly explaining his lonely sojourn in Domville's Wood and his trek through the night to fetch me from Nantwich.

"It is good to see you, Daniel," said the rector. "Thank you for coming and for bringing Gabriel back safely."

"Thanks are not necessary on a day like today," I said, "It's a sorry day when a father has to bury his sons."

The rector bowed his head and brushed a tear from the corner of his eye. "Aye, that it is," he said. "Sometimes, God tests our faith in the most terrible way. There was evil abroad in this place, Daniel. Some might say it was the Devil's work. I must comfort myself with the thought that John and Henry fought that evil with bravery. Now they are at peace in the bosom of our Lord."

I nodded in sympathy. "And the animals who did this?" I asked. "They are gone?"

"Aye. The Irishmen left early this morning with orders to march to Middlewich."

"Then God help the people of that town," I said, grimly. "And my parents? How are they?"

"Passably well under the circumstances. They are shocked, of course, and their clothes and goods have been stolen, but apart from that they are faring well. Your brother George is with them now. You should go and look after them."

"I certainly will," I said, "but first I would like to familiarise myself with what happened here."

"Then prepare yourself well," said the rector. "It is not a sight for the faint-hearted."

Fowler was not exaggerating. The scene inside the church was one of pure devastation. There was wood strewn all over the floor of the nave where the pews had been chopped into pieces, ready to put on the Irishmen's bonfire by the turret steps. However, the worst sight was in the entranceway beneath the tower, where great swathes of black streaked the walls, below which lay the charred embers of the fire used to smoke out the victims, several of whose bodies were propped up against the wall, some lying grotesquely, almost naked, with their throats cut and knife wounds in chests and backs. The floor was stained brown with dried blood, and the whole area stank with the sickly sweet smell of death. I staggered over to the opposite wall and retched violently. Such a terrible sight I had never seen before.

I could tell that the rector was on the verge of tears as Gabriel and I surveyed the bodies of our friends. He clenched and unclenched his fists in anger as he led us to one body after another. Suddenly, though, his eye was caught by one corpse propped up in a corner, slightly apart from the others.

"Wait a minute," he said. "Who is this? I don't recognise this person. Whoever he is, he wasn't with our defence party that day."

I stepped forward to take a closer look, and as I did so, my heart sank. I had been so preoccupied with the awfulness of it all, I had failed to notice what I had dreaded discovering all along. There, sitting with his head lolling sideways, exposing a neat cut to the throat, was the dead body of James Nuttall. Tied loosely around his neck was a crimson sash.

21

Barthomley, Cheshire – Tuesday,
December 26, 1643

I walked over to where Nuttall lay and inspected his body closely. Unlike the other corpses waiting to be buried, Nuttall was still fully clothed. I carefully removed the crimson scarf from around his neck and placed it in a pocket inside my cloak. It was, I noticed, of identical material to that found on the body of Ralph Brett. Nuttall's shirt was stained brown with two-day-old blood, but, as I fingered it, I realised that the garment had frozen to a crisp. Moving his head to one side, I saw that his throat had been cut from ear to ear. A small mercy, I thought. Once this had happened, he would not have taken long to die.

However, a glance at the dead man's hands revealed something more sinister. I noticed with a deepening sense of shock and disgust that Nuttall's fingernails had been neatly removed. The poor man must have been tortured before he died. I exhaled deeply, and, running my hand through my hair, I thought about the agony Nuttall must have gone through. I also wondered what information was so important for him to hide that he would have felt the need to endure such treatment and, indeed, whether he gave anything away. Even if he did, I conjectured, he could not have submitted easily, for the nails on both his hands were missing. James Nuttall had undoubtedly been a brave man.

As the implications of Nuttall's death started to sink in, my mind turned towards Simon. Where on earth was he? Whoever had sought Nuttall must surely also be seeking my brother. I swallowed hard as ice-cold anxiety began to spread up my spine.

"You look like you know this person, Daniel," said Richard Fowler, who had been eyeing me with growing curiosity.

"I do," I confirmed. "He is a friend and associate of my brother, Simon. Whoever killed him may be looking for Simon also. I'm afraid he may be in mortal danger. Tell me," I demanded, turning to Gabriel Broomhall, "has anybody been asking after Simon at all?"

"Are you jesting, Master Daniel?" said Gabriel, with incredulity. "The house has been full of Irishmen since late Saturday morning. Wait, though..." He hesitated a moment as if trying to recall something important. "Now you mention it, a man came looking for him on Saturday evening after Simon had left. Proper mean he looked, too."

"Can you describe him?"

"Oh – he was quite tall, a strong-looking fellow with a

short beard and black hair. That's what struck be about him, see. His hair was as black as the night."

I nodded and realised that Gabriel had given me a description of Jem Bressy.

"What did you tell him?"

"That Master Simon had long since left. He asked to come into the house to wait, but I said we did not know when he would return."

"And he left?"

"Yes. He said something about royalist soldiers being on the way. He wasn't wrong."

I took a closer look at Nuttall's corpse, and it struck me that, although his chest was covered in blood, there was none on the floor around his body.

"Here, help me flip him over," I said to Gabriel, and with some effort, we managed to roll Nuttall over onto his side. As I expected, the back of his breeches were torn and covered in debris.

"What's the matter, Daniel?" asked the rector, as he watched me pick small pieces of gravel and undergrowth from the rear of Nuttall's breeches.

"This body has been moved," I postulated. "I'll wager he was killed in the woods and dragged into the church. And you say no-one's been in the church since the massacre?"

"No-one has dared to stray from their homes," confirmed Fowler. "They've not been allowed to, either, if the truth be told. The Irish were billeted in most of the houses hereabouts. To my knowledge, no-one has been in the church between Saturday evening and this morning."

I own that I was beginning to feel somewhat overtaken by events, which seemed to be spiralling out of control. Although the question of what Simon and Nuttall were doing in Barthomley remained a mystery, my main concern was what had happened to Simon, who was surely in grave danger. I took a moment to sit on one of the few remaining pews amongst the shattered interior of the nave of the church and prayed silently to God that my brother might be delivered safely from whatever complexities he had become entangled in.

I also allowed myself another, more worrying, thought. Why the crimson scarf? Why did Nuttall's murderers not just leave the body in the woods? Why take the trouble of dragging him into the church and leaving him fully-clothed alongside the half-naked villagers, and why the need to identify the body with a marker to specifically connect him with the murders of William Tench and Ralph Brett?

The only reason that I could think of was that the perpetrator wanted, for some reason, to crow about the murder and perhaps to draw my attention to it. Another thought also struck me that chilled me to the marrow. Could the murderers perhaps have known that I hailed from Barthomley and that I would want to go there once the pillaging band of Irishmen was gone? If that were the case, I reasoned, they would know that Simon was from

Barthomley too and perhaps also where my family lived. With a growing feeling of apprehension, I decided what I had to do.

"Gabriel," I said, "we must get back to my parents. They may not be safe either."

I quickly gave my apologies to the rector and was about to leave the church when I caught sight of a familiar figure sweeping up rushes and fragments of splintered wood from the floor of the nave. To my astonishment, I recognised the slight and soberly-dressed physique of Hugh Furnival.

"Good morning, Mr Furnival," I said, failing to keep the element of surprise from my voice. "I did not expect to see you here."

"Why ever not?" replied Furnival, raising his eyebrow and suppressing a hint of a smile. "I am a Barthomley man like you. I imagine I'm here for the same reason – out of concern for my family. I trust yours are well and have survived this appalling act of butchery?"

I hastily apologised for my insensitivity and enquired after Furnival and Alice's respective families.

"My father died several years ago and my mother now lives with a brother in Manchester, but Alice's parents fared better than might have been expected. As they live a little way up the hill and were not on the main route, they have escaped being plundered, thanks be to God."

"That is indeed a blessing," I agreed. "And your plans now?"

"It is my intention to stay with Alice's family for a couple of days until it's safe to leave them. However, after that, I need to travel to Shrewsbury to deliver the news I had gathered in Nantwich and to help prepare our next newssheet. As you are here, perhaps I could ask you keep a watch over Alice's wellbeing whilst I'm away? Especially if the King's army besiege the town and I can't get back in." Of course, I agreed without reservation.

Engrossed in my own thoughts, I left Furnival to his sweeping and headed back outside the church, gesturing to Gabriel Broomhall to untether the horses and follow me towards the gate leading to Greenbank Farm. As I did so, I noticed the villagers place two bodies carefully into a single grave and start shovelling the frozen earth on top of them. Standing next to the grave, staring into the middle distance with tears in his eyes and his hands clasped in prayer, was Richard Fowler.

Not surprisingly, my family had locked, bolted, and barricaded the back door of the farmhouse, so it took much banging, shouting, and peering in the window before we heard the sound of voices and furniture being dragged across the floor. Eventually, the door opened to reveal my brother George standing in his undergarments.

"Daniel!" he exclaimed. "Thank the Lord you have come! We prayed all night for your safe deliverance. It appears our prayers have been heeded. And you too, Gabriel. You risked much by venturing forth in such bitter weather. We owe you a debt of gratitude."

George ushered us inside, where we found the whole family gathered around the fire – my father and mother, George's wife Ellen and their four children: daughters Ellen, Susanna, and Mary and their four-year-old son, Richard. The children had been allowed to keep their clothing, but the adults had all been forced to strip to their underwear and were now sat huddled on chairs, with sheets and sacking pulled tight around their shoulders to keep in the warmth.

I hugged my family one by one and told them I was relieved to see them safe, although in truth, it was deeply shocking to see them reduced to little more than a cowering, half-naked clump of humanity. It turned out that eight soldiers had billeted themselves within the house, including a boorish major called Connaught. To my brother's credit, he had shown the good sense to open his doors to the Irishmen and welcome them as though they were a group of avenging angels. He had sworn allegiance to the King and drank to the prospect of the defeat of the puritan traitor Brereton when it became clear that the Irish had been ordered to march to Middlewich to engage Sir William in battle.

George's decision to show no resistance had saved him a beating and stopped Ellen from being raped, but it hadn't stopped the Irishmen from taking their clothes and most of the food in the house. Still, they considered they had got away lightly. They had heard the horses being taken from the stables, but the rest of the livestock was still there. The children had been scared at the presence of eight soldiers with strange accents in the house, but they had behaved well and had not cried.

"You have been very fortunate," I said. "The barbarity these men have perpetrated in the church is something no man should see."

George nodded and explained they already knew what had happened because the soldiers had been boasting about it. I turned my mind to more practical things and managed to ascertain that my family had not been left totally without clothes and provisions. Before the Irishmen had arrived, George had thankfully had the foresight to hide clothes and some extra food in one of the outhouses behind a pile of hay bales, as he had realised the farm might be raided. However, he had not yet dared to go out to retrieve them for fear of the soldiers returning.

"And what of Simon?" I asked. "I understand he has been here?"

George nodded in the affirmative. "Thank God he wasn't here when the soldiers arrived, though," he said. "Simon left on the Saturday. He said he had business to sort out, but he has not yet returned."

I had to concur. I imagined Simon's reaction to the Irishmen might have been very different to that of my elder brother. At that moment, as though it were providence, we heard the noise of hooves outside. There was a momentary air of tension as we waited to see who it was, but this was immediately relieved as a familiar face burst through the door; that of Simon himself. Open-mouthed astonishment was quickly replaced by joy at the knowledge that Simon was still alive.

"Thank God you're safe," sobbed my mother, as she wrapped her arms around him. Simon wore a broad grin, although he seemed somewhat surprised to see me there.

"Why is everyone undressed?" he asked. "Surely it is not time for bed at this hour of the day?"

George was not amused. "Then you have not heard what has happened in Barthomley these last days?" he retorted, and proceeded to relate the events that had taken place in the church. I watched my younger brother's face pale and the smile vanish from his lips.

"And where in the name of Jesus have you been this past week?" I demanded. "I think you owe me an explanation."

Simon looked me in the eye. "It is quite simple," he said. "James Nuttall and I were asked by Colonel Booth to seek out Sir William Brereton in Middlewich and to provide him with important information."

"Information? What kind of information?"

Simon ignored the question manfully and continued talking. "Because of the dangers of travelling in these times, we decided to split up. James planned to go through Haslington and Sandbach. I was to take the road to Alsager and Holmes Chapel. When I arrived at

Middlewich, it became clear that royalist forces were amassing outside the town, and it was not easy to get in unobserved. It looks like there is going to be a battle there."

"So I understand," I said. "It will be the second time this year that the people of Middlewich have had to endure such a thing."

"Exactly. So I decided not to linger in Middlewich any longer than was necessary. I delivered my message to Sir William and set off back for Barthomley immediately. James must have been held up, for he had not yet arrived by the time I departed."

I looked at Simon and realised that he did not yet know about Nuttall.

"Simon, Nuttall is dead," I said. "His throat has been cut and he was left inside the church."

"Killed by the royalist soldiers?"

"No, by the same people who killed your friend Brett. He was left with a red scarf around his neck, just like Tench and Brett."

Simon paled. "Oh my God, then we need to get back to Nantwich fast." At this, he disappeared into my parents' cellar and emerged a couple of minutes later clutching a leather pouch. I looked at the pouch and glared at Simon. Things were getting more complicated by the minute.

"I think you have some things you need to tell me, brother," I said, icily.

Simon sighed. "Daniel, I have been trying to protect

you," he said. "Knowledge can be dangerous and *this* knowledge especially so. However, I think the time has come where I must involve you. I will explain on the ride back to Nantwich. Your horse is saddled, I believe?"

"Yes, of course," I said, "but-"

"Then we must go," insisted Simon. At that, I was whisked out of the farmhouse, leaving my disbelieving family behind.

We had been riding in silence for fully fifteen minutes before anything was said on the subject that was tormenting my emotions. I had barely had enough time to say farewell to my family before we were on the road and heading for Nantwich. I had quickly helped George retrieve the remaining clothes and food from the outhouse before mounting my horse and untethering the mount ridden by Gabriel Broomhall, so as to return it to Edward Shenton. Simon had been waiting for me impatiently by the front of the house, a determined look on his face.

"We must make haste, Daniel," he had insisted, before trotting off at a keen pace in the direction of Englesea Brook.

For my part, I was seething inside at the dangers my brother had exposed us to, but I noticed something different in Simon's face as we rode. His teeth were clenched tightly together as he stared, expressionless, into the middle distance. However, an occasional nervous twitch at the corner of his mouth betrayed the true state of his emotions. I realised that I was dealing with a determination bordering on obsession.

"It's a fine mix-up you have embroiled our family in," I began, hesitantly. "I think you owe us an explanation."

"And you shall have one," said Simon, calmly. "Where would you like me to start?"

"To be truthful, I'm tempted to ask you to begin by explaining what's in that leather pouch you carry, but I have a feeling I should hear the whole story first. Perhaps you'd better start at the beginning. I have a feeling everything starts with Ralph Brett. Am I right?"

Simon exhaled deeply, and, although the road was empty, he still took the precaution of looking anxiously over his shoulder before answering. "Ralph Brett," he said, "was a professional soldier and served in Europe for many years. As you know, he returned to Nantwich a few years ago, married and began to live a quiet life running his family business. But, as you are also aware, he had contacts in high places."

"You mean the Duke of Hamilton?"

"Precisely."

"But Hamilton is the King's man in Scotland. Are you telling me Brett is a royalist spy?"

"No. Exactly the opposite. Let me finish. Ralph is a loyal parliamentarian and the Duke knows that. In September, Ralph was contacted by the Duke and asked to travel to his lordship's estate in Scotland. As you will be aware, Parliament has signed an agreement with the Covenanters for the latter to provide military support in exchange for money and certain assurances about their Presbyterian faith. This is a disaster for Hamilton, as it is exactly what he was supposed to prevent. He knew that the King would be apoplectic once he became aware of Hamilton's failings. There have also been suggestions from those that would do mischief that Hamilton's closeness to the line of succession to the crown might give him good grounds to act treasonably."

"And is he a traitor?"

"The Duke is loyal to his Majesty, but he sees no reason to lose his head over a situation that is largely of the King's own making."

"And that is why Brett was summoned?" I demanded. "To what end?"

Simon patted the front of his cloak where he had safely secreted the leather pouch he had retrieved from my parents' cellar. "Ralph was given the contents of this pouch," he said. "It contains personal letters from his Majesty to the Duke, which reveal details of the King's business, particularly that in Ireland, which the King would not want to see in parliamentary hands. Ralph was told to hold on to these papers as a safeguard in case the Duke was incarcerated and held to account over the events in Scotland. I understand the Duke arrived in Oxford last week with his brother, and both were promptly arrested. We are now waiting for word from his lordship as to what to do next."

I looked in horror at Simon. "God's teeth, brother, and you saw fit to hide these documents in our house, putting our parents, our brother, and his family at risk?"

"I know," said my brother, putting his hands in the air in an attempt to placate me. "I'm sorry about that, but there was no alternative. Let me explain."

"I think you'd better. How on earth did you become involved in all this?"

"You know little of my political activities, Daniel," said Simon, "and perhaps it's better that way. James Nuttall and I first got to know Ralph as a result of conversations we held in taverns in Nantwich. After a while, he began to trust us as loyal supporters of the parliamentary cause, so when he was entrusted in this task, he asked both James and I to help him. However, as you know, someone in the King's employ appears to have found out that we have these letters and is trying his best to find them."

"Hence Brett's murder – and Tench's too presumably – although I fail to understand the nature of his involvement. Tench was a *royalist* spy. Why would Brett's murderer want to silence him? Had he turned his coat perhaps?"

"I don't think so," said Simon, "Ralph knew nothing of Tench – and what is the significance of the crimson scarf? Why tie scarves around the necks of both victims?"

I thought about this for a moment and turned to Simon. "They certainly allowed you to make a connection between Tench and Brett," I said, thoughtfully, "and probably also made you act quicker to make the Duke's papers secure."

Simon pulled on his reins to slow his horse down and looked at me with raised eyebrows. The suggestion that the murderer had deliberately used the crimson scarf to connect the two killings, in order to encourage Simon and Nuttall to act rashly, was clearly something that had not occurred to him before; certainly, it had not occurred to me.

"That's right," said Simon. "Once Ralph died, we realised we had to get the papers out of Nantwich, somewhere where they wouldn't be found. I thought here would be a good place."

"But that hasn't worked."

"No. Whoever killed Ralph and James clearly knows my connections with Barthomley. The papers are safer somewhere in Nantwich after all. That's one reason why we need to get back."

I considered Simon's point a while. "So who else knows about this?" I asked.

"Elizabeth, of course. But she and I, and now you, are the only people who know the location of the letters. Colonel Booth knows about their existence, though, or, to be more accurate, he knows we have important papers that could be of significant value to the parliamentarian cause but is not aware of their content or where they are being kept. Indeed, the Duke specifically asked for Colonel Booth to be informed about our task and provided us with a letter from him to Booth explaining that we were in possession of important papers and asking for his protection. However, Ralph was under instructions not to pass over the letters until specific instructions to do so had been received from the Duke. That is why James and I have been chasing around the countryside trying to conceal them, instead of the papers being already under Booth's protection. Now Sir William Brereton also knows. That was the purpose of my ride to Middlewich. The Colonel reckoned his superiors should be aware of the situation should Nantwich fall. If that happens and we hear from Hamilton, we are to find a way to get the letters to Sir William."

I hesitated and looked at Simon suspiciously. "What do you mean, 'we'? Apart from Elizabeth Brett, you are the only person left."

"Yes," said Simon. "That's why I need your help in this. We need to see Colonel Booth without delay."

"Hold on a minute," I began, indignantly. "What makes you think you can involve me in this?"

Simon looked at me, narrowing his eyes. "I'm sorry, Daniel," he said, "but you *are* involved. You are my brother, you have been investigating Ralph's murder, and you were attacked in Elizabeth's house the other night. Even if you weren't involved, the perpetrator obviously thinks you are."

I thought about that for a moment and had to agree

with Simon. I told him about the events on my trip to Hankelow, which I had so far refrained from relating. Simon whistled in surprise.

"That just goes to prove my point," he said. "So one of these men is dead and the second is this man, Bressy. But there must be a third murderer, surely?"

"Yes. There is a third person, but we don't know who that is. Hulse and Bressy remained by the earthworks after the murder, but someone else was heard by Lady Norton running away from the scene. Other soldiers caught sight of the third person too."

"Have you the slightest idea who this could be?"

"No, that is the difficult bit," I admitted.

"Could it perhaps be Thomas Maisterson or one of his gentlemen friends, like Roger Wilbraham?" suggested Simon.

"Possibly," I admitted, explaining the interest Maisterson had shown in the affair and his keenness to protect the interests of both Randle Church and Lady Norton. "That would certainly go some way towards explaining the connection of William Tench to this whole business."

"I'm not so sure," said Simon. "Tench has no direct connection to this as far as I am aware. How he fits into the whole picture is a complete mystery to me. Perhaps he had some relationship with Hulse, Bressy, and the third person. If we can solve this riddle, perhaps we'll be able to identify who's responsible."

I nodded and silently considered Simon's words. "But something doesn't add up," I said, eventually. "There's something about Maisterson that makes me think he's telling the truth. He seems just as concerned at getting to the bottom of this as you are. Perhaps he's just a good actor, but that's not my impression. It seems to me that Maisterson's main aim is making sure that his personal property is safe."

"But he did know that Tench was a royalist scout, right?"

"Yes, I think so, but he wouldn't discuss that."

"Hmm," said Simon, with a sardonic smile. "I wouldn't trust Maisterson as far as I can spit."

I could understand Simon's point of view but didn't say anything. I was confused and plagued by the strange sensation that the solution to the whole affair was plain enough but irritatingly just out of my grasp. I just could not see the wood for trees. There was also one other thing, which I did not understand and which had begun to nag at me.

"Simon," I said. "One more thing. Your friend Brett is now dead, so why not just hand the letters over to Colonel Booth and have done with the matter?"

"I thought about that, Daniel, but I couldn't do it," replied Simon, with a shrug of the shoulders. "Ralph's loyalty was to Hamilton, not particularly to Parliament. So he would have wanted us to follow the Duke's instructions to the letter, and Ralph was my friend, so why would I act against his wishes? There is also Elizabeth to consider. The Duke had promised a reward to Ralph, so for Elizabeth's sake, we need to keep to the plan. In any case, the result will be the same, regardless of whether Booth gets the letters now or later."

I might have guessed Simon would opt for the more difficult option, but I was in no mood to argue. "So what are we going to do with these letters now?" I enquired.

"Leave that to me," said Simon. "I know a suitable place."

I didn't question him any further. I was learning quickly that as far as Simon was concerned, it was better not to know any more than was necessary. The sconce at the end of Hospital Street was already in sight, so I made the decision to let Simon follow his instincts. At least the pouch would be out of my sight, and, if I didn't know where it was, I would not be in a position to inadvertently betray Simon. I made my way slowly back to Edward Shenton's stables with the horses, but an uncomfortable feeling was beginning to overwhelm me, the feeling that I was being pulled deeper and deeper against my will into an affair that had become totally out of control.

22

Folkingham, Lincolnshire – Friday,
December 29, 1643

The parliamentarian commander, Sir Thomas Fairfax,
smiled ruefully as he watched his men pull out of the
Lincolnshire village of Folkingham. Colours flew,
drums rattled, and wagons creaked as two thousand
eight hundred horse and five hundred dragoons wearily
shook off the fatigue of a long campaign and mobilised
themselves for the anticipated march. Spurring his
familiar white horse into action, he cantered down the
line of troopers and wondered how his men, all of whom
had served him with loyalty and distinction over the past
twelve months, would be able to cope with the enforced
march they were embarking on. The snow lay thick on
the local fenland. It was knee-deep in places, and his
cavalrymen needed rest, not an extended campaign in
the depths of midwinter.

The troopers, riding two abreast, recognised Sir
Thomas's slight frame, olive complexion, and long dark
hair and shouted "Hiya, Black Tom," by way of greeting,
as he made his way to the head of the convoy.

Fairfax was not an ostentatious man, erring towards modesty, and this was reflected in his attire. He wore normal chest and back plates over his buff coat, his rank betrayed only by the decorated shoulder straps on his armour and the empty brass plume holder fitted to the back of his helmet. He acknowledged the shouts with a wave of the hand.

The orders Fairfax had received from his committee were to march across the country to aid Sir William Brereton, who had suffered a debilitating defeat in Middlewich at the hands of Lord Byron and his Irish army, losing over two hundred men in the process. Brereton was now holed up in the nearby town of Sandbach, desperately awaiting reinforcements. Fairfax was aware that he would be tasked with helping Brereton relieve a potential siege of strategic importance, although in their haste to urge Fairfax to march forthwith, his superiors had forgotten to tell him exactly where he was supposed to be heading. Fairfax, in a manner true to his determined character, had not waited to be informed of his final destination before departing, but had sent a curt instruction for the information to be sent to him en route.

Sir Thomas had experienced an eventful year with mixed results militarily, but it had ultimately been a successful one, thanks to the determination and commitment of his men. His spectacular victory at Wakefield in May had been followed by disastrous defeat at Adwalton Moor in June at the hands of the Marquis of Newcastle and a frantic retreat to Hull, during which he had been shot through the wrist. In Hull, though, Sir Thomas and his father Ferdinando were secure, and they had managed to keep Newcastle occupied all through the summer and autumn. Then, in October, Sir Thomas had crossed the Humber and joined forces with a little-known Colonel in the Eastern Association called Cromwell, to win a decisive battle at Winceby, the day before the siege at Hull was raised. Finally, on December 20, Sir Thomas had joined with Sir John Meldrum to retake Gainsborough for Parliament.

How his men had achieved such staggering success against apparently superior opposition, Sir Thomas was at a loss to explain. Perhaps, he reasoned, it was all down to providence.

Despite their achievements, however, Fairfax's soldiers now badly needed a rest. They were tired, many were sick, their pay was badly in arrears, and food was short. Worse still, in the middle of winter, his men were living half-naked and in rags. His officers had even gone so far as to write to him to put their concern on paper. New clothing had been a priority, but his request for supplies and, in particular, clothing had fallen on deaf ears, and so Sir Thomas had been forced to use his own credit to buy new clothes for fifteen hundred of his men.

Never in the best of health himself, Sir Thomas also badly needed to recover from the hard campaign. His impressive and strong-willed wife, Ann, who had sworn to confront any danger her husband faced, had accompanied him for much of the campaign thus far, but now she had been sent to London to recuperate with their five-year-old daughter, Little Moll.

Sir Thomas would have dearly loved to follow them, but he had now been entrusted with even greater responsibility than before, having been given the power to draw together all regiments of foot in Lancashire and Cheshire to come to Brereton's aid. Sir Thomas's plan was to march through Leicester and Stafford, relying on intelligence to decide on the safest route. After combining with Brereton, he was then to head for Manchester, with a view to reinforcing further.

Fairfax rode towards the head of the column until he spotted a rider carrying his personal cornet, a green and white fringed square of silk displaying a yellow sun on a green background and containing an image of a bound bible. Fairfax signalled to the man riding behind the cornet-bearer, a major by the name of Rokeby, a well-built man with a full beard and a pockmarked nose.

"Are you sure it's wise, marching forth in such inclement weather, sir?" Major Rokeby asked, eyeing the dull, snow-laden clouds with trepidation.

Fairfax looked at Rokeby with a mild sense of irritation and gave him the answer he was expecting. "I would much rather be sat in front of a warm fire at Nun Appleton," he said, "That much is true. But God has ordained that we must endure more hardship before we gain the victory that will justly be ours. Whatever challenge awaits us in Cheshire, Major, make no mistake. We will prevail."

23

Nantwich – Monday, January 1, 1644

It was New Year's Day before Simon and I managed to speak to Colonel Booth, which was not in the least surprising, as he was preoccupied with other, more immediate matters. Dealing with two brothers professing to be in possession of unidentified and potentially spurious documents of unconfirmed interest to the parliamentarian cause was understandably lower on his list of priorities than coping with the aftermath of Brereton's disastrous defeat on St Stephen's Day.

Sir William's retreat from Middlewich and the loss of over two hundred men was a savage blow and meant that Booth could not count on any help from his superior officer in the near future. Worse still, Brereton's line of communication with Nantwich had broken down, and Booth was not able to ascertain whether reinforcements were on the way.

Meanwhile, the tension weighed down unbearably on the inhabitants of Nantwich. It seemed like the whole of the royalist army was closing in on us. On the day after the battle at Middlewich, messengers reported that the King's forces had besieged Crewe Hall. Despite defending gallantly and killing around sixty royalists, the sheer number of attacking soldiers, combined with a lack of food and ammunition, eventually forced the hall's garrison to surrender. On Thursday 29th, around a hundred and forty brave parliamentarians were herded into the stables and eventually imprisoned in Betley Church.

By the Saturday, about four hundred royalist soldiers had re-crossed the river to Wrenbury and surrounded Nantwich on that side, whilst the remainder were in Wistaston, Willaston, and other villages to the east. The result was that our town was effectively besieged, and the garrison soldiers had to be on constant watch to defend the town both night and day.

Wherever you looked from the town's earthen walls, clusters of grubby canvas tents were visible. Ensigns, the flags of the various regiments, fluttered in the breeze, standing out against the white of the snow. Around them were horses, oxen, carts, and soldiers, hundreds of them, settling down in preparation for the anticipated siege. Perversely, this had made me feel somewhat safer, my logic being that Bressy would not be able to get into the town any more. His unknown partner, on the other hand, was a different matter. Time would tell whether he had made it back into Nantwich before Byron's men had closed the siege.

The King's soldiers were not the only thing that had

closed in on Nantwich, though. The prospect of bad weather loomed large once again. On Saturday morning, large flakes of snow started falling, aided by a bitter easterly wind, which swept across the earthworks surrounding the town like a scythe. Sentries hunkered down behind the wooden walls, rubbing their hands together, trying to draw warmth from the torches lining the defences. The blizzard persisted all day and throughout the night. Snow drifted waist-deep in places and weighed heavily on the thatched roofs in the town.

There was no market on the Saturday. The snow would not have helped in the best of circumstances, but there was no way for people to get into the town. Fortunately, there was plenty of food available. In anticipation of the siege, livestock and food had been brought inside the walls, so for the time being at least, provisions were easy enough to come by.

For my own part, I had enough cheese to feed my family for a month but precious little to sell on to other townsfolk. Now that all routes out of town were closed, I was beginning to rue the fact that I had not made a bigger effort to recover some of the cheese that lay with my broken cart in Hunsterson.

The town had been uncharacteristically quiet since my return from Barthomley, so I had concentrated on spending time with my family. Mrs Padgett had scolded me for missing the Christmas festivities, which she had enjoyed on her own with Amy, but she had expressed herself relieved to see me return safely, as did Alexander and his family. Word had spread quickly about the events in Barthomley, so both Alexander and Mrs Padgett had been concerned for my safety, especially when the news began to spread about the battle that had taken place in Middlewich. They were also pleased to see Simon was safe, although Alexander showed some concern when I told him about Nuttall.

Simon himself had taken care not to be seen out and about. When we arrived back, he took himself off to his house, and I hadn't seen him since. I assumed the leather pouch with Hamilton's letters had been hidden somewhere safe, but I made it my business not to inquire as to where.

Meanwhile, notice of our impending meeting with George Booth had arrived the previous evening. A messenger boy had knocked on our door some time after dark and delivered a hastily scrawled note from Simon, bidding me to present myself at the Colonel's quarters in The Lamb at 10.30 am the following day.

The inn was a hive of activity when I arrived, bustling and busy with soldiers going to and fro, preparing themselves for the siege. When I presented myself, I was ushered into a small drawing room, where I found Simon already sat waiting. My brother gave me a nervous smile as I entered. We were clearly sat in Booth's operations centre, for a plan of the town lay open on the table and was covered in writing. A sentry stood guard by the door, watching us suspiciously. Presently, the sound of leather boots was heard from behind the door, and the Colonel breezed in. I was surprised to note that Booth, far from appearing distracted by the events in Middlewich, displayed an animated demeanour, as though the challenge posed by the siege had given him energy. This I took to be a good sign.

Booth smiled broadly. "Ah. The Cheswis brothers return," he said. "It is gratifying to see you both in one piece. I hear Barthomley has not been a place for the faint-hearted."

"No, colonel," replied Simon. "It has been the source of much evil these past few days."

"Byron has much to answer for," acknowledged Booth, "but I expected no less from him. No man of God should take pleasure in work like this, but he is a man who appears to enjoy such things." Booth gave me a sharp glance before continuing and Simon immediately caught on.

"There's no need to be on your guard, sir," he said. "I have fully apprised my brother of the situation. He is now working on our side. He can be trusted."

Booth looked at me askance for a moment and then nodded. "And Nuttall? What about him?"

"Nuttall's dead, sir. His throat was cut and his body dumped inside the church at Barthomley with the other victims of the massacre."

"So he didn't get through to Brereton. Did he talk, do

you think?"

"I don't know. He was certainly tortured, but it makes no difference. The papers we spoke of are safe."

Booth pursed his lips. "And what about you, Cheswis? Did you reach Sir William?"

"Yes, I did. He is now fully aware of the situation we find ourselves in. He asked me to tell you that he will look forward to taking possession of the documents once my Lord Hamilton has given his approval."

Booth nodded, seemingly satisfied. "These papers," he began. "I know not where you have secreted them, but surely they would be more secure under my safekeeping."

Simon's eyes flashed at me briefly, but his expression remained unchanged. "No, sir," he said, "Ralph Brett was under express orders not to pass this information on."

"But Brett is dead – you can pass these on to me."

Simon remained unmoved. "No, sir, Ralph was a loyal servant of the Duke of Hamilton and he engaged me as *his* loyal servant. You will get the papers soon enough. Besides, they are truly safer with us. What will happen if Byron takes Nantwich and you have these papers? They will fall once more into royalist hands. No, they are best kept in my safekeeping."

Booth looked slightly irritated and he slapped his gloves on the table in annoyance. "Very well, but both you and Mrs Brett are at risk. We don't know whether the murderer is still at large in this town."

"That is true," agreed Simon. "So what do you

suggest?"

The Colonel sat down at his table and leaned back thoughtfully in his chair, stroking his moustache.

"Here's what I think," he said, eventually. "I propose the two of you go and live in Mrs Brett's house for the time being until this matter is resolved. You can protect Mrs Brett from any further break-ins, and I will make sure a permanent sentry is placed at the front and back of the house."

Up to this point I had kept my silence and let Simon speak, but, faced with this outrageous suggestion, I had to step in and speak my mind. "I can't possibly agree to this, Colonel," I said. "I have a business to run, a family to look after, and I still need to fulfil my role as constable, not to mention the sentry duty I will be expected to perform."

The Colonel gave me an inscrutable smile and dismissed my objection with a wave of the hand. "That's true," he said, "but I'm more concerned about your individual safety and that of Mrs Brett. You will still be able to carry out your duties, but I need to be sure that you are all safe at night and not on your own outside of the main hours of daylight."

Ten minutes later, arrangements were in place for Simon and I to move into one of Elizabeth Brett's spare rooms, whilst a couple of soldiers were nominated as our permanent bodyguards. As I walked back to Pepper Street to gather my things, I wondered what Mrs Padgett would have to say about the nature of the arrangement. It was highly irregular, of course, but it did mean I would be able to spend more time in the company of Elizabeth Brett, the prospect of which, I admit, made me feel strangely pleased.

Surprisingly, Mrs Padgett did not seem in the least bothered at the prospect of me moving in with the young widow. It was, she reasoned, only a temporary abode, and, so long as I was there, I was out of the clutches of Alice Furnival. She even went to the trouble of helping me pack some clothes for my stay. Nevertheless, she made sure I realised what I would be missing by sitting me down with a warming bowl of her mutton pottage before allowing me to venture forth again into the snow.

It was with a certain degree of guilt, therefore, that, after dropping my bag off at Elizabeth Brett's, I decided that I should go and visit Alice. My promise to Hugh Furnival had been on my mind ever since my return from Barthomley, and it was beginning to weigh on my conscience that I had not yet got around to checking on her welfare.

Alice's brother-in-law worked in the legal profession and occupied a reasonably substantial residence on Mill Street, next door to the large brick mansion owned by the Wright family. On my arrival, I was shown into the drawing room by a lank-haired young servant, who promptly excused himself and left me to survey my surroundings. I was surprised at the nature of the furniture, which was modern and expensive-looking. There were several upholstered chairs and a gateleg table, next to which, against the wall, stood a fine carved oak coffer. Against the other wall, perched on a stand, was an intricately-designed tortoiseshell cabinet, which I presumed had been imported from southern Europe. On the walls, I noticed mounted candles in sconces with mirrors behind, whilst red silk curtains masked the windows. I was busy looking at the cabinet when Alice walked in.

"I see you are admiring my sister's taste in decoration," she said, announcing her presence.

"Your sister has very fine taste, my compliments to her," I said. "This cabinet is particularly beautiful."

"It's Italian, but purchased in London," she explained. "The house is newly decorated."

I was impressed and said so. "Your brother-in-law must be doing well to afford such luxury, especially in these difficult times."

"Edward is an excellent lawyer," said Alice. "There is always a need for good men in the legal profession."

I acknowledged this with a smile. "I have news from your husband," I said, coming to the point. "I saw him in Barthomley. He wishes you to know that he and your family are safe and that he will send further word to you once he is in Shrewsbury."

"You were in Barthomley?" she said, with interest.

"I have heard news that the Irish have laid waste to the village in a most cruel fashion, with many people killed. I hesitated to give these stories credence, but I was most worried, both for Hugh and my family."

"I have seen it with my own eyes," I said. "Twelve men stripped naked and murdered in cold blood. People who we grew up with. Reverend Fowler's two sons, Richard Steele and his boys, and my friends James Boughey and Richard Cawell."

Alice gasped and put her hand over her mouth at the mention of these last two names, as she had known them too when we were children.

"Poor James, poor Richard," she groaned. "How awful. And your family?"

"They are safe," I said. "Fortunately, my parents and George's family knew not to resist them. They have lost many of their possessions, but at least they are unhurt. Your parents are fine too. Stony Cross, it seems, was too far up the hill for the soldiers to be bothered with. By the time I arrived in the village, the soldiers had already left for Middlewich."

At that moment, I made a mistake I bitterly regret. I don't know what it was that made me react in that particular manner, perhaps it was the teardrops that had settled on her cheeks or the slight shudder in her voice, but I suddenly blurted out, "Oh Alice, don't cry."

This immediately made Alice burst into floods of tears, my reaction to which was to instantly take her in my arms and stroke her face as I would have done years before. I immediately pulled myself back, realising what I doing, but I feared I was too late. To my surprise, Alice tensed slightly, but didn't pull away, and smiled at me.

"I'm so sorry, Alice," I flustered, my face reddening. "I had no right to do that. You are another man's wife. I lost track of who I was for the moment."

"Daniel, it's alright," she replied. "There's no need to apologise."

"Yes there is," I insisted, horrified at my lack of decorum. "I should have behaved more appropriately. I have embarrassed myself and I should leave. However, your husband has asked me to check on your safety while he is away. I have promised him I will drop by periodically to make sure you are safe. If you need to contact me, you can leave a message with Mrs Padgett."

"Daniel, don't go," she implored, catching hold of my arm. It was too late though. I gently removed Alice's hand from my coat, thanked her for seeing me and stepped silently out of the front door. Once out on street I looked back and saw Alice staring at me through the window. I could have sworn there was a hint of a smile on her face.

As I walked back, my head was spinning in a whirlpool of mixed emotions. I was not happy about what I was feeling and cursed myself for my lack of control. However, there was something else that was bothering me. I had the nagging feeling that there was something about the building I had just left that was not quite right. My mind searched frantically for the answer, but I couldn't quite put my finger on it.

24

Nantwich – Tuesday, January 2 – Tuesday January 9, 1644

The next day, things started to get more serious for Nantwich. Firstly, the King's army took possession of Dorfold House, little more than half a mile from the sconce at Welsh Row End, and began to use it as accommodation for its officers, including, as it later transpired, Lord Byron himself.

The news that the house had been occupied without meaningful opposition was greeted with dismay by many in the town, not least because its owner, Roger Wilbraham of Dorfold, unlike his younger cousin and namesake from Townsend House, was a vehement supporter of the parliamentary cause and had already spent time in Shrewsbury as a prisoner of his Majesty. I wondered what humiliations he had been forced to endure, having had to submit to his home being invaded by a group of preening cavaliers.

The small company of soldiers sent out by Colonel Booth to guard Acton's church fared somewhat better. Under the command of Captain Sadler, the group defended the church bravely and with no little skill, despite being fired upon by royalist cannon. They even managed to kill the canoniere and several other soldiers, including some who'd taken refuge in a dwelling by the church. Unfortunately, they also killed the widow who lived there and five others living nearby.

Faced with increased pressure from Byron's men, Colonel Booth issued orders that the earthworks should be maintained day and night by soldiers and townsfolk alike. Even the women were told they needed to defend the town if necessary and were put on standby to line the walls with pans of hot brine, especially in the areas within a hundred yards or so of the wich houses, from where brine could easily be brought.

It was also the first full day of my sojourn in Elizabeth Brett's house. Simon and I shared the bedchamber normally occupied by the youngster, Ralph, whilst the boy moved into his mother's room. My brother and I took turns to use the room's only bed, the other sleeping on rushes on the floor. We soon started arguing, for Simon is one of the untidiest people I know, and it was not long before he had driven me to distraction by turning the room into a jumble of his clothing and other possessions. In the end, I developed the habit of tidying his clutter myself.

Colonel Booth, I was relieved to note, had kept his word and made sure two sentries were placed outside the house day and night, whilst soldiers guarding the earthworks to the rear of the Bretts' back yard were ordered to keep a special look-out to make sure that the house did not come under threat. Simon and I were even offered bodyguards to watch over us whilst we were at work and on sentry duty, although both of us decided that was taking things too far.

Mrs Padgett, meanwhile, having got wind of my secret visit to Alice, had changed her opinion and was now less than pleased with the arrangement.

"A man ought to be able to sleep in his own bed at night," she muttered when I dropped by to see her the morning after I moved in. "Your duty does not extend this far, living with a young widow when her husband is barely cold in his grave. It's morally wrong, so it is."

I suspected her reaction had more to do with her not having anyone to mother whilst I was away, and so I told her firmly to stop being such an incorrigible scold.

"It's only for a short time," I said, "and Simon is with me in any case."

As it happened, I saw very little of Simon during the following week, his absence at Barthomley having created a backlog at Simkins' workshop that required his almost constant presence there. I, on the other hand, had no cheese to sell and there was little I could do at the wich house. It was too cold to venture outside for no reason, and so the time between my constabulary and sentry duties was spent, for the most part, trying to amuse Elizabeth's young son.

I thanked God for the presence in the house of a spinning top with nine pins, which I set up in the hall, moving the table to one side. After an initial shyness, the boy eventually came out of his shell and spent many an hour whooping and bawling, as he sent the pins flying across the floor. Elizabeth scolded us playfully for making a mess of her hall, but she seemed glad that someone was able to occupy her child.

Considering she had just lost her husband, I found Elizabeth Brett to be most agreeable company. Being alone in her presence for hours at a time, I had to force myself to admit that I found her to be extremely attractive. I realised it was inappropriate to feel that way for a woman who had buried her husband but two weeks before. In any case, it would be impossible that she could return any such feelings at this stage, so I tried manfully to banish such ideas from my thoughts. After all, there was still the issue of Alice to resolve. I continued to be disturbed by my indiscretion of a couple of days previously and did not trust myself to act differently given the same situation again. Alice had, after all, been the love of my life, and her presence, it seemed, had always been there, getting in the way of any other relationship I might have wished to develop. It seemed hard to understand how this might change, given that she was now living in the same town. It was all very disturbing, so I tried to concentrate on other matters, which generally brought me once again to the issue of how to solve the mystery of the murders of

Tench, Brett, and Nuttall.

One afternoon, I was sat playing with Ralph and his ninepins when I caught Elizabeth watching us.

"I'm sorry," she said, her face reddening, "I didn't mean to stare. It's just that you remind me of my husband, the way you're playing with Ralph."

I froze and looked back at her, embarrassed. "I didn't mean to upset you," I said.

"How could I possibly be upset? I loved my husband and you've reminded me of happy times I had. How can I be upset about that?"

I thought about that for a moment. It felt strangely pleasing that I had elicited this kind of response from Elizabeth, but I didn't trust my emotions, so instead I opted for a strictly practical response. "Your life has been turned upside down, Mistress Brett," I said.

"Call me Elizabeth, please. Your brother does."

"Very well. Your life has been placed in turmoil with these events. Have you had any more thoughts about what you will do once this siege is over and the Duke of Hamilton's letters are out of your hands?"

"I don't know," said Elizabeth. "I had thought to sell the drapery business and use the money to set up a small haberdashery of my own. I have already had an offer from Gilbert Kinshaw to buy the business, once the current situation has stabilised. I have a mind to accept his offer."

There were absolutely no grounds for questioning

Kinshaw's motives in making such an offer, I reasoned, for Kinshaw was one of the town's larger merchants, with interests in several areas, not just salt. Nevertheless, this revelation intrigued me. Kinshaw had been present at William Tench's funeral and had drawn my attention to John Davenport's fraudulent misuse of walling rights. Now he was sniffing around Elizabeth Brett too. Could it possibly be that Kinshaw was the connection between Brett and Tench? I resolved to find out.

Over the course of the following days, news began to filter in from outside Nantwich, and it became clear that the royalists were tightening the noose around the town. On the 4th of January, a group of royalists besieged and captured nearby Doddington Hall, the hundred-strong force there succumbing with little resistance, despite having plenty of food and ammunition.

There was better news on the Saturday, when a group of soldiers from the garrison ventured outside the town and came back with seven of the King's carriages laden with goods and provisions. Celebrations did not last long, though, for the royalists were so enraged that they set fire to and destroyed a number of barns and cottages located just outside the earthworks.

During this period, I kept my promise to Hugh Furnival and visited Alice twice. On the first occasion, Alice's sister and her husband were present, so I was only able to communicate with her at the door, but on the occasion of my second visit on the following Tuesday, they were both out and I was invited in. Still feeling somewhat embarrassed, I began by apologising to Alice for my impropriety the week before.

"There is really no need to apologise, Daniel," she said. "I am flattered you still feel something for me after all these years."

I didn't know how to respond to this, so I simply said what I was feeling. "If only you knew how much I've torn myself inside out over that time," I said. I wasn't sure whether I had said the right thing, but Alice looked at me with an expression which I interpreted to be one of pity.

"I'm sorry it didn't work out for us," she said, "and I'm sorry you feel betrayed. The fact is, you weren't there, and I fell in love. Hugh has been a good husband to me, but it doesn't mean I don't still have feelings for you, even after such a length of time."

I was not sure whether this was what I wanted to hear or not. Perhaps she read as much in my face, for she quickly added; "I'm also sorry it has affected your life so much. Let us hope for a quick resolution to this war, so Hugh and I can return to Shrewsbury."

I nodded while simultaneously trying to read in Alice's face the meaning behind her words. Was she suggesting adultery? I couldn't be sure, but I dared not believe it either. My mind was telling me that Furnival had taken Alice from me in the first place, so there was no reason to feel guilty about taking her back. Nevertheless, the situation felt wholly improper. In the end, it was Alice who was first to speak.

"You seem to have a lot on your mind at the moment," she ventured.

"Yes. It's not just my fear of how this siege might end. I am entrusted with solving three murders and getting nowhere."

"*Three* murders?" she asked, raising her eyebrows in surprise. I realised I hadn't told her about Nuttall, so I told her the whole story, leaving out what Simon had said to me on our ride back.

"So you are concerned for your brother, too. Is there anything Brett, Nuttall, and your brother knew or were hiding from you? Hugh told me your brother is very politically aware and a fervent supporter of Parliament."

"Yes," I admitted, "although his support is based not particularly on religious grounds – more on support for the new political ideas promoting equal rights for all. As for whether he's hiding anything, I cannot say."

Alice nodded and then said, "If you ever feel the need to get any of this off your chest, you'll always find a welcome here, Daniel."

"I know," I said, and was grateful for the offer, although I own that my gratitude was far outweighed by my consternation as to what such a welcome might entail, and whether Hugh Furnival might approve of such an arrangement.

I suspected he might not but was ashamed to find

myself wondering what it would be like to find out. It was not in my nature to cultivate such a relationship with a married woman, but the new, sophisticated Alice was as beguiling as the old one was sweet and innocent. I feared I was beginning to fight a losing battle.

25

Nantwich – Tuesday, January 9, 1644

I didn't have long to wait to get first-hand confirmation of Gilbert Kinshaw's interest in the Brett's drapery business, for shortly after my return from Alice's, Kinshaw's portly frame presented itself on Elizabeth's doorstep. My brother and I had been careful not to spread the word about where we were lodging, so Kinshaw was somewhat taken aback when he saw that it was I who had opened the door.

"Constable Cheswis," he said. "I did not expect to find you here. You are on official business, I take it?"

"Of course," I said, realising any other answer would provoke unnecessary scandal. "Mr Brett's murderer has not yet been apprehended and, until he is, Mrs Brett is in danger. My brother and I are providing the necessary security."

Kinshaw looked knowingly at me. "And the two soldiers on guard outside? Why are they there, may I ask?"

"That question you had best address to Colonel Booth," I answered. "It was he who provided us with the sentry guard. And what can I do for you, Mr Kinshaw?"

"I would speak with Mistress Brett," he replied, attempting to propel his considerable frame through the doorway. "I have business to discuss with her."

I blocked him off; no mean feat, as he was considerably heavier than me. "If this is about purchasing her husband's business," I said, "it is less than a month since he died, and you have made no appointment. Could you not perhaps show a little more consideration and wait outside? I will check whether she's available."

Kinshaw glared at me, the colour rising in his cheeks. "Not that it's any of your business, of course, but as you appear to already know about my affairs, I should point out that this issue has already been discussed with Mrs Brett. I merely wished to make sure that the continuation of the business is assured and that Mrs Brett receives a fair price for her assets," he said.

Before I could offer a sarcastic riposte, Elizabeth had appeared in the doorway behind me. "Let him in, Daniel," she said, and I reluctantly stepped aside. I stood over by the wall and waited for Kinshaw to speak.

"He is staying here?" asked the merchant, straightening his doublet and clearly trying hard not to lose his temper. Elizabeth ignored the question.

"This won't take long, Mr Kinshaw," she said, calmly. "I haven't yet made a final decision on my husband's affairs. I would like a little more time to consider your proposal, if I may. There are some issues that need to be resolved before I can make a final decision, and the speedy completion of these is not being helped by the current predicament this town finds itself in. I will certainly take due account of your kind offer, but perhaps if you were to return, say, in three weeks' time, I may have better news for you."

Kinshaw gave a gruff acquiescence. "Please don't take too long about it, Mrs Brett. The offer won't be there forever." With that, he turned on his heels and made for the door.

"Just one moment, Mr Kinshaw," I said, barring his route to the exit. "I have a couple of questions, if I may."

"Very well. Be quick about it then," he said. "I don't have all day."

I took a deep breath. "The last time we met, we were at the funeral of William Tench, where you spoke of a potential fraud carried out in relation to walling allocations by a man who appears to have been blackmailed by the murder victim. Despite this, no action has been taken as yet by the Rulers of Walling against John Davenport. Now you appear at the house of another victim's wife trying to carry out a business deal. Tell me, Mr Kinshaw, what is the connection between William Tench and Ralph Brett?"

Kinshaw gaped at me, eyes wide open. "You think I had something to do with these deaths?" he blurted. "I'd be very careful what you say if I were you, Master Cheswis. My dealings with Mrs Brett are strictly on a business footing. I have interests in the drapery trade, and so I see advantages in buying Mrs Brett's business. Davenport, meanwhile, will get what's coming to him in due course, believe you me." And with that, Kinshaw stalked out of the door, slamming it behind him, leaving Elizabeth and I staring at each other, dumbfounded.

Kinshaw's curiously outlandish response was one of the things I discussed with Alexander that evening over a tankard of strong ale in The Red Cow Inn, a busy and well-appointed tavern located on Beam Street, about halfway between my friend's house and my own temporary abode. I had not seen Alexander for several days, and at first he was somewhat perplexed at my insistence that he should call for me at the Bretts' house and accompany me home afterwards. Unfortunately, the need to keep Simon's secret precluded me from giving Alexander an explanation of my reasons for taking such precautions, although he freely accepted that my safety would be significantly easier to secure if I was to remain in the company of somebody of his physical stature. The atmosphere in the tavern was lively, but we managed to find a quiet corner by the door where we could not be overheard.

At first, our conversation focused on the enquiries I had asked Alexander to make regarding my suspicions that James Skinner had been stealing my cheese, and it quickly became clear that my friend had drawn a blank on that score. Skinner's family had a reputation for being rough and ready, but no-one appeared willing to say anything against the youngster.

"I would forget about it, if I were you, and concentrate on more important things," said Alexander. "He's probably pinched some cheese for his immediate family, but there's nothing you can prove."

I thanked Alexander for his efforts. To be honest, I had almost forgotten about my suspicions, and, after all, it would have been churlish of me to have accosted someone who had saved my life over the paltry matter of a few pieces of cheese. Our conversation eventually moved on to more important issues and, more specifically, Kinshaw's curious behaviour.

"From what you say, there is absolutely no evidence connecting Kinshaw to these murders," said Alexander, in between mouthfuls of bread and roast meat. "The only thing that can be proved is that both Kinshaw and Tench knew about Davenport's fraud and that Tench is dead."

"Quite," I agreed, "and the fact that Tench is now dead is perhaps a good reason why Kinshaw hasn't acted on the fraud accusations. He would not want to become embroiled in blackmail allegations."

"That's true. How does Brett fit in, do you think?"

I could not, of course, answer this question without imparting knowledge that it was safer to be ignorant of and which I was, in any case, not at liberty to divulge, so I simply told Alexander that I had discovered that

Brett, Nuttall, and Simon had been privy to information of importance to Parliament, which was why the Bretts' house was under protection.

"It's for the best you know no more than that," I said to Alexander, who looked at me doubtfully. "What we need to establish is who is behind the plot to target his wife and friends."

"Which brings us back to Kinshaw."

"Exactly," I said. "The connections between Kinshaw and the first two victims are strange and appear unrelated, but they do give him a motive, blackmail in one case and pecuniary gain in the other."

"But if Kinshaw is involved, and for these reasons, the issue of the crimson scarf becomes a mystery. There is no reason to suspect him of being a royalist intelligencer."

"That's right. The same applies to Nuttall's murder. To draw a connection with Kinshaw, we would need to show that Kinshaw was not around on December the twenty-third, the day of the atrocity in Barthomley."

"Not necessarily," pointed out Alexander. "We know that Bressy is the murderer's hatchet man. He was certainly outside of Nantwich on the twenty-third. What's more, only he and Hulse were around when they tried to murder you. It does not follow that the third member of this group had to be present when Nuttall was murdered."

I mused on this for a moment and had to admit that Alexander's logic was impeccable. "Kinshaw is not the only suspect, though," I said. "The other conundrum is Maisterson and Wilbraham and their group of clandestine royalists. They insist that their motive is only to protect their property and that they don't know anything as far as the killings of Tench and Brett are concerned."

"And yet Maisterson clearly knows that Tench was a scout."

"Yes, but they won't discuss this any further with me."

"Don't you find that suspicious?" asked Alexander, pushing the remains of his food away and belching loudly.

"I don't know. Yes. Maybe. His wife works for Randle Church, so perhaps it's not so surprising Maisterson and his group knew what he was up to, and, if their true motive is simply to protect their property and status, it would be understandable if they didn't want to draw attention to the fact they knew about his activities. There's something odd about Tench, though. He doesn't fit in. He seems to have been acting largely on his own, but there must be a connecting factor between him and everybody else."

"What about Tench's wife? Did she reveal anything when you spoke to her?"

"No," I replied, "but I can't help feeling that she's important in some way. There's something I've missed, but I can't quite place it."

Alexander wiped his mouth with his sleeve and leaned back against the wall on his stool. "Then you need to find out what the connection is," he said, simply. "I take it this means you need me to make some discreet enquiries?"

"Indeed I do," I said, beckoning over a serving girl to refill our tankards. "I need you to look into all business, political, or personal connections between Kinshaw, Maisterson, Wilbraham, Lady Norton, Randle Church, and all of the victims, to see if any as yet unknown link can be established."

"Leave it to me," grinned Alexander, evidently delighted to be given this responsibility. "We may not have found your cheese thief, but our murderer may yet be within our grasp!"

26

Dorfold House, Cheshire – Wednesday,
January 10, 1644

The man who would become known as the "Bloody Braggadoccio" looked through the upstairs window of the fine red brick mansion he occupied and contemplated the scene developing below him. Lord John Byron had been well-ensconced in the comfortable surroundings of Dorfold House for several days, much to the chagrin of its owner, Roger Wilbraham of Dorfold, who stood in the courtyard in front of the house, remonstrating loudly with one of Byron's captains and gesturing towards an artillery train, which was making its way laboriously across the grounds of the house towards a gap in the trees and the field beyond. Seventeen pairs of oxen stomped and snorted, their chains rattling, as they dragged the great gun carriage carrying the cannon that would be used to pound the Nantwich defences. Behind it, following the deep ruts in the semi-frozen earth created by the first gun carriage, was a second train hauling a mortar. Accompanying both was the mass of humanity required to move and operate heavy ordnance

– gunners, fireworkers, drivers, pioneers, and craftsmen, all marching to positions behind the trees, where they would be in full view of Welsh Row.

Byron fingered his moustache and smiled to himself as he watched Wilbraham, who was almost incandescent with rage at the damage the artillery train was causing to his property. He had little sympathy for Wilbraham, for he was a traitor and deserved everything that was coming to him. However, Wilbraham was also a gentleman and, for that, against his better judgment, Byron had granted him the right to remain in his own property, whilst it was in use by his Majesty's forces.

Byron turned away from the window and focused his attention on the other matter of concern to him; namely, the whereabouts of Lord Hamilton's correspondence. He was not particularly enthused about the efficiency of the intelligence agent that had been entrusted to recover the letters. The agent's hired muscle had failed to find anything at Brett's house, and one of them, Hulse, had been stupid enough to get himself killed in trying to eliminate the Constable, whose persistence in trying to identify his agent had been a grave cause of concern. Still, Brett and Nuttall were dead, so the number of people with the knowledge and opportunity to do anything with the letters was rapidly decreasing.

Despite this, the Cheswis brothers were becoming a major thorn in his side. Byron had hoped his men would find what he had been looking for hidden in the depths of Greenbank Farm. However, Bressy and the other soldiers who had returned to the Cheswis's farm had ransacked the place from top to toe and still found nothing. The parents and the brother were clearly ignorant of anything to do with the matter, for threats to kill the children had elicited no information at all. They had searched the house and the cellars thoroughly, but to no avail.

Nevertheless, he reasoned, if the papers were not in Barthomley, it was comforting to know that they would, in all likelihood, still be in Nantwich. And if that was so, they would not be going anywhere. With a smile of self-satisfaction, he realised he had time on his side.

He had already issued a summons to Colonel George Booth to surrender the town, which, as he had expected, had been refused. He had heard that Fairfax had been despatched to Manchester and that he and Brereton would eventually arrive to confront him, but he knew this would not happen for at least two weeks. After all, Fairfax needed to rest his men and gather together enough foot soldiers willing to march with him and Brereton to Nantwich.

In the meantime, Byron's large ordnance would shortly be in place, ready to start raining fire and terror on the local townspeople. Byron was in no hurry. He would take his time and slowly bombard and starve the puritan rebels into submission. The raid on the King's carriages had been a setback, for sure, but the people of Nantwich could not hold out for ever, and, just when they had run out of food, ammunition, and will to fight, he would attack. All he had to do was to wait until his forces took over the town, which they surely would, then the Cheswis brothers would be captured and hung as traitors, and the King's letters would be safe.

27

I was in the vicinity of Welsh Row when the shooting began. The streets had been quiet, for by now most regular business in the town had ceased. Men no longer dared venture from the town walls for fear of an attack by the enemy, who were now encamped all around the town, their fires and tents visible for all to see. I had finished my sentry duty and was on the way back home for a meal and some rest, but decided to make a brief detour past my wich house to check it was secure. It was eleven o'clock at night, and the townsmen and soldiers I had left manning the earthworks were settling down for what they thought would be a peaceful night. I skirted the earthen walls until I came almost to the banks of the Weaver, keeping to the light provided by the torches on the walkway. I then headed down behind the wich houses on Great Wood Street and along the side of the common cistern, carrying my musket in front of me.

It was a dark night. The waning crescent of the old moon had not yet risen above the horizon, and the inky blackness of the brine lake gave off an aura of gloomy malevolence, relieved only by the occasional flicker of light emanating from the taverns on Welsh Row. I had just finished checking the locks on the door of my wich house, when the brooding silence was broken by a deafening boom coming from the direction of Dorfold House.

I stopped in my tracks and instinctively cupped my hands over my ears, realising immediately the significance of what I had heard – mortar fire. I looked over the roofs of the buildings on Little Wood Street and noticed that the sky was filled with glowing orange lights, which were getting nearer by the second. Meanwhile, shouts of alarm were heard from the earthworks to my right, and I realised that the royalists were shooting large, red hot iron bullets into the town. I barely had time to react before one of the red balls thudded into the ground twenty yards to my left. Three more splashed into the cistern, whilst numerous others buried themselves into the wich houses on the other side of the water.

Once I was sure all the bullets had fallen to earth, my first reaction was to run through Strawberry Hill and onto Welsh Row, where people had already started to mill out onto the street. Brine workers, many of them women, were emerging from the tenements, buckets in hand, heading for the timber wich houses on Little Wood Street.

"Check for fire!" shouted someone. "Line up with the

buckets by the cistern." I gazed into the gloom and saw the familiar figure of John Davenport organising the workers into teams. I knew only too well the urgency of the situation. If one of these wooden buildings caught fire it would only be a matter of minutes before the whole street was ablaze.

A couple of minutes later, the booming report of the mortar was heard again. This time, though, the bullets rained down on an area closer to the edge of town. I joined the queue of brine workers by the cistern and helped pass buckets along a line to extinguish a small fire in one of the wich houses. However, after ten minutes or so it became clear that my fellow brine workers had events under control. I thought to return home to the relative safety of Pepper Street, but something told me to head up Welsh Row to where the bullets were falling with increasing regularity. As I made haste in the direction of the sconce at Welsh Row End, I heard several more explosions and was forced to take refuge behind a wall as the glowing red balls flew over my head.

As I passed the gates of Townsend House, a figure darted down the pathway and tried to hail me. I waved as I recognised the squat, bearded figure of Will Butters.

"What's the matter, Will?" I shouted.

"We need help, Master Cheswis," he called, the urgency etched in his voice. "The shot these cavalier bastards are sending over has set fire to a hovel of kidds. We need to put it out or the whole damned building will go up in smoke." I followed Butters round the back of the house, and, sure enough, a wooden shack full of faggots used for fuel had caught fire and was burning merrily. Worse still, the wind was throwing red hot smuts in the air and blowing them in the direction of the house.

Thanks to Will's efforts, a number of people from nearby houses had already appeared in the grounds of the house and were frantically passing buckets of water along a line to extinguish the flames. Among them, I noticed, were many women brine workers, including John Davenport's daughters, Margery and Martha. I also noted the presence of Robert Hollis, the owner of the barn near to where Tench's body had been found, Edmund Parker, the landlord of The White Swan, and Edward Yardley, who, like me, appeared to have just finished sentry duty.

"Christ's robes, Will," I said, as another explosion reverberated in the distance. "This is the very image of hell. Where is Roger Wilbraham?"

Butters paused to watch a shower of bullets fly overhead, several of which buried themselves in the ground nearby, causing the train of helpers to dive for cover.

"Master Roger retired to his bedchamber this morning, sir," shouted Butters, trying manfully to make himself heard above the commotion. "He has a sore fever and has not been able to venture forth without being overcome by uncontrollable shivers. He's heazing like a dog, sir, if the truth be told. The doctor has already been to attend to him and has administered what medicine he can but he'll be bedfast for a day or two yet, I'll warrant."

"If anything is guaranteed to raise him then this is surely it," I said, ruefully. "This is enough to raise the dead."

Cursing, I joined the train and started passing water rapidly along the line. Meanwhile, many more people had seen the fire and were flooding into the grounds, so that within the next ten minutes several human chains had formed, each passing buckets along as they attempted to put out the blaze. Every couple of minutes or so a fresh boom reverberated across the countryside, forcing everybody to take cover behind walls, round the side of the house, or curled up on the ground.

After a while, it seemed that the shots were getting more frequent and more targeted, and we realised with horror that Byron's gunners had seen the fire and were deliberately trying to kill the people putting it out, men and women alike.

"Sweet Jesus," growled Butters, as we took cover yet again. "These Irishmen are nought but a bunch of barbarians. God help us if they break through our walls. If they're prepared to shoot at innocent women now, what kind of mercy can we expect, if we let them break this siege?"

I nodded in agreement and scrambled to my feet again as soon as the barrage of bullets stopped.

Eventually, almost imperceptibly, the fierceness of the blaze started to abate, and at last it began to feel like the fire was under control. This was just as well, because we had been there the best part of an hour, and many of the people tending the blaze were beginning to show a dangerous degree of nonchalance towards the missiles that were being propelled towards us. As the flames began to die down, I found myself stood in the human chain next to Margery Davenport. In between passing buckets of water across, I called to her and asked how her father was faring.

"A little improved, thank you," replied the girl. "He is better for being out of jail, but he is still morose and depressed. I can't say why. It's a mystery to us."

I began to wonder whether it would be ill-mannered to ask Margery how much she was aware of her father's activities whilst he'd been a Ruler of Walling, but, as fate would have it, all such lines of enquiry became superfluous, for at that moment, something happened that will live with me for the rest of my life. Once more, we heard the boom of the mortar as the gunners completed their firing cycle, but this time, for some reason, perhaps it was fatigue, we carried on passing water to each other without having a care for the red hot lumps of metal that were heading our way. I turned away from Margery to grab the bucket from the person on my left and heard a brief whistling sound next to me, followed by a dull thud. As I turned back to face Margery, I was confused to find she was no longer there. I looked down and realised with horror that she was lying on her back at my feet. A piece of cannon-shot the size of an egg had hit her full in the chest, and blood was pumping out of a gaping wound in her breast. She tried momentarily to get up, but couldn't, and collapsed, motionless, as her life blood ebbed away into the snow.

There was a moment of shock as people took in what had happened, followed by a piercing shriek as Martha rushed over to where her sister was, her face as white as a sheet.

"Margery, Margery!" she howled, before turning helplessly to the crowd of onlookers. "Somebody get a physician," she wailed, but everyone could see that such action was pointless. I bent down to help Martha up and lead her away. Meanwhile, Will Butters stood and watched, with a face like death, as the dull red piece of metal that had killed my friend's daughter lay hissing in the snow.

Twenty minutes later, John Davenport stood by the rear wall of Townsend House with his fist in his mouth, silently weeping over the inert body of his daughter. Margery had been laid to one side of the gardens with a sheet over her, whilst her father was fetched from Little Wood Street. Martha, meanwhile, was led home to her mother. My friend cut a lonely figure as he stood sobbing in the shadows cast by the Wilbrahams' great house, his back illuminated by the flickering glow from the fire, which had still not quite been extinguished. His body heaved as I approached him, and I laid my hand on his shoulder.

"I'm so sorry, John," I said. "I was with her when she died. She was standing right next to me. I don't think she felt anything."

Davenport looked up as I touched him and grimaced, anguish etched on his features. "This is all my fault, Daniel," he lamented. "Divine providence is what it is. The Lord knows I am guilty of something I shouldn't have done, and now he is punishing me."

"You must not allow yourself to believe that," I insisted. "This is due to the King and his murderous artillery. No-one else. You can't blame yourself."

"Oh, but I do," said Davenport, "and I shall be damned for evermore for my sins."

"Not if you believe what the puritans say," I ventured. "They would have you believe that if you are destined to be damned, you will be damned whatever you do, but if you are to be saved, what you do has no import whatsoever."

Davenport snorted and turned to look at me through narrowed eyes. "Damn the fucking puritans," he seethed, "and damn the cavaliers too. Just wait until I get hold of the bastards who did this to Margery. Someone will pay for this, dearly." Behind me, buckets were still being passed urgently along the line of people stretched across the lawn. Several of them turned round, staring as Davenport spoke, for his voice had risen to a dangerous level. I put my hand on my friend's arm to calm him, but he shook it off with a shrug.

"I'm sorry, Daniel, I'd like to be on my own if I may," he said, stalking off down the garden in the direction of the outhouses, pigsty, and stables. Reluctantly, I let him go and set about helping the others sort out the fire, which was still angrily spitting embers into the air.

The royalist bombardment carried on for at least a couple of hours more and was not just limited to Welsh Row. Cannonballs were also shot over the river, damaging properties in Barker Street, High Street, and Pillory Street. One crashed into the stables at The Crown and killed a couple of horses. People were consequently out and about in the town putting out fires until three in the morning. Eventually, the blaze at Townsend House was extinguished, but the pile of kidds was burned and useless.

After a while, I noticed Davenport walk past me, head down and with a preoccupied look on his face. Making sure he kept himself apart from the remaining helpers, he sat down on a garden wall, oblivious to what was going on around him, and started talking to himself in low muttering tones. I decided to leave him alone in his grief and surveyed the scene around me.

There seemed to be little more that I could do that evening. The bombardment had finally died down, allowing the exhausted townsfolk to slowly filter away back to their own houses. I was just about to head back home myself, when I became aware of a commotion emanating from round the back of the stables. Suddenly, a couple of male servants came running round the front of the building.

"Constable, come quick," one of them shouted. "There's something you should see."

With a sigh, I allowed myself to be led wearily round the back of the house and into the stables. The horses were whickering nervously. One of them was sweating and kicking out at the wall. Clearly, something had disturbed them. After being in the brightness of the snow and the firelight, I had to adjust my eyes to the dark in the dingy stable block. However, I was gradually able to make out shapes in the corner of the building. The servants pointed out what looked like a sack of vegetables, but as my eyes adjusted to the dark, my heart lurched and I groaned with horror, for I realised I was looking at the dead body of Will Butters, his throat neatly cut from ear to ear.

Perhaps it was the incessant and debilitating boom from Byron's mortar that disoriented me so, or maybe it was just the sight of so much gore in such a short space of time, but I must have been standing in silence for fully two minutes contemplating the bloody scene in the stables before I came to my senses. As my eyes got used to the light, I could see that the stable floor had begun to resemble the interior of a butcher's shop, for Butter's blood had flowed freely, soaking his shirt and jerkin, and had seeped into the piles of straw covering the floor where he lay. It was not until one of the servants, both of whom had been shuffling their feet nervously, coughed lightly and asked what I would like them to do, that I managed to pull myself together.

I quickly sent one of the servants into the house to fetch an oil lamp, instructing him not to reveal the atrocity that had just happened to those still milling around the garden. When he returned five minutes later, I set about inspecting the gruesome-looking cadaver that now lay before me. The stables were bathed in a dull, unearthly light, accentuating a strange aura of malevolence that seemed to have pervaded the area. The atmosphere was made even more unsettling by the strange angle of Butters' neck, which made him look as though he had just been cut down from a gibbet. In the chaos and commotion of the evening, I had not noticed when Butters had taken his leave of the firefighters on the lawn, but, bending down to inspect the gaping wound in his throat, I realised that the attack had only just happened, for the body was still warm, and the bloodstains that drenched the victim's shirt were still wet and bright red. I also noticed with interest that the murderer had left no crimson scarf this time. Perhaps, I speculated, the perpetrator had been forced to leave the scene of his crime in a hurry.

"How did you discover him?" I asked, turning to the

two servants, who had introduced themselves as Thomas Dodd and Joseph Rowley.

"We had both been cleaning the kitchens, sir," said Dodd, a muscular, sandy-haired man in his mid-twenties. His colleague, a callow-looking youth in his late teens, looked on nervously, biting his nails, not sure where the conversation was heading.

"Why so late?" I asked.

"We'd been patrolling the walls all evening, like yourself," came the curt response. "It's the only time we could get to do it. Our responsibilities in this house don't end just because George Booth tells us we need to stand on the earthworks in the freezing cold for hours on end. After that, of course, we had been helping to put out the fire with the other servants. Once it became clear that the fire was under control, we went back inside to finish our duties."

"And what happened next?" I pressed.

"The kitchens at Townsend House open out to the rear of the house," explained Dodd. "I had just opened the back door, as I was planning to take some food scraps out to the pigs, when I thought I saw a movement over by the stables. A few seconds later, I heard the sound of struggling and a crash as though men were fighting. I called for Joe here, and we went over together to investigate. We'd just entered the stables, when a figure appeared out of the dark like a bat out of hell – barged straight through between us, he did. We had no time to react, otherwise we'd have given the villainous malt-worm a good kicking. Raddled his bones good and proper, we would have."

"That's right, sir," added Rowley, encouraged somewhat by his friend's bravado. "The bastard disappeared in the dark round the side of the house. We came in here and found Mr Butters like this."

"Were you able to see what this man looked like?" I asked, more in hope than expectation.

"No, sir," said Dodd. "'Tis a matter of regret, but it was too dark, and he was too quick. He didn't seem to be a very big man, though. Although he was plenty agile enough, that has to be said."

Having extracted all the information I could out of Dodd and Rowley, I decided it would be for the best to get the body out of the stables. So Dodd and I carried Butters outside, with a view to lying him on the ground next to Margery Davenport, whilst Rowley was dispatched to find the coroner. By the time the body had been brought around from the stables, though, the people at the front of the house had begun to realise what was going on, and a general hubbub had started to build. I looked into the crowd and was relieved to note that Alexander Clowes had turned up.

"I heard what had happened to Miss Davenport and figured you might need me," he said, simply, as he lumbered over towards where I was standing.

"Thanks," I said, with gratitude, "You can start by

helping us with this body."

Alexander took one look at Butters, and his face turned grey. "Zounds, Daniel, is there no end to this?" he exclaimed, looping his formidable forearms around Butters' shoulders and allowing me to take one of his legs from Dodd. Butters was quite heavy to carry all the way from the stables, even for three of us, but we completed the task as efficiently as we could.

Just as the body was placed on the ground next to Margery, I heard a voice from the crowd behind me. "Are you going to arrest the person who did this?"

I looked over to where the voice had come from and saw the perpetual smirk of Edward Yardley, who was looking at me intently from behind a group of women.

I hesitated. "At this point, I don't think we can ascertain-"

"You know exactly who is responsible for this," said Yardley, coldly, nodding to the hunched figure of John Davenport. The crowd were listening intently now, and all eyes turned to the brine worker, who was still sat on the garden wall, mumbling incoherently to himself. "We all saw him walk round the back of the house towards the stables, and you heard the threats he made – 'Someone will pay for this,' he said – and who was the person who brought his daughter here, who he'd blame? Will Butters, that's who."

A murmur went round the group, and Alexander shot me a quick glance. I had to admit that Yardley had a point, and yet I knew that Davenport was not responsible for Butters' death. Nevertheless, I sensed that the situation was becoming dangerous. Davenport also appeared to notice a change in the mood of the group and sat up suddenly, his face bearing a worried expression as he began to emerge from his trance.

"No, no, no," he said. "You've got it wrong. I just went round the back to have a few moments to myself. This has nothing to do with me!"

"Listen to him," said Yardley, warming to the task. "You've got the evidence you need. He's murdered William Tench, and now he's murdered Will Butters. Are you going to let him get away with this or is Davenport too much of a friend to you for you to do your duty?"

The crowd assented, and I heard a few shouts of "arrest him" and "stretch his neck, constable!"

"Of course I'm going to arrest him," I said, taking the bull by the horns and motioning to Alexander, who took a couple of rapid steps towards Davenport. The brine worker protested loudly as his arms were fastened behind his back.

"What are you doing?" shouted Davenport, fearful of the crowd. "This is nothing to do with me, I swear."

I walked over to Davenport and hissed at him under my breath. "Quiet, you fool. Can't you see when you're in danger? These people would have your neck in a noose in five minutes if I were not here. I know you're not responsible, but we need to get you out of here. Let's walk and I'll explain on the way to the jail."

"Not the jail, I can't go back there." Davenport started to protest, but Alexander had placed a knee in the small of his back and started propelling him towards the gate.

We were halfway down Welsh Row towards the bridge before anyone spoke, but it was Davenport, still struggling, who broke the silence. "Are you going to tell me what all this is about?" he hissed. "And are you going to untie me?"

Alexander waited until we had crossed the bridge before pushing Davenport up, face-first, against the wall of the first building on the East bank of the river.

"Stop your confounded struggling and listen to me," I said in exasperation, as Alexander held Davenport's arms behind his back in a vice-like grip. "I've just realised what's going on – something Yardley said. I know you're not a murderer, but you have to trust me on this. You are the prime suspect for the murder of Tench and Butters, and so for your own safety I'm going to have to lock you up again – but don't worry, I'll make sure your wife knows what's going on. In the meantime, I think I know how to get to the bottom of this mystery."

The jailer was not accustomed to being raised at three in the morning, so it took a little while before the heavily-bolted gate swung open and we were able to hustle Davenport in through the entrance.

"It is indeed a pleasure to see you again, Mr Davenport,"

said the jailer, with a wry smile. "Am I to assume you enjoyed staying here so much you couldn't keep away?"

Davenport said nothing, but stared coldly at the jailer through narrowed eyes.

"Just make sure you look after him and that he's kept in reasonable comfort," I said, pressing a shilling into the jailer's hand.

The jailer closed his fist around the coin and looked at me curiously. "The best that Nantwich can offer – just for you, Master Cheswis," he said, as he led Davenport, scowling, to his cell.

"Are you going to enlighten me?" asked Alexander, as we emerged into the cold night air.

"Certainly," I said. "It's obvious when you think about it. I don't know how I could have been so blind. When Yardley accused Davenport, he referred only to the murders of Tench and Butters."

Alexander looked at me nonplussed and scratched his forehead. "And the significance of that is what, exactly?"

"We've been blinded by the issue of the crimson scarf found on Tench, Brett, and Nuttall's bodies, but the truth is that the scarf is actually an irrelevance. Think about it. The scarf found on Tench's body was a ceremonial sash obtained somehow from Randle Church. The fact that it was found around Tench's neck is not necessarily an indication that he was murdered for his espionage activities. It may have been a ruse to make us think that. The next two scarves, on the other hand, were much more ordinary in nature. I believe the second two murders were made to look like they were committed by the same person as the first, probably to confuse us. No wonder we have had difficulties in working out Tench's connection with Brett and Nuttall."

"You mean, you think we're looking for two unconnected murderers?"

"Precisely. I don't know who committed these murders yet, or precisely why – or why John Davenport is being framed. But one thing's for sure. We have time on our side. Neither of the perpetrators is going anywhere. We just have to wait, and sooner or later, one or both of them will reveal themselves."

28

Nantwich – Thursday, January 11 – Thursday January 18, 1644

And so the waiting game began. I resigned myself to watching in anticipation for a sign that might lead me the murderers of Tench, Brett, Nuttall, and Butters, although, if the truth be told, my mind was more focused on the besieging force that sat menacingly outside the town walls than on making any more progress with my investigations.

Much of the following week passed by without major incident, although victuals were now beginning to become scarce throughout the town. The taverns had begun rationing ale, and food was rapidly running out for townsfolk and soldiers alike. There was also a desperate shortage of fodder for the livestock that had been brought inside the walls for safekeeping, and it was fast becoming clear that we would soon have to resort to killing our cattle and pigs, if we were not to go hungry. After that, it would be the turn of the horses.

As for Elizabeth, she was also beginning to run out of food, although she made sure as best she could that young

Ralph always had a full belly. The rest of us reduced our food intake to one meal a day, and as a result, I began to be aware of a constant gnawing hunger that plagued my insides. Nevertheless, I thanked the Lord, for I was better off than many, due to the store of cheese that I had managed to keep aside.

When I was not on sentry duty, I passed the time and took my mind off the hunger by playing with Ralph, who had become quite attached to me. Simon, for some unaccountable reason, seemed hugely amused by this and teased me mercilessly.

"You look like the proper family man," he said to me one morning, as I crawled across the hall floor with Ralph on my back.

"Nonsense," I said, allowing the boy to climb off and gesturing for him to run off to his mother, who was in the kitchen. "I just enjoy the boy's company."

"I can see that," said Simon. "Maybe when this siege is over you should marry Elizabeth."

"What?" I said, shocked. "Whatever has made you think that?"

"I'm teasing you, brother, but it's only half in jest. Have you not seen how Elizabeth looks at you?"

"Nonsense, man. Her husband's barely been buried a month."

"Just think about it, Daniel," said Simon, more seriously now. "Elizabeth is as sweet as a nosegay, I'm sure you'll admit. Many a man would be pleased to have her as a wife. I know she holds you in affection. Don't let an opportunity like this pass you by."

"Nevertheless, I scarcely think-"

"And if your reaction has anything to do with Alice Bickerton," he warned, "then I counsel you to think again. That women is married to Hugh Furnival, and whatever games she is playing with you, she has no intention of things being any other way than what they are. Don't be caught for a fool."

I considered what Simon had said. I had to admit that I liked Elizabeth, but Simon was right. As long as Alice was around, there was always going to be something inside me which would not let me free.

As January rolled on, the weather remained ice cold. Intermittent snow showers regularly topped up the white blanket that had covered the fields for nigh on six weeks already. It was a wearying experience, but the townsfolk understood that it would not last forever. It had become clear that the siege was turning into a battle of wills to see whether the town could last out until Brereton arrived with reinforcements. We realised that before he did, Byron would want to attempt to storm the town, and so a growing trepidation began to envelop the town as the certainty of an attack grew.

This belief was strengthened by a summons made by Byron to the townsfolk of Nantwich on Tuesday January 16th, which was read out by the town crier at different points in the town during the morning of that day. The first I heard of it was when I caught the familiar sound of Alexander's bell-ringing echoing down Pepper Street, calling people to meet in the square. When I got there, I found an expectant and somewhat animated crowd of several hundred souls consisting of townsmen, women, and soldiers bustling around the town crier, who, together with Colonel George Booth, was flanked by two halberdiers.

"These are the words of my Lord Byron," began the town crier as I took up a position behind a group of off-duty pikemen.

"A pox on the miscreant bastard," shouted one of them, to general cheers from his comrades.

"To the inhabitants and commanders of the town of Nantwich," continued the town crier, ignoring the interruption. "Whereas I am certainly informed as well by divers of the soldiers who are now my prisoners, as by several other creditable persons, that you are not only in a desperate condition..."

A chorus of jeers drowned out the town crier's next words, forcing him to stop his speech temporarily. "We'll manage," was the response from several people, whilst one of the pikemen in front of me bellowed; "Not as desperate as them sat out there freezing in the snow."

The town crier waited for the hubbub to die down and then continued. "...That you are not only in a desperate condition, but that the late summons I sent to the town hath been suppressed and concealed from the inhabitants thereof, and they most grossly abused, by being told that no mercy was intended to be shown by this army to the town, but that both man, woman, and child should be put to the sword; I have therefore thought fit once more to send unto you, that the minds of the people with you may be dispossessed of that false and wicked slander, which hath been cast upon this army."

Shouts of "not true" and "shame" filled the air.

"And I do charge you - as you will answer Almighty God for the lives of those persons who shall perish by your perfidious dealings with them - that you impart and publish the said summons I sent to the people with you; and that you yield up the town of Nantwich into my hands, for his Majesty's use, and submit yourselves to his Majesty's mercy, which I am willing to offer unto you. Though I am confident that neither by yourselves, nor by any aid that can come unto you, there is any possibility for you to escape the hands of this army. If you please to send two gentlemen of quality to me, the one a commander, the other a townsman, whereby you may receive better satisfaction, I shall give safe conduct and hostage for their return. I do expect a present answer from you - John Byron."

The crowd erupted in a barrage of obscenities at Byron's arrogance, but I noticed that not all the crowd were jeering. There were several worried-looking faces amongst the throng. Once the noise had abated somewhat, Colonel Booth stepped forward.

"People of Nantwich," he said. "You have heard Lord Byron's summons. In the name of God and Parliament, here is my riposte." The crowd fell silent again as Booth continued speaking.

"We have received your last summons, and do return this answer that we never reported, or caused to be reported, that your Lordship, or the army intended any such cruelty; we thinking it impossible for gentlemen and soldiers so much to forget humanity: and if any have informed you otherwise, it is their own conceit, and no reality. Concerning the publishing of your former summons, it was publicly read amongst the soldiers and townsmen, as your trumpeter can witness; and since that time, multitudes of copies of it have been dispersed among the townsmen and others; and from none hath it been concealed and detained."

"Too right it hasn't!" shouted one of the pikemen.

"For the delivery of this town, we may not with our consciences, credits, or reputations, betray that trust reposed in us, for maintaining and defending this town, as long as any enemy shall appear to offend it. Though we be termed traitors and hypocrites, yet we hope and are confident that God will evidence and make known to the world in his due time – though for the present we should suffer - our zeal for his glory, our unstained and unspotted loyalty towards his Majesty and sincerity in all our professions - George Booth."

Amidst unrestrained cheering at Booth's words, I

turned to my right and saw that Simon had appeared at my shoulder.

"Well, if it was not the case before, there will now certainly be a reckoning," he said, a hint of resignation in his voice.

"Aye, let us hope Brereton gets here in time," I replied.

The reading of the statements certainly seemed to have motivated the town, for, on the same day, several companies burst forth from the garrison to attack the King's army where they had built walls and dug in earthworks of their own, driving them away with the loss of only one man and gaining a considerable amount of clothes and ammunition. It was temporary comfort, though, for the cannonade from Dorfold House began again the following day, striking fear once more into the hearts of the townsfolk.

Byron's men must have discharged their cannon nearly a hundred times and, although the artillery fire did not cause much damage to property, the intention was obvious. At daybreak on the Thursday morning, therefore, the townsfolk of Nantwich waited for the assault they knew would shape their future.

It was five in the morning. The air was icy cold but perfectly still, as every spare man – soldier and townsperson alike – stood in the grim darkness of the pre-dawn, ready to face the anticipated onslaught, the earthen walls illuminated only by the line of torches which flickered intermittently along their perimeter. Most men stood on the walls and in the sconces at the end of each street, chatting quietly or smoking their clay pipes. The tension was palpable. With the town having turned down Byron's summons and suffered a day of bombardment, it was clear that an attack was imminent and the most likely time for that was dawn.

I had been sent to a position in Wickstead's sconce, so named because it was next to the garden of Richard Wickstead, one of the town's leading merchants, and was located down by the river on the North side of Welsh Row. Simon and Alexander were with me, as were many of the other recruits who had been trained up, including James Skinner and his brothers. In order to guarantee a force of equal strength along the town defences, the townsmen were interspersed with soldiers from the garrison, and I was glad to see the figure of Jack Wade on the wall next to me. Patrolling the wall behind him was Sergeant Bradshaw.

"So this is what it comes down to?" I said, by way of greeting.

"Don't be misled by the size of their force," said Wade, gesturing into the gloom beyond the walls, where, despite the darkness and the freezing mist hanging like a pall over the river, the royalist soldiers could be seen manoeuvring into position along the river bank. "These walls are built to hold. I'll wager these Irishmen have bitten off more than they can chew."

"Let us hope that that is so," I said.

The garrison soldiers and the male townsfolk were not the only people on the walls, though. The women of Nantwich were also prepared to fight. In anticipation of the struggle to come, the wich houses along the side of the river had begun to boil brine, and a team of women stood ready with buckets, waiting to fling the boiling liquid on any attackers. I looked over towards the Davenports' wich house and caught sight of Ann Davenport, her expression fixed in a look of steely determination, organising some of the women into a line, ready to pass buckets up the ladders to the top of the walls. I glanced to my right and caught sight of Elizabeth, who, having left Ralph with Mistress Johnson, was standing thirty yards away, ready for action at the top of one of the ladders.

The first we knew that something was about to happen was just after five, when a single piece of ordnance was discharged from Acton. Immediately, raucous shouts of "For God and King" echoed through the air, and groups of green-uniformed soldiers began to approach the walls. I noticed that many of the first wave of attackers were carrying scaling ladders. Intermingled amongst them were musketeers.

"Those are firelocks," said Wade, in my ear. I looked and saw he was correct, as no glowing match was visible to betray their location.

"Hold your fire – don't waste your musket balls," shouted Sergeant Bradshaw. "You'll barely tickle them at this range." The women, however, started to ferry buckets of brine along the line for the women on the top of the wooden platform.

Eventually, the firelocks arrived within range and quickly organised themselves into formation. We knew exactly what was coming next. When the royalists fired their first volley, we would have to duck, and that would be the cue for the other soldiers armed with scaling ladders and snaphanches to charge for the walls. Our orders were to shoot the attackers whilst they were within range, then let the women pour water on them once on the ladders. Each alternate man inside the sconce was to stand back from the edge and to blast any attacker who emerged over the top.

Simon and I managed to get a couple of shots off before the scaling ladders were put against the walls. I took aim at the firelocks fifty yards away and pulled the trigger, my nostrils filling with the now-familiar stink of sulphur. I glanced to my right and saw Skinner doing the same. Along the riverbank, a piercing scream went up, and one of the greencoats tottered and collapsed into the water. Despite a volley of fire from the firelocks, nobody was hurt in the sconce, although a ladder appeared to my left, as if out of nowhere. Simon and I tried to push the ladder over but couldn't do so without making my head a target for the firelocks below. With horror, I felt the ladder vibrate as one of the attackers made to climb up it.

Suddenly, I saw Elizabeth and another woman scuttle

between us and tip a bucket of water over the wall. With relief, I heard a blood-curdling yell from a few feet below as someone received a bucketful of boiling brine in the face. The women were now passing buckets along the line as fast as they could.

The shooting and the boiling brine were effective, but after a few minutes it became clear that the number of people climbing the ladders was too large. Suddenly, a shout went up as a hate-filled face appeared above the wall on the right of the sconce. Wade aimed his musket and fired. The musket ball hit the royalist just below the eye, and his head exploded in a shower of blood. For a split-second his destroyed face stared at us, then it disappeared over the edge, taking the next soldier with him.

More soldiers began to appear one-by-one, our musketeers shooting them as they appeared over the parapet. One stumbled into the sconce, fell to his knees and then tried to get up, but was smashed over the head by Elizabeth with her heavy wooden bucket. He was then run through by one of the soldiers with a sword. Anyone else who was lucky enough to escape a musket ball in our vicinity was clubbed by Alexander with the butt end of his weapon.

Things were happening so fast that it became difficult to keep track of what was going on, but it was clear that Wickstead's sconce was not the only place that was being attacked. Immediately across the river at Wall Lane, the earthworks were under attack from a regiment clad in bright red uniforms, whilst sounds from across the river to the right suggested that Pillory Street End was also coming under pressure. The melee inside Wickstead's sconce continued for nearly an hour, until the floor was littered with dead royalists. Meanwhile, the more fortunate ones who had been injured or surrendered had been hauled down from the sconce and were being guarded.

During a break in the assault, Wade and I looked over the parapet and saw the captain of the group of firelocks attempting to rally his men. Wade squinted and turned to me. "You know what," he announced, "If I'm not mistaken, that captain there is the same fellow who took Beeston Castle."

"Are you sure?" I asked.

"I'd recognise him anywhere," grinned Wade. "What I'd give to bag him."

I looked at the Captain just in time to see him rally his troops for an attack. At that point, a hundred firelocks all charged for the walls, and we braced ourselves for further hard work and bloodshed. I glanced to the right and saw James Skinner, his eyes fixed in concentration, step up to the wall as the Captain charged at the head of his men. He took careful aim and fired as the Captain got within fifteen feet of the sconce. The Captain stopped in his tracks, gave an audible gasp and grabbed at his stomach, before crumpling head first into the side of the earthworks.

"Captain Sandford's down," came a cry, and the rest of the flintlocks hesitated. The rest of us inside the sconce took aim and fired, three or four of the royalists falling under the volley. The rest took fright and retreated as fast as their legs could carry them, leaving the scaling ladders behind. These were rapidly hauled up by the townsfolk and soldiers, in order to stop any more assaults.

Sounds from other areas of Nantwich had also subdued and were being replaced by cheers and shouts of "For King and Parliament". It was clear that against all the odds, the royalists had been repelled from there too. Meanwhile, in the half light of dawn, we could see the royalists retreating in the distance, dragging their dead with them, although many dead and injured still lay on the ground outside the walls.

I looked over to see if I could find Elizabeth, for I'd lost track of her. To my relief, I found her collapsed, exhausted, against a wall, sweating profusely and breathing heavily, but safe. I had a quick look around and saw that there were a couple of injuries amongst the town's defenders, but miraculously, no-one in the sconce had been killed.

Skinner, meanwhile, was being congratulated by Sergeant Bradshaw for shooting Sandford, whose dead body was hauled up into the sconce and stripped. I walked over to inspect the corpse and noticed that several pieces of paper were sticking out of the dead man's pockets. I unfolded one of them and started to read.

"Fucking papist bastard," said Wade, aiming a kick at Sandford's leg. "Serves the motley-minded miscreant right."

"I wouldn't be so sure, Jack," I said. "Listen to this. Appearances can be deceptive."

I smoothed out Sandford's note and read it to Wade. "To the officers, soldiers and gentlemen in Nantwich : Gentlemen, let this resolve your jealousies, concerning our religion. I vow by the faith of a Christian, I know not one papist in our army. And, as I am a gentleman, we are not Irish, but true borne English and real protestants, born and bred. Pray you mistake us not, but receive us into your fair esteem and know we intend loyalty towards his Majesty and will be no other than faithful in his service. Thus gentlemen believe from yours, Thomas Sandford."

Wade snorted, but I could see I had made my point.

"Sandford was a brave man," I said, handing the letter to Sergeant Bradshaw. "It's a shame that such men have to die. A curse on this war." Shaking my head, I picked up my musket and headed towards the bridge."

29

Pendennis Castle, Cornwall – Thursday
January 18, 1644

*T*he Duke of Hamilton sat thoughtfully in his chamber at Pendennis Castle and stared out at the view over Falmouth. The weather in this far-flung extremity of England was wild and stormy, clouds scudding rapidly across the sky. A number of small boats at anchor on the Fal estuary bobbed precariously, the wind whistling past their masts. Behind them, on the east bank of the river, rising starkly against the angry sky, was the twin castle of St Mawes. The Duke sighed and contemplated the bad fortune that had plagued him in recent months.

Since he had been arrested and removed to Cornwall, he had been treated with respect and had enjoyed some degree of comfort. However, he had not been given any idea of when, and if, he was going to be released and feared he may eventually end up with his neck on the executioner's block, especially if his rival Montrose had anything to do with it.

The King, as he had expected, had been furious when the Duke and his brother, Lanark, had arrived in Oxford, and both had immediately been placed before a court of inquiry. He could not complain, of course. The inquiry had been carried out thoroughly and with dignity, but with the witnesses including Montrose himself and other Scottish noblemen of considerable standing, there was only ever going to be one outcome. His Majesty, to be fair, had shown a substantial degree of reluctance in banishing him to the depths of the South-West, but he had done it, nevertheless. Lanark, on the other hand, had fared better. Having managed to escape from custody, he had high-tailed it back to Scotland and had cast his lot with the covenanters.

Hamilton surveyed his surroundings. Pendennis Castle was a mighty fortress built by Henry VIII, consisting of a circular keep approached via a drawbridge and portcullis and surrounded by a lower curtain wall. The whole construction was defended by a formidable outer defence with angular bastions. The castle was considered impregnable, being constructed on a narrow headland on the west bank of the River Fal, and surrounded on three sides by sea. There was no way he was going anywhere. Reluctantly, he had accepted the necessity of the back-up plan that had been instigated on his behalf.

It had not been easy, but Michael Forbes, the loyal servant who had followed him to Oxford and then on to Cornwall, with the express intention of helping the Duke, should he be incarcerated, had managed to bribe one of the servants at Pendennis to smuggle a message inside and a sealed letter from the Duke out. Forbes was now on his way to Ralph Brett in Nantwich. If all went well, the King's letters would soon be in the hands of those that could make best use of them, and, God willing, he would be freed from his prison, to be one day, perhaps, heir to the throne.

30

*Nantwich – Thursday, January 18 – Wednesday
January 24, 1644*

Once the walls were secured, it did not take long before the full details of the royalists' abortive dawn raid began to emerge. Byron's men had attacked the town at five different places simultaneously, but, thanks to the bravery and discipline of the garrison force and our own redoubtable townspeople, they had been repelled everywhere, taking great losses. Overall, nearly four hundred royalists had died in the assault.

The largest slaughter had taken place at the sconce at Wall Lane End, where the bulk of Byron's red regiment had been destroyed. Many officers and men, including a Lieutenant-Colonel, had been slain or wounded and cast into the river, but around eighty had also perished at Pillory Street End, whilst lesser numbers died at the sconce on Hospital Street and at the end of Beam Street near Lady Norton's. Remarkably, only three townsmen had lost their lives.

A number of Byron's officers and men had also been taken prisoner, and from them it was learned that a substantial proportion of the royalist troops had deserted, despite the fact that the soldiers arriving from Ireland were battle-hardened and well-used to the discomforts of a winter siege. The revelation helped considerably towards sustaining the morale of those who were defending the town.

Despite the magnitude of the royalist defeat, though, the siege continued to hold, and the euphoria of the victory was very quickly replaced by the numbing realisation that nothing had really changed. Food was now dreadfully short, and much of that which was available was prioritised for the garrison soldiers, in order to keep them fit for fighting. The decision had been made to begin slaughtering the cattle that were being held inside the walls, and every second night a communal roast was organised, although the amount of meat per person was strictly rationed. Ironically, there would have been no shortage of salt, had there been any meat left for the butchers to preserve.

Hay was also in short supply and reserved for the horses, leaving the town's cattle with no food at all, although the townsfolk knew full well that, if the siege continued for much longer, there would soon be no cattle left for this to be a problem anymore. For the first time, with no-one able to get in or out of the town, the people of Nantwich started to wonder how long they could hold out.

Oddly enough, despite the effectiveness of the siege,

Hugh Furnival had managed to find his way back into Nantwich. The first I knew about it was when his newssheet, *The Public Scout*, started appearing around the town. Simon, being very attuned to such things, had seen it in one of the taverns and made a point of bringing me a copy. In it was a brief account of the murders of Brett and Tench, as well as various pro-parliamentarian reports on what was happening elsewhere in Cheshire and Shropshire.

The very next day, Furnival himself turned up at Elizabeth's house with Alice in tow, to thank me for my attentions while he was away. Knowing my partiality to such things, Alice brought a small pork pie with her, which was particularly surprising and very much appreciated, given the shortage of victuals in Nantwich. Her husband, she explained, anticipating the severity of conditions within the town, had managed to carry a limited amount of food in his baggage, and she had made sure to put a little aside for me.

"How did you manage to get past the royalist pickets?" I asked Furnival, amazed that he had managed to get through at all.

"It was certainly not easy," he answered, "but, when I arrived in Audlem, I heard about the bombardment and realised that an attack was imminent, so I took lodgings there and decided to wait it out. If it hadn't been for the fact that Alice was here, I would have gone back to Shrewsbury and waited for the siege to end. In the event, after their failed assault, I was able to use the confusion of the royalist retreat to ride through the line of fleeing soldiers."

I had to admit I found it impressive that Furnival had managed to achieve such a feat, but it was something I spent little time mulling over, for I had other things on my mind, not least the fact that I had made no further progress on the murders. There was no sign of Bressy and therefore no apparent threat to Simon and myself. Consequently, I had begun to come to the conclusion that he was no longer in Nantwich. At the same time, nothing had emerged to shed any light on the unfortunate circumstances in which John Davenport found himself. I was beginning to think that I was never going to get to the bottom of either matter, when suddenly, like a bolt from the blue, a breakthrough finally came on the Wednesday, six days after the royalists' disastrous assault on our town. It came as the weather broke to milder air and leaden skies, as if it had blown in with the breeze.

For weeks, the fields had been covered by a thick blanket of white. Even in the town, the snow had been a foot deep in places, piled up in drifts against walls and houses. Within a couple of hours, though, the snow had turned to slush and mud as the ground thawed. Great puddles lay everywhere, and the main thoroughfares turned to a morass of mud and filth. The Weaver, meanwhile, was slowly rising.

It was late afternoon, and I was with Alexander in the

main square mending the pillory, which needed new hinges, when a number of off-duty soldiers walked past. Amongst them was Jack Wade, who acknowledged me as he passed and came over for a chat.

"Good afternoon, Master Cheswis," he said, cheerfully, in his strange Birmingham accent. "It's not the weather for such work, I would suggest." I looked up at the sky and realised that it had begun to spit with rain. I needed to finish the repairs on the pillory quickly before it started to rain properly.

"Aye Jack, that's true," I replied. "but no better for soldiering either, I'll wager."

"You're in the right of it, sir," said Wade. "The earthworks are as slippery as the skin of an eel. I could barely keep on my feet this afternoon."

I spent a couple of minutes discussing the weather with Wade and was just about to continue with my repair and bid him good day, when Hugh Furnival walked past in the opposite direction and shouted a greeting to me. I returned the compliment and thanked him once again for the gift of the pie, of which I had made short work.

"Good afternoon, sir," chipped in Wade, who was staring at Furnival with a surprised look on his face. "I have not seen you around town before, but I am glad to see you returned from Beeston safely." Furnival stopped and squinted through narrowed eyes at Wade. For a moment, I thought Furnival didn't know the soldier, but suddenly his eyes widened in recognition and he said,

"Yes, thank you. I am well-recovered," before marching off down the High Street with an uncomfortable look on his face.

"You know him?" I asked Wade, my curiosity awakened by Furnival's strange response.

"Of course. He was the guest staying in the upper ward of Beeston Castle when it was attacked. I believe he is a relative of Captain Steele. At least, that is the argument Captain Sandford used as a bargaining tool to get Steele to surrender the castle. I haven't seen him since that day."

My heart jolted as I immediately realised the significance of what Wade was saying. I grabbed hold of him by the arm.

"Jack," I said, "think carefully. Can you remember which soldiers were on duty in the upper ward when it was invaded?"

Wade thought for a moment and said "I think so. There was Sergeant Wilkes, plus about seven sentries, Jack Bromley, William Sparke, Henry Pickering, Richard Clegg, John Williams, Nat Hulse, and Jem Bressy." Wade counted out the names on his fingers as he spoke.

"I knew it," I said, and turned to Alexander, who, in the meantime, had finished the repair to the pillory by himself. "I know who murdered Brett and Nuttall – who the third man is. It's Hugh Furnival. No wonder he managed to get past the royalist pickets so easily." With a flash of memory, I then realised what had been bothering me about Alice's sister's drawing room, and everything fell into place.

"My God! The curtains," I said, looking at Alexander's puzzled face and realising I had made no sense. "Alice's sister has new red silk curtains hanging in her drawing room," I explained. "I'll wager those curtains are a match for the material used in the scarves we found on Brett's body."

Alexander and Wade looked at me. "And I'll bet Furnival is the customer who Brett had planned to meet on the morning of his death," said Alexander, realising where my train of thought was heading.

"Precisely," I said. Then a thought struck me. "Alexander, Elizabeth Brett and Simon are in danger."

"But there are two sentries placed outside the Bretts' house," said Alexander.

"I know," I said, "but two sentries are not many, and Simon may not be home at this time."

I turned my attention to Wade, who was looking at us as though we were madmen. "Jack," I said. "I need your help. You must come with us. I'll explain on the way, but first we must pay a quick visit to Thomas Steele."

31

Nantwich – Wednesday January 24, 1644

Considering the misery of his circumstances, Thomas Steele appeared to be in a much more sanguine frame of mind than would have been expected, and I remarked as such to the Captain as I stood in the middle of his cell, the doorway framed by my two breathless companions.

"Gentlemen, I think you may be confusing ebullience with acceptance and resignation," said Steele, with a thin smile. "I am to be tried for treachery and will no doubt be found guilty of that accusation. Even if I could prove I did not surrender to Sandford out of treachery, I will still be found guilty of cowardice – so whatever happens, this sad state of affairs will cost me my life. That being the case, I see no reason for spending my remaining days in a fog of despair. I will soon be in the arms of the Lord, so that is certainly something to be joyous about."

I smiled, finding his acceptance both admirable and horrific at the same time. "Captain Steele," I said, coming to the point. "When Beeston castle was attacked, you had a guest staying in the upper ward of the castle.

Could you tell me who that was?"

"Certainly," replied Steele, "that was Hugh Furnival. He is a brother to my wife, Jane."

I remembered it now. Furnival did have an older sister, and I vaguely remembered her from my youth, a thin, pale-faced girl with angular features. I could have been no more than eight years old when she was married and left Barthomley for good. "Why do you ask?" he said.

I did not want to burden Steele with the knowledge that he was in jail on account of his brother-in-law's treachery. I was also aware of the pressure of time, so I avoided a direct answer.

"It is a long story, and I will return to relate it to you, but right now time is of the essence. I'm afraid I must leave you. We need to locate Mr Furnival as a matter of urgency."

"I understand," he said, looking at me curiously. "But promise me you will return. I enjoyed our conversation about the cheese business. Your enthusiasm reminds me of me when I was younger."

"I give you my word," I said, and headed for the door of the cell, my thoughts already on the whereabouts of Furnival and the safety of my brother and Elizabeth Brett.

Whilst we were inside the jail, the rain had begun to fall more heavily, and as Alexander, Wade, and I marched down Pepper Street and Beam Street in the direction of

Elizabeth's house, great globules of water splashed down on the cobbles, adding to the rivulets of melt-water which flowed into the central drain running down the middle of the street. One or two of the householders had used the novelty of running water as an opportunity to brush the filth from the front of their houses and stood with stiff brushes, directing streams of detritus into the sewerage channel. A trickle of water ran down the brim of my hat and down my neck. The downpour was soaking me to the skin, but at least, I conceded, the town would be cleaner for it.

When we arrived at the Bretts' house, we were greeted by a scene of confusion. One of the guards was propped up against the wall, nursing a head wound and holding a bloody towel to his head. The other soldier was standing on guard, whilst Elizabeth stood by the front door, talking in an animated manner with Mistress Johnson. I took one look at Elizabeth's face and realised she had been beaten too. Red marks were visible on her cheeks, and there was an angry-looking swelling underneath her eye, which she was dabbing gingerly with a handkerchief.

"Furnival," she said, simply, when she saw me coming.

"I know," I said. "What happened?"

"You'd better ask *him*," she said, glaring at the first soldier, whose eyes were staring sheepishly at me from behind the folds of his towel.

"Bastard hit me over the head, sir," he complained, his eyes flicking to and fro between Elizabeth and the second soldier.

"You mean you turned your fuckin' back on him, you beef-witted scut," growled the second guard. "I was round the back, sir," he explained, turning to me, "but, by the time I got here, he'd barricaded himself inside the house, with Mrs Brett."

I gave the first soldier a withering look of my own and turned my attention to Elizabeth. It did not take a genius to work out what had happened next.

"Did you tell him anything?" I asked, almost without thinking.

"No, of course not," retorted Elizabeth, her eyes flashing dangerously. "What do you take me for? Furnival wanted to know whether the documents were with Simon. I refused to answer, but he guessed the truth anyway."

"And how long did this take?" I asked.

"Not long. The soldiers managed to find a way in at the rear of the house, and Mistress Johnson heard the commotion and came running too, but, by the time they arrived, Furnival had made good his escape."

"And Simon is not here," I observed. "Do you know where he is?"

"Yes, he's with Rose Bailey."

"And does Furnival know this?"

Elizabeth grimaced and gave me a worried look. "I don't know," she said. "I certainly didn't tell him, but Furnival's demeanour was not of a man who was unsure of what he was doing."

I looked at Alexander, whose jaw was set with a look of grim determination.

"We must go, Daniel," he said, propelling his considerable frame through the front door, into the pouring rain, leaving Jack Wade and myself trailing in his wake.

Rose Bailey lived with her parents in the furthermost of the little row of cottages which stood next to the Bretts' more substantial brick house, so it only took a few seconds for us to splash our way through the puddles to get there. However, her front door stood ominously ajar, and, as we approached, a sharp clattering noise reverberated from round the back of the cottage, followed by a yell of pain and a gruff curse. Inside the building, muffled noises of alarm could be heard. Wade shot me a quick glance and reversed his musket, now useless in the rain, in order to brandish it as a club. Alexander, meanwhile, stepped forward and kicked at the front door, sending it flying back on its hinges with a crash.

At first, the main room looked empty in the dim candlelight, but, after a few seconds, a movement under the table caught my eye. I peered into the gloom and gasped as I realised what I was looking at. Sat facing inwards, each gagged and with their hands securely tied behind them around the table legs, were Simon, Rose Bailey, and her mother. I rushed over to the table with my knife and deftly sliced through the piece of cloth that bound Simon's mouth.

"It's Hugh Furnival," spluttered my brother, "and he's just left."

"We know," I said, as Alexander and Wade untied Rose and her mother, who began to draw great rasping breaths, and claw at her cheeks. Rose merely sat speechless, her eyes bulging from behind her mass of auburn curls.

"He's got the letters," persisted Simon, as he struggled to his feet, his hand rubbing the back of his neck in agitation. "We must get them back."

Furnival, it emerged, had entered the house with a pistol and forced Simon, at gunpoint, to tie up the two women, before being bound himself. He had then gagged Rose and her mother and threatened to cut their throats if Simon did not reveal the location of the letters. I thanked the Lord that Rose's father had been out manning the walls, for his presence would surely have resulted in bloodshed. I looked behind Simon and saw the raised floorboards, where Furnival had reached to get the pouch holding the King's correspondence.

"He was here only a couple of minutes ago," said Simon. "If we're quick, we can still catch him. I think he escaped through the back."

"What do you mean, we?" I said, with incredulity. "You're staying here. Take care of your woman; she needs comforting, and there are three of us."

Simon opened his mouth to protest, but at that

moment, the high-pitched tone of pistol shots resonated from behind the house, followed by a cacophony of angry shouting. Without a further word, Alexander, Wade, and I left Simon to care for the women and ran out through the back door, immediately tripping over a pile of kidds, which lay strewn across the cobbled yard. It had clearly been the sound of Furnival colliding with the stack of firewood that we had heard just before entering the house. Ignoring the mess, we charged through the morass that was the Baileys' backlands until we reached the earthworks, which ran fifty yards behind the house. Mounting the ladders to the wooden palisade, we observed several soldiers firing pistols over the wall into the distance.

"What's happened?" I shouted down to one of the musketeers, who stood, smoking a pipe, at the bottom of the ladder.

The soldier squinted up at me and blew plumes of smoke into the air. "They escaped over the side," he said. "We thought they were here for sentry duty, but they simply climbed the wall and slid down the earthworks. They were fifty yards away before we had time to react, and our muskets are useless. The matches are all wet." I glanced at the soldier's weapon, which stood propped against the ladder. The normally glowing matchcord had clearly long been extinguished.

"They?" I asked, catching my breath.

"There were two of them," said the soldier. "A man and

a woman, though at first I took the woman for a young boy, given the dark."

I peered into the darkness beyond the earthworks, and after a moment or so I was able to make out two figures making their way across Beam Heath towards the river bank. With a start, I realised that it was not only Furnival who had escaped. He had taken Alice with him.

Beam Heath was a sprawling area of common ground located to the north-east of Nantwich, which is generally used for the grazing of livestock. In peaceful times, it had been a fair, well-used pasture, but it was now little more than a wasteland. The livestock that normally grazed there had all been brought into the town for safekeeping, whilst its cottages and barns had been reduced to empty shells, burned out or knocked down by the men of the garrison to prevent the royalists from using them as cover.

It was not a place to be frequented on a night like this, but there was no choice. Borrowing pistols from the men on the wall, the three of us leapt over the side of the earthworks and slid down the greasy slope into the ditch at the bottom. It was now a truly filthy night. It was teeming down, and the ditch was already a foot deep in icy-cold water, which slopped over the tops of our boots as we waded through. I looked ahead, through the sheeting rain, and could just make out the dark silhouettes of Furnival and Alice. Furnival was struggling laboriously across the saturated ground, having to help Alice occasionally as she stumbled.

Bracing myself against the rain, I led my small group after them, in a north-westerly direction, towards the river bank, which was just as well, as to the north-east I could clearly see the camp fires of Byron's men amidst lines of white tents, which seemed to stretch all the way to the Beam Bridge, three-quarters of a mile from the town.

Furnival, I noted, did not aim directly for the stone bridge that usually crossed the Weaver at this point, for he knew full well that this had been dismantled by the garrison soldiers. Instead, he aimed directly towards the river, with a view to following it downstream, in order to find the temporary crossing that he knew had been constructed by Byron's men. Following their path, we plodded through the fields of slush, mud, and melt-water, but found that we could not go as far as we had expected, as the Weaver had started to burst its banks. Whereas the river was normally a slow-moving, sedate stream, today it had become a raging torrent, a black mass of unstoppable water forcing its way inexorably northwards. We marched resolutely along as dry a line as we could manage and saw that we were gradually gaining on Furnival and Alice. However, we also realised that it would be touch and go whether we would catch them before they reached the bridge.

The crossing hastily erected by the royalists was little

more than a series of wooden platts tied with rope to stakes set either side of the stream, and, as it came into view, we saw that the wooden structure was heaving and creaking in protest at the powerful torrent of water that was passing beneath it.

"That bridge looks like it's about to depart for Liverpool any minute," said Wade, as we got nearer.

"You're in the right of it, Jack," said Alexander, "but I don't think we should wait around to see. We're not going to catch them now, and we've come too far! We need to go back, now!'"

A dull pain gripped my innards as I realised that Alexander was right. The line of royalist camp fires was no more than a hundred yards away, and, with trepidation, I saw that our chase along the river bank had begun to attract the interest of some of the figures stood by the tents. Up ahead, Furnival looked anxiously round and seemed to waver momentarily as he reached the wooden bridge. He then turned round and shouted something in my direction, waving his arms at me. I thought it sounded like "Save yourselves and go home," but I couldn't be sure, for Furnival's words were caught by the wind and disappeared into the murk of the night.

It was too late, anyway, and I realised with horror that we were going to be captured. Suddenly, a group of about ten soldiers broke out from the line of tents and started to advance towards us. I shouted to Alexander and Wade to look around for cover, but before we could find anything, a volley of musket fire reverberated through the night and Wade screamed out in pain, falling to the ground.

"Sweet Jesus," screamed the soldier. "Firelocks. Bastard shot me in the foot." I was relieved that Wade wasn't more badly hurt, but I immediately realised that the game was up and yelled for quarter. There followed a tense thirty seconds when I didn't know whether I would live or die, but, eventually, a burly-looking sergeant strode up to me and jabbed me in small of the back with his musket.

"Move it, rebel," he said, gruffly, shoving me unceremoniously in the direction of the tents. I glanced round and saw that Alexander was receiving the same treatment. Wade, meanwhile, was hoisted roughly to his feet, bellowing with agony as he realised he was unable to put any weight on his leg. The Sergeant saw this and immediately strode over to Wade, aiming a kick at his bad leg, which sent him sprawling with a sickening scream into the mud. Then, with a nefarious grin, he pulled his pistol from its holster and jabbed it into Wade's neck.

"I suggest you tell me who you are, you roundhead shitbreech," he growled, "or I will blow your brains from here to Chester." To my right, Alexander struggled in the grip of the two men who were holding him and was rewarded with a sharp musket butt in the small of the back. Fortunately, at that precise moment, Furnival stepped forward, as if from nowhere.

"Fine work, gentlemen," he said, addressing the

Sergeant. "Please make sure these men are kept secure and delivered to Dorfold House on the morrow. They are traitors and will be dealt with as such by my Lord Byron." I was grateful for the intervention, but realised that Wade was starting to shiver with shock.

"Our friend needs attention, Furnival," I ventured. "Will you not show mercy and make sure he receives it? He is a regular soldier and has no part in our business."

Furnival looked at Wade with withering contempt. "He is also a fool. He would have done better to keep his own counsel. No doubt he will regret it tomorrow. Very well," he added, and addressed the Sergeant. "Please make sure the soldier's wounds are treated and that he is made warm." The Sergeant looked at Furnival disbelievingly for a moment, but eventually acquiesced gruffly and hoisted Wade to his feet again.

"I'm afraid I must bid you farewell, Cheswis," said Furnival, turning his attention to me. "You have failed, although I will give you your due. You are a persistent fellow." My gaze fell on Alice, who appeared behind Furnival, a look of barely-suppressed horror on her face.

"Tell me one thing, Furnival," I said. "Why go to all this trouble to hide your loyalties?"

"It was no great plan. I was the proud owner of a printing press when the King was stationed in Shrewsbury, and he summoned me to help him. As I have said before, my role as a publisher is to write what the public wants to hear, so I have no problem with reporting a parliamentarian viewpoint. But it does not change my loyalty to the Crown. His Majesty suggested I could well serve him by continuing to report in this manner as a cover for other activities he might wish for me to carry out. When your brother's friend Brett brought these papers back to Nantwich, I was summoned as the ideal person to get them back."

"And the best person to distribute *Mercurius Aulicus* also, I presume," I added.

"Naturally. As the publisher of *The Public Scout* nobody would suspect me of being the source of *Mercurius Aulicus*."

"And certainly not of being a royalist spy," I added.

"That is true," said Furnival, stepping forward until he was no more than a couple of feet from me, and I could feel his hot breath on my face. "But tell me, Cheswis. How did you work out that I was responsible for the deaths of Brett and Nuttall? You could not have deduced that simply from knowing that I helped Sandford gain access to the inner ward at Beeston Castle."

"No, but the knowledge that Hulse and Bressy were also in the inner ward at the time allowed me to put together the final pieces of the puzzle, and I was suddenly able to see how the two murders were planned and executed. I knew there was something about the drawing room in Alice's brother-in-law's house that was important, but I couldn't quite work out what it was – until I learned about your connection with Hulse and Bressy, of course, and then it came to me in a flash."

All this time Furnival stood looking at me with a flicker of a smile touching the corner of his mouth. "Pray explain," he said.

"Certainly," I said. "The key was the newly hung curtains. Where would the silk cloth for those have come from but from a mercer? You bought the material from Ralph Brett and used the excuse of paying for it to lure him to his death. You waited for him by Lady Norton's back gate, but because he was an ex-soldier and could take care of himself, you made sure Bressy was with you. When Brett arrived, either you or Bressy clubbed him over the head with a rock and the two of you then dragged him across Lady Norton's garden to the gate by the earthworks, where Hulse was waiting. Fortunately for you, it was misty, so nobody on the earthworks had noticed that Bressy had abandoned his post. After all, Hulse was still there. It was only when you staged a fight to draw their attention that the other soldiers saw what was happening. You then clubbed Brett again to make sure he was dead and hit Bressy in the face with your staff to make it look as though he had been fighting with you, before making good your escape through Lady Norton's garden.

"The curtains," I continued, "also gave you an idea of how you could create an alibi for Brett's murder. The curtains were bright red, the same colour as the scarf that William Tench's murderer had left on his body.

When Alice told you about Tench's murder, it occurred to you that if you could make me think that the same person killed Tench, Brett, and anyone else you needed to dispose of, then you would be in the clear, for you were not in Nantwich when Tench was murdered. You therefore had some scarves made up from the material left over from the curtains and used them during the murders of Brett and Nuttall."

"But you weren't fooled by that," stated Furnival.

"No. The scarves made from the curtains were good, but they were completely different to the high quality ceremonial sash used in Tench's murder, which I already knew had belonged to Randle Church."

"Very perceptive," said Furnival. "Is that all?"

"No. I then had to consider the circumstances surrounding Nuttall's death. Why, I wondered, was it necessary to leave a scarf on the body of Nuttall? Few people in Barthomley would have connected the scarf with Tench. The obvious conclusion was that the murderer knew my family lived in Barthomley and fully expected me to arrive there at some point, in search of my brother Simon. I should really have put two and two together when you appeared at St Bertoline's church the day after the murder. You and Bressy, I presume, were lodging at Stony Cross Farm the whole of the time that you were in Barthomley."

"You appear to have it all worked out," said Furnival, taking a step backwards to stand once more beside Alice.

"It is a pity that we are on different sides in this conflict, for you would have made a fine intelligencer."

I chose to ignore this comment and instead turned my attention to Alice. "And you," I said, unable to hide the betrayal from my voice. "You would use the affection I held for you as a means to help your husband in this manner? Are you not ashamed?"

Alice moved to open her mouth, but Furnival raised his hand to quiet her. "My wife's involvement in this was not planned," he said, "but when we discovered that your brother and eventually you were both involved in this business, it seemed that we could do no other than use it to our advantage."

"God will judge you both accordingly," I said, looking him straight in the eye.

"That he will, but he will be judging you rather sooner, I think," he said.

Furnival turned to the Sergeant again. "My colleague is with you somewhere, I believe?" he asked. "He said he would wait near the bridge."

"Aye, sir, he has been called for," said the Sergeant. At that moment, the group of soldiers parted and Jem Bressy stepped through.

"Ah, Bressy," said Furnival. "I trust you are faring well. It's time for me to depart and deliver the news of this success to Lord Byron."

"Yes, sir," said Bressy. "You do not wish to wait awhile until the rain eases?"

"No. His lordship should not be kept waiting, and the sooner I reach the warmth of Dorfold and escape this filthy weather, the better. However, my wife may remain with you under the hospitality of the Sergeant and his men. I will entrust you with the task of making sure that she is delivered safely to Dorfold House and that the prisoners are kept secure. I will deal with them properly on the morrow."

"Yes, sir."

"And Alice, I will see you tomorrow, my love," he said, embracing his wife.

"Hugh. I don't think-" she began, but Furnival was already on his way, striding over to the wooden bridge, Bressy at his heels.

Furnival took one look back and waved before striding onto the wooden platt, which wobbled and weaved on the surface of the water. Unsteady on his feet, as Bressy paused, hesitantly, on the bank, Furnival stepped slowly across the bridge with deliberate footsteps. But as he arrived at the half-way point, a particularly violent gust of wind caused the bridge to wobble more than it had done before. Furnival put his hand out to steady himself, but his foot slipped on the greasy surface of the wood, and slowly, despite waving his arms in a circular motion, Furnival tipped backwards, flinging the pouch in the air as he lost control of his body. Time stood still for what seemed like an eternity before Furnival landed on his back, cracking his head on the wooden platt, and the pouch was gobbled up greedily by the river. Furnival lay motionless for a couple of seconds, as soldiers ran towards him from the camp, but then he rolled slowly over the edge, his body immediately being consumed by the raging waters.

At that precise moment, one of the ropes snapped on the bridge, and there was a sickening crack as the bridge support timbers split in two, sending foot-long splinters flying through the air. Bressy, who had one foot resting on one of the platts, was forced to dive for cover, sprawling headfirst along the side of the riverbank. In a matter of seconds, the entire bridge collapsed into the river and was carried off downstream as though it had never existed. There was a momentary silence as the wood disappeared and the watching people took in what had happened. Then, just as I was contemplating the irony of Furnival's final words to me, the only thing I heard was a long, horrible scream, one that I hadn't heard for many a year. I didn't need to look to know from whom it came.

32

Beam Heath and Dorfold House,
Cheshire – Thursday January 25, 1644

Alexander and I endured a miserable night on Beam Heath. We were placed under armed guard in a tent, so at least we kept relatively dry. However, away from the fires it was still uncomfortably cold, and we slept only fitfully. As I tossed and turned, I wondered what it must have been like for Byron's men before the thaw, having to sit outside in freezing temperatures for days on end.

After an hour or two, Wade was returned to us, still in shock and drifting in and out of consciousness. His foot had been cleaned up and dressed and his lower leg put in splints, but I knew that the main danger was the risk of infection from the musket ball. He needed proper attention from a physician. Even then, we realised, the prospects for saving his foot were not good. Wade lay inert on the floor of the tent, mumbling to himself in a state of semi-delirium. Huddling close to him, Alexander and I made our best efforts to keep him warm.

During the night, we listened to the incessant chatter

of our guards and learned that Fairfax and Brereton had been on the march from Manchester. Byron's troops would have to fight the following day, and this gave us at least some grounds for optimism. Byron's orders had been to get all the royalist troops back to the Acton side of the river, but, as this was now no longer possible, the force on Beam Heath, under the command of his brother, Sir Robert Byron, would have to walk around Nantwich as far as Shrewbridge, a mile south of the town, in order to cross the river and join with the rest of the forces at Acton.

I eventually drifted off to sleep but was jolted awake from fitful slumber by the pungent smell of leather. I opened my eyes to see one of the burly Sergeant's bucket top boots planted firmly on my chest.

"Move it, roundhead," he growled. "Time for a walk."

I struggled groggily to my feet and was hustled unceremoniously out of the tent. I was pleased to be greeted by a bright and breezy morning with warm, spring-like air and white clouds scudding across the sky. Although the fields remained saturated with water, the rain had stopped, and the overcast skies of the day before had been replaced by bright sunshine. It felt as though a weight had been lifted from everyone's shoulders, but perhaps it was just the knowledge that today was the day of reckoning for Nantwich, and that one way or another, the siege would be lifted. Whilst the rest of the force decamped, Alexander and I were placed under the watchful gaze of a group of grinning pikemen, who taunted us with their bread and cheese whilst our own stomachs grumbled in protest. Wade, meanwhile, was still in no fit state to travel, so he was put on a cart with some of the injured from the previous week's raid.

The walk to Acton was planned to take in Dorfold on the way, and it proved to be as laborious as it was long. The flooded water meadows and the need to stay far enough away from Nantwich to avoid being attacked meant that a huge detour was necessary. The sodden ground, meanwhile, meant that the carts and artillery kept getting stuck in the mud. As the convoy toiled through the saturated landscape, it quickly became clear that Byron's men had decamped just in time, for, in the distance, a number of townsfolk, having realised that the force on Beam Heath had been isolated from the main body of Byron's army, had ventured forth from the earthworks to destroy the royalist defences, to grab any hay left by Byron's men, and to set fire to any remaining barns, to prevent them from being used again. Up ahead, I caught sight of Alice riding with Sir Robert Byron and his officers and cursed at my bad fortune.

In the end, it was a good six mile walk to Dorfold. We crossed the river at Shrewbridge but had to make many detours to avoid the flooded fields. It was approaching midday, therefore, before we passed by Bull's Wood, and the red brick façade of Dorfold House came into view.

We had approached Dorfold from the south along a

narrow bridleway, which skirted by the house to the east and eventually led to The Star Inn and Acton's church. A hundred yards or so to the east of the house, the bridleway met a path which led to the front of the house. At the junction, Robert Byron halted his men, for the route to Acton was bustling with officers heading from their quarters towards the church, where the majority of the lower ranks were billeted. Amidst the organised chaos, an artillery train was trying to haul a huge cannon and a mortar through the mud, churning the ground in front of the house into a morass. I realised that this must have been the ordnance that had bombarded Welsh Row and gave a silent prayer of thanks that the guns were now being moved away.

From a distance, I saw Sir Robert Byron converse with one of his officers, before riding off towards the house, closely followed by Alice. I watched, intrigued, as a well-dressed officer with shoulder-length brown curls and a fine gold and green doublet appeared at the top of the steps leading to the doorway of the house. Both Byron and Alice dismounted from their horses and approached the newcomer, although Alice, looking pale and drawn, seemed unsure as to her position and held back slightly. I watched, transfixed, as the two men embraced each other, and I realised that I was looking at none other than Lord John Byron, the leader of the royalist forces in Cheshire.

I was woken from my reverie by the sight of the burly

Sergeant and two of his pikemen, who appeared suddenly at my side.

"Time for you to get what's coming to you, rebel," said the Sergeant, with a sadistic smile. "Follow me."

Alexander and I were led in the direction of the house, encouraged by the two pikemen, who prodded us in the back as we went. Up ahead, I saw two more soldiers carrying a stretcher, on which lay the motionless body of Jack Wade. We were brought to a halt at the foot of the steps to the house. I glanced up towards the doorway at Alice, who reddened slightly and turned her gaze away from me. Lord Byron, meanwhile, had descended the steps and was looking at me close-up, his countenance fixed in a steely glare.

"Well, well," said Byron to his brother. "These base rogues are responsible for the demise of our friend Furnival, you say?"

"Indeed," said Sir Robert. "In fact, this one is one of the Cheswis brothers."

Lord Byron raised an eyebrow and looked at me with renewed interest.

"I will look forward to renewing my acquaintance with you after I have put Fairfax and his followers to the sword," he said. "In the meantime, you will remain here as a guest of his Majesty, King Charles."

Alexander, Wade, and I were taken upstairs to an oak-panelled bedroom and locked in with a guard placed outside the door. Things could have been worse, for we were at least able to wrap Wade up warmly in one of the beds. We were also given a bowl of pottage and some bread each, which went some way towards relieving the gnawing hunger which had been gripping my insides. The rough handling afforded to Wade in the act of depositing him on the bed was a blessing in disguise, in so far as it had woken him sufficiently to allow me to spoon-feed him some pottage, which seemed to revive him somewhat. However, no sooner had he emptied his bowl than he fell again into deep slumber.

Alexander and I would both have been grateful for the small mercy afforded by sleep, but we were far too agitated for that. Instead, I sat on the floor of the bedroom, hugging my shoulders, and wondered what had brought me to this juncture. I prayed fervently that Fairfax and Brereton would overcome Byron's Irish army, for I knew with certainty that unless that happened, Alexander and I would be hung as spies, probably that evening. I felt a numbness inside my stomach as I considered this eventuality. I thought about Alexander's young family and Mrs Padgett and Amy. How would they fare without us? I thought about Elizabeth Brett and her son, but most of all, I thought about Simon, who would no doubt be sought out by Byron to suffer the same fate as Alexander and I.

I must have been sat for at least two hours consumed in these thoughts, for the clock on the mantelpiece was indicating fully three o'clock when I heard a key in the lock, and a familiar mass of blond ringlets appeared around the side of the door.

Alice smiled nervously and put a finger to her mouth to stop me from talking. "Quickly," she said, "you only have a few moments. Follow me."

I was dumbfounded, but despite my confusion, I nudged Alexander in the ribs, and we were both on our feet in an instant.

"Don't worry about your friend," she said, gesturing towards Wade, who had not stirred. "Lord Byron has a good physician here. I will make sure he is well taken care of."

I looked over at the bed and shook my head vehemently.

"We can't leave him here, Alice," I said. "He is here on my account. If we desert him now, he will be hung as a spy."

"That won't happen," insisted Alice, with a frown. "He was wearing Brereton's colours. He will be considered as no more than an enemy prisoner. You know how it is. If he recovers from his injuries, he will be invited to join Byron's army. That is not such a bad fate. Don't be a fool, Daniel. You need to come, now."

I took one last look at Wade, before nodding briefly and following Alice out of the door onto the landing, where I was amazed to see two unconscious guards propped up against the wall.

"A sleeping draught," explained Alice, "administered

with the help of Roger Wilbraham of Dorfold. Don't worry about the guards. They will wake up in a while."

"And the rest of Lord Byron's men?"

"Lord Byron himself is in Acton, facing the parliamentarian army. He and his colleagues have more important things to worry about right now than two fugitives."

"But what if Byron wins the battle and returns this evening? How will you explain this to him?"

"I won't need to, Daniel," said Alice. "Wilbraham is strong for Parliament and Byron will assume he is responsible."

"And Wilbraham?"

"He will not betray me. I have helped him secure your escape."

I nodded and followed Alice along a corridor, down a set of stairs, and into the kitchens. Standing there waiting was Wilbraham, who smiled and indicated towards a door, which led out to the lawns at the side of the house.

"Gentlemen, you may leave this way," said Wilbraham. "Be careful crossing the lawns. There are still a number of soldiers guarding the house. Once you're in the trees you should be safe, but be sure to stay clear of the royalist artillery. There may still be some ordnance in place, directed at the town."

I nodded my thanks to Wilbraham and turned to Alice. "Why are you doing this?" I asked.

"Daniel. I have known you a long time and, despite

what you think of me in this moment, I still have feelings for you. Hugh's death is not your fault. I would not have you and your friends hung as spies on my account. Now go quickly while you have the chance."

I needed no second bidding. The next moment, Alexander and I were sprinting across the lawn, heading for the safety of the trees.

33

Hurleston, Cheshire – Thursday
January 25, 1644

*S*ir Thomas Fairfax stood on the high ground at
Hurleston, a mile to the north-west of Acton, and
clicked his teeth in annoyance. In the middle distance,
across a dip in the landscape, he was able to identify
the massed forces of Lord Byron's royalist army blocking
the road to Nantwich, and he did not like what he saw.
Fairfax's scouts had informed him that Sir Robert Byron's
men on the east bank of the Weaver had been stranded
away from the rest of the royalists by the swollen river,
due to the collapse of the only bridge north of Nantwich
– and yet, judging by the ensign clearly visible ahead,
Sir Robert's men were already moving into position on
the royalist left flank, positioning themselves between
Fairfax's army and Acton's church. Fairfax's plan had
been to attack Byron, but now that he was able to see the
strength of the royalist army, he was no longer convinced
of the wisdom of such a move. He had therefore halted his
force and called his most senior officers to an impromptu
Council of War.

"Gentlemen, our guns and carriages have been too slow," he said, addressing the select band of eight men standing in front of him. "We no longer have the numerical advantage. How do you propose we proceed?"

Fairfax ran his fingers through his hair and observed the reactions of his colleagues. The first man to speak was a square-jawed officer of roughly his own age, clean-shaven save for a thick, dark moustache that adorned his upper lip. "We should attack Byron's army now, Thomas, while we have the chance. His men have been sat in the snow for nearly a month. They are not as strong as they look."

Fairfax stared at Sir William Fairfax, and a narrow smile formed on his lips. "Thank you, cousin," he replied. Fairfax did not doubt Sir William's courage or his commitment to serving God and the parliamentary cause, but he was looking for more than mere bravado.

"I knew we should have remained in Lancashire," said a tall man in his early thirties with a clean-shaven, narrow face and black shoulder-length hair that lay flat over his head but bushy across his shoulders. Next to him, an older, smaller, and more rotund man nodded vigorously.

"Sir John, you should be in no doubt that your interests will be best served by ensuring that Nantwich does not fall," snapped Fairfax. Sir John Booth and Richard Holland were the commanders in charge of Fairfax's Lancashire Regiments, and it had taken some degree

of persuasion to convince them that a winter's march to South Cheshire was good idea.

Of the five remaining men, four remained quiet. They were Colonels Assheton, Bright, Copley, and Lambert. However, the fifth, a slightly-built man with thin, pinched features, stepped forward and spoke calmly and with authority.

"You are right, Sir Thomas," he said. "There is no need to risk all by attacking a superior force. We should head directly to Nantwich, relieve the garrison and then attack Lord Byron with a combined force."

"And how do we do this, Sir William?" asked Fairfax. "The road ahead is blocked."

Sir William Brereton, Commander of Parliament's forces in Cheshire, pointed across the fields in a south-easterly direction. "There is a narrow lane about a mile distant called Welshman's Lane. If we cut across the fields, avoiding the road altogether, we can bypass Byron. Once we have reached the lane, it is but a simple walk into Nantwich."

Fairfax considered Brereton's words carefully. Leaving the road would be a slow and risky manoeuvre, requiring his men to haul artillery across sodden fields and cut their way through hedgerows. Then again, nothing he had encountered on his march to Nantwich had been straightforward.

The first setback had been the point-blank refusal of Colonel Hutchinson to join him with a troop of horse quartered at Nottingham, a reinforcement he had been counting upon. Fairfax had then marched across to Stafford and Newcastle, where he had managed to make contact with Brereton. However, Byron had attacked his men, leaving Brereton and Fairfax with no option but to march north to Manchester, where they had spent two weeks trying to recruit foot soldiers. In total, they had managed to assemble nearly 3,000 infantry to make a combined force of 3,550 horse and 3,000 foot. Included among the Manchester recruits were some of the men who had served under him during his disastrous defeat at Adwalton the previous year. He had burst into tears when he saw their haggard, half-naked state and had immediately set about taking care of their welfare.

He and Brereton had departed for Nantwich on 21 January, clashing with one of Byron's pickets at Delamere Forest before billeting at Tilston. That had been the previous night, and now, this morning, he had already had to subdue a small force at Barbridge, five miles from Nantwich, before marching on to his current position, well aware of his tardiness.

Fairfax considered Brereton's suggestion for a few moments before deciding that the risk involved in carrying out a march across the face of the enemy was less than attacking them head-on. The column of soldiers, therefore, left the road with the guns and baggage train in the van, the pioneers cutting a channel through the hedges. Immediately behind them was Colonel Lambert's horse and Brereton and Assheton's foot. Fairfax himself was in the centre, followed by Booth and Holland's foot and Sir William Fairfax's horse bringing up the rear.

At first, he thought his plan was going to work, but it did not take long for him to realise that Byron had identified what the parliamentarians were trying to do and was aiming to cut them off at their point of maximum vulnerability. To Fairfax's dismay, he noticed that the two royalist wings had begun to orchestrate a wheeling action, in order to attack his column from both the front and rear simultaneously. Realising he was trapped and that he had no hope of reaching Welshman's Lane, Fairfax ordered Booth and Holland to turn to face the enemy that was about to descend upon them from the rear, whilst watching as Brereton and Assheton were attacked from the front. With resignation and no little degree of frustration that he had lost the opportunity to fight the battle on his terms, Fairfax realised he had no option but to turn his whole army round, organise it, and fight. It was just after half past three in the afternoon.

34

Acton, Cheshire – Thursday January 25, 1644

It was a sprint of no more than thirty yards into the thick but narrow band of woodland that bordered the east side of Dorfold House, but, in my heightened state of agitation, it felt more like two hundred. Concealing myself behind the trunk of an oak tree, I glanced back towards the house and was able to ascertain with relief that we had not been spotted by any of the remaining guards, who, I realised, must all have been stationed on the Acton side of the house.

Alexander and I waded through the sodden undergrowth to the other side of the woodland, beyond which lay open fields stretching all the way to Nantwich. It was clear why Byron had chosen this place to stand the artillery that had bombarded the town a fortnight previously, as from here the earthworks at Welsh Row End were no more than half a mile away. Having seen the royalist artillery train hauling cannon and mortars from the scene earlier that morning, we did not expect to find any remaining ordnance in place. Nonetheless, we approached the edge of the trees warily, just in case any of Byron's men had remained behind. It was as well that we did, for, although the heavy artillery had long since been removed, the route back to Nantwich was now blocked by a group of around a hundred infantry, who were loitering meaningfully on the main road with the obvious intention of preventing a breakout from Welsh Row. Alexander and I slid carefully back into the trees to make sure we were not seen.

"What do we do now?" breathed Alexander, removing his hat to reveal a wrinkled forehead lined with beads of sweat. It was a good question, the answer to which was not immediately obvious. Heading straight for Nantwich was clearly out of the question, as, in truth, was the alternative option of retracing this morning's steps back to Shrewbridge, for even this carried a considerable risk of being spotted crossing the open fields. What concerned me more, though, was whether it was a good idea to be marching back to Nantwich at all. If we were to return to our homes and Byron was victorious, Alexander and I stood to be arrested and hung.

"I think caution is called for at this point," I said. "I say we stay here in the wood and see what happens." The decision proved to be the correct one, for at that moment, I became aware of an increased volume of shouting from the direction of Acton, followed quickly by the roar of Byron's field artillery.

"The fighting has begun," I said. "Let us see if we can get a better view." Taking care to stay within the line of the trees, we skirted northwards in the direction of the road to Tarporley, until we reached the edge of the woodland. From here, the vantage point was much better. Not only could we still see back to Nantwich, but we also had a clear view across the fields to the north.

The sight was magnificent but terrible at the same time. Two or three hundred yards away and facing away from us, down the slope, was Byron's army, spread across several fields. The standards of the various companies fluttered in the breeze as they started to manoeuvre into position. I calculated that Alexander and I were located somewhere between Byron's centre and right flank. Through gaps in between the raised pikes of the royalists, I could see the parliamentary army lower down in the distance and realised that they were trying to march across the face of the royalist position.

"Looks like Fairfax doesn't want to fight," I said. "He's trying to reach Nantwich."

"Aye," said Alexander, with a grimace, "but he's not going to make it. His pioneers are stuck in a bloody hedgerow."

I strained my eyes and stared beyond the royalist right flank towards the head of the parliamentary force and saw, with trepidation, that Alexander spoke the truth. Fairfax's pioneers and artillerymen had stopped and were frantically trying to cut a hole in the line of hedges that criss-crossed the field. They were now being attacked by cavalry on the royalist right flank.

Meanwhile, movement in the distance suggested that Byron's left flank, the furthest away from where I stood, had attempted to follow suit.

"He'll have to fight," exclaimed Alexander, "otherwise he'll be surrounded."

My friend, I realised, was right. Parliament, in some confusion, was being attacked on three sides. The only positive thing, from the parliamentary point of view, was that the royalist cavalry was having difficulty operating effectively, due to the sodden ground and the small enclosures they were operating in.

As the minutes went by, however, I gradually began to realise that, although the royalists had initially held the upper hand, Parliament was holding firm. The cavalry on Parliament's right flank had begun to rally, and the ensign of Sir William Brereton's foot, which I recognised in the middle of the left wing, began to make an impression against the pikes and muskets of the royalist right. Strangely, through all of this, the royalist centre had held back, barely engaging with the enemy.

The battle was now at its loudest; artillery, musket, and sword drowning out voices. So, when the bells began, I almost didn't hear them. It was the sharp ears of Alexander, attuned to such things, that picked them up first.

"Daniel, listen," he shouted, grabbing my arm. "They know!"

I listened carefully, and, sure enough, above the noise

of the battle, I could just make out the sound of St Mary's church bells being rung back-to-front, a coded sign which we both knew was a call to action. The garrison and townspeople of Nantwich knew what was happening and were coming to help.

"Now we'll see what these Irishmen are made of," said Alexander, as we watched the road which led to the end of Welsh Row. After a few minutes, we observed soldiers breaking out via the sconce at the end of the street and over the walls and ditches surrounding that side of the town. I was amazed. In the distance, men flooded over the walls like ants until they numbered nearly a thousand, engulfing the unfortunate royalist guard in a matter of minutes. Once Byron's men had surrendered, the garrison men started to march up the road towards where Alexander and I were standing.

Turning my attention once again to the main battle, I realised that the royalist centre had begun to retreat, so that the parliamentarian centre was beginning to separate the royalists' left and right flanks, falling into the flanks of both their wings. It also seemed that the parliamentarian horse was beginning to beat Byron's cavalry away from the lanes that enclosed the fields in which the action was taking place.

Alexander turned to me and smiled. "It looks like Fairfax's boys are beginning to take control," he said.

"Thank the Lord for that," I replied, and looked down the road towards Nantwich at the column of men, which was now almost upon us. At its head was Colonel Booth, on his fine bay gelding. Behind him were the soldiers of the Nantwich garrison and the men of the Nantwich trained bands. As they came within fifty yards of us, Alexander and I stepped out of the trees onto the roadside and waved our hands frantically in the air. It took a few moments for those in the van to recognise us, and one or two musketeers lined us up in their sights, suspecting a trap. However, a shout went up; "It's Constable Cheswis and Bellman Clowes. Hold your fire, men."

Within a few seconds, Colonel Booth pulled his horse alongside us and halted. "Well, sir," he said, by way of greeting. "I did not envisage finding you here. You'll have a story to tell, I'll wager?"

"We do, Colonel," I said, "but it can wait until the matter at hand is resolved. Can we be of assistance?"

"You most certainly can," said Booth, spurring his horse forward. "You may join our rear. I'll send a rider back to pick up a couple of spare weapons." With that, Booth summoned over a cavalry officer, who quickly galloped back towards the town and secured a couple of muskets, bandoliers, and swords from the weapons taken from the royalist prisoners, who were now being led away into town. Five minutes later, we were able to tag onto the end of the column, which was now heading rapidly towards the rear of the royalist force. As the column marched past I caught sight of James Skinner and his two brothers, eyes alight and focused in front of them. One of the brothers saluted me as he marched past, but Skinner himself didn't even see me, his face a mask of concentration.

Our group of townsmen followed Sergeant Bradshaw, who headed straight for the rear of the royalist centre, which was already in retreat. Positioning ourselves behind a hedgerow, we started firing at a line of green-coated musketeers, several of whom collapsed to the floor screaming, causing their neighbours to wheel round in panic. In the melee, several royalist officers, realising they were being attacked from two sides, were frantically trying to rally their troops and to reposition some of their pikemen. As I reloaded my musket, I caught sight of a familiar face wielding his sword and threatening any of the wavering royalists who looked like they were ready to flee.

Jem Bressy didn't notice me because he had his eyes on other things. He had recognised the Skinner brothers, who stood to the left of our group, next to a gap in the hedgerow. Aided by several of his colleagues, Bressy waited for the Skinners to empty their muskets before charging headlong into their midst.

"I know you," roared Bressy, jabbing his musket butt into James Skinner's solar plexus. "Your shooting eye is among the best, you can be of use to us."

Before any of his brothers could react, Skinner was grabbed by Bressy and two others and muscled away back into the royalist lines.

"No! Jim!" screamed Skinner's brothers simultaneously, but it was to no avail. Within seconds, James Skinner had disappeared from view. The elder of the two brothers made to charge off into the midst of the royalist hordes, but, spotting his intentions, Alexander grabbed him round the neck and hauled him back behind the hedgerow. Bradshaw, who had seen Bressy's act of bravado, was over in an instant.

"Stay back here, you fool," he screamed, spittle showering the elder brother's face. "Do you want to get yourself fucking killed? Concentrate on shooting as many of these bastards as you can."

Fighting back tears, the two brothers picked up their muskets and started to reload.

The battle did not last much longer. Within a few minutes, the parliamentarian centre and our group met in the middle and separated the two halves of the royalist army. The royalist left flank, which I later discovered to be Robert Byron's regiment, gathered together what infantry it could from the centre and left the battlefield as quickly as it could in the direction of Chester. Many of those trapped on the battlefield surrendered on the spot, whilst the remnants of the royalist right wing, surrounded on three sides, was slowly pushed back until those who could still run were forced to flee up the hill, back in the direction of Acton's church. Byron's army was now fully routed, and, for the first time, I started to realise that we would be able to return safely to Nantwich that evening.

The whole battle had lasted no more than an hour and a half.

Dusk was falling as the remaining royalists enclosed themselves in Acton's churchyard. In utter confusion, many of them surrendered rather than resist any longer and were put under armed guard. The remainder barricaded themselves behind the church's substantial walls, hoping that we would retreat back to Nantwich in the dark.

However, Fairfax and his men were in no mood to let the royalists off the hook that easily. With the tension of the past weeks finally released, the men of the garrison combined with Fairfax's troops to build huge fires in the field known as the Lady Field, opposite the church, and sat down to wait for the last of the enemy to surrender. Many of Fairfax's troops broke up into groups and began to hold impromptu prayer meetings. I listened in the darkness and picked out the soft melody of a psalm spreading across the battlefield.

Let God arise, let his enemies be scattered: let them also that hate him flee before him.

As smoke is driven away, so drive them away: as wax melteth before the fire, so let the wicked perish at the presence of God.

But let the righteous be glad; let them rejoice before God: yea, let them exceedingly rejoice.

A strange irony, I thought, that such music should be coming from a killing field, where so much godlessness had just taken place, while there was no music coming from inside the church.

35

Nantwich – Friday January 26, 1644

The scene in Nantwich the next morning was one of unrestrained celebration. People teemed out onto the streets in jubilation, and much ale was consumed in the taverns. By mid-morning, farmers and tradesmen had started to come in with foodstuffs to replenish the stocks reduced during the siege. With Fairfax's troops, as well as the garrison soldiers, flooding the town, Nantwich was full to the brim.

There was also the matter of the sixteen hundred prisoners taken, many of whom were marched into the town amidst loud jeering and imprisoned in St Mary's church, guard being maintained by the garrison soldiers. Many of these prisoners would eventually take up arms for Parliament, but not before they had created an unholy, stinking mess in the besieged church. Mats and rushes would need to be burned, pews cleaned, and the floors brushed. In the meantime, church services would be held in the Crown Gallery, in Townsend House, and at Lady Norton's.

The defeat and the loss of half his army must have been

a severe loss to Lord Byron, for among the prisoners were some of his most senior officers; Major General Gibson, Sir Michael Erneley, Sir Francis Butler, and others.

As for myself, I had not slept a wink. During the long night, I spent some time with James Skinner's brothers, who, distraught at the loss of their sibling, had been unable to join in with the general rejoicing.

"What will happen to Jim, do you think, Master Cheswis?" asked Jack, the elder brother.

"I don't know," I replied, truthfully. "My guess, though, is that he'll be made to fight in Byron's army. I hope for his sake he accepts. It will be better for his prospects than if he refuses. Things could be worse, you know. Most of *these* prisoners will end up fighting on *our* side. Most of them have no more love for the King than they do for puritans. So long as they're paid, most soldiers will fight for either side, especially if the choice is between a full stomach and a damp cell."

I looked at the younger brother, Robert, and realised I had done nothing to lighten their mood. There was little I could say, so I settled for telling them I would do my best to find out what had happened to their brother.

Next, I had to cope with Colonel Booth, who sought me out in the Lady Field once the action had died down. As I anticipated, Simon had already informed him about Furnival's role in the affair, and he congratulated me on my timely intervention the night before. However, the news that Furnival was dead and that Hamilton's documents were lost was not welcomed with quite as much enthusiasm.

"That is disappointing," he said, clicking his teeth in irritation. "Is there any chance, do you think, that the papers might be recovered?"

"I confess it highly unlikely, sir," I said. "The Weaver was a raging torrent last night, and, as the papers were thrown into the air by Furnival as he fell, they could be anywhere between here and the Irish Sea - that is if they are in a fit state to be read at all."

I didn't tell Booth about what had happened to Alice, nor about how we escaped from Dorfold, which was my next destination. As soon as the Colonel had excused himself, I attracted Alexander's attention and we headed off back down the road towards Dorfold House, grateful to escape the Colonel's presence, even though I had expected Booth's wrath at the loss of Hamilton's documents to be greater than it was.

A number of royalists had retreated back to the house during the fighting and several had been killed, the remainder having been rounded up and made prisoner. Curiously enough, though, of Alice there was no sign. This particular mystery was quickly solved by an audience with Roger Wilbraham of Dorfold, who explained that, having seen what Alice had done for Alexander and myself, he had given her the opportunity to escape once it became clear who had won the battle. Alice had not needed to be asked twice. Borrowing a servant's clothes and taking only a winter cloak with her, she had fled in the middle of the night.

Alice, though, was much less of a concern than Jack Wade. Fortunately, the royalist physician had been able to treat him before the house was recaptured, but, to my despair, I discovered that he had been unable to save Wade's foot, which had been amputated above the ankle. He was now propped up in bed, sleeping off the liquor he had been plied with, his stump swathed in bandages.

I felt ransacked with guilt about Wade's situation. The young man had followed Alexander and I at my bidding, and now he would be a cripple for the rest of his life. I had no idea how I would make it up to him. Once daylight broke, Alexander and I borrowed a cart from Roger Wilbraham and transferred him back to my house in Pepper Street, so that Mrs Padgett could care for him full time. He was my responsibility now, and I swore that, if nothing else, I would make sure he was nursed back to health.

Mrs Padgett was delighted to see me still in one piece but less pleased to see the patient I had brought with me. Consequently, she spent the next quarter of an hour muttering and moaning about being constantly at my beck and call when I didn't even appear to live under the same roof as her any more. Despite this, we managed to get Wade comfortable in my chamber upstairs, allowing Alexander to take his leave and return to Margery and his children.

"You are a soft touch, Daniel Cheswis," complained Mrs Padgett, as I made my way downstairs and headed for the kitchen. "We cannot take responsibility for this young man."

"Nonsense, woman," I snapped. "Jack has lost his foot because of me. It is my duty to look after him."

"But another mouth to feed," insisted my housekeeper. "How will we cope?"

"We'll find a way," I said. "We always do."

I wasn't sure what food I would find in the kitchen, but, having not eaten for the past twenty-four hours, I was truly famished. To my surprise, I saw some bread and boiled bacon in the middle of the table and headed straight for it.

"So you've been out already I see," I said.

"Food is still hard to get hold of," replied Mrs Padgett. "The whole town wants feeding, not to speak of all the extra soldiers and prisoners. They even brought in over a hundred women prisoners, many of them armed with knives. You know, if I didn't know better, I could have sworn Alice Bickerton was amongst them."

Hiding my surprise at this turn of events, I looked at Mrs Padgett curiously and noticed a hint of a smile appear at the corner of her mouth. I said nothing but took a knife to the bacon and sliced at it venomously.

As I ate, I realised that there were still plenty of issues that I needed to take care of. Firstly, I needed to check that Simon and Elizabeth were safe. Then, there was the issue of the two unsolved murders. In the excitement of the battle, I had almost forgotten that John Davenport was still locked up and that I was no closer to finding out who had been responsible for the two killings that had taken place on Welsh Row. Hugh Furnival had murdered Ralph Brett and James Nuttall, but the deaths of William Tench and Will Butters still remained a mystery. As if to mirror my thoughts, at that moment there was a knock at the door, which Mrs Padgett opened to reveal the figure of Thomas Maisterson. I bid her let him enter.

"Good morning, Master Cheswis," he said. "I have heard something of your escapades last night. It is good to see that you are still in the land of the living, although by the look of you, only just."

I ruffled my hair and realised how right he must have been. After one night sleeping rough soaked to the skin and another night with no sleep, I must have looked a rare sight.

"It is true. I have endured some singular discomforts and I am indeed fortunate to be alive. I think I have the brave soldiers of this garrison to thank for that. They were instrumental in Parliament's victory last night. I trust you, yourself, are well?" In truth, Maisterson also looked as though he had not slept for a while.

"I survive," he admitted. "I will not be seeing my Lord Byron in these parts for a while, I'll wager, but at least our property remains safe, and the people of this town have not suffered as they might have done, had the town fallen. Indeed, I understand some of the property lost at Beeston has been recovered."

I nodded in agreement. "You have sought me out, Mr Maisterson," I said, turning to the matter in hand. "With what can I be of assistance?"

Maisterson looked at me seriously. "Randle Church and I have uncovered some information you may be interested in," he said, mysteriously. "I would suggest you present yourself at Mr Church's house at one o'clock, and you may learn something that will help you identify the person who killed William Tench and Will Butters." And with that, he drew his cloak around him and swept out of the house.

I must confess that Thomas Maisterson's words intrigued me, and I was sorely tempted to follow him straight down the street. First, though, there was something that I had to do. Shoving the last piece of bread into my mouth, I thanked Mrs Padgett and strode out through the front door in the direction of St Mary's.

The church, as was to be expected, was in a considerable state of confusion. Groups of royalist soldiers sat under armed guard on the ground outside the entrance waiting to be admitted, whilst townsfolk milled around the outside of the square, jeering and taunting the prisoners. I weaved my way through the crowds to the main door and asked who was in charge. I was directed to a middle-aged captain wearing Fairfax's colours, who was chatting and joking with a group of guards.

"Yes? What is it, constable?" he asked, when I introduced myself.

"I'm looking for a woman," I announced, and was immediately greeted by a chorus of jeers from the officer's companions.

The Captain saw the joke and made the most of it. "Who isn't looking for that?" he said, "but I wouldn't waste your time here. I wouldn't want to be seen swiving wi' any o' this lot. Not unless you want to catch the pox, that is."

"He looks proper desperate, sir," said one of the guards. "Happen it makes no difference to 'im."

"Aye," added another. "Mebbe his yard's already riddled wi't pox." This predictably produced a gale of lewd laughter, which I ignored.

"Captain, I understand you took some women prisoners yesterday," I persevered.

"Aye, and a bigger bunch of harlots and slatterns I've not seen in many a year. What of it?"

"There's one woman I'm particularly looking for in connection with the murders that took place here recently," I explained. "I have a suspicion she may be among them. May I take a look?"

The Captain's eyes widened and he whistled in surprise. Waving the guards away, he drew me to one side where no-one else could hear. "These women were part of a women's regiment," he said. "I'm under orders not to let anyone be moved until I'm told otherwise. It would be a grave risk to let you in there."

I understood immediately. Reaching into my pocket, I extracted a shilling and thrust it into the Captain's fist. "And there's another one for you, if I find who I'm looking for," I added.

The Captain accepted the coin and motioned for me to follow him. He brushed aside the guard on the door and led me into the interior of the church, which was already a sight to behold. The nave was heaving and beginning to smell like a cesspit. Injured soldiers lay strewn across the pews, whilst others sat morosely in the aisles. The Captain led me through the throng of prisoners until we reached the south transept, which had been separated off from the rest of the church. There, a group of sorry-looking women were sat, contemplating their fate.

"They didn't look quite so sorry for themselves before we brought them here," said the Captain, drily. "Give a woman a knife and they can be as fearsome as any man, which one or two of our men found out to their cost." I ignored the Captain and scoured the faces, which, not expecting visitors, looked up at me with curiosity. At first I didn't see her, but then my eyes focused on a hunched figure looking down into her skirts and trying to shield her face.

"I have her," I announced, striding purposefully through the group of women and hauling Alice roughly to her feet. "Just do as I say," I growled, looking straight into her eyes and hoping that Alice understood what I was trying to do. Grabbing her by the arm, I led her out of the transept, giving the Captain the other shilling as I did so. Alice started to struggle and aimed a swinging kick at my ankles, so I was forced to twist her arm behind her back and grab her roughly by the hair.

"Alice – keep walking if you value your freedom," I hissed, almost inaudibly. Alice stared at me momentarily, and this time she went limp, allowing me to propel her down the aisle and out into the open air. Once beyond the cordon of soldiers guarding the church, I relaxed a little but still kept hold of her arm, marching her across the square and into Pepper Street.

"I think that makes us even," I said, eventually.

"I'm impressed," said Alice, with a pout. "I wish you were as assertive as that ten years ago."

I looked at her askance but said nothing.

"Where are we going?" she asked.

"To my house in the first instance," I replied, marching her down Pepper Street and in through my front door. Mrs Padgett was tending the hearth when we entered. She turned round and gasped at the sudden intrusion.

"What are you doing bringing that woman here?" she exclaimed, horrified.

"Don't worry, Mrs Padgett," I said. "She won't be here long. Ready Demeter, would you please, and pack a bag with whatever provisions we can spare." Mrs Padgett looked at me as if I were mad, but she did my bidding and disappeared out towards the back door.

"Sit down, Alice," I said, motioning to the armchair by the fireplace.

Alice obeyed and looked at me meekly. "I suppose I should thank you," she said. "Why did you do that, after what I've done to you?"

"I trust God will let me know in his own time," I answered. "You knew everything your husband was up to, didn't you?"

"Most of it," said Alice, "but it was never meant to be like this, I swear. The plan was simply to recover the letters from Ralph Brett. Then we found out your brother was involved."

"And why did you copy the murder of William Tench?"

"That was my idea. I knew about Hugh's plans for Brett, and, when I found out about Tench, I thought using the material from the curtains I bought would confuse the issue and hide our involvement. That was a mistake because it meant *you* became involved." She sighed. "If I am punished for my involvement in this, I deserve everything that God has in store for me. I still cannot believe that you haven't left me to my fate."

"Alice, I have loved you more than life itself. I have suffered for years thinking what could have been, had only I stayed in Barthomley. I cannot see you imprisoned, raped, killed or cast out into the winter with nothing but the clothes you are standing in, assuming they even allow you that. You have done me a great wrong this last month, but I cannot live with myself if I allow that."

Alice started to get to her feet and tried to take hold of me by the hand.

"No, don't do that, Alice," I said, forcing her back onto her seat. "I have realised this last two days that our union was never meant to be. Fate has decreed it so. It cannot be any other way."

"That may be so," she said, "but I want you to know that I never intended things to work out this way. Despite what you think, I still have feelings for you. I feel a pain in my gut when I think of the hurt I caused you. I didn't mean to break your heart, but you must understand I fell in love with Hugh and have loved him ever since. He was a good husband to me."

"Yes, I see that, and that is why I now realise there never could be a future for us."

Alice looked at me for a moment and then nodded, looking down into her lap.

"Where will you go once you are out of Nantwich?" I asked, after a few moments.

"My children are in Shrewsbury," replied Alice. "I have to go there. As long as Parliament does not come looking for me, I will be safe there and will inherit Hugh's assets."

"George Booth does not understand the level of your involvement in this, and he will not hear it from me," I promised.

Alice smiled gratefully. "I owe you a great deal," she

said.

"No. You owe me nothing. You saved my life at Dorfold House. You were not to know that Fairfax would prevail. If Byron had returned victorious, Alexander and I would have been hung as spies."

Walking over to the cabinet by the wall, I put my hand in one of the drawers and extracted a small leather purse. I took out a guinea and handed it to Alice.

"Mrs Padgett will give you my horse," I said. "You can reimburse me when you are able to do so."

"I will send money to my sister with instructions to pay you back, once I am in Shrewsbury," she replied. She then hesitated for a moment before adding, "You are a kind man, Daniel Cheswis."

"Perhaps too kind," I said, pursing my lips.

At that point, Mrs Padgett came back in, ignoring Alice completely. "The horse is ready, Master Daniel," she said. Thanking her, I led Alice to the backlands, where Demeter was tethered.

"Thank you, Danull," she said, kissing me on the cheek. Taking hold of the reins, she hoisted herself into the saddle and, with a wave, she was gone.

36

Nantwich – Friday January 26, 1644

It was Marion Tench who answered the door when I presented myself at Randle Church's mansion at one o'clock. The widow looked at me with suspicion as I explained my reason for being there, and, at first, I thought she wasn't going to let me in. However, after a moment's hesitation, she thought better of it and bid me enter and take a seat in the hallway. She disappeared into the drawing room and emerged a few moments later with Maisterson, before retreating into the kitchen with a worried look on her face.

The drawing room was brightly lit, with a view over the rear garden and stables towards the earthworks, which were visible a few yards behind the rear wall. Randle Church was sat in the same armchair as during my last visit. This time, however, there was a third person in the room, a pale-faced maid, who Maisterson introduced as Bridgett Palyn.

"Good morning, Master Cheswis," said Church. "I trust you are recovered after your exertions on the battlefield?"

"I thank you for your concern, Mr Church," I replied. "I am quite well, although I confess, a little weary. I have not slept for nearly two days and then only in a field."

"Then we will not detain you long," he said. "You will be wondering, no doubt, why you have been summoned here."

"Mr Maisterson informs me that you may have some information relevant to my quest to discover who murdered William Tench and Will Butters."

"That is indeed so. At least, we believe that to be the case. We have been concerned these last days about the unfortunate deaths that have occurred in our town, all of which have been servants of those of prominent townspeople, who would be loyal to the King, or relatives and friends of those servants. We wished to allay any suspicion that we were in some way involved. Indeed, our motive in all of this has merely been to protect our property and position within the town. We have, therefore, carried out some investigations of our own, particularly into the unfortunate demise of Mr Tench. In doing so, we questioned Bridgett, who is a maid in my kitchen here, and from whom I elicited some interesting information."

I glanced at the nervous young girl before me, who looked as though she would have preferred to be elsewhere and was clearly intimidated in the presence of Church and Maisterson. Somewhere in the house, a door banged to.

"Pray continue," I said.

"Perhaps Bridgett would like to explain what she saw on Wednesday evening," suggested Maisterson. I turned to the girl, who smiled nervously, her fingers twirling the dark hair that protruded from under her coif.

"If it pleases sir, it was late evening. I was washing the crockery and cleaning up the remains of the evening meal, when I heard a noise at the back door. Before I could go to see what it was, Mrs Tench strode through the kitchen and opened up the door. There was a man waiting for her there, and they left together. I wouldn't have thought anything more of it, but when I left for home half an hour later, as I walked past Mrs Tench's front door, I caught sight of them through the window, embracing."

"I'm sorry," I said, turning to Maisterson, "I don't see the significance of this."

"Let the woman finish, Cheswis," he said.

"And did you recognise the man?" I asked.

"Yes sir, it was Edward Yardley," she said. "I know him because I live near Great Wood Street. The rest of my family are brine workers, you see."

Maisterson and Church both looked at me, and I considered what Bridgett had said. It was certainly of interest that Yardley and Mrs Tench were having a relationship. It was also, perhaps, understandable that she had found a source of solace to help her come to terms with her widowhood, even if Tench had been dead little more than a month, but there was nothing to suggest that they had been lovers before Tench's death, although, I admitted to myself, that may have been the case. I still didn't understand what Church and Maisterson were driving at. The only connection between Yardley and Tench was Yardley's obvious antipathy for John Davenport.

"Forgive me if I'm being a little dense," I said to Maisterson. "Is there something I'm not understanding here?"

Maisterson raised his eyebrows. "That may well be so, Master Cheswis," he said. "I had you for someone more perceptive. You omitted to inform us of this during your investigation, but a little research of our own has revealed that your friend Davenport left money for Tench at his place of work the day of his death."

"So you know Davenport was being blackmailed?"

"We had figured it out, yes. We don't know what his secret was exactly, although it will be something to do with walling rights, but, quite frankly, that's not a matter for us to investigate. It's an issue for the Rulers of Walling."

"But how would Tench have got hold of the information?" I asked.

"Well that's obvious isn't it?" said Maisterson. "From Gilbert Kinshaw, of course. He is a Ruler of Walling and Marion Tench is his sister. Kinshaw was her maiden name."

I reeled. It all started to fall into place. No wonder Kinshaw got so angry when I asked him the connection between Tench and Brett. He thought I was getting close. It was then that the full horror of the story hit me.

"So if Yardley and Marion Tench were lovers, they would have a motive for killing William Tench."

"Precisely."

"And it also explains how Mr Church's sash ended up around Tench's neck."

"Exactly. She stole it from me," said Church, "though the Lord knows why. It has only served as a means of incriminating her."

With a start, I suddenly realised what had been nagging me about Marion Tench's words, the day after her husband's death. When she said that 'her family would take care of it', she meant that Kinshaw's role as a Ruler of Walling would allow him to blackmail Davenport.

"So blackmail was used as a means of making it look as if Davenport had a motive for the murder?"

"Master Cheswis, you are getting there eventually," said Church.

"Alright," I said. "So that explains the murder of William Tench. What about that of Will Butters?"

"I think you'll find that was a spur of the moment decision," said Maisterson. "Think about it. Why did Yardley need to commit another murder?"

I stared at Maisterson, and the solution came to me in

a flash. "Why, because Davenport had not been found guilty of the murder of Tench, due to the confusion caused by the demise of Brett and Nuttall. Yardley had to find another way of incriminating Davenport. When he saw Margery die at Townsend House, he saw another motive for Davenport to commit murder and acted on instinct, killing Butters immediately. There was no sash this time because he didn't have one – it was too short notice."

"There you have it, sir," said Church, slapping his thighs with delight. "I knew you'd get there in the end."

"I would have fetched Marion Tench at this point," said Maisterson, "but I think you'll find she has just left. I heard the back door close a few moments ago."

I stared at Maisterson in alarm. "You mean you have let her escape," I exclaimed, "knowing full well that she was a murderess?"

Maisterson shrugged nonchalantly. "It is not my responsibility to apprehend criminals, Master Cheswis," he said. "That is your domain. But there are not too many places that she can go. I would hazard a guess that, if you raise hue and cry, and are quick about it, she will not get far."

I rose to my feet, realising I would have to move fast, but a thought suddenly struck me. "Just one thing," I said. "Why does Yardley hate John Davenport so much?"

"You wouldn't necessarily know this, because you have only been in the town for ten years," replied

Maisterson. "The reasons lie back in the time before you moved here. Ask your housekeeper, Cecilia Padgett. She was a neighbour of the Yardleys for years. If you do that, all will become clear."

As I ran back home, I began to realise that Mrs Padgett was not the only person that I needed to consult. With the revelation that Edward Yardley and Marion Tench had colluded in murder came a clarity of thought which I had not previously thought possible. The fog, which had addled my brain for the past seven weeks, began to lift, and I remembered the conversation I'd had with John Davenport on the day Ralph Brett's body had been found.

"He deserves everything he gets, that one," Davenport had said of Yardley. "He's just like his father was in that respect." How could I have been so stupid as to miss the significance of those words? It was just a hunch, but one that I needed to investigate. Quickening my step, I marched across the square to the Booth Hall and banged on the door.

The Bailiffs clerk, Ezekiel Green, was somewhat less accommodating than he had been on my previous visit, which was not particularly surprising, given what was going on in the town that day. Nevertheless, he listened to my request politely and went to fetch the court rolls for the ten years previous to those I'd checked before. It took me a while to find what I was looking for, but, eventually, I came across an entry from 1625 in the specific book of court rulings that dealt with the infringement of walling issues.

> *10 October 1 Carl 1, 1625 – Mr Jeremiah Yardley*
> *– for failing to repair the pavement outside his*
> *wich house, when so asked to do – 39 s 11 ½ d*
> *and the forfeiture of 3 days walling*

I turned the page and immediately came across another entry from six months later.

> *17th April 2 Carl 1 1626 – Mr Jeremiah Yardley*
> *– for possessing a wich house, whose chimney*
> *being faulty and of great danger to themselves*
> *and the whole town – we order the chimney be*
> *taken down and replaced in a manner so to avoid*
> *danger of fire, in addition to a penalty of 39s*
> *11 1/2d. In addition we require a surety of £6*
> *against further transgressions.*

A further look in the walling records revealed what I already knew to be the case. One of the Rulers of Walling for the 1625-26 period was William Davenport, father of John. I now had one further piece of evidence to show the antipathy between the Yardleys and the Davenports, but as yet I had not managed to find a motive for murder. However, although I had only discovered half the story, I knew who would be able to reveal the rest of it to me. It was time to talk to Mrs Padgett.

My housekeeper was busy baking. She had been out around the town that morning and had already made sure she had bought an ample supply of the foodstuffs and other provisions that had begun to find their way into the town. I came straight to the point.

"What can you tell me about Jeremiah Yardley?" I asked. "I understand you were a neighbour of his nearly twenty years ago."

Mrs Padgett turned round and looked at me in surprise. "Jeremiah Yardley? Why yes. That was a sad story fit to melt the iciest heart," she said.

"Sad?" I asked. "In what way?"

"I was newly-wed at the time," related Mrs Padgett. "As you say, Jeremiah and his wife were our neighbours. Kindly people they were too, but they had several sickly children – I believe only Edward, the eldest, survived, and they found it hard to make ends meet. The problems began to arise shortly after King Charles came to the throne. Sixteen-twenty-five was the year of the corn shortage, and many townsfolk found life hard. Jeremiah and his family owned two or three wich houses, but they didn't have the money to maintain them. The Rulers of Walling fined him for not repairing the street outside one of the wich houses and for not maintaining one of the others sufficiently. Times were hard, and Jeremiah had no money to pay the fines or pay for the repairs. He had to sell one of his wich houses to pay for everything, which in turn reduced the amount they could earn. He had to sell it at a very low price too. It all became too much for Jeremiah, I fear."

"And what happened?" I asked.

"Jeremiah was so beside himself with shame and worry that he took his own life. His body was found in the river. Jeremiah's wife had to bring up Edward on his own."

"I can imagine that was a strain," I said. "And who bought Jeremiah's wich house?" I asked, already knowing the answer.

"Why, I believe it was William Davenport," she said. "I believe he bought it for his son – your friend, John Davenport."

So that was it. Yardley had been harbouring a grudge against the Davenport family for nearly twenty years. It was all very neat. Edward Yardley and Marion Tench had murdered William Tench so that they could be together, and it had been engineered so that it appeared that Davenport had carried out the murder, the aim being to see Davenport hung as a revenge for Yardley's father's death all those years ago. When Ralph Brett was murdered, though, the plan went awry, because Davenport's presence in jail gave him an alibi. The murder of Butters was merely a desperate, bungled attempt to incriminate Davenport again.

It was then that I realised the need for urgency. Marion Tench had been in Randle Church's house while Church and Maisterson were relating their suspicions to me, but she had gone by the time I left. As if to confirm my worries, at that moment there was a loud knock on the door and a breathless Alexander burst into the house.

"Come quickly, Daniel," he said. "There has been a disturbance at the Davenports' house."

It took no longer than five minutes for Alexander and I to race through the Swine Market and across the town bridge to the Davenports' house on Welsh Row, but by the time we arrived, a small crowd of curious onlookers had already assembled outside. When they saw my face, the crowd parted to reveal Ann Davenport sat on the front doorstep, clutching her arm and being comforted by neighbours. Ann appeared to be nursing a wound on her left bicep, around which was tied a bloody bandage. She looked like she had seen a ghost.

"It's not what it looks like, Daniel," she said, tremulously, struggling to her feet.

"What is, Ann?" I said, trying to take in the scene around me. "What has happened?"

"I think you should take a look for yourself, Master Cheswis," interjected one of the neighbours, who had been standing by the door, his hand resting on Ann's shoulder. I glanced nervously inside the house, and what I saw made my heart lurch. Inside the hallway, an overturned cabinet lay on its back, its door half ripped off its hinges. Remnants of food and broken plates lay strewn across the floor as though the room had been ransacked. Worst of all, though, lying face down behind the cabinet, was the inert body of Marion Tench. I picked my way through the debris and turned the body over onto its back. The floor was covered in blood, and a slit down the front of Mrs Tench's skirts revealed a large wound in her abdomen and groin area. A large knife lay discarded near the body.

"God's Bones," I exclaimed. "Is there no end to this slaughter?"

I turned to Ann, who buried her face in her hands and started sobbing. "She tried to kill me," she wailed. "The knife is hers."

I walked over to pick up the blood-stained weapon lying on the floor and noticed that the handle carried the coat of arms of the Church family. Marion Tench had obviously grabbed the knife from Church's Mansion, before heading directly for the Davenports' house.

"Why, in God's name, was she here?" I asked.

"It was Bridgett Palyn's doing," replied Ann, in a quivering voice.

I looked at her with incredulity. "Bridgett Palyn? What has Randle Church's maid got to do with this?"

"You know Bridgett and our poor Margery were friends?" said Ann, squeezing the bandage round her arm tighter. "They were inseparable. Margery's death hit Bridgett just as hard as it has us. Last night, Bridgett came to me and told me she had seen Edward Yardley and Mrs Tench embracing. I put two and two together and realised who had murdered William Tench, and why so much trouble had been taken to make it look as though John was responsible."

"And so you confronted Marion Tench?"

"No, although I can't deny it was on my mind to do so. No. Mrs Tench had realised that I would be told about the relationship, and so she came to try and persuade me not to tell anybody."

"You mean she offered you money?"

Ann shrugged and nodded. I laughed out loud at the unfortunate symmetry of the situation. The whole sorry affair had begun by William Tench blackmailing John Davenport. Now it had ended with Tench's wife offering to pay the Davenports back.

"It's no laughing matter," said Ann, as the crowd broke out into a low murmur at my odd behaviour.

"I'm sorry," I said, "I did not mean to make merry at the expense of others, I was merely contemplating the irony of the situation." Ann glared at me through knotted eyebrows.

"So what happened next?" I asked.

"Well, she became more insistent," said Ann, "and then I asked her whether she would have me protect a murderer. At that point, she realised that I knew everything."

"At which point, the mood changed, I'll wager."

"She started to shout and scream at me and throw things around. She smashed my plates, emptied the contents of my kitchen over the floor and tried to break my furniture. I grabbed hold of her to try to stop her."

"She speaks the truth," cut in one of the neighbours. "The noise was enough to wake the dead. Several of us came running, but when we got here it was too late." I turned back from the neighbour to face Ann.

"She pulled out a knife from under her skirts, the one you see on the floor. She slashed my arm with it. I stepped back and stumbled over the fallen chair. I was on my back on the floor and she was about to kill me."

"So what stopped her?"

"I was lucky. I grabbed a cooking pot that she'd thrown on the floor and smote her with all the force I could muster, square on the shins. She shrieked and dropped the knife, but she wouldn't back down. She still came for me, so I grabbed the knife and plunged it into her guts. She stopped coming at me after that."

"That's when we came in," said the neighbour. "Ann was on the floor, holding her arm."

"Ann," I said, "We know now that Edward Yardley murdered William Tench and tried to place the blame on your husband. We also know why. We know about Yardley's father and the bad feeling between your two families."

"It's a burden we've had to bear for years," said Ann. "Yardley has been a blight on our lives."

"Well, he won't be for much longer – at least once we track him down," I said.

"And what about John?" she asked. "He is still locked up with that traitor in your pox-ridden jailhouse. Are you going to free him?"

"You have my word," I promised, "but first I will need to raise hue and cry in order to track down Yardley. The guards at the sconces will need to be alerted."

"Then do your duty, Daniel," said Ann. "But do not linger. It's time this nightmare was brought to an end – for all of us."

37

Nantwich – Friday January 26, 1644

Davenport was sat hunched and morose in the corner of his cell when Alexander and I arrived at the jail on Pillory Street to set him free. He was still wearing the clothes he had been arrested in two weeks earlier and stank of filth and sweat. The bloodstains on his shirt from Margery's body had now faded to a dirty brown, and his face, normally clean-shaven, carried a mass of sixteen-day-old stubble. Unsurprisingly, though, he brightened up when I told him about Yardley.

"I told you that man were an evil bastard, Daniel," he said. "You have arrested him, I take it?"

"Not exactly," I admitted, "but the guards on the sconces report that he has not left town, nor will he, now that they have been alerted. In the meantime, there is a guard at your house, so he won't show up there either."

Davenport pressed his lips flat and looked at me suspiciously. "At my house?" he said. "Why would he go there? He knows I am locked up in this rat-infested jail cell."

I sighed and explained what had just happened in

Davenport's kitchen, watching as his demeanour changed again, first to shock and then to anger. "Then I must go to comfort Ann immediately," he said, fixing a flinty stare at the wall behind me. "Just make sure you catch Yardley before I do."

"I will do my utmost," I assured him. "He cannot hide for long."

"And what about Kinshaw?" added Davenport. "He may not have murdered Tench, but he was involved in the cover up."

I unlocked Davenport's chains and shoved him in the direction of the cell door. "Go home to your wife, John. She needs you," I said, "and leave Kinshaw to me."

With the most urgent matters now attended to, I realised that I had been back in Nantwich for most of the day but had still not shown my face at the Bretts' house, where Simon and Elizabeth would be waiting for news. I therefore walked round to Beam Street and noticed that a guard was still in position at the front of the house. In all the confusion of the day, I realised that no-one had bothered telling Simon and Elizabeth that they were safe to roam the town. Simon saw me approaching through the window and opened the door as Elizabeth came running downstairs.

"Ah, the stranger returns," said Simon, sardonically. "I hear you've been back most of the day. You didn't feel the urgency to release us from our prison here?"

"Aren't you going to ask how I am?" I countered, ignoring the jibe. "Alexander and I are lucky to be alive."

"It's good to see you're safe," said Elizabeth, "but we've been worried about you."

"I'm sorry, Simon," I said. "A lot has happened. I will explain. Firstly, Furnival is dead."

Simon swallowed hard and wiped the back of his hand across his forehead as he considered the implications of what he had been told. Elizabeth gave out a sharp cry and sat down at the table.

"Dead? How so?" demanded Simon. I explained the chase across Beam Heath and Furnival's efforts to cross the temporary bridge. Simon pursed his lips when I explained about Wade.

"I am sorry for him," said my brother. "How does he fare?"

"He will survive, but he will no longer be able to walk on two feet. He rests at my house."

"And the Duke's letters?"

"Lost," I said. "They lie in the Weaver somewhere between here and the sea."

"That is a shame," said Simon, sadly, his shoulders sagging with disappointment. "We could have saved many lives, if we had been able to reveal the duplicitous nature of this King. Let us hope his true nature is revealed soon. And what of Furnival's wife?"

I related the story of our march to Dorfold House, the manner of our release, our involvement in the battle and

Alice's final escape to Shrewsbury.

"Then she is out of your life for good. The Lord be praised for that," he said, exchanging a brief glance with Elizabeth.

"And what about Booth?" he continued. "How did he take the loss of the papers?"

I thought about that for a moment and had to admit that the Colonel's reaction was curious. "Oddly enough, he did not seem too upset," I admitted.

"I thought as much. You see, if the King's letters had reached London, Brereton would have taken much of the credit for their delivery. As it stands, though, depending on whether he passed my message on to others, he gains no benefit, at best, and a shower of criticism at worst."

I have to admit that this was an entirely new consideration for me. "Why on earth would Booth want to see Brereton fail?" I asked, incredulously.

Simon smiled and gave me a look that seemed to border on pity. "Daniel," he said. "You really don't have much of a feel for local politics, do you? Think about it. Brereton is a puritan and far too radical for Booth, who is a moderate, politically speaking. In addition, Booth comes from a family that is above Brereton's in the social scale. Before the war, political influence in Cheshire was in the hands of the baronets, men like Booth's grandfather, Old Sir George Booth. Now, however, power is entirely in Brereton's hands. He has surrounded himself with a group of cronies who sit on local committees and control everything. He even has a way of by-passing decisions, should he need to. The last thing Booth needs is for Brereton to get credit for the delivery of Hamilton's papers. He would end up with even more power."

I was amazed at the depth of Simon's knowledge and was just about to tell him so, when I glanced out of the window and caught sight of the portly figure of Gilbert Kinshaw making his way to the front door. Simon caught sight of him too and looked over at me.

"Today is not the day for this," he said. "I'll get rid of him."

"No. Leave it," I said. "He and I have some unfinished business." I strode over to Elizabeth's front door and swung it open, just as Kinshaw had finished speaking to the soldiers on guard. The pre-prepared smile that adorned his face vanished abruptly as he realised who stood before him.

"Ah, Mr Cheswis," he said. "You are still here?"

"That I am," I replied, "although I must confess I am surprised to see you here again today. You have presumably not heard yet about your sister?"

"Marion?" said Kinshaw, frowning. "What of her?"

"She lies dead on the floor of John Davenport's house, having attacked his wife with a knife. Her lover, Edward Yardley, is in hiding, wanted for the murders of William Tench and Will Butters."

Kinshaw's eyes widened as he took on board what he was being told. "Marion. D-dead?" he stammered. "You mean she was killed by Ann Davenport? Are you going to do your duty, Cheswis, and make sure the Davenports pay the price for their crimes, or do I need to go to the High Constable about this?"

"Enough, Kinshaw," I snapped. "You can't pull the wool over my eyes on this. William Tench was murdered by Yardley and your sister. They had Tench blackmail Davenport about his fraudulent walling activities to make it look like Davenport had a motive to kill Tench. And there is only one person who could have told Tench about Davenport's secret. And that's you! You're involved in this up to your neck, Mr Kinshaw."

Kinshaw bridled. "You can't prove any of this," he said.

"I would welcome the opportunity to try," I retorted.

"And you, sirrah," said Kinshaw, "are the town constable. I have provided you with the information you needed to conduct an investigation against Davenport for fraud, and yet you have done nothing about it, preferring to push the responsibility back to the Rulers of Walling. This wouldn't be because Davenport is your friend, would it? I'm sure the Deputy Lieutenants would have a view on this."

At this point, Elizabeth, who had been listening to the conversation open-mouthed, stepped in. "Mr Kinshaw," she said, smiling sweetly. "I'm sure you have not come here today to argue with Mr Cheswis. I presume you have come to talk to me about your offer to buy my husband's business?"

Kinshaw turned to her. "You are right, Mistress Brett. I must offer my apologies for using your house in which to conduct this unseemly argument."

Elizabeth waved him away with a brush of her hand. "You do not have to apologise, sir," she said, "but I do have a proposal."

"I'm listening," he replied.

"You have made me an offer for my husband's business," said Elizabeth. "I think it is worth more than you have offered, but it is still a considerable amount. I will sell the business to you at the price you offer, but there are some conditions. Firstly, you will not conduct any proceedings against Mr Davenport through the Walling Committee. You will forget that any such transgressions took place and let Mr Davenport and his family live their lives in peace. Secondly, you will drop any accusations against Mr Cheswis or inferences that he has carried out his duties in anything other than a completely proper manner. Do we have a deal?"

A smile played on the corner of Simon's lips, but both Kinshaw and I were dumbstruck.

"You would do that for him?" said Kinshaw.

Elizabeth didn't answer but merely repeated the question. "Do we have a deal?"

Kinshaw hesitated for a while and then looked at me out of the corner of his eyes. "Very well," he said. "I'll have my lawyers draw up the contract." He stepped forward and shook Elizabeth's hand. "It has been a pleasure doing business with you, Mrs Brett. I'm not sure you have the best of the deal, but you have a certain style, I think."

Elizabeth nodded at the compliment.

Kinshaw turned towards the door but then stopped. "Just one thing," he said. "How do I know you won't go back on this arrangement once the business is in my hands?"

"That is because you will provide me with a signed, open-ended, legally binding agreement to sell the business back to me at the original selling price. I will keep this document safe, and use it only if you go back on our agreement."

"And how do I know that you won't use the document anyway?"

"You don't," said Elizabeth. "You'll just have to trust me."

Kinshaw looked at Elizabeth for a moment, and then his face broke into a smile. "By the saints, madam, you strike a hard bargain," he said, "but you have certainly earned my respect. I do hope this is not the last time we do business together. It has been an enlightening experience".

I could still hear him chuckling as he waddled his way past the guard out onto the street. As he did so, Elizabeth turned round and headed for the kitchen where Ralph Junior was playing. Simon watched her go and then laid his hand on my shoulder.

"Brother," he said. "Such a thing I did not expect to see. I think you have a choice to make. Make sure it's the right one."

As Simon and I watched the figure of Gilbert Kinshaw receding down Beam Street, my eye was caught by the sight of a figure on horseback making his way slowly in the opposite direction. He was dressed in a buff coat and wore a wide-brimmed hat with a fine feather in it. He stopped outside Elizabeth's house and dismounted.

"Good day, sir," he said. "I would speak with Ralph Brett. I trust I am in the right place."

"You are, sir," I said. "May I ask in what connection you seek Mr Brett?"

"My name is Michael Forbes," said the horseman." I bring a communication from my master, Lord Hamilton. I have ridden from Falmouth, where he is held prisoner." Simon and I exchanged a quick glance.

"I think you may be disappointed, sir," I said, "but you had better come in. Mistress Brett is at home."

"I'm afraid my husband was cruelly murdered in December," said Elizabeth, once Forbes was seated in the hall. Forbes looked crushed at the news and sat frowning for what must have been at least a minute, stroking the feather in his hat.

"May I speak to you in confidence in front of these gentlemen?" he asked, once he had recovered his composure.

"Yes, of course. These gentlemen are close friends of mine and of my husband. Their business is my business."

"Very well," said Forbes. "Your husband visited my master at his family home in Kinneil in October, where he entrusted him with a package of documents. Do you know anything about this?"

Elizabeth shook her head. "No sir, I knew he had been in Scotland. He told me he had been to Edinburgh for trading purposes. He was a mercer. I know of no trip other than to there."

Forbes nodded. "So he did not confide in you as to the nature of his visit to the Duke?"

"I'm afraid not. He didn't discuss his business affairs with me. I know he served under his lordship in the Palatinate, but beyond that I know little of his time there."

"And would he have had any close contacts he may have confided in in Nantwich?"

"I'm afraid not," said Elizabeth. "My husband was killed after meeting someone early in the morning near the town's earthworks. We still do not know why he was killed, but I think you may have answered the question."

"And you do not know the whereabouts of the documents of which I speak?"

"We have been through all of my husband's business documentation since his death," said Elizabeth. "I can assure you we found nothing of the nature such as what you describe."

"Then my journey is wasted," said Forbes. "I am

sorry for your loss." And with that he shook Elizabeth's hand and left the house, leaving Elizabeth, Simon, and I to contemplate what might have come to pass, had he arrived two days earlier.

38

Nantwich – Saturday January 27, 1644

*I*t was market day in Nantwich, and the weather was unusually mild for the time of year. White clouds scudded across the sky and the sun shone, casting its warmth over the stallholders in the square. It was like a spring day, and the optimism that such a day brings was reflected in the mood of the populace.

The town reverberated to the sound of tradesmen hawking their wares. Farmers drove their cattle through the Beast Market, hens and geese were led noisily up the High Street, fish was being laid out on boards. Everyone in Nantwich would eat well for the first time in weeks. Today, the town's bellman would not be ringing to announce a death, but to report glad tidings.

Three officers stood in the square, surveying the scene; an olive-skinned senior officer, a thin man with pinched features in plain puritan garb, and the broad-shouldered commander of the garrison. All three men bore a self-satisfied demeanour. They were overseeing their people, the people whose safety and livelihoods they had assured. However, although they acknowledged the *plaudits of the townsfolk with good grace, their minds were already on their next move, on campaigns that would secure the future of the whole country, not just a small town in Cheshire.*

Slightly less self-satisfied were the two gentlemen, one in his forties, the other in his early twenties, who had emerged from the morning service held in the gallery of the Crown Hotel. The older man looked at his watch and checked it against the church clock. They were glad that there had been no slaughter – no looting and pillaging, but their minds had already turned to more personal concerns, not least how much they would be sequestered for their support of the King.

Meanwhile, in a house on Pepper Street, a middle-aged woman was busy cooking, having already been out in the market to secure the best of the goods on offer. She was back in the environment she loved best and sang merrily as she worked. Things could not have turned out better. The master of the house had returned, and the young injured soldier he had brought with him had turned out to be most appreciative of her efforts, flattering and flirting with her as she nursed him back to health.

"Mistress," he said, "you're fit to capture the heart of any young man with cooking like that!" She knew it was a joke, but nevertheless, she was happy.

The young soldier was in much better spirits, having got over the shock of his injury. The stump, where his foot had been, would take some time to heal, but the wound appeared to have no infection. He was not out of the woods yet, but at least he was looking to the future. He would be doing no more soldiering, but he had been spared life as a vagrant and beggar by the generosity of the master of the house, who had offered him an apprenticeship in his salt and cheese business, an offer he had readily accepted with gratitude. He had certainly fallen on his feet, or in his case, on one foot and a stump. He laughed at the joke and resolved to use it in the future when describing his good fortune.

Not so happy were the two brothers sat on the wall by the churchyard contemplating the whereabouts of their younger sibling and praying for his safety in the hands of the royalist army. To his credit, their brother's employer had sworn to help free him from the King's service. They had not expected a gesture of that kind, and although they would hold their brother's master to that promise, they had agreed that henceforward they would willingly forego the weekly supplies of stolen Cheshire cheese to which they had become accustomed.

Even less happy were the two men sat in opposite cells in the town jail in Pillory Street. The disgraced army captain had already been tried and condemned, and he knew he would be shot once the garrison commander turned his mind to him. The salt worker in the cell opposite expected no better. Caught trying to escape over the earthworks at Welsh Row End, he was to face trial for the murders of a tanner and a domestic servant.

He knew he would not get the privilege of a soldier's death. All he could expect was the hangman's noose.

Meanwhile, in another part of the town, one of the town's constables strolled through the throng of people. Holding his right hand was a five-year-old boy, who skipped along with excitement and tugged at the man's sleeve every time he found something of interest.

Next to him walked a young woman, the child's mother, who, with a hint of a smile on her face, watched the child and saw her future take shape in front of her. The Constable noticed the smile and returned the compliment. It was a day of release, new directions and change – a day for decisions, and on this day and in this place, Daniel Cheswis made his choice.

Author's Note

The Battle of Nantwich was crucial in changing the direction of the Civil War in Cheshire. Although the altercation, which took place on January 25th 1644 on the fields near Acton, was low in casualties (only 300 died in the battle itself, less than the number who perished during the failed assault on January 18), the effect on the war in the area was significant. Byron's infantry force was demolished, and henceforward, Nantwich was left in relative peace, the war's focus switching to Chester. Never again did the royalists hold so much ground in Cheshire.

The main three parliamentary leaders depicted in this novel all benefitted from their role at Nantwich.

After the battle, Sir Thomas Fairfax returned to Yorkshire, where he went on to improve his military reputation still further, particularly at Marston Moor, to the point that in January 1645 he was appointed Commander-in-Chief of the New Model Army. Sir William Brereton also retained his command and became one of only three commanders to be specifically exempted from the Self-Denying Ordinance. Colonel George Booth continued to play an active part in the

Civil War on the parliamentarian side. He served as an MP in the Protectorate but was eventually to play a leading role in the Restoration.

Lord John Byron continued to lead the royalist cause in Cheshire until the end of the First Civil War but sailed away into exile in 1646. He died in Paris in 1652.

Other military personnel mentioned in the story were also real people.

The resourceful and efficient James Lothian, captured in the skirmish at Burford on December 17th, was the subject of a prisoner exchange shortly after the Battle of Nantwich, and he continued to play an active role on the parliamentary side in Cheshire and North Wales.

The unfortunate Thomas Steele was executed in Tinkers Croft on Monday 29th January 1643. Steele was a cheese trader and hailed from the Sandbach/Weston area. He did marry a Jane Furnival from Barthomley, although her brother in the story, Hugh Furnival, is a fictitious character.

Steele's nemesis, the valiant but ultimately doomed Thomas Sandford, did capture Beeston Castle by climbing the castle walls with eight of his firelocks in a daring act of bravado. It is considered possible that treachery was involved, although the nature of events in the upper ward as described in the novel, are the product of my imagination. What is true is that Steele entertained Sandford and his troops afterwards, an act which led to the former's downfall. Sandford died at Wickstead's sconce on 18 January, reportedly shot by a 15-year-old with a musket.

John Connaught, the bloodthirsty captain responsible for the infamous massacre at Barthomley, eventually paid for his deed with his life. He was executed in 1660 at a trial, in which he protested his innocence. The victims mentioned in the story were all real people.

The story also mentions a number of the prominent townspeople of the time.

Thomas Maisterson was the head of the oldest of the traditional Nantwich families. He was sequestered heavily for his support of the royalist cause and died in 1652.

Randle Church died in 1648 at the age of 86, having survived his son and grandson. His fabulous house on Hospital Street, Churches Mansion, is still standing and today houses an antiques shop.

Lady Margaret Norton passed away in April 1644, a couple of months after the battle. Her property eventually became the town prison and was demolished in 1767. A row of almshouses now stands on the site.

Roger Wilbraham of Townsend House, depicted here as an inexperienced 20-year-old, lived to become the High Sherriff of Cheshire and was one of the town's most respected forefathers and benefactors. He lived until 1708. Roger married his cousin, Alice, daughter of his namesake, Roger Wilbraham of Dorfold, who also makes a brief appearance in the book.

Daniel Cheswis and his immediate family, as well as most of the common soldiers and townspeople mentioned in the story, are invented characters, but several are based on real people.

The Comberbachs were the most prominent family of tanners in the 1640s, and the town bellman at the time was, indeed, called Alexander Clowes. The cannon attack on Townsend House on Jan 10th did result in the death of a young woman called Margery Davenport, the daughter of a John Davenport, whilst contemporary reports of the Jan 18th assault tell of the bravery of the women-folk of the town and in particular of a heroine called Brett.

Finally, the person with whom the story begins and ends, the Duke of Hamilton, remained in captivity in Pendennis Castle until 1645, when he was released and came back into the King's favour. He was often accused of disloyalty because of his ancestry, but there is no real evidence of this. The plot described in the novel is entirely fictional. Hamilton fought again for his King and was ultimately rewarded with the same fate. Like Charles I, he met his end in 1649, on the executioner's block.

Acknowledgements

Thanks are due to a number of people, without whose input, my idea for portraying the events surrounding the Battle of Nantwich could not have been brought to fruition.

Firstly, on a practical front, I have to express my gratitude to Matthew and his team at Electric Reads, who guided me through the publishing process with enthusiasm and professionalism. Special thanks are due to Tom, who edited the manuscript, and Vanessa, who designed the cover.

Many thanks also to Cliff Astles, who allowed me to use his photograph of the 2013 Holly Holy Day battle re-enactment as part of the cover design.

I am indebted to my brother, Mike Wilson, Dean of the School of Media and Performance at University College, Falmouth, who read my manuscript and provided me with advice from an academic viewpoint, and to Colin Bissett of the Sealed Knot, whose in-depth knowledge of the Civil War in Cheshire was invaluable in helping me avoid a number of historical errors.

And finally, a special thank-you to my wife, Karen, who proofed the first draft of the book and didn't get too annoyed, when I spent weekends writing instead of doing the garden and DIY jobs.

Bibliographical Notes

In carrying out the historical research for *The Winter Siege*, I consulted a great many books covering the Civil War Period including memoirs, manuscripts and letters written by a number of the main protagonists in the struggle to gain control over Cheshire in 1643 and 1644. Several sources, however, deserve particular mention.

Anyone writing about the history of Nantwich will, at some time, have referred to James Hall's *A History of the Town and Parish of Nantwich or Wich Malbank in the County Palatine of Chester* (1883). It is by far the most comprehensive work on the history of the town and is particularly detailed on the Civil War.

Also most helpful in gaining an understanding of 17th century Cheshire politics and the events leading up to the Battle of Nantwich were *Cheshire 1630-1660 – County Government and Society during the English Revolution* by JS Morrill (1974) and *The Civil Wars in Cheshire* by RN Dore (1966)

For information on farming and cheese production in the seventeenth century I used Charles F Foster's *Cheshire Cheese and Farming in the North West in the 17th and 18th Centuries* (1998), whilst Joan R Kent's

The English Village Constable 1580-1642 (1986) was invaluable for information on the responsibilities of the local constabulary in Stuart times.

Hall is particularly informative on the development of the salt industry in Nantwich and the reasons for its eventual decline. However, I also referred to *The Salt Industry* by Andrew and Annelise Fielding (2006), particularly for the layout of the walling area around the common cistern in Great Wood Street and Little Wood Street.

For help with Cheshire dialect words, a useful reference tool was *A Glossary of Words used in the Dialect of Cheshire* by Lieut. Col. Egerton Leigh MP (1877). Leigh's glossary was based on an earlier attempt to produce a Cheshire Glossary by none other than Roger Wilbraham.

And finally, it would be remiss of me if I failed to mention the two main contemporary accounts of the Civil War in Cheshire, these being Thomas Malbon's *Memorials of the Civil War in Cheshire and the Adjacent Counties* and Edward Burghall's *Providence Improved*, largely plagiarised from Malbon's account but interesting nonetheless, especially for the picture Burghall paints of life in Cheshire in the 1630s and early 1640s. Both Malbon and Burghall make brief cameo appearances in *The Winter Siege*.

Glossary

Backlands   The area behind a house, back garden

Bangbeggar   One whose duty it is to drive away
             beggars

Barrow   Conical baskets, in which salt is put to
          rain

Bear ward   Bear tender

Bum bailey   Sherriff's officer, constable – used as a
             term of derision

Cankered   Ill-tempered

Channel lookers   Officials responsible for making sure
                   people cleaned the streets in front of
                   their houses, shops and buildings

Cheshire acre   A Cheshire acre is equal to a
                pproximately 2.11 statute acres

Fire lookers	Officers responsible for fire prevention
Flam	Nonsense
Flett cheese	Cheese made from skimmed milk
Heazing	Coughing
Jagger	Coal seller
Kidds	Faggots, firewood
Kindling	A fixed allocation of time allowed for salt making, equivalent to four days
Lating	The process of bell ringing to invite people to a funeral
Leach Brine	Brine, which drops from salt in drying and is preserved to be dried again
Lead (relating to wich houses)	A salt pan
Leave-looker	Market inspectors, weights and measures officers
Loot	Wooden rakes used to scoop out salt

Lossell	A lazy good-for-nothing
Making Meet	The allocation of walling rights and setting salt prices
Rulers of Walling	Annually elected inspectors of the salt works
Runagate	An idle person
Sconce	A star shaped fortification
Ship (relating to salt making)	A hollowed-out tree trunk used to store brine
St Martin's Summer	Indian summer
Swiving	Having sex
Theet	A wooden pipe used to transport brine into a wich house
Walling	Salt making
Wich house	A salt house
Yard	Euphemism for the male sexual organ

Made in the USA
Columbia, SC
07 January 2018